I0585953

THE THREADBARE QUEEN

The Rising Wave

MICHELLE DIENER

ECLIPSE

ALSO BY MICHELLE DIENER

FANTASY NOVELS BY MICHELLE DIENER

Mistress of the Wind

The Rising Wave series:

The Rising Wave (Prequel Novella)

The Turncoat King

The Threadbare Queen

Fate's Arrow (Due late 2022)

The Dark Forest series:

The Golden Apple

The Silver Pear

SCIENCE FICTION NOVELS

Sky Raiders series:

Sky Raiders

Calling the Change

Shadow Warrior

Class 5 series:

Dark Horse

Dark Deeds

Dark Minds

Dark Matters

Dark Ambitions (A Class 5 Novella)

Dark Class (Due out 2022)

Verdant String series:

Interference & Insurgency Box Set

Breakaway

Breakeven

Trailblazer

High Flyer

Wave Rider

HISTORICAL FICTION NOVELS

Susanna Horenbout and John Parker series:

In a Treacherous Court

Keeper of the King's Secrets

In Defense of the Queen

Regency London series:

The Emperor's Conspiracy

Banquet of Lies

A Dangerous Madness

Other historical novels:

Daughter of the Sky

To receive notification when Michelle Diener's next book is released, you can sign up to her new release notification list.

ABOUT THE THREADBARE QUEEN

A conqueror's victory is never assured . . .

The Rising Wave may have taken control of Kassia, but hot on the heels of their victory, Luc receives word from one of his spies that the Jatan, emboldened by the Kassian army's withdrawal, have crossed the border. More worryingly, they haven't just moved into northern Kassia, but also east to his home region of Cervantes, and with all the Cervantes warriors with Luc in Kassia's capital, cementing their hold on power, his home is vulnerable and defence-less. He has no choice but to leave Ava to secure Fernwell, gather forces, and head north, to try to push the Jatan back to their side of the mountains.

A queen's safety is never a given . . .

Finally, after months of trying, a minion of the Speaker of Grimwalt's court manages to snatch Ava from under the noses of her friends and allies, off the streets of Fernwell and onto the back roads to Grimwalt. Ava has to struggle against an insidious assault on her vitality and magic, fighting a power that isn't just strong, but malevolent.

Nothing is set in stone—neither defeat nor victory . . .

As Ava tries to escape her captors and Luc races to defend his homeland, they draw closer and closer to each other, until finally their paths cross, as it always seems to do. As they once again face their enemies together, they will have to use all their strength to salvage the victory they've worked so hard to accomplish.

The Threadbare Queen is the second book in the Rising Wave series. The series begins with The Rising Wave, a prequel novella, and continues with The Turncoat King. Look out for Fate's Arrow, coming in 2022.

CHAPTER 1

Eavesdroppers never hear any good of themselves.

That little gem from her mother echoed in Ava's head as she slouched against a wall in the main square in the city of Fernwell, across from a small stall selling fruit.

Her father had disagreed with that saying, pointing out the pragmatic uses of eavesdropping in his and her mother's professional capacity as trade envoys for Grimwalt, but the saying had stuck in Ava's mind.

She twisted her lips in a wry smile.

It had certainly held true of the conversations she'd overheard on the streets of Fernwell.

She had yet to hear a good word.

She would have to tell Luc later that there was even less good being said about him.

"When that interloper killed the queen—"

"No." A middle-aged man cut the speaker—a woman with a basket of vegetables and fruit over her arm—off with a chop of his hand and decisive shake of his head. "I was there, the Turncoat King didn't kill the queen."

"Aye. I was there, too. It was the princeling who killed his aunt.

They turned on each other like the scorpions they were." A second man leaned over the display and plucked a large orange from the pile, lifting it to the light to check it for bruising. "Not to say the Turncoat King's not dangerous."

"Got a hold over the new queen, way I hear it." The woman passed over the coins for her purchase and pursed her lips.

"We sure she has a right to the throne?" The stall holder hadn't spoken up yet, but now Ava lifted her head to look at him, interested.

She hadn't heard many questioning her claim to be queen.

A cart rolled down the street, drowning out the conversation and blocking her view, and Ava ducked around it to get closer, careful with her footing on cobbles still wet with afternoon rain.

Though the cold rain from earlier had eased, she had the hood of her cloak up against the still-damp wind, but even if she hadn't, she would have been invisible.

She kept a short distance between herself and the small group, even so.

"The old queen acknowledged her." The man slipped his orange into a bag. "By holding her prisoner for treason, she made it clear the princess was her niece. But she acknowledged her as she lay injured on the street, too. With her dying breath."

"So I heard," the stall holder said. "But I don't know a person who knew of her before the queen suddenly had her as a prisoner."

"She was shut away up north by the Herald himself, way I heard it." The first man shrugged. "She looks like a Valestri to my eyes."

"You've seen her?" The woman sounded surprised, and a little bitter. "Hasn't so much as stepped out of that palace in the two weeks since all that nasty bloodshed, that I know of."

Ouch.

Ava looked down at her magic-worked cloak and felt a tug of guilt. She should be a visible, approachable leader.

Not slinking through her city like a wraith.

Still, she justified her current slinking on the grounds it gave her the opportunity to hear the honest opinions of her new subjects.

Here on the streets, unaware of the presence of their new queen, the good citizens of Fernwell spoke freely.

Certainly more freely that the slick, desperate nobles in the palace.

The landowners and titled few were desperately trying not to notice that their time had come to an end.

It had been two weeks since she, Luc, and General Ru had taken Kassia's capital city. Perhaps that wasn't long enough for some to understand that change had arrived.

Luc found it hard to bear their overtures, their pretense that everything was going to carry on as it had.

Ava had had to steer him away too many times to count from the sycophants who tried to pretend that it was all business as usual, albeit under new management.

They must know it wasn't, and yet they persisted, as if they could change their new reality by simply pretending it wasn't happening.

As for the men and women of Fernwell that she encountered on the streets, most voiced their suspicion that whatever she and Luc were cooking up was going to be the ruin of them all.

Luc told her that attitude was to be expected. When had the citizens of Kassia ever had a decent leader, he'd asked her?

Ava couldn't answer. Didn't know if they had one now.

She wanted to be good. Or even just mildly competent. And she also wanted to pass the mantle on to someone else as soon as possible.

The problem with that was Luc.

He had fought almost his whole life to bring down her aunt and cousin. She wouldn't throw away his victory by handing things over to idiots.

Speaking of idiots, up ahead, obscured by the crowds, someone gave a shout.

It sent a ripple of worry through her.

This was the other reason she had to justify her daily escape from the palace.

She had saved at least three lives since they'd taken Fernwell. Maybe more with her covert wanderings.

The small group at the stall broke off their conversation and began moving toward the source of the commotion.

Ava increased her pace, weaving through the gawkers enticed by the prospect of a confrontation.

Given the number of Rising Wave soldiers present in the city each day, and the equal number of Kassians who chafed under the new order, Ava was surprised there weren't more fights.

General Ru and Luc had ordered their people to deescalate, to take the high road, but even so . . .

She burrowed through a crowd of spectators to find two Cervantes soldiers, Luc's people, standing in a small open circle. With them, but slightly to the side, was a Venyatux soldier, a woman she recognized all too well.

Catja. One of General Ru's personal guards.

Facing them, fists clenched, was a massive man.

He looked unkempt, as if he was sleeping rough or had been on an all-night bender and had stumbled into the street after spending some time unconscious on a tavern floor.

"You will need to apologize." The Cervantes soldier who spoke to the man was not someone Ava knew personally, but she recognized her.

Her partner—because they had been told to always move about the city in pairs—was a tall, battle-scarred man who stood loose and calm beside her.

He almost looked bored, but Ava could feel the potential for violence coiled within him.

She felt the faint buzz from her cloak, a strong message this was a highly volatile situation.

If she threw the cloak off and stepped in as herself, as Queen Ava of Kassia, would that help the situation, or merely stoke tensions even higher?

So far, she had managed to avoid revealing herself in these situations. Better they never knew she'd been here, and better no one noticed her appearing out of thin air.

That would not help her popularity. At all.

The last thing she needed was whispers about her Grimwaldian heritage.

The big scruffy Kassian turned his head and spat on the ground. "This is my city. I won't be apologizing to anyone."

The crowd almost audibly drew in a breath.

Because it wasn't their city any more.

That was the root cause of all these confrontations.

She may be the former queen's niece, but she wasn't Kassian. As the stall holder had said, no one had even heard of her until a few short weeks ago.

It meant confusion and distrust reigned.

Ava drew out a small piece of fabric, pulled the threaded needle woven into her sleeve out, and began to embroider the fine cotton.

She tried to keep the sense of urgency out of her fingers, but it was hard to do when she saw the two Cervantes soldiers step forward in a way that said they were going to make the Kassian apologize.

"Wait." Catja spoke up from her position beside them. "He isn't worth any trouble."

The Cervantes both turned to look at her, and the crowd pressed a little closer.

The delay gave Ava time to finish her rough design.

She shouldered her way through the tightening line of spectators and stepped into the open circle.

She was confident enough in her magic that she believed she wouldn't be noticed on a busy street, but in a small space with hundreds of eyes on her . . . she worried. But as she moved toward the Kassian, no one shouted out, no one commented on her presence at all.

Except . . .

She thought she saw a man turn toward her, eyes narrowed as if trying to work out what he was seeing, but she had no time to keep an eye on him.

Things were about to get violent.

She stepped close to the Kassian, smelled the puff of stale ale and body odor coming off him, and forced herself to lean in.

"Here," she said, pressing the scrap of fabric into his hand.

"What?" He looked down at it, then gave a sudden heave of his chest. He looked around, wild-eyed, for an escape. "Need to—"

A few of the people around him seemed to understand what he needed to do. They began scrambling back, out of his way, and he pushed wildly through the narrow path that opened up to him, lunging for the wall of the closest building and bracing against it as he vomited.

Most of the spectators seemed to realize the show was over, and began to drift away.

Ava stepped closer to the Cervantes and Catja.

"You shouldn't back down over something like that," the Cervantes woman was saying to Catja. "It breeds disrespect if it's allowed to go unchallenged."

"We've been told to deescalate." Catja didn't disagree, though.

"There was no deescalating that one." The big Cervantes man spoke for the first time. "He was going out of his way to provoke."

Ava didn't doubt it.

She was about to step away, to continue her walk, when she felt a familiar frisson against her skin as her cloak told her of the approach of someone with power.

Some of it given by her.

Sewn into his very skin.

"Commander." The Cervantes woman's voice was clipped and respectful.

Ava turned to face the commander of the Rising Wave without surprise.

She was developing more and more awareness of Luc, the longer they were together.

He glanced at her, a quick flick of the eyes that told her he knew full well she was there, and then he turned to his two soldiers.

"Dirk, Finola." He addressed them. "Catja." He acknowledged the Venyatux soldier with a nod. "What happened?"

"That one called Catja a Venyatux witch." Finola pointed to the Kassian, who had finished throwing up and was now leaning, pale and weak against the wall, eyes closed. "Said General Ru was a sorceress, and Catja was her witchy handmaiden."

Luc's gaze cut to her again, just for a moment, and Ava could see the banked amusement in his eyes.

Very funny.

There was no official ban on spell casters, but she had always been warned there was a social cost to spell casters revealing themselves, and in her mother's and her case, actual danger in doing so.

Finola's original warning to Catja was right. Accusing General Ru and her soldiers of sorcery was a sign of disrespect. It would need to be dealt with.

"Is he in trouble?" A woman spoke up from the much smaller crowd that remained. They had stepped back from the Kassian, who was still leaning, slack-mouthed, with eyes closed, against a wall, but Ava sensed they were unwilling to leave him, as if they feared something would happen to him.

"He a friend of yours?" Luc asked her.

She seemed unsure how to answer. She half-lifted a shoulder. "I know him. Wouldn't call him a friend." She glanced over at the man, now bent over with hands on his knees, his skin tinged with gray.

"But yet you're staying to see he's all right." Luc kept his voice neutral.

"Been rumors." The woman half-shrugged again.

"Rumors?" Luc's attention sharpened, and so did Ava's.

"That people who talk back to the soldiers disappear."

"Which people?" Finola spoke up, tone indignant.

The woman flicked a look at her, shook her head. "No specifics."

"And what do these rumors say happens to these unnamed victims?" Luc asked.

The people who up until now had stood around the woman began drifting further away, leaving her out in the open, on her own. She noticed it, and went still, shook her head.

"They don't, exactly. They just say it's revenge. For the Chosen camps."

She was now completely on her own. A few people were still within earshot, but most had disappeared completely, and those who were still visible looked ready to melt away.

"Where did you hear these rumors?" Catja asked.

Like she'd done when Finola had taken over the questions from Luc, the woman looked at Catja with a quick flick of surprise, and Ava wondered what she found so surprising. Perhaps that Luc was not controlling everything, that he allowed his companions a voice.

He was right. Fernwell had not had good leaders up until now.

"People talk in the taverns. The speculation can get . . ." The woman looked at the Kassian, who had finally straightened, "more than a little wild."

"What's your name?"

Luc's question didn't seem to surprise her.

She had done what she thought was the right thing, watching over a fellow Kassian, and she had now come to the Turncoat King's attention. She seemed resigned when she lifted her head.

"Yvette."

"You are a courageous woman, Yvette. And I can tell you there are no Kassians being abducted and disappeared by the Rising Wave."

She hesitated, then gave a nod. "And him?"

"You can stay while I speak to him. And that's all I'll be doing."

She nodded again, and stayed put, to see it through.

Ava agreed with Luc. This woman was courageous.

"His name is Redmayne." Yvette put her hands behind her back, as if standing to attention, and Ava wondered what her role had been before Fernwell fell.

Luc gave her a nod of appreciation, and then stood in front of Redmayne. "You tried to pick a fight with my people."

Redmayn lifted blurry eyes to meet Luc's. He rocked a little, from side to side. "I don't feel well."

Ava suddenly realised he was still holding the scrap of fabric, and she might not have worked as sophisticated a spell as she could have, given the time she'd had to do it in.

She moved back beside the Kassian and tugged the fabric from his fingers.

When she lifted her head, Luc's gaze sharpened, and she saw he was fighting a grin.

He had just realised how she'd neutralised the confrontation, and he found it funny.

"Take a deep breath and I'm sure you'll feel better."

Redmayne narrowed his eyes. "I do suddenly feel better. You're not a sorcerer are you?"

"If I *was* a sorcerer, would I be using my power to make you feel better?" Luc asked him.

He thought about it for an amusingly long time. "I reckon not."

Luc stared at him for a beat. "Don't let me catch you picking fights with my soldiers again, Redmayne."

Redmayne was just canny enough to realize he had been given an out, and he took it, backing away and then turning to shuffle off down the street.

"Are we in trouble?" Finola's question was soft, for Luc's ears only.

The final dregs of the crowd had moved on, and there weren't many people standing close by, but still, Ava could see she didn't want to chance being overheard.

Yvette watched Redmayne stumble away and then with a quick, final look at Luc, tucked back into the stream of pedestrians going about their business, careful not to bring any more attention to herself.

"You're not in trouble." Luc stepped closer to the wall, out of the main thoroughfare. "Confrontations are inevitable. Just report each incident. If there's a pattern emerging—"

"There is." Catja interrupted him, voice as soft as Finola's. "This isn't the first time I've been called a spell caster in the last three days. Someone is making a concerted effort to spread rumours that we're sorcerers, kidnappers and monsters."

"Not unexpected." Dirk lifted broad shoulders. "Who likes being defeated in battle?"

"True, but these have a more . . . organized smell to them." Catja tugged at her braid. "This is strategic."

Luc's face remained neutral, but Ava thought she noticed the skin around his eyes tighten.

"I'll speak to General Ru tonight," he said. "We need to be the ones controlling the narrative here." He dismissed the three soldiers with a nod and waited until they were no longer visible before he turned back to Ava, gave her a long, hard look, and then began to walk toward the palace.

Ava fell into step with him.

"Will I look like I'm talking to myself?" he asked.

She actually didn't know. "Maybe. Or they'll see me, but as an indistinct figure. I'm not sure. We'll have to ask General Ru, or Oscar and Deni." The only three people other than Luc who knew her secret. "How do I look to you?"

He glanced over at her, but only for a moment, and then faced forward again, as if he were a man on his own. "Beautiful, as always."

She gave a snort of laughter, and was suddenly sorry she couldn't hold his hand. It would make people wonder about the mental fitness of the Commander, though, and that wouldn't do.

"You think I'm insincere?" His question was careful, and she focused on his face, suddenly aware there was an undertone to his voice.

"No. I know you think that, but I meant, before, on the plains, you could sense me, but not see me. Now you seem to be able to see through the workings in the cloak. You looked straight at me."

He had always been able to sense her presence when she was wearing the cloak. It had come between them before, reminding him as it did of the terrible mind games that had been played on him in the Chosen camps where he'd grown up.

They had overcome that. Luc had been able to set the horror of those experiences aside.

And now he seemed able to overcome the magic, to a degree.

"You look like a shadow." He glanced over at her again.

She wondered if that was because she wanted him to see her. How responsive was the magic she had worked into her cloak?

She dismissed that train of thought, because they were passing a narrow, dark alley, and it was empty.

She reached out, grabbed Luc's sleeve, and tugged him into it with her.

They stopped just a few steps from the alley entrance, but in deep shadow.

Ava lifted her cloak on either side, and stepped in to embrace him, covering all but his head with the magic-worked cloth.

He leaned back against the wall, and she leaned into him and lifted her face to his.

"I can see you properly now," he said. "Perhaps because I'm surrounded by the cloak, too."

She nodded at that, interested but ignoring it for the moment to address more important issues.

"You are always sincere," she said, then couldn't help the smallest twitch of her lips. "Unless you're talking to one of the nobles and then—"

He bent down and kissed her, cutting off her words.

When he lifted his head, his eyes locked with hers. "Why are you sneaking out, Ava?"

It hurt him.

She could see it in his face.

She didn't want that. Felt a twisting in her gut at the thought.

"The walls close in sometimes. And I don't want to be a whiney baby and interrupt your discussions with General Ru when they do. So I go walking, but keep myself safe with the cloak."

He sighed. "I don't want you to feel that way."

"I know." She shrugged. "I have been out of a dungeon cell far less time than I was in one. I'm sure it'll get better."

"And you want to go back to Grimwalt." He didn't make it a question.

She looked down, her gaze fixing on the brooch that held his cloak at his throat, and pressed her forehead against his chin. "The kidnapper sent by the Speaker of the Grimwalt court said my friends were imprisoned."

"He was trying to hurt you." Luc ran a hand down her back.

"I . . . yes. But I don't think that means he was lying." She had thought about it ever since the Speaker's emissary had taunted her with it, before Luc had killed him.

"Even if he was telling the truth, you don't know which friends, and you don't know where they're being held."

"It's Tomas and Velda." She had other acquaintances in Grimwalt, friends from her teenage years when her parents had spent time at court, but she had travelled with her mother and father on their trade missions, or stayed home on the border with Venyatu for schooling, far more often that she'd been at court.

She did not have many Grimwaldian friends her own age, and then she'd been imprisoned by her cousin.

It was definitely Tomas, her grandmother's estate manager, and Velda, her grandmother's housekeeper. They had helped her escape Grimwalt, and they had paid the price for it.

She wondered what had happened to the pack of dogs she had stolen from the Kassian general who'd overseen her captivity. Tomas had taken care of them after she left Grimwalt to find Luc, but if he was imprisoned, they had no one.

So, yes. She wanted to go back, for many reasons. And knew, all too well, that she couldn't leave just yet.

"How do we find out who he meant, if he was being honest at all?"

Luc using the word 'we' soothed her.

She wasn't in this alone. She knew it in her head, but sometimes her heart needed reminding.

She had been on her own for a long time before she met her warlord.

"Tomas was going to take Velda and the dogs to a friend. I don't know who that was, but I'm sure the local village innkeeper would have known both Tomas and Velda. I could write to her and ask for information."

"Then let's do that." He brushed his lips to her forehead. "The reason I came looking for you might offer an alternative way, though."

She hadn't known he'd specifically come looking for her, but she wasn't surprised. "What other way?"

"A trade and diplomatic envoy has just arrived from Grimwalt."

She suddenly remembered the glimpse she'd had of a man staring at her in surprise when she'd stepped into the tight circle of the crowd earlier.

She'd been too focused on solving the problems created by Redmayne to worry about him before, but now that worry sat heavy in her stomach, weighing her down.

She did not need a rumor to start about her being a spell caster. For one, because it was true, but also, it put a target on her back. Her cousin had held her and her mother for years, trying to force them to work magic to his advantage.

Her mother's experiences as a young woman, kidnapped and traumatised for the same reason, had colored Ava's entire life.

"Was one of them a man in his mid-thirties, short brown hair, a scruffy beard, in a black cloak?" She lifted her face to Luc's and he frowned down at her.

"Not that I noticed, but they may have had servants or assistants who weren't presented at the court." He touched her cheek. "Why?"

"Someone like that seemed to notice me when I was handing

the spell to Redmayne. I saw him look in my direction, and he was surprised."

Luc tugged at the hood of her cloak. "Was this up?"

She gave a slow nod.

"So if he was able to see through the invisibility spell, he might not have gotten a good look at who was inside the cloak?"

"Perhaps." It was something to hope for.

"And he might have only seen what I see. A dark, shadowy figure."

She hoped that was true.

"And even if he did see you, he only knows you were wearing a spell-cast cloak. Not that you created the spells on it yourself." Luc tugged at the wool tunic he wore beneath his own cloak. The spells woven into it were protective, making it impossible for an arrow, knife or sword to pierce it.

"That's true." She'd forgotten many rulers bought spell-worked items for protection, for advantage. Who was to say she hadn't done the same?

Her hands trembled, just a little, as she let the thought settle on her. She had spent so long under the threat that any use of her magic that wasn't specifically for her cousin's use could get her killed, it clouded her thinking.

She leaned against Luc completely, and his arms closed around her.

"You help me see more clearly," she whispered.

A shout from the street, someone calling Luc's name, snapped both their attention back to reality.

Ava pushed back from him with effort, forced herself to give him room to step past her, back into the main thoroughfare.

"No more hiding in the shadows for you," she said.

He smiled at her, but his face was taut. He was feeling the stress of winning the war almost more than when he was leading the Rising Wave toward Fernwell.

"I'll see what this is about, and then meet you at the palace," he said. "The general and I told the Grimwaldians you were busy and we'd meet later this afternoon."

Then he was gone, and she stepped out after him, saw it was Rafe calling him, a small cohort of soldiers from both Venyatu and Cervantes behind him.

Ava watched as Luc bent close to Rafe and then turn toward the city gates with him. Most of the Rising Wave was camped just outside the city walls.

She wished she could follow.

But she had duties of her own, and she would need to think about what she may need to work into her clothing to shield against a Grimwaldian envoy, some of whom could possibly see through her protections.

It was not something she'd had to worry about before.

She might consider avoiding them, just to be safe, but one or more of them may know what had become of Tomas and Velda.

She would not waste this opportunity to find out what had happened to her friends. So she would take the time to think of a way to loosen their tongues and tell her what they knew.

CHAPTER 2

As he followed Rafe toward the city gates, Luc forced
himself not to look back.

He wanted a last look at Ava, but as far as everyone
else was concerned, she wasn't there.

That was good, he knew. It protected her.

It bothered him that she thought someone had seen through
her spell earlier.

He turned to Rafe. "Were you the one who met the Grimwaldian delegation at the palace gates?"

Rafe nodded. "The guards wouldn't let them through, and
someone called me to deal with them."

"How many were there? When they were presented to me,
there were only six."

Rafe's gaze sharpened. "There were six at the gates. The four
senior diplomats and two assistants. You're saying there are more of
them?"

"They didn't make it across the whole of Kassia, from the
northern border to the south, without at least a few guards for
protection."

Rafe swore softly. "I should have thought of that immediately.

Just the diplomats presented themselves at the gates. They must have left the rest of their group somewhere in the city."

"That would be my guess." Luc kept his eyes on their surroundings as they walked through the last line of buildings before the gates out to the open fields to the north of the city. No one paid them any more mind than usual. "Did they say where they are staying?"

Rafe rubbed the back of his neck. "No. I assumed they'd be given rooms in the palace."

Luc shook his head. "No Grimwaldian will have that much access to Ava. Not while I'm alive to prevent it."

"Understood." Rafe glanced at him. "There was someone in Herron's old palace rooms last night. The guards heard the rattle of drawers opening and burst inside, but whoever was there managed to escape. The window was open and there was a rope dangling down into the gardens."

Luc kept his stride even, not letting any sign of his deep unease show. "Bold of someone to break in under our noses. Was anything taken?"

Rafe lifted his shoulders. "Nothing obvious. I've spoken to Raun-Tu, and we've made sure the gardens are patrolled now, too. And the cliffs. I found another rope at the far end of the garden, thrown over one of the walls built on the cliff. They came up from the sea, got a rope over the wall into the garden, and then another one into the Herald's rooms."

Someone who had inside knowledge, then. It would be impossible for a random thief to know which rooms had been Herron's.

"They wouldn't have gone to that trouble and then not taken anything. We just don't know what, yet." That worried him.

Rafe grunted in agreement.

One thing bothered him almost as much, though. "Why am I only hearing about this now?"

Rafe rubbed his chin. "Because there was no sense waking you. It was over, and there was no immediate threat. You were with Ava, and we . . . I . . . thought you could do with a little time off."

His temper had been more than a little stretched since he'd had to start dealing with the Fernwell city council and the nobles, Luc admitted to himself. He needed to rein himself in, before no one told him anything at all.

They reached the arched gate and nodded to the guards. Rafe lifted his hand to a small group of soldiers standing around a fire pit.

"Frederik!"

The young soldier turned and came to attention, then jogged over to them, expression eager.

The scar on his cheek was a thin, silver line against the warm brown of his skin. Luc studied it, and thought Ava would be relieved to know the scar was still visible.

Frederik noticed him looking and touched a fingertip to the scar. "It's fully healed, Commander."

"So I see."

Rafe waved off the conversation with a chop of his hand. "Get a partner, and go find where the Grimwaldian envoy that arrived today went after they presented themselves at the palace."

"Yes, sir." Frederik seemed delighted. "Covertly?"

"Covertly." Rafe's eyes narrowed. "Be discrete. Find out how many of them there are, and if you can, what they've been up to since they arrived."

Frederik rushed back to the group he'd been standing with, and collected Talura, a young soldier from the Funabi forces who'd been part of a team Luc had led in the past. The two of them raced past Luc and Rafe, back into the city.

"Almost painfully eager," Rafe said, with a shake of his head.

"He's loyal. And eager isn't a bad attribute."

"We were never eager," Rafe said.

"We were pressed into service, stolen and forced to fight. We were never going to be eager." Luc had made the Kassians pay for that, but nothing could bring back his childhood.

Rafe grunted in agreement and they walked in silence toward the main tent.

Outside, a horse had been tied to a pole, and Luc realised why Rafe had said so little about why he was urgently needed in the camp.

He had sent watchers to keep an eye on the Jatan border when the Rising Wave had started moving toward Fernwell.

The Jatan had been very conveniently keeping some of the Kassian forces occupied at the time, fighting border skirmishes, and he'd wanted to know if or when that situation changed.

He recognized the colours woven into the saddlebag as being those of one of his scouts.

He said nothing, but Rafe caught his eye and the look that passed between them was a mix of excitement and dread.

As Luc stepped through the tent flaps, Dak was the first person he saw. His lieutenant stood beside a table, and the rider of the horse, hair sweat-soaked, cloak stained with travel, leaned against it beside him.

"Kym."

She turned, her face lighting up at the sight of him.

"I won't embrace you, Commander. I stink. But it's good to see you."

"You heard we won." He hoped that's why she was here.

She shook her head. "I heard about your victory when I reached Bartolo, not that I trusted the news completely, but that's not why I came looking for the Rising Wave."

Luc's gaze met Dak's, and his friend gave a tiny shake of his head.

Kym caught the exchange, and blew out a breath. "You know the Kassians withdrew most of their forces on the Jatan border to try and crush you before you reached Fernwell?"

Luc nodded.

"For the first week after they left, the Jatan were just grateful for the reprieve. I think they were on the verge of collapse. But they slowly realised the Kassian forces were gone for good, not just licking their wounds nearby."

Dak looked worried. "Kym says they've started to encroach on Kassia."

Kym nodded. "They have. You need to decide how much you're comfortable with them taking, because I watched them for the first two days of their advancement, and they didn't look like they were stopping."

"You said they were near defeat when the Herald moved his army away to take on the Rising Wave?" Luc wondered why they were being so bold, if so. An army on its last legs was not wise to take territory it couldn't defend.

Kym nodded. "I think they've lost a lot of their experienced warriors, and perhaps the older ones who are left are hungry for revenge, and there are some young, green leaders promoted out of necessity. They're moving way beyond their capability to defend their position, but they're also getting excited about their progress. If you don't nip it in the bud, they're going to start feeling like the bits they've taken are really theirs to take." She fidgeted, and then looked down.

"What is it?" Luc watched her carefully. She was holding something back and he wondered why.

When she lifted her head, he could see the strain around her eyes and mouth.

"Some of them broke off from the main spearhead." She worried her lower lip with her teeth. "I think they were headed for Cervantes, but I didn't have time to both follow them and get here to give you the news."

It would have been a hard choice to make. Luc tilted his head. "What about the other watchers I set on the border? Joacim, Mande and . . ." He tried to remember the last name.

"Farvela," Kym said quietly. She lifted both shoulders. "I haven't seen any of them in well over a week. None of them came to our last scheduled meeting. That's when I decided I had to come to Fernwell. To let you know what was happening. I was stretched too thin."

"You did the right thing. Go bathe, rest and eat. And I'm sorry, but you'll have to lead us back to where you think the Jatan have gone." Luc thought about it. Every day's delay was dangerous. Especially if they were headed for Cervantes.

All the Cervantes soldiers were here, part of the Rising Wave force that had taken the Kassian capital. The villages and camps of his home were completely undefended.

They had given up their strongest to bring an end to Kassian rule.

If the Jatan thought to replace one foreign power with another . . . for a moment, exhaustion and despair drained his strength, and he forced himself to shake them off.

He had taken the Kassian stronghold of Fernwell. He could take some green Jatan officers with more ambition than strength and sense any day.

"I'll see you have all you need." Dak put a hand on Kym's shoulder. "Luc's right. We'll have to go head them off."

With a nod, Kym followed him out, and Luc stood in silence for a moment. Rafe said nothing, and the only sound was the *snap snap snap* of the tent canvas in the brisk wind.

"There was a night, two years ago," Rafe said into the silence. "We were about to fight the Venyatux. The Kassians thought we would fight their battle for them, that the threat of harm to the youngsters still in the camps would keep us in line."

Luc turned to look at him.

Rafe smiled, a crooked lift of one side of his mouth. "I considered taking my own life, that night. Having that control over myself at least, if I had nothing else."

Luc's felt a chill grip him at this admission.

Rafe lifted a hand, a silent request to be allowed to continue without interruption, and Luc gave a nod.

"You came into the sleeping tent at maybe two or three in the morning. I could see you had been running or riding hard, that you'd gone somewhere and come back." He gave a chuckle. "When you said you'd snuck into the Venyatux camp and made a deal with them . . ." Rafe lifted both hands, palms up. "I had never heard of anything so brilliant. But for me, the biggest, most amazing gift you gave me in that moment was my control back. And when we went out onto the field the next morning, and instead of attacking the Venyatux, turned on the Kassians lined up behind us on the field . . ." Rafe sighed. "Nothing will ever compare. Not even taking Fernwell by having the gates simply open to us, and being invited in. You have never led us astray since that night on the eve of battle, and you will not lead us astray now."

"Everyone is tired. We've fought almost continually since that night you describe. And when we haven't been fighting, we've been on the move." Luc knew the Cervantes needed a break. A time to come to terms with everything that had happened.

Not just in the last two years, but since the establishment of the Chosen camps, the systematic abduction and internment of a generation of children.

He sucked in a breath, thinking of all the young Cervantes he'd been able to liberate from the Chosen camps after that fateful day when he'd negotiated with the Venyatux, and turned on the Kassians.

The day he'd become the famous Turncoat King.

He had had no childhood.

He would fight to the death to ensure those children he'd managed to set free did.

Which meant heading north and stopping the Jatan in their tracks.

It didn't matter if he was tired. He could sleep when whatever threat to the Cervantes was dead.

CHAPTER 3

Ava nodded to the Rising Wave soldiers on guard in the
halls of the palace. She walked the passageways at a fast
clip, heading from her and Luc's rooms to the old queen's
study. General Ru wanted them to meet before she graced the
Grimwaldian envoy with her presence.

She enjoyed the flutter of her dress against her skin. She had
chosen fabric of pale green silk, and it was unadorned. It looked
thin, almost weightless.

Fortunately, the current fashion of layered sleeves, each layer
slightly longer than the layer above, made it easy to hide workings
on the innermost layer, flush against her skin.

She had also worked the inside of the strip of fabric that delin-
eated the waist of the dress.

And finally, she had fashioned undergarments for herself. A
tight bodice and short shorts. She had found the finest, stretchiest
linen, cut on the bias, and she had embroidered every inch of available fabric.

The undergarments gave her a similar sense of security to her
cloak, which she couldn't wear indoors without raising eyebrows
and suspicions.

They had a second, unexpected benefit, though.

They seemed to fascinate Luc.

She was approaching the former queen's study, and Raun-Tu, one of General Ru's top lieutenants, opened the door for her.

She met Luc's gaze as he looked up at her entrance, and she thought some of what she'd just been thinking remained in her gaze, because his eyes widened and heat flared within them.

He gave her a long, slow smile, but she found her own lips were incapable of moving.

"Problem?" Raun-Tu asked her, and she realised she was blocking the entrance.

"No." She cleared her throat, but before she stepped all the way in, she turned and whispered a request in Raun-Tu's ear. He nodded and closed the door behind her.

"Something's happened." She could see maps on the table, and despite the surge of desire she had just shared with Luc, she could see he was tense. More tense than usual.

"One of my spies from the Jatan border just came back to report." Luc closed his eyes and rubbed the back of his neck.

"And?" She felt a sinking feeling in the pit of her stomach.

"And we have a problem." The general's words were measured, but Ava wanted to laugh at them.

Just one problem?

She thought they had at least four or five, and that was before whatever news Luc's spy had brought with them.

Before she could respond, General Ru lifted a hand, opened a drawer in the desk beside her, and pulled out a thin, braided rope of dark brown thread.

Ava had made it brown to match the wooden boards of the study.

The general held the two ends together, one in each hand, and threw the loop that she'd created outward, bending down to a crouch and laying the rough circle that was formed on the floor, careful to cross one end over the other so there was no gap.

She stepped into the ring, and Luc and then Ava joined her.

No one could hear a word that was said now.

"What is it?"

"The Jatan have invaded the north west." Luc's words were quiet.

They should have anticipated that, she supposed. With the Kassians no longer there to hold them back, the Jatan would have no reason to stay on their side of the border.

"Should I send a missive to their leaders, demanding they retreat?"

Luc look up in surprise at that. "Do you think that will work?"

She lifted her shoulders. "I've met a few Jatan when I traveled with my parents on their trade missions. They're not unreasonable. I've even been to Jatan once before and while I assume a strongly worded letter won't stop them, it will set out our position, and let them know we intend to defend our borders. It may slow them down."

"They may have assumed a Cervantes, Funabi and Venyatux alliance would have no interest in the land on the Kassian side of the Jatan border. Writing to let them know we do object may well give them pause." General Ru gave a slow nod. "It's better to do it than not."

"Write it, then." Luc's mouth formed a grim line. "And I'll take it with me when I ride north."

"You're going up to the border?" Her stomach sank, and she found herself suddenly short of breath. "Is it that bad?"

When Luc's gaze met hers, she saw that yes, it was that bad.

"My scout saw some of them turn, headed for Cervantes," he said. "And there is no one in my homeland to stop them. Every soldier is here in Fernwell."

A spike of fury rose in her.

How dare the Jatan? How dare they use the sacrifices of the Cervantes to advance themselves?

She pushed back her shoulders. "I will come with you, and I will make them regret it."

Before Luc could respond to her, Raun-Tu tapped on the door and leaned in.

"Grimwaldians." His voice seemed to come from far away.

The general turned, giving a nod to her lieutenant and stepping out of the circle. "Where are they?"

"I've put them in the waiting room to the side of the throne room." He withdrew.

Ava stepped out of the circle herself and bent to pick up the braided rope. It bothered her that Raun-Tu had poked his head into the room while they were using it.

The big lieutenant was used to constant access to the general, and also to the more informal set-up of the Rising Wave camp, where tents were the only structures.

Still . . .

"What does Raun-Tu know about the rope of silence?" she asked as she slid it back into the drawer. Then felt stupid calling her thin, woven length of thread something as portentous as the rope of silence.

General Ru gave Ava her full attention. "Good name," she said. "He knows nothing. But if he does notice it, or if I need to use it in his presence, I'll say it was left behind by the Grimwaldians who tried to capture you. He already knows about the binding ropes that weaken a body that I kept from that incident, and that there was a strange silence for some of the time during which they tried to drag you away."

Luc touched her shoulder, and she realised how stiff she was.

She forced herself to relax. "I suppose that's the best we can do."

"He's my lieutenant, Ava." General Ru lifted her shoulders.

What she meant was, she needed to use it, and Raun-Tu would eventually see it. It was what it was.

The leader of the Venyatux army was a pragmatist, Ava knew. And she used everything she had around her to maximum advantage.

Ava had made the rope only two days ago. The general had started using it immediately.

She had only herself to blame.

She sighed.

"Wear the crown when you meet the Grimwaldians." The general nodded to her aunt's crown, set on a stand on the desk.

Ava grimaced. She had worn it twice, at the two formal meetings they'd had so far with the nobles and city elders.

It was uncomfortable.

Luc lifted it up and she took a step closer so he could set it on her head.

It was filigree, not too heavy, but her aunt's head was a little smaller than her own, so it pressed into her temples.

She stepped out into the corridor.

"Don't look so put out about playing queen." Raun-Tu grinned at her.

He used to be her commanding officer, back when she'd been pretending to be a Venyatux soldier, and he still hadn't gotten used to her being the queen of Kassia.

She hadn't, either, to be honest.

She smoothed her expression to something neutral and unreadable. "Better?"

Raun-Tu's grin deepened, and he held out the two scrolls she'd requested he find for her. "You wanted these?"

"I'll take them." Luc reached for them and lifted his brows. "We're going hard with them?"

General Ru had been fussing in the study, and she stepped out as Luc spoke, her eyes going wide at the sight of the scrolls. "I see. No quarter given, I take it?"

"We could pretend we don't know about these, but that's just more game playing. I want to confront them with the missives, and see their reaction." She didn't know if this was the right way, if there was a better strategy, but the honesty of it appealed to her. She couldn't very well play games anyway if she wanted to ask them where Tomas and Velda were being held.

The scrolls contained offers and promises from the Speaker of the Grimwalt Court to her aunt, the former queen of Kassia, which made it clear the Speaker was on her aunt's side in the conflict with the Rising Wave, even though at the time, Grimwalt's border had been closed to Kassia.

The Speaker's cooperation, however, had been contingent on money and influence. The scrolls laid bare an ugly streak of greed and hubris.

And if she, Luc and the general had intercepted the scrolls en route to her aunt and changed the wording a little to insult the queen and make her less likely to cooperate with the Speaker . . . well, that didn't negate the original intention of the missives.

"I agree. No games." Luc tucked the scrolls under an arm and held out his other to her. She slipped her hand through the crook of his elbow and let him lead the way to the throne room.

When she was seated on the ornate throne her aunt had used, with Luc on one side of her, the general on the other, the doors to the chamber were opened and the Grimwaldians walked through.

The room was clad in peach marble, veined with cream and gold, and the back of the throne was carved into a cresting wave.

Every time Ava sat on it, she had to admit she felt a sense of satisfaction at the symbolism.

Her aunt had been brought down by an army calling themselves the Rising Wave. She had asked Luc if his mother had told him about the carvings in the throne from the one time she had been received by the queen and that is why he had given his army the name that he had. He had looked at the throne thoughtfully and shaken his head.

"I can't remember," he'd said. "But maybe. Maybe it lodged in some corner of my mind."

No torches or lanterns were necessary in the throne room, even though the afternoon was winding down to dusk.

The windows were long and wide and caught the sun as it sank, orange and fat, so that the marble glowed and the room seemed to shimmer with golden air.

The Grimwaldians traversed the long carpet from the door to the foot of the dais, where they came to a halt. Raun-Tu and the three guards he had assigned to stand with him, one Cervantes, one Venyatux and one Funabi, drew themselves straighter as the envoy approached, and Raun-Tu moved subtly, making it clear they would go no further.

"Your highness." The leader of the delegation was familiar to Ava.

She'd anticipated some of the group would be.

She'd spent years in and out of the Grimwalt court. Not long enough to form close ties, but enough to form acquaintances.

She couldn't quite place the man who addressed her, but she knew she had seen him before.

"You might remember me, your highness, I am Julian Furte. I was a friend of your parents."

"And yet, I hear my family is out of favor in Grimwalt now. And that I am considered a fugitive. I would be interested in hearing what my crime is."

Furte blanched, and then his cheeks flushed. "Where did you hear that?"

"A reliable source. And of course, the man who tried to abduct me on the orders of the Speaker of the Grimwalt court mentioned something along those lines, as well."

Two of the diplomats in the envoy drew in audible breaths at her pronouncement, and looked back toward the door.

Raun-Tu's people stepped closer, blocking their way.

"I . . . know nothing about that. If someone claimed the Speaker was trying to take you against your will, they were lying." Furte's tongue darted out to wet his lips.

"They weren't lying." She leaned forward. "The Speaker sent me numerous requests to attend court when I managed to free myself from Kassian imprisonment, and when I declined, he sent two people after me. They pursued me all the way to Fernwell."

Furte turned to his little entourage. "Did any of you know of this?"

Blank faces stared back at him, but Ava thought one of the assistants looked a little nervous.

"And then, of course, there are these." She gestured to the scrolls Luc was holding, and Raun-Tu walked up the steps and took them from Luc and handed them to Furte. "I found them in my aunt's study after the Rising Wave took the city."

Furte gave one to a colleague, unrolled the other, and they read in silence. It grew and grew, until Ava felt the weight of it.

She watched the group carefully.

Some of them might really not be aware of the machinations of the Speaker. Some might be under his sway. But she was growing surer by the moment that woman who was clearly an assistant, her dark hair pulled back in a low bun, her clothing more plain and severe than those of the diplomats, had known exactly what she was walking into.

She had courage, at least, Ava thought.

The woman didn't know what kind of a leader Ava was. She also had the infamous Turncoat King, and the fierce General Ru of the Venyatux army, standing on either side of her.

The assistant might have been serving herself up for death, for all she knew.

And yet she had come anyway.

"I can hardly believe what is written here," Furte said eventually, into the silence. He passed the scroll to another in the group.

"I concur. If we had known these scrolls existed, we would have approached you in a completely different way." The woman who had read the second scroll's voice trembled slightly. "I am Renata Ewing, your highness, and I was a friend of your mother's." She drew herself up. "I helped your grandmother persuade the court to close our border to Kassia in retaliation for your mother and father's capture and death. I would never have stood for anything that is written on this parchment."

"The two spies in the Venyatux column mentioned in the scrolls, were they the two who pursued you to Fernwell?" Furte seemed to be connecting things very quickly.

"We can only assume so. They disappeared when the Rising Wave was close to Fernwell, and one of them broke into my rooms in the palace after we took the city, and tried to abduct me at knife-point."

Luc crossed his arms over his chest. "Before I killed him, he said he was acting on the Speaker's orders."

"He was lying." The assistant, the one Ava was sure found none of these revelations a surprise, hissed the words.

"He was the same person who tried to abduct me from my grandmother's estate, on the Speaker's orders again, before I joined the Rising Wave." Ava leaned back on the throne and wondered how her aunt had stood sitting on it for hours on end. It was hard and extremely uncomfortable. "He mentioned it when he tried to abduct me from the Venyatux column on the way to Fernwell, as well. I believed he was telling the truth. What reason would he have to lie?"

"Why would the Speaker be so fixated on getting you to court?" A third member of the envoy spoke for the first time. "Did he say?"

"No." Ava tilted her head. That was the truth, although she knew all too well the reason for it. He wanted to use her magic skills for his own benefit. "I thought you could enlighten us." Would they tell her the truth if they knew it?

"We had no idea. If we had any inkling . . ."

"You would have turned tail and run for home," General Ru said in a calm voice.

"Perhaps." The fourth diplomat of the envoy was an old man, and he spoke quietly, with dignity. His words brought down the tension better than any protestation of innocence could have. "My name is Guran Hur and I can see things are not what we were led to believe."

"What were you led to believe?" Ava asked, looking at him directly.

Before he could answer, as his mouth opened to speak, the young assistant pushed Furte to one side and raised her arm, aiming for Guran Hur.

Raun-Tu shoved her, hard, and she fell, landing badly on her side.

Ava heard the thump of her body connecting with the marble floor, the wheeze as she struggled for breath.

Ava rose to her feet, focusing on the object in the woman's hand.

She had assumed it was a knife, but it looked like a tarnished silver spoon.

"Stay back." The woman managed to draw breath to speak, and she waved the spoon at them, pain in her voice and on her face. She moved awkwardly, as if her arm was broken, and got her knees under her.

She looked as if she wanted to rise to her feet, but her skin had taken on a gray tinge and instead she bent her head down to her knees and concentrated on breathing. She slipped the spoon from the hand of her broken arm to the other.

"Is that a spoon?" General Ru asked, astonished.

"That's what it looks like." Renata Ewing glanced at Ava. "It is probably something more dangerous."

Ava had already guessed that, but she saw Renata was making sure to be helpful and cooperative.

"Janice. What is this about?" Guran Hur's voice was soft.

Instead of answering, her lip trembling, her eyes wild, Janice threw the spoon at him. Her aim was off, she was throwing with her non-dominant hand, and it missed Guran Hur and hit the third diplomat, the one who had yet to introduce himself.

He crumpled to the ground, his eyes bulging, his face twisted in fear. It seemed to Ava he tried to scream, but nothing came out of him but the rattle of constricted breath. He twitched, as if batting something away and then lay still, completely unmoving.

Raun-Tu had unsheathed his sword and he used it to flick the spoon away. It skittered across the slick marble and came to rest against a wall.

All eyes turned back to Janice, but she had lain down herself,

Ava saw. Her eyes were closed, and she had curled up, in a foetal position. She seemed to no longer be a threat to anyone.

In the silence, Ava heard Janice's breath rattle in her chest, and then a sigh.

She ran lightly down the stairs of the dais and approached.

Luc's hand was suddenly on her shoulder. He said nothing, but she understood the warning clearly enough.

"I think she's dead," she said into the quiet. She crouched down, looking carefully at what Janice might have in her hands.

Nothing.

"She just laid down and died?" General Ru was disbelieving.

"Someone bespelled her." Furte sounded angry. "Someone set her on a course of action and made sure she would die when it was done, so she couldn't give them away."

"What course of action, though?" General Ru's voice was harsh in the quiet. "Stopping one of you answering a question was hardly a solution. She couldn't have been sure she could kill all of you, and she must have known we would stop her."

That was true.

Ava wondered why Janice would give herself away like that. She might have been able to silence Guran Hur before he spoke, but she surely understood killing the other three diplomats and her fellow assistant would have been nearly impossible under the circumstances.

"Was there something you know that the others don't?" she asked the old Grimwaldian.

Guran Hur was looking at the spoon, and he turned to answer her. "Maybe I do."

"Then maybe you need to start talking."

CHAPTER 4

S ome of the Grimwaldians could well be lying about what they knew.

Luc watched them from his position behind Ava, who was seated at the large table in the chamber off the throne room, where her aunt had previously entertained her favorite courtiers and visiting dignitaries.

It was a lavish space in the palace's inner sanctum, and Luc could see the venue was not lost on the Grimwaldians. They were being given a level of trust that they surely had not earned.

The other assistant had been led away by one of Raun-Tu's guards, babbling as he went that he had no idea what Janice had planned to do. He hadn't even liked her.

He was probably harmless, but Luc was not going to risk Ava, so he had taken a moment to murmur in Raun-Tu's ear to let the man loose outside the palace and make sure he was followed.

Raun-Tu's eyes had gleamed as he gave a slight nod and beckoned one of his guards to him.

The three diplomats sat along the opposite side of the table, and all of them looked nervous.

"So, what do you know?" The general cut to the chase.

Luc knew she understood his urgency, his need to leave as soon as this problem was dealt with to intercept the Jatan.

Rafe was busy putting a unit together, sourcing supplies, but the main issue now was not how quickly they could be on the road, but what to do about Ava.

She thought she could come.

Wanted to come.

And Luc knew all too well that would be problematic.

They had only just taken Fernwell.

The queen could not abandon it now.

"You have to understand, when we left Grimwalt just over three weeks ago, we didn't realize the Rising Wave had taken Fernwell." Furte spoke first, and Luc wondered about the dynamics of the envoy. Furte had put himself forward every time they'd spoken as a group, but it was Guran Hur who'd been targeted by Janice, and Guran Hur whose words seemed to carry the most weight.

"You would have known before you arrived, though," Luc said. "And even if you didn't know we had been successful, you must surely have known you were walking into a war zone."

"We were told we would be allowed in to Fernwell and would have the ear of the queen when we got here." Guran Hur leaned forward, hands clasped together. The scrolls Ava had shown them lay on the table, unrolled, and Hur nodded toward them. "Having read the missives from our Speaker to the former queen of Kassia, I understand now why he thought we would be given safe passage by her."

"Even so," General Ru had decided to sit beside Ava, rather than stand, and she leaned forward herself, "how could you be sure Fernwell wouldn't be surrounded by the Rising Wave, or your path blocked by us?"

"We couldn't. We were prepared to wait at a safe distance until . . ." Renate's voice trailed off.

"Until?" Ava asked.

"Until Kassia defeated the Rising Wave." Renate ducked her head in embarrassment. "I am not sure why we were so sure that is how it would be, but thinking back on our reasoning now, that's the only outcome we considered."

"And when you reached Fernwell and found the one outcome you hadn't considered had come to pass, you came in anyway." Luc studied their faces. "And you asked to see the queen. But not the queen you were expecting when you set out."

The three sat still and looked at each other in surprise, as if just realizing now how strange their behavior was.

"I can't explain it." Furte shook his head. "When you put it like that . . ."

"It's like we were living in a strange bubble." Renata rubbed at her temple. "I don't know what to say."

"The wagon driver." Guran Hur said the words as if he were being strangled. "It was . . ." He swallowed hard, fighting for air, and eventually leaned back in his chair, weak with some invisible effort.

Everyone in the room had come to attention when they saw his struggles. No one touched him, though.

The old diplomat blew out a breath. "I can't remember, but it seems I'm the only one who even knows what's been forgotten, so perhaps that is why Janice tried to kill me."

Because after the Rising Wave took Fernwell, the point was no longer to get money or influence from the old Kassian queen, but to take Ava back to Grimwalt.

Luc would bet his trusty sword the wagon driver or someone riding with the envoy was the one tasked with abducting her. And in order to have a solid reason to get into Fernwell, to have access to Ava, they had kept the diplomats in the envoy befuddled and pointed toward the city and a meeting with a queen. Whichever one happened to be on the throne.

They needed to find that cart driver.

He leaned across and touched the general's shoulder, a silent request for her to be on guard with Ava, and strode out of the room.

He made his way to the stables, where Rafe was shouting orders as horses were led out and saddled. The light of the day was almost completely gone and torches lit the cobbled space, dancing light and shadow over the chaos.

"You need to send someone to find the Grimwaldians' wagon driver. He's the one to watch."

Rafe made a face. "How important is this? There's a lot to do, if we're going to ride tonight."

"Very important, but as you won't be the one left behind searching for him, hand it to someone you trust. There are a lot of soldiers doing nothing, give whoever you hand this to the authority to draft as many people as they need to find him. And tell them to beware. I think he's a spell caster. He's responsible for the mess in the throne room."

Rafe looked at him blankly. "What mess?"

Luc felt a sudden, grudging respect for Raun-Tu. The general's lieutenant had kept things very much contained.

"Two dead."

Rafe's whole body tensed. "What?"

"It's dealt with. But be warned, the wagon driver seems the likely culprit. The envoy was bespelled and they used a magic-worked spoon."

Rafe looked like he wanted to chuckle at the mention of the spoon.

"It killed the person it was used against." Luc's words didn't quite dispel the skepticism on Rafe's face but he sobered up.

"Magical utensils. Got it."

It was Luc's turn to make a face. "I know it sounds ridiculous. I'm assuming that's how the Grimwaldian got the spoon past the guards and within throwing distance of Ava."

Rafe's face was completely serious now. "How do we know what's dangerous?"

Luc shook his head. "It's impossible to know for sure. Just tell whoever you send not to accept anything from them, and beware of anything they've got in their hands."

Rafe nodded. "When do we leave?"

Luc thought of Ava, and the weight of his responsibility pressed hard on him. "As soon as I can square things here."

"We'll have an extra companion for some of the way. Kikir has been talking about returning home to report on the Rising Wave's victory and the alliances he's made with us and the Venyatux, and he asked if he could accompany us until he needs to turn north toward Skäddar."

The Skäddar warrior had been a useful ally, and Luc had no concerns about him being part of the unit. In fact, it would be a shame to lose such an accomplished fighter before they reached Cervantes.

"He's welcome."

Rafe tapped a fist to his chest and left, and Luc made his way back to the antechamber.

A month ago, while he'd waited for Ava to join him from Grimwalt, he'd felt like heaving the responsibility for the massive army off his shoulders and going to look for her.

He'd had to force himself to stay where he was, to lead the column, and she had come to him, just as she'd promised, bringing a sense of home and peace with her.

It would be hard to leave her here. Especially as he knew she would fight the idea of him going without her.

And yet, he couldn't see another way for this to work.

When he reached the chamber it was clear the meeting was over. Everyone was on their feet.

The general stood beside Ava, and Luc saw his heart's choice looked a little amused at the protective stance General Ru had taken.

Ava could look after herself, he knew. But it eased something in him that the general would watch her back.

"Where are you staying in the city?" Ava asked Guran Hur.

"I . . ." He looked over at the others, and they seemed equally unable to answer.

"Then we will organize a place for you close by to the palace." The general shared a look with Raun-Tu and he nodded.

Luc approved. Better to keep the envoy away from the rest of their entourage. Especially if they were so befuddled they didn't know where they were staying.

As they were led out, Renate Ewing reached out a hand to Ava, and before Luc could stop her, she gripped Ava's arm.

"Your mother was my friend. I'm glad to see you alive and well, because your grandmother and I feared the worst for you when word came back that your parents had been killed."

Luc did not relax, even though Ava placed her own hand over Renate's and patted it. "Perhaps one day we can sit together and talk of my mother. Remember her."

The woman nodded and then followed her colleagues out of the room.

Ava waited until they were gone and her posture drooped. "They are so confused, they don't even know where they are staying. There is no way I'll be able to find out from them where Tomas and Velda have been taken."

"And yet, they didn't seem confused at all when they got here." The general was skeptical.

"They were probably told the same thing every day, and it burrowed into their minds, so the spell caster needed to do less and less work to keep them ignoring reality. We pulled the loose thread, and the whole construct has unraveled. Things like where they are staying, where their luggage is, that requires them to be present in the now, and they haven't been in the now for a few weeks, is my guess."

The general hummed, but she didn't contradict Ava. "You're ready?" she asked Luc.

"Ready?" Ava turned, eyes wide. "We're going now?"

"No." Luc saw the general slip out of the room and take the guards with her.

Good.

They would need privacy for this conversation.

Ava was frowning at him, but not because she was confused. She was bright enough to have worked out he didn't mean her to come with him.

She said nothing, looking up at him. She was working through it herself. When she finally came to the same conclusion as him, she sighed, leaned against him.

"I can't leave. You have to go."

"Yes." The word was hard to get out.

His arms were around her, and she burrowed closer. When she lifted her face to his, he could see tears in her eyes.

"I don't like this."

"I know."

"How soon will you be ready to go?" She tried to step back, he could see it was to show him she accepted and understood, but he held on to her.

"Rafe is organizing things. Soon." He nuzzled her hair, unwilling to waste even a moment with her.

"I need to work a few things for you."

He wanted to protest, to keep her with him for the short time they had left, but he would be a fool ten times over to stop her.

He had seen first hand how valuable the workings she made could be.

He forced himself to loosen his hold and step back. "Half an hour, maybe a little more, and then we'll be off."

She nodded, drawing herself up. "I'll work until you come to let me know you're going."

He brushed his lips across her forehead, and then she was gone in a swirl of green silk.

He didn't see a single stitch of embroidery on her dress.

Knowing his heart's choice, she had hidden them away. And he realized they hadn't even had time to talk about what her magic had told her about the Grimwaldians.

They wouldn't have time before he left, either.

Things were moving too fast.

And while he hadn't exactly enjoyed the aftermath of his victory over Kassia, he realised he dreaded having to leave.

His life had been a series of doing things he dreaded, he acknowledged as he strode out of the palace to the stables.

Maybe one day he would be able to say no to whatever it was that was asked of him.

Unfortunately, that day wasn't today.

CHAPTER 5

"I thought you'd be more difficult about it." General Ru turned back to the palace, and given Luc and his unit of eighty soldiers were out of sight, Ava turned with her.

"I wanted to be." But there was no one to blame, other than the Jatan. And Luc was the one going off to deal with them. "There was no other choice."

"No. Things are wobbly enough with you here, imagine if the queen disappeared? We also have the Grimwaldians to deal with. You need to be careful there. I don't trust them." General Ru stepped through into the big open space at the entrance to the palace.

"Luc has people watching them, and Rafe has appointed Eckhart to coordinate and look for the wagon driver." She didn't know Eckhart well, but she'd traded pleasantries with him over meals on the road with the Rising Wave, and he seemed competent.

Rafe wouldn't have chosen him otherwise.

Massi and Revek had gone with Luc, and she couldn't help but think he'd taken them because it was easier for her that way.

Both of the Rising Wave lieutenants had had problems with Ava when she'd come into Luc's life. Things were better now, but there was a lot of unspoken history between them.

Dak, Luc's third lieutenant, had been chosen as the head of the Rising Wave in Luc's absence. Ava wondered if he was happy or sad to have been left behind.

He'd come to say goodbye to Luc, but had left to go back to the Rising Wave camp immediately.

He promised he'd be back the following evening to have dinner at the palace with the general and herself, so they could plan their next moves in Luc's absence.

It was not something she was looking forward to.

Her aunt had run Kassia with less and less input from her councillors as she'd become more and more paranoid, and Ava's cousin, Herron, the Queen's Herald, had made decisions behind her back that had led to the Rising Wave's decisive victory.

The way Kassia was run had to change.

She had always thought Grimwalt had a good system, that Kassia could benefit from learning from it. It was ruled by input from all its people, theoretically, but since she'd escaped, and learned first hand the overreach of Grimwalt's Speaker, its system clearly needed a few tweaks, as well.

The Venyatux had a similar structure to Grimwalt, with a council that elected a leader. The Skäddar didn't even appoint a leader to make decisions. It was done by a collective.

But after her aunt's long influence, it was taking people time to understand a shift in governance was coming, and to put forward ideas.

She had come away from each meeting with the community leaders and councillors feeling further behind than when she'd started.

The problem was they kept trying to work out her angle, sure she was tricking them in some way. And they kept nervous, wary eyes on Luc and the general, as if sure a bloodbath was imminent.

It drained her of energy and made her feel like getting on a horse and riding away back to Cervantes with Luc, letting Kassia rot.

Too many sacrifices had been made for that to be an option, but a queen who didn't want to be a queen could dream, couldn't she?

She made her way to her rooms, then stood by the window and wondered what to do.

There was plenty of correspondence from Kassia's neighbours, all stiff and panicked, seeking information from her about how things would proceed.

She couldn't really tell them until she knew herself, and she could not bear the thought of tackling them now.

Not while her heart and her head were with Luc, racing toward the north.

She saw someone had left her a tray with soup and bread, some cheese and fruit, and she sat and forced a few spoonfuls down, but she had no appetite.

Luc would try to reach Bartolo tonight sometime before midnight, where they could rest the horses and gather more supplies.

She couldn't sit and write, or even read, as if her body was with them, riding in the night.

She paced restlessly, and then stood by the window again, listening to the sounds of the city below and beyond the walls.

A light tap on her door was a relief.

"Captain Eckhart is below to speak with you." Talika, one of the guards often on watch outside her rooms, gestured to the stairs.

"I'll come down." She was glad of the distraction.

Eckart was waiting for her in a small room off the main entrance. It had a fire place and comfortable chairs, as well as a small dining table. She, Luc, the general and whichever of their lieutenants weren't on duty met here often in the two weeks since they'd taken the city.

"Eckhart." She clasped a fist to her chest in greeting. "I haven't seen much of you since we took Fernwell."

Eckart gave a lopsided smile. "I've been tasked with decommissioning the Kassian guards and soldiers. I've been arranging new work for them, so we don't have hundreds of unemployed trained killers wandering around."

Ava had been involved in the process, but only in as much as she'd made funds available for reconstruction projects and rebuilding. Her aunt, it seemed, hadn't been inclined to spend money on keeping her city maintained.

It made for a useful outlet for the Kassian soldiers and guards either in the city or those limping back from the battlefields. Right now, no one in the Rising Wave was prepared to trust or accept Kassian soldiers into their ranks.

But everyone had been in agreement they couldn't simply cut them loose, either.

Eckart would have been busy.

"Rafe asked you to coordinate the watch on the Grimwaldians?"

Eckart nodded. He was broad shouldered, his face always serious, but his light brown hair was curly and it framed his face and gave him a sweet, friendly look.

"Frederick and Talura have been watching the envoy since this afternoon, and Rafe added more watchers to the group since the incident in the throne room." He paused. "Can you tell me exactly what that incident was?"

His voice changed a little when he asked, coming out stiff, as if he were insulted he hadn't been given all the information.

But he would know there were some things it was better to keep quiet about, and she had never known him to be territorial.

The workings in her dress spiked, warning her.

"A magic spoon was used to kill one of the diplomats."

"Are the diplomats still in the palace?"

She shook her head. "Raun-Tu has them somewhere safe. We are more interested in the people who accompanied them. The wagon driver, any other assistants or helpers."

She kept talking, but she was wary. She didn't understand everything her workings were telling her.

Eckhart didn't mean her harm, but he was dangerous to her. There was a dissonance that sat uncomfortably on her skin.

"Frederik and Talura found where they're staying. In an inn off the main road. I went in to speak to them, see if I could find the wagon driver that Rafe told me is the prime suspect."

Again, she felt a tug of warning. If he were enspelled, he wouldn't personally mean her harm, but would be dangerous to her, wouldn't he? It was the only thing that made sense.

And there was only one way to find out.

"Can I see the beautiful thing you have in your pocket?" she asked. She was guessing about the pocket, but he wore no cloak and had nothing in his hands. Janice had used a silver spoon, maybe Eckhart would be carrying something similar.

Eckart hesitated.

Ava was sorry she had no thread and fabric on her. She had come straight down from her rooms, still in the green silk dress, and it had no pockets.

It left her not exactly defenceless, but she had no thread to work, no way to counter whatever spell was exerting its influence over Eckart.

Because if there was nothing in his pocket, if he wasn't enspelled, he would have already said so.

He put a hand in his pocket, a frown on his face, and pulled out a fork.

He looked at it for a moment, the expression in his eyes one of wonder, and then he threw the fork at her.

She had enough protections to slide out of the way, so it hit the wall with a ting and clattered to the floor.

She was tempted to trap it under her shoe, but she couldn't remember if the spoon Janice had thrown this afternoon had touched the skin of the diplomat it had killed. She had a feeling it hadn't.

The magic might be able to affect her, even through her sole, so she stepped clear of it.

"You found the wagon driver," she said.

Eckhart blinked. "Did I?" He ran a hand over his face and then spun slowly in place, as if trying to orientate himself. "I can't remember."

"What does the fork do?" The spoon had killed the diplomat instantly, but if this was meant for her, then maybe it wasn't lethal. So far the Speaker of the Grimwalt court had tried to take her alive. She was no use to him dead.

"The fork?" He blinked at her. "What fork?"

She pointed to it, and he stared at it for a long time. "Rafe said to look out for magical utensils. He made it sound funny."

"They spelled you to throw it at me." Or was it at her? Perhaps it was meant for someone else. Especially if it was deadly.

The general, perhaps? Or Luc?

It was common knowledge that Luc was the head of the Rising Wave. It would have been him Eckhart would have come to if he hadn't left for the border. If whoever had given Eckhart the fork hadn't realized Luc had left the city, it could have been a ploy to get rid of one of her most powerful lines of defence.

Eckhart wanted to argue that he hadn't been spelled. She could see it in the way his lips pursed in a mulish slant. But the fork lay there, and eventually he closed his eyes. "What happened?"

"What do you remember?" She had seldom had a chance to ask someone what they recalled from a spell casting. Most of the workings she gave her friends and allies were protective, passive in that they demanded nothing from their recipients, but the ones where she forced people to act against their will, she had never had the chance to ask them what they thought was happening at the time.

"I was asking after a wagon driver. I was a little annoyed, because I had a lot of other work to do. More important work, I thought." He sent her an apologetic glance. "The staff seemed to be confused about who was staying there. The Grimwaldians had taken rooms there, Frederik had been watching them for a couple of hours from across the street, so it seemed strange that they would say there were no Grimwaldians in lodgings." He rubbed the back of his head. "The innkeeper and her family were spelled, too?"

Ava nodded. "Probably."

"And then I spoke to someone . . ." he trailed off again, and for the first time, she saw fear in his eyes. "I don't remember anything about it, except that I knew I was finished my work. That I could go report in, because everything was sorted out."

"When did this happen?" She hadn't expected that.

"It was dark, like it is now." Eckhart rubbed his chest. "I don't know." His gaze went back to the fork. "What do we do with that?"

"Handle it with care."

"The magic will fade in time, won't it?" Eckhart asked.

"I'm no expert." And that was the truth, amusingly enough. She was learning as she went. "But yes, I think so."

There was a wooden box on the side table, filled with parchment and pens, and she emptied it out and used a poker from the fireplace to scoop the fork into it and close the lid.

"Do you feel compelled to do anything," she asked Eckhart as she set the box on the table.

"To you, you mean?" He looked a little sick. "No."

"This isn't your fault, Eckhart. It's the fault of the spell caster, and maybe even Rafe for making a little too light of the assignment."

"What about Frederick and Talura? Might they be enspelled?" He worried his lip. "They're the ones who told me which tavern to go to."

She hadn't thought of that, and she should have.

"I'll check." This was something she would need to do in her cloak, with all the protections at her disposal, as well as enough thread and strips of fabric to work a counter spell, if she could.

She let Eckhart go, telling him to steer clear of Frederik until she'd seen him. To go get some rest. He looked haunted when he left her, and she was sorry for it.

He was a victim in this.

She scooped up the box and went looking for the general, who she discovered was out at the Rising Wave camp, talking to her lieutenants about the Jatan encroachment.

But checking on Frederik and Talura couldn't wait.

She didn't know if they had been enspelled or not, but they could be a danger to those around them, and none of it was their fault.

Ava couldn't help but think it was hers.

She would have to go find the general. Not only would she want to know what had happened with Eckhart, but it would be foolish for Ava to check on Frederik and Talura without letting someone know what she was going to do.

Just in case.

And the general, Oscar and Deni were the only ones she could tell, other than Luc.

She took the box upstairs, made sure the guards understood no one was to open it or even touch it, and put it away in a drawer.

When she was back in her trousers and shirt, she slipped out of the palace in her cloak, nothing but a shadow among the many thrown by the torches and lanterns in the streets.

It wasn't that late yet, people were still about, but the night was winding down.

It soothed some of the buzzing beneath her skin to be walking in the cool air.

For a long time she had been locked away, and just the fact that she could step out and go where she wanted, unchallenged, was a gift.

Up ahead, from a narrow side alley, someone cried out, a sound of pain and surprise.

Ava slowed her steps, coming level to the entrance and looking down the narrow space, but it was too dark to see anything.

The cry came again, low to the ground, as if the person was lying in the street.

Ava stepped into the alley and moved carefully forward, one hand to the wall, trying to see what lay ahead.

Something soft dropped down on her from above, and she went still, reaching up a hand to feel what it was.

Her fingers encountered rough hessian, and she pulled at the net she realised had been thrown over her, scrabbling hard and fast to get it off her.

The workings in her cloak flared to life, and then she found herself frozen in place.

This had happened once before, when someone had thrown fire at her and her cloak had burned.

It was a strange sense of vertigo—she felt off-kilter and dizzy, but couldn't move.

When her cloak had burned, she'd thought her inability to move had been caused by her protective workings reacting to something they couldn't counter. They hadn't known how to help her, and so they'd kept her in place.

It was not good that she felt the same way again. Whatever this net was, it wasn't the fire that had burned her cloak before, but it must contain something that was confusing her protections.

And whoever had thrown it had been able to see her, even though she should be invisible to most eyes.

The net suddenly tightened around her thighs, and as it did, she recalled the man from earlier that day, his quick frown as he caught a glimpse of her in the crowd.

At least one person *could* see her.

And they had clearly tracked her. Tricked her into entering this alley.

Something in the net ignited as she gripped the ropes and tried to pull them up.

Pain flared all around her, white hot and blinding, and Ava fell.

CHAPTER 6

S he came awake to the rattle of wheels over stones.

It was dawn, or just after, because pale gray light seeped between the gaps in the rough wooden walls that had been knocked together to form an enclosed cart.

She was alone in the back, and no longer caught in the net, but something weighed her down.

She had felt its like before, when the Grimwalt Speaker's agents had tried to take her from the Rising Wave. General Ru still had it, a thin black rope that seemed to suck the energy and will out of a person.

This could be the same one, but as she was sure the general wouldn't be careless with the one she had, there must be two of them.

The rope bound her hands and wound around her neck, and it burned where it touched her skin.

She was wearing a rough shift, not her own clothes.

She wanted to sit up, but the energy-sapping rope made that impossible, and she found it difficult even to turn her head to see if she could work out which direction the light filtering into the cart was coming from.

They were going north, it seemed.

No surprises there if the Grimwalt Speaker was involved.

The cart finally moved from the stony road to something smoother, and she heard the sound of water.

The cart slowed, and then came to a stop.

Although she needed to relieve herself and wanted some idea of who had her, when she heard the creak of someone standing from the driver's seat, and the thump of him jumping down, her heart beat harder, fear and panic warring for a place in her chest.

There was a creak of sound as the ill-fitting door at the back of the cart opened, and a man stepped up from the ground to look in.

It was difficult to see him properly and he was backlit by the just-risen sun, but as her eyes adjusted, she saw he was the man from yesterday who'd seen her in the city. He still wore his black cloak. His eyes were light brown and his scruffy beard held a few strands of gray.

He looked her over impersonally, holding a long knife in a gloved hand.

The space was so small, he only had to shuffle in to loom over her, using his gloved hands to unwind the rope into a tight coil.

She took her first proper breath since she'd woken, and the knife slid, cool and deadly, against her throat.

"Now, I'm going to let you out, and you're going to give me no trouble."

She wondered, as she pushed herself off the thin, lumpy mattress and got to her feet, if he knew she was a spell caster.

He was a little afraid of her, she could see it in the way he held himself, even though he was head and shoulders taller.

He moved back as she pushed herself to her feet, and her knees buckled, tipping her forward.

He swore and stumbled back, almost falling down the steps.

She stayed on her knees, head bowed, and dry heaved a few times.

She couldn't think clearly, but she knew she was not well.

It frightened her, how not well she felt.

"Don't throw up in here. I don't want to clean it."

She vaguely heard anger in his voice, and she thought it was because he felt foolish, jumping back as if she was going to attack him when she couldn't even stand.

He stepped back inside, reaching up to set the magical rope on a shelf and taking another rope down.

"Lift your arms."

She did as he asked, deciding it would do her no good to defy him now, when she was so weak, and she really wanted to go outside.

The rope was already looped at one end, and he tugged it over her hands, down her arms and to her waist, tightening it so that it was snug as a belt.

It wasn't magical. It was just a normal rope.

The relief of that choked her and made it hard to breathe.

The man jumped down to the ground, and she followed slowly, taking the steps, to find he had pulled the cart off the road, between the trees on the bank of a river.

The Bartolo?

They would have to cross the Bartolo if they continued north, and if they'd been traveling all night, then this could well be it.

She bent over, catching her breath, and looked around to see if there was a second person.

It had taken at least two people to capture her. One to lure her into the alley, the other to throw the net.

But it looked as if the driver was alone.

"If there's even the smallest tug on the rope, I'll drag you back to me and cut you." He spoke without any heat, and she believed him all the more because of it. "I need to get you to someone as fast as possible, and I can't have you causing me any delays. If I have to hurt you to keep you obeying me, I will."

"Can I have my clothes?" she asked him as she followed him to a small stand of trees to the left, her legs still feeling weak and shaky.

He turned and gave her a sour look. "I was told to destroy every stitch of your clothing. I threw it all into the sea. You're lucky to have on what you've got."

What she had on was a rough cotton shift that looked like it had been cut from a sack.

"Did you make the spoon and the fork?" she asked as he herded her amongst the trees. She wanted to know if he was a spell caster, or just someone sent to fetch her who'd been given access to the weapons he had so far used.

He grunted, neither confirming or denying. "Go around that tree. Don't try anything or—"

"Or you'll cut me."

He flashed her a look. Grunted again. "Be quick. We have to move."

She moved around the trunk, out of his sight, and wondered how she was going to get herself free.

Luc wasn't coming for her. He wouldn't even know she was missing.

The general would, but she might only now be discovering that Ava was missing.

The wagon driver had hours and hours on anyone who might come after her.

This was up to her.

She leaned against the tree, pushing through the fog in her head to think. If she was going to escape, she would have to do it when she was like this. Tied but not magically weighed down.

She had no needle and thread. No workings to help her.

She would have to get innovative.

"She's gone." General Erdene Ru could see Ava had not slept the night in her room.

The guard was nervous. She had not done anything wrong, though, and she was used to fair treatment, General Ru noted with approval. She didn't tremble or try to make excuses.

Luc of the Cervantes was a good commander.

Erdene would have never entered into an alliance with him if it had been otherwise.

Since the first night he'd come creeping into her camp, on the eve of battle with the Kassian army, to propose a plan so audacious, so delightfully underhanded that she had had difficulty keeping her delight and agreement in check, she had been very partial to Luc.

"She asked after you, General Ru. She was looking for you." The guard rubbed her palms down the sides of her thighs in agitation. She was about seven or eight years younger than Erdene herself, and Erdene wondered what her story was. Why she was fighting in the Rising Wave.

"And she said something about a box?" General Ru stepped into Luc and Ava's room with interest. She hadn't been in here yet, her own rooms were in another wing.

"She showed us the box and said we were not to even touch it, that it was dangerous, that it had a very dangerous item inside." The second guard stood stiffly to attention.

"I don't see a box." Erdene walked to the large chest of drawers to one side of the door.

"Do you think—" The first guard swallowed what she was going to say as Erdene began to open the drawers, her eyes wide in shock at the invasion of Ava's privacy.

"The queen of Kassia has disappeared, and she warned you about a dangerous box before she did. I think it's worth finding it, don't you?"

They said nothing as she opened another drawer and then stood back.

"Is that the box?"

They peered closer. Nodded.

"Don't open it."

Erdene turned to find one of the Cervantes captains at the door. She recognized him as the soldier in charge of decommissioning the Kassian soldiers.

He had always reminded her of a happy puppy, golden brown

curls and friendly eyes, but he didn't look his usual eager, accommodating self this morning.

"You know what's inside it, Eckhart?"

Eckhart nodded. "A magic fork."

The guards didn't react, except with mild amusement and disbelief, so Erdene guessed Raun-Tu had managed to keep most of what had happened in the throne room a secret, but she went very still.

The spoon had killed in an instant. No wonder Ava had warned her guards to not even touch the box.

"I think you and I need a word." Erdene nodded to the guards, dismissing them, and waited until they were outside to wave her hand at the door.

The captain closed it.

"What do you know?"

"I need to talk to Ava." The captain looked around, as if expecting to see her.

"We can't find her. It seems she's disappeared." Erdene watched his face as she spoke, and she saw him jolt at her words, and his golden brown skin lost some of its color.

"Ava was going to find you. Going to tell you what had happened with me and the fork. I heard her ask someone where you were as I was leaving."

"What had happened?" Now they were getting somewhere.

"I was assigned to look for the Grimwaldian wagon driver who came into the city with the diplomats. Rafe told me it was important I find him, but that I was to be careful of magical utensils."

Erdene lifted a brow.

Eckhart gave a brief nod. "He made a joke of it. He didn't understand the true danger."

"But now you do?"

Eckhart sighed. "I was enspelled, Ava said. She didn't blame me for it."

"What did you do?" Although Erdene was beginning to guess.

"I threw the fork that's inside that box at her. She managed to duck."

Erdene bet she had. The queen of Kassia was the strongest spell caster she had ever come across.

She had noted with interest that Ava had yet to realize how strong she truly was.

She must have had enough protection sewn into her clothes to make any assassination attempt difficult, if not impossible.

If assassination had been the aim. So far, they had tried to capture her, not kill her.

"What happened after that?"

Eckhart rubbed a finger down the bridge of his nose. "She asked me some questions about what had happened to me when I went to find the wagon driver, and we both became worried about the two other soldiers who had been investigating the whereabouts of the Grimwaldian contingent."

"Ava wanted to check on them?"

Eckhart nodded. "But she was going to speak to you first. Not go looking for them without help."

So Ava had been taken on her way to find her, Erdene thought. Someone had followed Eckhart, perhaps, and waited to see what havoc he managed to wreak with his fork.

"Do you remember anything before you were enspelled?"

Eckhart told her the name of the tavern, the order he'd received to find Ava and report to her. "I don't remember being given the fork, or the instructions to throw it at her." He ran a hand over a face that was pale and drawn.

"They would have had multiple plans in place." Erdene gave him what comfort she could. "It might not have been her you were meant to attack. It could have been Luc, or even me." The more Erdene thought about that, the more likely it seemed.

"I didn't mean to attack anyone."

"Perhaps enspelling you was simply them taking advantage of the situation to create chaos. They hoped they'd have a better chance of grabbing Ava if things were unstable."

"Why didn't she take a guard with her when she went to the camp to look for you?" Eckhart's expression was haunted.

"She thought she was safe." Erdene couldn't say that no doubt Ava had been wearing her protective cloak. Somehow, the Grimwaldians had found a way around her protections, though.

"If it was the Grimwaldians, are they taking her back to Grimwalt?" Eckhart asked.

"That makes the most sense. But they've had almost half a day's head start." That didn't mean they shouldn't go after them.

They would.

But aside from the danger Ava was in personally, her disappearance from the palace was not good for Fernwell, and for the Rising Wave. Not good at all.

CHAPTER 7

Someone joined her captor sometime after they'd left the town of Bartolo.

Ava was aware they had crossed the bridge that was the entrance to the town on the south west, and driven through the main thoroughfare and out the far gate.

If only she could have moved or called for help.

There were people who would help her here, including Bartolo's mayor, but that was why her captor had checked the rope was secure on her before he'd gone through the town, no doubt.

She'd lapsed into a semi-conscious state after a while, but the sound of hooves stirred her, and she became more aware, hoping for rescue, hoping even for a stranger who might realize something was wrong.

Then she heard the rider call a greeting and the soft murmur of voices, and understood her abductor had been joined by a co-conspirator. Maybe even two.

Hope drained from her in a sickening rush.

Another watcher meant less opportunity to escape, and she was not doing well with the rope.

Perhaps it was because of her own innate magic, or perhaps

anyone would be the same, but it felt as if it was sapping not only her energy but her body as well. She thought she was thinner, and not just because she hadn't eaten.

She'd had no appetite when the driver had offered her some bread earlier and had only sipped a bit of water.

That had been hours ago.

One of the few things she could gauge was the movement of light through the cracks and gaps in the ill-made wooden covering over the cart, and it was close to sunset.

She closed her eyes, as she had done most of the day, too exhausted to keep them open, and didn't realize the cart had stopped until light spilled into her narrow prison as someone opened the door.

She didn't have the inclination or the energy to look and see who it was.

Someone gave a shout, and she thought she heard an argument, before the wagon driver came in, gloves on, and unwound the rope.

She wondered if he expected her to get up and relieve herself or drink some more, but she had no energy to do either. She simply lay, aware of the reprieve but unable to care very much.

She heard more shouting, and then a man, not the wagon driver, came in, picked her up roughly, and took her outside.

There was a fire, and the cart had been pulled off the road into a small copse of trees.

She was dumped on the ground near the fire, and the feel of the slightly damp, springy grass was a balm to her.

She lay quietly and kept her eyes closed.

When she woke again, the two men were sitting with a woman, talking quietly by the fire as they ate. Something had been roasted over the fire, and she wondered if she would vomit as the smell hit her and made her lightheaded.

"You're a fool, Sirna. A coward and a fool." The man who'd carried her from the cart crouched beside her when she tried to roll on her side, lifting her up, and she retched a little, but there was nothing in her stomach to come up, and she collapsed back down, panting.

"No one said—"

"No one should have had to say. It was for capture and going through Bartolo only." The man stood and when he returned, he had a cup of water which he held to her lips. "She's a valuable commodity. You almost killed her because you wanted an easy time. A prisoner who wouldn't even need watching."

Ava took the water a tiny sip at a time, but his words made the reason for his concern clear.

He was no ally. He wanted her in working condition to exploit, nothing more.

She managed half the cup, and then lay back down, content to simply be, without the draining, sucking weight of the rope.

"The orders were to leave Dimitri in Fernwell, so I had to deal with her on my own and drive the cart. It would have done us no good if she'd escaped."

"You could have tied her up with normal rope. That is hardly difficult to think of." The man put the cup to one side.

"She's coming back into focus," Sirna said, his voice pitched at a whine.

"Only because I got to her in time." The man straightened, looming over her. "There's no way I can take her with me on the horse in the shape she's in. That alone is going to earn you a black mark in the Speaker's book."

That sounded like the plan was for him to take her with him on the massive horse she could now see hobbled beside the cart.

She couldn't be sorry that wasn't possible, but she was sorry about the reason for it.

"She might be better in the morning." Sirna sounded more hopeful than convinced.

"I'm not waiting until the morning. I need to leave now. I was expected in Taunen today, and it's a hard three day ride just to the border as it is. You took longer than we thought to trap her, and I'll be facing the Speaker's temper as it is."

"She was in the palace, surrounded by guards. I did well to get her at all." Sirna was angry now, and a little afraid; she could hear it in his voice. "And we traveled through a war zone just to get to Fernwell."

"I'll tell him, but it won't save you from his anger about overusing the rope. Even if you don't use it on her again, she'll barely be whole by the time you get to Grimwalt."

"Evelyn and I were going to go east, through Venyatu and home. Not to Grimwalt. That was the agreement."

"The agreement was you would be well-paid to secure her, unharmed, so I could take her to Taunen. She is not unharmed."

The woman, Ava guessed she was Evelyn, spoke for the first time. "Weren't you going to hold her in front of you on your horse anyway?"

"Not as a dead weight." The man was beginning to get angry. "And that plan was conceived when I thought you'd bring her out over a week ago. Even using the Focus, which I got for you at great risk, not to mention cost, you still got her late, and you kept her in the rope. I don't have time to ride with an unconscious hostage all the way to Taunen, late as I am already."

"Fine. I'll take her to the Grimwalt border. No further. Not all the way to Taunen." There was a defiant thread to Sirna's voice.

The man thought about it. "All right. For your own wellbeing, that might be wise. But if you use the rope on her again—"

"I won't use it."

"Good. You've been warned, Sirna. If she's damaged when you get to the border, there will be consequences, and I won't protect you."

"It'll take at least a week, maybe more, in the cart. She'll be fine by then."

"She better be." The man bent to pick up his cloak and swirled it over his shoulders. "You'd be wise to keep him straight, Evelyn. You might just be included in whatever punishment the Speaker deems fit if she's not able to sit up by herself."

"Leave Evelyn out of it. She helped you, didn't she? Pretended to be your captive in Bartolo. What's the Speaker want with this one, anyway?" Sirna stood, brushing crumbs off his shirt.

"I don't know. I don't want to know." The man loosened the ropes hobbling his horse and fitted the saddle back on. "I suggest you be just as incurious."

None of them knew?

Ava had thought Sirna was the one who'd made the spoon, fork and rope, had enspelled Eckhart, but clearly not.

If he hadn't known how much damage the rope would do to her, that made sense.

She didn't trust he wouldn't use it again, though.

He would do whatever he thought he could get away with, as long as it made his own life easier.

Maybe Evelyn would stop him, although she still didn't know how the woman fit in.

The man seemed to come to the same conclusion. "Maybe I should take the rope with me. Its owner wants it back as quickly as possible. And the net."

"And leave me with no way to keep her quiet if things get dangerous?" Sirna's whine was back. "You don't think they'll be sending someone after her?"

"You know that's what Evelyn and I were making sure wouldn't happen in Bartolo. Whoever comes looking for her will head down river. We put on a good show to ensure it. You'll have a clear run."

So that's why he and Evelyn had come from behind. They'd been laying a false trail.

But the general knew the Grimwaldians were involved. She wouldn't easily be fooled by a false trail, Ava was sure of it.

She turned her head to look at the firelight and noticed her hand seemed a little translucent.

Fear at the sight of it sharpened her concentration.

She hadn't realised Sirna had meant she was literally coming more into focus.

She had been fading away in a real sense. The rope must absorb its captive, somehow.

She knew she could make a working that had the same effect of sapping someone's strength, without the damage, and she couldn't help but wonder if the damage was on purpose.

Someone very nasty had made this.

"All right, I'll leave the rope with you, but you'll hand it over with her when you get to the border."

"You can have the net back." Sirna stood and walked to the cart, coming back with a dark bag. "Is it supposed to glow when it's used?"

The man took the bag, put his hand in, and then frowned. "The magic's been stripped from it. Did you destroy her clothes and shoes, like I told you to?"

"I threw them in the sea. They're gone."

"Then she's no more dangerous than anyone else. No need for the rope unless you absolutely have to keep her quiet. If she wanders off, which I doubt, given the state of her, you still have the Focus to track her down. It's foolproof, made out of something from her past." He tied the black bag to his saddle and then turned sharply. "What about the tea?"

Sirna went still. "There's not much left of it."

"Is that so?" The words were soft and dangerous.

Sirna stood looking at him for a moment, then turned and stomped back to the cart.

Ava heard him rummaging around and then he came back holding a tin.

"This had better be everything that's left." The man opened the tin and peered inside. "If there is any hint you've taken some—"

"I swear, that's all that's left."

The man slid the tin into the black bag with the net. "I'm warning you one last time, Sirna. There'll be no mercy if she's too damaged for whatever the Speaker has in mind for her. And no payment, either."

At the mention of payment, Sirna bridled. "I did the job. And I need money for the road. The agreement was thirty gri."

"The agreement was that you'd get her last week, and she'd be in one piece." The man turned back to his saddle bag, pulled out a small pouch. "Here's five gri. You'll get the rest when you reach the border. Only if she's in good condition."

"That's not what was agreed. She's right here, isn't she? Alive and well. *And* I'm taking her to the border, which wasn't in the plan. I should be getting more for that."

"I'd keep that attitude to myself, if I were you." The man swung up on his horse and then he was gone, yipping to his horse to hasten its step.

"You're *not* me," Sirna murmured.

Ava didn't know whether to be glad of that or not. At least, for now, the rope was off her.

She had a chance.

But aside from the rope, she realised there were other things in Sirna's arsenal.

This Focus the man on the horse spoke of.

It sounded like Sirna had used it to track her. It was possible he hadn't seen through her invisibility workings on the street in Fernwell at all, he had simply known she was there, even though he couldn't see her. That might be why he'd seemed so confused at the time.

He must have been waiting outside the palace gates, and been able to follow her easily through the crowd.

She wondered what the Focus looked like, and how the man on the horse had acquired it.

Maybe someone had broken into her grandmother's house and taken something from her room.

It made her even more afraid for Velda and Tomas.

Tomas had said they would leave and stay away for a while for their own safety, but since the Speaker's henchman had taunted her with the news that friends of hers were imprisoned, she had feared he'd been talking about Velda and Tomas.

And knowing the sheer level of harm the Speaker seemed willing to do when it came to her, she worried they were far from safe.

She closed her eyes at the thought.

She was far from safe, herself.

She needed to escape. To save her friends and return to Fernwell.

And she knew enough about statecraft to understand that this was not the time for the queen to vanish.

CHAPTER 8

They rode hard.

Luc could feel the urgency in all of them, the fear that they had given up so much, only for the prize, the safety of their people, to be compromised.

Massi rode on one side of him, Rafe on the other.

Revek brought up the rear of the eighty-strong unit, and the distance wasn't just strategic. He kept away from Luc, and Luc didn't object, or even feel that bothered by it.

He should, though. He and Revek had been like brothers.

But that was before.

Before he had tried to kill Luc. And then, more inexcusably, Ava.

Ava, the one who had most reason to dislike Rev, though, had been the one to excuse him. She told Luc he hadn't been able to help himself, and he was a victim.

That was something Revek was probably struggling with. He was aware he'd been used.

They had all been victims for too long in the camps, and none wanted that to define them.

Maybe time would ease the tight knot of distrust and hurt in him for his old friend.

He hoped he could be the kind of leader who didn't hold a grudge. But maybe the closer the friend, the deeper the feeling of betrayal, even if the blame wasn't solely on Rev's shoulders.

A whistle came from up ahead.

One of the scouts calling to let them know there was danger coming up.

Luc drew his sword almost at the same time as Massi notched an arrow in her bow and Rafe hefted his own sword.

All around him, others readied their bows or drew their own weapons.

They spread out, all talk ceasing, slowing their mounts, so that what had been a tight, fast column poured into the surrounding trees and bush like the slow glide of spilled honey.

Luc had not been part of the big clash between the Rising Wave and the Kassian forces. General Ru had led that offensive.

He had been sneaking through the hills, making sure the magical flares the Queen's Herald had acquired to burn the Rising Wave and most of the countryside down would never be used.

He hadn't realized he'd missed this feeling of purpose and focus as they approached an enemy.

He rode ahead, and Massi and Rafe kept pace with him.

The scouts waited for them near a stand of trees.

"Soldiers," Erinne said, voice a soft whisper. She was fast and light, the perfect scout, and her mount danced beneath her, still eager to run. "They look like stragglers from the Kassian army."

Luc waited for the first line of horses behind him to catch up and twirled a finger in the air.

They streamed right and left, surrounding the group.

A faint sound of a bird call let Luc know when they had closed the circle, and he moved forward, his big horse making it necessary to duck under a few branches as he found himself in a wide clearing.

The soldiers were expecting them.

They were on their feet, weapons in hand, but they looked ragged and thin in the face.

One of them stepped forward, and Luc watched him as he took in Massi, Rafe, then Luc, and glanced behind him.

They knew they were surrounded, that much was clear.

"You going to kill us?" he asked eventually.

"No."

That set him back on his heels.

"What then?"

"You Kassian army?" They clearly were, but Luc asked anyway.

"You must know the answer to that." One of the other men in the group called out.

Luc inclined his head. "Go to Fernwell. You'll be decommissioned, given work."

"What'll the Turncoat King say about that?" the leader asked.

Rafe chuckled. "You're talking to the Turncoat King."

That quietened them all down.

"What are you doing here, then?" someone else asked.

Luc ignored the question. "Were you part of the Kassian border force that came up behind our supply train?"

The leader gave a slow nod. "Spent six months on the Jatan border. We were close to crushing them."

"So I hear." His words seemed to give the Kassian soldiers some succour, because they relaxed. "And then you escaped General Ru. That's hard to do."

"She came up behind us. We thought we had the element of surprise. Turns out General Daikin was wrong about that." The leader of the group sounded bitter. "He wasn't right in the head, that one. Not at all."

Luc remembered the name. Remembered the man.

Daikin had been in charge of the fortress close to the border with Grimwalt where Ava had been held prisoner. The general had hunted him and Ava down when they'd escaped.

Ava had bested him while Luc was badly injured, and Haslia, the traitorous spell caster who'd been working as a spy for Daikin, had confessed to Luc that the Kassian general had never forgiven Ava for it.

"I heard General Daikin died on the battlefield," Luc said.

"We heard that, too." The leader lifted his shoulders. "Don't care either way."

Luc made a careful note of how many stragglers stood in the clearing. "Do you know how many more of you there might be out here?"

"Haven't seen anyone else out here." The leader met his gaze squarely, but Luc had the feeling he was lying.

That was okay. He didn't expect trust or truth from men who had been his deadly enemies until two weeks ago, after which they became his conquered enemies.

"Are you really saying we won't be imprisoned if we turn ourselves in?" One of the men in the group called.

"I'm giving you my word on it, if you hand in your weapons and make no trouble. There is plenty of work available in the rebuilding of Kassia, and every soldier who wants to sign up is accepted."

"You're headed for Jatan, aren't you?" The leader spoke softly for the first time, although more from surprise than in an effort to limit who heard him.

"And if I am, do you have any advice for me?" Luc asked.

The man nodded. "I reckon I do. They'll put up a brave front right to the bitter end, that lot. They won't lose face for anything. They could be bleeding out, close to death, and as long as they think you don't know it, they'll pretend they're the ones about to score victory."

"I'll keep that in mind." Luc touched his horse's flank, and it began walking, skirting around the group. "Go well."

Rafe and Massi followed, and Luc sensed the surprise and relief from the soldiers as they realised they were really not going to have to fight.

"Seems wrong, just letting them be." Massi spoke as soon as they were out of sight, amongst the trees.

"They couldn't believe it, themselves. Did you see the surprise?" Rafe asked.

"That wouldn't have been a fight, it would have been a massacre." Luc wasn't interested in massacres.

And he hoped the Jatan felt the same.

That if they had reached Cervantes, his people still stood, unharmed.

Or he would have to change his position.

CHAPTER 9

The problem with their victory was it had been easily come by.

Not that easily, Erdene Ru conceded; she'd had to take on an army on the plains, Luc and Ava had had to thwart an ambush with magical flare fire, and Raun-Tu and Massi had neutralised the soldiers hiding in Bartolo, which had been the only safe place for the Rising Wave to cross the river.

She had told Luc just before she'd left with most of the Rising Wave to take on the Kassian forces in battle that it would be a feat long remembered and spoken of.

She'd been right.

However, when they'd reached Fernwell, most of the hard work had been completed, and then the Queen's Herald had done them the favor of attacking his aunt in the street, and the old queen had done them the even greater favor of having her guards kill her nephew in retaliation, and then proclaiming Ava her successor with her dying breath.

It meant the Rising Wave's hands were clean of regicide.

Used to being ruled by a queen, and with no army left to insist otherwise, the citizens of Fernwell had opened the city gates on

Ava's orders and let them in.

But now that queen was missing.

Erdene looked around the table at her three lieutenants and Dak, the temporary head of the Cervantes and Funabi contingent of the Rising Wave, and crossed her arms over her chest.

"We are going to lie."

There was no immediate reaction to that.

"How can we? There are still servants working in the palace who were hired by the old queen, although we've gotten rid of most of them. Someone will talk." Heival scowled as if those servants were in front of her right now.

"They need to be removed."

"It's too late." Fervanti shook her head. "The guards called you when they found her missing, and some of the servants were in earshot. By now, they'd have gossiped to the others, and perhaps people beyond the palace walls."

"Then we say we found her. She went out to the camp to see Deni and her friends, because she was missing Luc, and spent the night there." Erdene didn't think that was a bad story, actually.

Dak lifted a shoulder in agreement. "Even if they don't believe it, as long as we stick to it, what can they say?"

"They can say she isn't here. If she isn't missing, why isn't she back in her rooms?" Heival flicked her long braid behind her.

"But she will be back in her rooms." Erdene crouched down, pulled a key from her pocket, and unlocked a drawer. The necklace she drew out had belonged to the man who'd tried twice to abduct Ava. Luc had killed him, and the necklace had become the property of the Rising Wave.

"What is that?" Dak sounded so suspicious, Erdene had the feeling he knew exactly what it was.

"It changes the appearance of the wearer. The Grimwaldian spy who was in our column, who tried to take Ava from the camp, and then from the palace, used it for himself, to hide in plain sight because Ava knew his face."

"The one who got into the palace by making himself look like one of the guards?" Fervanti held out her hand for it, and Erdene gave it to her.

"How does it work?" Raun-Tu leaned closer to peer at it, then stepped back as Fervanti slid the necklace over her head.

"Who do I look like?" she asked.

"Yourself." Erdene frowned. She didn't know how it worked, but it couldn't be that difficult. "Think about looking like someone else."

Fervanti's face wavered a little, and then Erdene found herself looking at a close approximation of herself. Only older and more tired looking than she really was.

There was a beat of silence. Dak coughed.

Erdene frowned.

"Try looking like Ava," Heival said, and there was a slight wobble to her voice, suspiciously like suppressed laughter.

The false face wavered, collapsed back to look like Fervanti, and then shimmered into something that looked a bit like Ava, but not quite.

"She doesn't look like that," Dak said.

"She doesn't have to look exactly like Ava, just more or less like her from a distance." Erdene didn't think anyone could pass off having a conversation as if they were Ava.

"Fervanti is too tall to be Ava, anyway. We'll need to find someone who's closer to her body shape." Raun-Tu narrowed his eyes, as if mentally considering who amongst his soldiers might be suitable.

"The one who guards her rooms," Erdene said. "She's the right height, and a similar shape." The guard Erdene had noticed a number of times was older than Ava, but that wouldn't matter if they were using the necklace to change her features.

"Talika." Dak nodded slowly. "She also already knows Ava is missing, so we wouldn't have to bring in someone new to the secret."

"Get her down here." Erdene had the sense that they couldn't afford any delay.

The Rising Wave had the advantage here. Two thousand battle-hardened soldiers surrounded the city and had access to it through the open gates, but she'd heard the rumors circulating about people going missing, and that she and some of her people were spell casters.

Someone was fomenting trouble, stirring the pot, and the disappearance of the queen would play right into their hands.

If things were not exactly running smoothly right now, at least there was no violence. Once the killing started, it was hard to go back.

People were unforgiving when standing over the bodies of their loved ones, no matter who had started the fight.

She needed to find who was undermining the Rising Wave with the people of Fernwell. And she needed to create the illusion that nothing was wrong in the palace.

A guard knocked at the door, and Raun-Tu opened it, took the scroll that was held out.

"News from Deni?" She had sent Deni, Oscar, and Taira with a small, tight-knit group of Ava's old Venyatux unit to Bartolo.

Ava had to have been taken by someone from the Grimwalt envoy, and so it made sense they'd head for Bartolo, cross the river, and then travel north east toward Grimwalt itself.

Raun-Tu unrolled the scroll and stood still as he read it. He handed it to her.

"They reached Bartolo, but a few people saw someone who looked like Ava, cowed and bullied by a man. They got into a boat that was travelling downstream, toward the coast."

"That's the opposite way to Grimwalt." Fervanti shook her head.

"A little too obvious, surely?" Heival said.

"A false trail?" Dak asked.

"What else? They think to make us confused, but if they are from Grimwalt, they will be headed back to Grimwalt." Erdene was sure of it.

"They await your orders in Bartolo." Raun-Tu's lips formed a thin line. He was frustrated, but Deni could not have done anything else.

"Send a messenger and tell him to go north east, following the road to Grimwalt. And to try and make up the time lost."

Raun-Tu stepped out, his feet silent, even on the squeaky marble that seemed to be everywhere in this pretty, impractical palace.

"We need to send a message to Luc." Dak had said this to Erdene before, but she'd asked him to hold off until they had more news.

It was a delaying tactic, and she turned to him now, realizing she would have to lay her cards on the table. "We can't do that."

There was silence.

"He would want to know." Heival stated the obvious.

"And when he does, what will that mean for him?" Erdene asked.

"It would tear him in two." Dak spoke softly. "He would want to find her, but he could not yet have reached the border to see what the Jatan are up to. So Cervantes would still potentially be in danger."

"He would be honor bound to check on his people and make sure they're safe." Fervanti rubbed between her breasts, as if her heart hurt. "It would be a terrible burden to give him."

Dak swore. "And still, he will never forgive me for not telling him."

"No. It's me he won't forgive." But Erdene was prepared to take that risk. She'd once told Luc that leaders sometimes had to make hard decisions. This was one of them.

Dak shook his head. "You, too. But me, as well." But he didn't argue further. Erdene would have to corner him later, and make absolutely sure he wasn't going to break down and send a messenger out.

But looking at his miserable face, she guessed he'd accepted that she was right about this.

"What if they don't have her?" Fervanti asked. "What if she's dead?"

"They haven't tried to grab her so many times because they want to kill her," Erdene said. "They want her for something."

"What could they want her for? They're risking a war with us if we can prove they took her." Heival's words shocked the others. They hadn't thought about the ramifications of Ava's abduction other than through the lens of Fernwell, and the stability of the city. Not to mention worry over their friend.

"War over Ava?" Dak spoke slowly.

"She's the queen of Kassia," Heival said, looking at him as if he was slow. "What would any country do if their monarch was kidnapped?"

Absolute silence blanketed the room.

They had been outsiders for so long, it took a mental shift to see themselves as the ones in power.

"Why would they risk it, then?" Fervanti asked, voice whisper soft.

Erdene didn't answer, but she knew.

And she was very afraid for everyone if that risk paid off.

CHAPTER 10

"I don't see why she gets to sleep in the cart." Evelyn's voice was a whine in the background.

Ava didn't want to go back into the cart anyway, despite the chill of the night air and the cold of the dew on the ground. The further from Fernwell and the warmth of the sea they traveled, the colder the temperatures, but she did not want those rough wooden walls enclosing her again.

It had brought back the trapped feeling that came with years spent locked in a cell.

"If you sleep in the cart, love, I have to stay awake all night guarding her. You'll have to drive and be with her on your own during the day while I sleep."

Evelyn thought about that. "We could use the magic rope. Don't listen to what *he* says. He likes frightening people."

He sighed. "Don't think I'm not tempted, but she was looking a little fuzzy around the edges toward the end there. I don't want the Speaker after me. And I want to be able to go back into Grimwalt when I need to in the future, without looking over my shoulder the whole time."

"*He* threatened that. We don't know if it's true."

"I'll keep you warm under the stars. It's just until the border." Sirna's voice changed tone. Not wheedling—it was stronger than that—but persuasive, giving Evelyn a chance to accept the reality for herself, without him having to force the issue.

Ava couldn't see her face, but she guessed the woman was pouting.

"Let's make a bed for ourselves." There was a little too much cheer in Sirna's voice, and Evelyn grumbled under her breath, but she helped him.

Ava was content to lie where she was as they moved about, even if the thin shift was getting damp and clinging to her skin from lying on the ground. The movement of air around her, the vastness of the sky above, was worth the price.

"I'll think of a way we can do it," Evelyn said, as they eventually stood over Ava and Sirna pulled her to her feet. "Don't think I won't."

Ava simply closed her eyes against her hard, angry face, and Sirna had to bodily lift her into the cart.

She heard the click of a padlock key turning, and understood she had been shut in, but this time, there was no rope dragging her down.

She could sense it, though.

It sat on the shelf above her. It felt as if it were probing for her living spirit, like a snake licking the air, and she shifted away from it, taking a blanket and curling up on the floor at the end of the bed, right by the door.

When she slept, she dreamed of Luc, calling for her in the forest, and she couldn't answer because a snake had wrapped itself around her and was squeezing out all her air.

EVELYN FORCED HER TO GET UP EARLY, AND EVERY STEP AVA took made her joints creak, as if she had become an old lady.

Sirna tied the long, blessedly unmagical rope around her waist to let her relieve herself, and she barely had the energy to stumble deep enough into the woods to be out of sight.

When she came back, panting, with perspiration on her brow from the effort of the short walk, he didn't untie her. Instead, he had her sit next to him on the driver's seat, and Evelyn disappeared inside the cart, where it was far warmer.

The air was cold enough to hurt as she breathed it in, and her breath came in puffs. She still only had on a rough-woven shift, and she shivered uncontrollably.

"Evelyn, get her a blanket." Sirna eyed her with dislike, as if her teeth were chattering to annoy him.

"Can't you get me some clothes?" Ava hunched over, trying to trap the warmth of her body. She needed shoes, too.

"Where from? Evelyn hasn't any to spare. And what with? I haven't been paid what was agreed." He sounded bitter about it. "And *himself* made me destroy what you were wearing."

Evelyn had referred to the rider as *him*, now Sirna was calling him *himself*. They either didn't know his name, or he'd threatened them with dire consequences if they spoke it.

She closed her eyes against the disappointment, and drew up her knees, hugging them tight.

"Evelyn!"

"She won't die of cold." Evelyn's sulky voice wafted through the badly fitted planks.

"If she's coughing and sick? And some idiot soldier at the border decides to use that as an excuse to keep some of my gri because she doesn't look in good condition?" Sirna half-turned in his seat. "All for the application of a blanket?"

Evelyn said nothing. She didn't like being admonished. Who did? But there was obviously only so much sulkiness Sirna was prepared to take.

"Now!" His voice was a whip crack, and the horses moved nervously at the fury in his voice.

"Then slow down so I can give it to you." Evelyn's tone was cool.

Sirna's grip on the reins tightened to white knuckles, but he treated his horses well, Ava saw. He didn't yank, he eased, so they were soon at a walking pace.

Evelyn hopped down and walked to the front, tossing the blanket up to Ava.

She was still not herself, not by a long way, and she nearly fumbled it and dropped it back on the ground. But she managed to hold onto one corner and pull it up. She settled it around her shoulders in relief.

She didn't thank Evelyn, and neither did Sirna, and after waiting for a moment for some token of gratitude, Eveyln turned on her heel and stalked back to the rear of the cart.

Ava didn't look over at Sirna, and he didn't say anything. From the corner of her eye she saw him rubbing at his growing beard, then he twisted in his seat and wrapped the end of the rope that was around her waist over and over the back of the driver's bench, knotting it tight enough she wondered if he'd be able to undo it later.

Slowly, the warmth of the blanket seeped into her skin, and she felt more able to look around and see where they were.

She also tested the limits of the rope.

Sirna had given her a little bit of room for movement—some of the rope lay loose by her side—but she guessed the farthest it would go would be to allow her to stand up, no more.

Given the state of the road they were traveling on, she worried about what she would do, how she'd get to safety, if the wheels gave or the horses bolted.

Especially as she no longer had the agility or the strength of only a few days ago.

The Rising Wave hadn't taken any of the merchants' roads on its way to Fernwell. They had forged their own path across the plains.

The road Sirna had them on now clearly was a merchant track, although not the main one. She'd heard Sirna tell Evelyn it was a back road he took often to avoid the Kassian army.

It wasn't well-maintained, and Sirna had to stop and clear the path of fallen branches a few times.

He was fit but not overly muscled, and he had a twitchiness about him, as if he were never able to rest.

She thought, with a spike of dark humor, that his conscience must be bothering him, but it was only amusing because it clearly wasn't true. He was likely more worried about being caught by the people General Ru would have sent after her than any regret for what he'd done.

The sun shone down warmer than it had been for a few days, and she found her eyes closing and her body relaxing.

They came to a bend in the path around midday and she roused herself from her doze to see the gleam of reflected sunlight on water up ahead.

The road dipped, and in the distance a clearing lay off to the side of the road. The open space fell away in a shallow slope into the river, and four covered carts, some blocking the way ahead, had stopped there for a midday meal.

"Shit." Sirna slowed the horses and then brought them to a halt.

"What is it?" Evelyn finally emerged from the back, coming around on Sirna's side. She shielded her eyes against the glare, and swore softly herself. "What do we do?"

"We can't go back. And there's no room to go past." Sirna looked over at Ava. "What are we going to do with you?"

Good question, Ava thought.

Her heart started to pound, because the spelled rope would look pretty tempting as a solution.

"If we use the rope, we could say she's ill." Evelyn said exactly what Ava thought she'd say.

"If we use the rope, she fades away." But Sirna was thinking about it, she could see. Even if just as a short-term solution.

"What if we use some of it? Just one end?" Evelyn gestured to her. "Tie it around her waist like a belt and put the rest into a bag at her hip."

"You've been thinking about this." Sirna's brows lifted as he secured the reins.

"I told you I wanted to sleep inside." Evelyn held his gaze, a challenge in her eyes.

"It might be a short-term solution." He started untying the knot he'd made earlier, then unwound the rope and tugged her toward him. "Come on," he said to Ava. "No matter what, I can't leave you up here."

No, he couldn't. From her lack of proper clothing, to the blanket around her and the rope, she looked exactly like what she was—a prisoner.

That would, at the very least, raise eyebrows.

She felt a rise in dread with every step she took to the back. She wanted to turn and run. To scream for help.

Evelyn came along behind her, not quite crowing, but smug enough that Ava felt a flare of hatred for the woman.

"Go and get it, then, Evie." Sirna held fast to the rope at Ava's waist when they reached the back, hidden from the view of the small caravan up ahead.

Had they even noticed Sirna's cart, yet?

Evelyn swung up into the back and Ava saw her don the gloves.

Fear and panic engulfed her, and she heard herself panting like a cornered animal.

She must have moved back, her full focus on Evelyn donning the gloves, so the cold blade of Sirna's knife was a shock against the warm skin of her throat.

"I don't want to hurt you, but I can't have talk about a prisoner. I know what kind of hornet's nest I've stirred up, taking you. I should have been rid of you days ago, but there's nothing I can do about it now. You keep your mouth shut, and you'll get to the border in one piece. After that, I don't much care."

But would she be in one piece?

As Evelyn brought out the rope, Ava thought its magic felt even stronger than it had before, a dark light dimming the sunlit day, looking for bright clean energy to devour.

Was that just her imagination, she wondered? Or a result of being caught in the rope for too long?

She flinched away from it as Evelyn lifted it up, and the knife nicked her neck.

"Careful." Sirna shook her, a vicious, impatient rattling of her teeth. He lifted the knife away, but it hovered just within her periphery.

"Do you have a bag to put the rest in?" Sirna asked Evelyn.

She sighed, set the rope on the ground, and went back into the cart.

Ava shuffled back. It seemed to her that one of the coils moved closer to her feet.

"It's absorbed too much of my energy." She kept her voice low, but urgent. "It's semi-alive."

"Don't talk nonsense." Sirna lifted the knife a little higher, but he stepped back, eyeing the coils suspiciously.

"Don't put it against my skin." She tried to think of ways to mitigate this disaster. "It will leech me through my clothes, but slower. It won't be as bad that way."

Sirna hesitated. "Maybe."

He didn't trust her. Ava didn't expect anything else, but she hoped Sirna's fear of *Himself*, the man from Grimwalt, would make him consider what she had to say.

Evelyn came back out with a rough bag that looked like it was for foraging the forest for berries, mushrooms and nuts. The strap was long enough to be worn across the body, and she lifted the rope and stuffed it in. She suddenly cried out as one of the coils touched the bare skin of her wrist above the gloves.

"What is it?" Sirna frowned at her as she lifted her arm and rubbed it.

"It hurts where it touches." She glared at it, then at Ava, and Ava thought just a little bit of doubt, of caution, was reflected in her eyes.

"Give me the gloves. You hold the knife." Sirna sounded angry, as if he blamed both her and Evelyn for the situation, when it was all of his own making.

They swapped places, Evelyn gripping the knife too tight, and yanking on the non-magical rope around Ava's waist as if she were about to run.

That was a joke. She could barely walk.

Sirna pulled out one end of the rope carefully from the bag and reached around her with it.

Evelyn moved so there was no chance of it touching her again, and she dragged Ava back with her.

"Careful." Sirna's voice was a hiss of displeasure.

"It wasn't on purpose." Evelyn steadied, though. But Ava thought she saw anger in the way her hand gripped the knife hilt.

They certainly weren't a happy duo. If they ever had been.

Sirna didn't ask Ava to lift her shift up, and she felt tears gather in her eyes when she realised he was going to keep the rope on the outside of her clothing.

She might even have Evelyn's reaction to the rope touching her to thank for that.

Sirna was nervous of it. More nervous than he'd been before.

He tied it in a knot in front of her, and then shifted the knot to her hip and lifted the bag over her head so it lay across her chest.

She could feel the rope's frustration at the barriers between her and it, but it still sipped from her, drawing her energy through the rough weave of her shift and the bag.

Her head spun, and her knees collapsed beneath her.

Sirna's shouted something, and then her head lolled against his arm.

She didn't know what he did after that.

She didn't care.

CHAPTER 11

Deni felt a sense of unease as he left Bartolo.

"Stop grinding your teeth." Oscar looked over at him. "It's making me even more tense.

"It's just, I've never known anyone to get the better of her." Deni remembered the first time he'd met Ava, riding with a whoop of joy toward the Venyatu column, face wreathed in smiles.

She'd been so happy to see them.

He'd been aiming an arrow at her at the time, and she had talked her way around his guard, relaxed him and befriended him, all before they'd reached the long train of soldiers and carts.

He'd never regretted it. Even if nothing she'd told him at the time had been the truth.

He couldn't help the grin that stretched his lips at the thought of how she hadn't been a poor shepherd from the mountains, she'd been the princess of Kassia.

She'd saved his life, along with the whole of the Rising Wave, from burning alive from the magical flares the Queen's Herald had been planning to use on them.

So how had someone gotten the better of her?

"You think we're dealing with a powerful spell caster?" Oscar was chewing a piece of dried meat, and the words came out indistinct.

"Or her abductors are using something that has a powerful spell embedded in it." He understood now that it wasn't necessary to be a spell caster yourself to use a spell. The protections Ava had embroidered into a scrap of fabric and given to him had saved him from an arrow to the chest once, and he hadn't even known what it was he'd tucked into his tunic.

Oscar was the only other person who knew her secret besides Luc and the general.

He knew it was why he'd been sent to look for her. The general wanted people who could help her hide her abilities and nature. And she had included some of Ava's friends in the team to help them.

If someone else had to learn what she was, at least it could be one of the soldiers in the unit she had been assigned to when she'd been pretending to be a simple soldier in the Venyatux army. If anyone would be inclined to keep her secret, it would be them.

Only, he knew the temptation to talk would be strong. It was unlikely all of them would keep quiet.

"We don't talk about . . ." He didn't finish his sentence, and Oscar looked over at him, frowned, and then gave a nod.

"No. Let's try to keep our little circle exclusive."

They were riding up front, a little way ahead of the others, and Taira rode up beside them. "This is the opposite way they said she went." She looked as strained as Deni felt.

"I know. But I have to believe it's a diversion." He'd split them up anyway, sending five of his team down the river, following the trail that had been left by the man accompanied by a cowed woman in a cloak, head bowed, who had gotten on a boat for the coast.

He knew in his gut sending them that way was a waste of time, but he didn't think he'd forgive himself if it turned out his gut was wrong and she could have been saved. So he'd split the group up, and now it was just himself, Oscar, Taira, Carrie and Tras.

"Deni's right." Tras and Carrie had caught up and Tras was

adamant. "There is no way Avasu would stand for the kind of treatment the witnesses say they saw her submit to without fighting back. If they brought her through here, it was hidden from sight and tied up or unconscious."

Cassie gave a nod. "I agree that the description of what they saw seems suspicious. Why would her abductor strike her when she was on the boat, out of reach of help, exactly when there were a good number of witnesses on the shore? It had to have been someone pretending to be her to set a false trail."

"And if it isn't?" Taira rubbed at her temple.

"Then Froen and the others will find her." Oscar kept his tone upbeat, but Deni knew he was just as worried as the rest of them.

Avasu seemed invincible.

She had sacrificed herself for him, Luc and Oscar up in the hills, allowed herself to be captured, and she had still gotten out of it. Not just intact, but with the keys to the city gates in her hand.

For her to disappear from the streets of Fernwell and be spirited away without a trace seemed utterly improbable.

"Strong magic is at work," he said, and realised he'd spoken out loud.

Every eye was on him.

They needed to know, to be warned, he decided.

"The only way they could have done this was using some magical trickery. We all know Avasu is no easy mark. If they got her, they did it with magic."

"Why did they take her, though?"

No one answered Taira's question.

Deni and Oscar knew, but admitting that would lead to admitting to other things. Which they could not do.

Deni fingered the tunic he wore, which Ava had embroidered for him before they'd gone into battle.

Oscar wore something similar.

Avasu had protected them. Was still protecting them. They could do no less than rescue her.

Luc hadn't trusted the Kassian soldiers when they'd said there were no other groups like them in the area.

The clearing showed signs of perhaps double the number they'd seen, the flattened ground where soldiers had slept, and piles of cups and plates beside the fire pit that had amounted to many more than the men they'd spoken to.

He sent the warning to everyone in the unit and wasn't surprised when the scouts picked up trails indicating small groups had come this way, sometimes only ten minutes ahead of them.

It meant they had to stay alert through what should have been the easy part of their journey, still deep within Kassia.

"Do you think they'll attack?" Kikir, the Skäddar warrior, asked as they passed yet another clear trail, freshly broken branches indicating someone had been through here less than half an hour before.

"Not if they're sensible." Luc kept his tone dry, because people who felt threatened were not always sensible.

Kikir sent him a look of surprise, saw his expression, and gave a small grin of agreement. He was wearing the scarf Ava had embroidered for him around his neck, the pattern in blue and green now more clear and sharp than the lines on his face, which had faded a little over the weeks since he'd joined the Rising Wave.

He noticed Luc looking at the scarf and touched it with his fingertips. "They won't believe this when I get home. No one has ever sewn this pattern into cloth."

"Is there a reason for that?" Luc asked. Ava had told him the pattern indicated that Kikir was the Skäddar's top warrior, the best they had to offer.

"Only one person gets this pattern drawn on their face each year, so perhaps that is the reason." Kikir let his hand drop back to the reins of his hardy mountain pony. "It will be much admired. I might have to give it to the next person who earns the honor."

He didn't look pleased by the idea, but Luc knew he wouldn't wear it if he no longer held the rights to the marks on his face.

"I will speak to the Collective as soon as I get home and I'll tell them about this new move the Jatan have made. Although I'm sure the generals will already be aware of it. If I can send you help, I will."

When Luc heard General Ru had asked the Skäddar to watch the Jatan border for her, in exchange for more trade opportunities in Venyatu, he'd been impressed.

He had neither the connections nor the reach at the time to ask himself. And nothing to offer on the trade front.

They had still been just a mismatched group of soldiers, marching toward Fernwell.

His own missives to the Jatan themselves had gone unanswered.

The Jatan's neighbors, the Skäddar, were an excellent second choice.

And in answer to General Ru's request, the Skäddar Collective had sent their best warrior to see what the Rising Wave was up to, to negotiate a deal, and no doubt learn as much about their tactics and weapons as he could.

Kikir had fit right in. He had become a friend to the Venyatu, and General Ru had even given him a prominent role in the battle she'd fought on the plains against the Kassian forces that had been diverted from the Jatan border.

Kikir, however, was a single warrior. Luc didn't know how much influence he would wield when he reached his home.

Anything was better than nothing, but he would not expect help until he saw it with his own eyes. But he would not be so rude as to say that out aloud.

"Thank you," he said, instead. "Your soldiers would be most welcome and appreciated."

Kikir nodded and they rode in silence for a few minutes.

"You must miss Avasu." Kikir glanced at him. "She is certainly one surprise after another. Strong and fierce." He gave a sudden chuckle. "The stories I will carry back to Skäddar about her will earn me many cups of milk beer."

Luc tapped his heart with two fingers and brushed them downward. "I am lucky." It went without saying that he missed her.

He worried about her, too.

He wanted to know she was safe, and he couldn't do that out here.

He knew she was as strong and fierce as Kikir said, but there were ways she could be taken. And they had tried to take her so many times.

He was frightened one day they'd succeed.

To those who knew her secret, her magic, she was a font of power and gold.

She had been locked up for a long time by someone who had wanted to wring every drop of magic from her for his own ends and she'd been free a lot less time than she'd been imprisoned.

He knew all too well it could happen again.

"You're worried about her?" Kikir must have read his face.

He nodded. "Someone from Grimwalt has sent people twice to get her, and there was an incident yesterday with the Grimwaldian envoy. I worry they'll try again."

Kikir must have heard something about it, because he nodded. "Skäddar shares a border with Grimwalt. I'll keep my ear to the ground for information on who is behind these attempts, and write to you if I discover anything."

"Thank you." Luc already knew who was behind it and why they wanted Ava so badly, but that was Ava's secret and he would never reveal it. He certainly appreciated the offer, though.

A whoop up ahead alerted him to trouble, and both he and Kikir unsheathed their swords as they rode forward, more cautious now, checking to see who was around them and how far out the unit was spread.

Rafe and Kym, the scout from the Jatan border, were riding to his right. To Kikir's left, Massi had drawn her bow.

An arrow flew out of the trees in front of them, and for a moment Luc worried it was aimed at Massi or Kikir.

But it was coming for him.

He didn't change his horse's stride, or try to duck. Instead he signalled to Massi to work out where it came from and shoot back.

The arrow skimmed his shoulder on its way past.

"My friend, you have ice in your veins, like a good Skäddar from the high mountains," Kikir called. He gave a yip of excitement and urged his own horse to keep pace.

Luc wondered if Ava had given the Skäddar any protective working. Perhaps the scarf, although he wasn't sure about that.

If she hadn't, he was remarkably lucky, as he and Luc burst through the trees unscathed, although Luc had never doubted his own safety for a moment. He had been shot at from a few paces away before and walked away without a scratch on him thanks to Ava's workings.

They'd surprised the attackers with their headlong race.

The attackers must have expected the Rising Wave to slow or take cover, not charge ahead, and they were still trying to get down from the trees when Luc and Kikir reached them.

Massi, with her bow drawn back, was not far behind them.

These weren't the same ragtag soldiers from the clearing, Luc saw immediately.

They were far more put together, their uniforms were complete, no mishmash of jackets and pants.

Luc kept them from moving away from the tree by steering his horse back and forth, and then a large number of his unit caught up and the attackers were completely surrounded.

They had shot at him, not any of the others, which would imply they knew who he was. But he'd learned through long, hard experience it was better to let your enemies talk first.

"We meant no harm." One of the two men set his bow down on the ground and backed up against the tree, hands up with palms facing out.

Massi actually laughed out loud at that.

The soldier started at the sound, and then cringed. "I mean, we thought you were going to attack us."

Luc said nothing, and the silence ticked over, the sound of wind and the squeak of bark rubbing against bark the only sound for a long moment.

"Do it, then!" The second man shoved forward, chest out, and slapped a hand over his heart.

"Do what?" Kikir wanted to know.

The man looked at him, eyes wide as he took in the markings on the Skäddar warrior's face, and then gazed at them all, suddenly uncertain.

"Kill us."

The place on his arm where Ava had sewn health and strength back into him as she closed the deep cut with needle and thread, and the now-smooth place on his chest where he'd been shot with an arrow, told him there was danger in believing this act.

These men were not frightened strays, lashing out in self-defence, waiting for a killing blow.

"Who knew I was coming? Who got you to wait up in the tree to shoot me?" he asked. He kept his voice quiet, implacable, and the one who was cringing against the tree went still and looked up at him.

He just caught the glimpse of surprise before it vanished again behind the guile.

On either side of him, his own people went still at his words.

"I recognize them." Revek moved his mount between Luc and Kikir and came to a stop shoulder to shoulder with Luc. "They're from Fernwell. I saw them there about a week ago. They were causing trouble with some of our people."

The one who'd slapped his chest in false bravado went pale beneath the gold of his skin, and glanced at his friend.

"They're clearly not the same as the bedraggled group we left behind us," Luc agreed. "Their uniforms are Fernwell crisp. I bet they guarded the gates or stood as the Queen's guard before the city fell to us. They were never on the Jatan border, or fighting us in Bartolo or in the hills."

"So, shall we kill them?" Kikir asked cheerfully. "They seem to expect it." He grinned.

The man who'd thumped his chest swallowed, and backed away.

"Well?" Massi sounded impatient. "My arrow is notched."

Luc looked over at her. Her face was impassive, but he could see a sparkle of amusement in her eyes. She was enjoying herself.

It warmed something in him.

"If you want—"

"No!" The one against the tree stepped forward, hands out.

"It's fine for you to try to kill me, but I mustn't return the favor?" Luc asked politely.

"Put like that," Massi said, and lifted the bow to aim.

"We know things." The chest-thumper glanced wildly at his friend and then back. "We were just following orders."

"Whose?" Luc was tired of this game now. Either they talked, or he would kill them himself. He would not leave them at his back to strike again. He was in too much of a hurry.

His feelings must have shown on his face, because the two men drew together and began to babble out a story.

A story of being recruited off the streets of Fernwell after they had the run-in with some Rising Wave soldiers that Revek had witnessed.

The tale gave Luc pause. "This sounds quite organized." He shared a quick look with Massi. "And after you're gone, whoever's gotten you out of the city spreads rumors that the Rising Wave have abducted you."

"We don't know anything about that." Chest-thumper turned out to be someone called Gert, and his friend was Raymon.

"Blaming us for what they're doing themselves." Rafe shook his head at the hypocrisy of it.

"Let me be sure I have this clear. You were taken out of the city. Driven out here into the countryside in carts with others they collected, and told to wait until I came through?"

"Not just you." Gert tugged on his jacket. "Any Rising Wave soldiers. But a messenger came earlier this morning, said you might be coming this way, toward Jatan . . ." He trailed off, realising mid-sentence he might not be doing himself any favors.

Luc focused on their uniforms. They seemed too neat for a week of living rough out in the open. "Where are you staying?"

"There's a small manor house." Raymon waved vaguely to the east. "We were put up there."

Now things were starting to make sense.

The fucking nobles.

Luc hadn't liked a single one of them from the start, although Ava had steered him clear of outright antagonism. He knew, and they knew, that their power was about to be snuffed out.

This was something he both understood and would relish dealing with.

If only he had time.

The safety of the Cervantes was more important than this.

"Which noble?" he asked.

They looked at each other again, and Massi let her arrow loose. It embedded itself into the tree behind the men, the fletched end of it poking between them.

He could see them look down at it, and by the time they looked back up, Massi had another arrow notched.

"Lord Cynera."

"I have a message for Lord Cynera." Luc saw a hunted look come into both men's eyes at the notion of delivering a message when they had clearly failed in their mission. He didn't think they would take a message to Lord Cynera. They'd head straight back to Fernwell and quietly join the ranks of wall builders under Captain Eckhart.

He sighed. Looked over at Rafe. "Can you get me some parchment and something to write with? These idiots aren't going to give Cynera anything. We'll have to deliver it ourselves and then be off."

Rafe nodded and wheeled back toward the pack horses that brought up the rear.

"What about these two?" Massi asked into the silence that fell. "We don't trust them to deliver a message. We can't trust them at our back. It's best we kill them."

"I swear. I really swear, we will go straight back to Fernwell." Raymon looked like he was about to faint.

"It's just . . . we were angry that we lost so easily. That you just walked into the city and took it." Gert rubbed over his heart nervously. "We wanted to fight back."

"Easy? Did you talk to the soldiers camping in squalor not an hour from here?" Kikir asked. "The ones I met on the plains in battle and defeated before we crossed the Bartolo and made our way to Fernwell? Or how about the magic flares your brave Queen's Herald hid in the hills, to burn the whole country down, including your own villages and towns?" His disgust was clear.

"We didn't think any of that was true, at first," Raymon said.

"At first?" Luc asked.

Raymon gulped. "We've spoken to those men you mentioned, at that camp they've made. But even when we knew most of the stories were true, we'd already said we would . . ." He heaved in a breath. "Stand watch and shoot whoever from the Rising Wave came past."

"How many of you are there?" Revek had been watching the trees and their surroundings the whole time.

"Twenty. It isn't a fighting force. We're meant to keep to the trees and shoot down on you. Lord Cynera thought you'd exact reprisals at the villages you passed, and that would help him stir up discontent."

"You were fine with that, were you? Reprisals in the villages caused by your actions?" Massi looked like she was no longer amused.

"I don't . . ." It was as if the idea had simply not occurred to Gert. His voice trailed away.

They really were idiots.

"You will hand your weapons to Kym and walk in front of us, calling off your friends until we get in sight of Cynera's manor house. If one more arrow is let loose, whether it lands or not, Massi will shoot you, if I don't hack off your heads first."

So they made their way, almost slower than he could stand, through the trees and copses to the east, with Gert and Raymon calling an end to their mission.

Massi and two other members of the unit who were excellent archers loosed a few arrows each when it looked like someone didn't want to lower their bow, so three came down from the trees with injuries.

Luc had finished writing his message, a little rough because he'd penned it while riding, by the time the manor's gate was in sight.

They had herded the whole twenty Kassian soldiers ahead of them.

Luc gave a whistle to call a stop. He moved ahead of the Kassians and turned his mount to face them. "You can go in with me and explain what happened, or you can go your own way. I can tell you now that the nobles are about to lose everything. If they promised they could pay you, they were lying. If they promised they could offer you land in exchange for services, they were lying. And anyone who attaches themselves to the nobles will go down with them. Am I very clear?" While he was speaking, everyone had stopped jostling and murmuring to each other to watch him. He hardly had to raise his voice at all.

There was a beat where no one moved, and then one of the men turned and started walking back the way they'd come, through the horses and the Rising Wave unit, into the forest toward Fernwell.

His action seemed to spur the others, and within a minute, no one was left.

"Rafe, find someone light and fast to go back to Fernwell and let them know about this; about the possible danger to anyone in the Rising Wave who passes this way if we haven't found them all, or if some of them creep back here to do Cynera's bidding. But wait until I come out from delivering my message. Let's see what Cynera has to say."

He studied the unit before him for a moment, noting with pride the easy, confident way his people sat on their horses, weapons drawn, just waiting for his word.

He hoped Cynera was getting a good look from his high windows.

He rode through the open gates, and Revek and Massi were suddenly on either side of him.

He said nothing, but he was happy to have them there. Even Rev.

"I'll go, if you want me to," Rev said as their horses crunched up the crushed stone of the drive.

"Go where?" He didn't understand what he meant.

"Back to Fernwell with the message."

Luc turned to him in surprise. "You'd go back?"

Rev managed a small smile. "I'm not saying I want to. But I will, if you'd prefer me out of your sight."

Luc said nothing as they approached the door, but the hard, tight feeling in his chest loosened for the first time since Revek's lover, Haslia, had tried to kill Rev to stop him from sharing anything she'd told him.

It was clear she had told Revek things that would have been useful to the Rising Wave and dangerous to Kassia, and equally clear that Revek hadn't passed that information on.

It had been hard to get over what seemed like a betrayal, but Ava had assured him that if Revek couldn't recall what had been said, Haslia had probably spelled him to forget, and her attempt to kill him was simply her tying off loose ends.

Before he could speak, the door opened, and a terrified man stood in the doorway.

"Get out! Get away from here! This is the property of Lord—"

"Lord Cynera, I know. I am the Commander of the Rising Wave. I would very much like to speak to Lord Cynera, immediately."

The man stared at him, white lipped, panting, close to fainting with fear. "He . . . He isn't here."

"And where is he, then?" Massi asked politely.

The man's eyes darted to her, and fixed on her, almost with relief. Massi had always looked friendly, except when she was pointing an arrow at you. "He's in Fernwell. He left four days ago."

They might have passed him coming through the gates as they were leaving, Luc thought. However he'd found out, Cynera had obviously sent one of his people back to set up this ambush.

"Well, it looks as if one of my people will have to deliver this to him in Fernwell, then." Luc tapped the missive on his thigh. "And a word of warning. If you shelter one more Kassian soldier in this manor, when I return from my journey I will raze this house to the ground. Do you understand?"

The man's eyes widened at the mention of soldiers and slowly nodded.

"Treason is an ugly, ugly crime," Revek said, and there was a slight catch to his voice. "And those convicted of it are subject to the full force of the Queen's law."

"To be honest," Massi leaned down a little toward him, "I would not want to be associated with a traitor for anything. I'd pack my belongings and run, if I were you."

The man crept back, step by step, until he was through the door, and then slammed it in their faces.

They turned their horses and moved at a trot back to the gates.

"I don't think you are a traitor, Rev. And I know you weren't responsible for what happened. It's just hard to get my heart to agree with what my head already knows." He reached out and put a hand on Rev's shoulder. "I know you want to protect our home, and I wouldn't ask you to play messenger instead."

Revek blew out a breath. "Good." His voice was thick.

"And now, can we finally be a family again?" Massi asked, and the exasperation in her voice made Luc chuckle.

By the time they reached the gate, he realized the hard knot in his chest was gone.

CHAPTER 12

"Are you all right?" The whisper was light and high—a child's whisper.

Ava turned her head and opened her eyes.

She was lying on a pile of straw on the ground, a short distance from a fire pit. Night had fallen, and people sat on logs set around the fire, chatting and laughing.

"Where are we?" she croaked.

"Near the river." The little girl who answered was hunched down on her haunches, her light brown hair a fluffy cloud around her face.

Near the river told Ava precisely nothing. They had been near the river when Sirna had put the magic rope around her waist, but she assumed they weren't still in the same place.

Sirna had obviously decided traveling with the caravan had some benefit to him.

She wondered what story he'd told them about her.

The rope was still in place—she could feel the subtle pull as it bled her dry—but Sirna had taken the bag with the rope in it off her and set it down a little way away from her. It was probably why she was capable of waking up.

"That is ugly," the little girl said, pointing to where the rope lay between her and the bag. "It's eating you up."

"I know."

"Why don't you take it off?" the little girl asked.

"I can't touch it with my hands." She looked down at her shift. To her surprise, she saw someone had wrapped a shawl around her shoulders. Maybe she could cover her hands with the shawl and pick the knot at her waist apart.

She tipped her head to get a better view of the campfire, and saw Evelyn and Sirna were sitting directly in front of her, with their backs to her as they faced the fire.

She pulled down the shawl, sliding it from under her back and shoulders, until it covered the rope at her waist, and carefully, with her fingertips, pulled at the knot.

The magic of the rope nipped at her fingers, and she had to lift her hands off, as if she were touching a hot iron.

Her arms felt heavy, and if she hadn't known she had gone fuzzy around the edges before, she would have dismissed the strange distortion around her hands as a trick of the light.

She went back to the knot. She pick, picked at it until it became too much, even through the shawl, and lifted her fingers away. Pick, pick, lift.

It wasn't as if she'd forgotten the girl, she'd just needed the rope off her more, so when thick gloves were placed on her chest, she blinked up in surprise.

The little girl put a finger to her lips. "They're my da's. He uses them when he melts iron in the fire." She paused. "I have to put them back quickly, so hurry."

Ava tried to slide her hands into them. It was much harder than it should have been, and with an impatient click of her tongue, the little girl helped her put them on.

The rope seemed to know she was trying to free herself.

She felt its pull on her energy grow, and her head slumped back on the ground, but she would not give up. She would not.

She let her head rest on the sweet, fresh hay, eyes closed, and picked at the rope by feel, pushing the shawl off her and tugging and working the rope until she felt it give.

"Stand back," she warned the girl. She hadn't opened her eyes, but she sensed the child was crouched close by, watching. "Stand well back."

She finally had the end of the rope in one hand and she managed to open her eyes and lift her head. She carefully set it down onto the ground and sat up.

It was a struggle, but she managed.

The world whirled around her for a moment, and she had a second's panic that she would fall back down on the rope that now lay behind her.

A small hand touched her shoulder, steadying her, and she felt tears sting the back of her eyes in gratitude. "Thank you," she whispered.

She inched forward on her behind, getting more distance from the rope, and then leaned forward, got up on her hands and knees, and turned back to face her tormentor.

The end of it fluttered, as if in a breeze. Except there was no breeze.

She didn't want to, but she crawled back, the gloves still on, and carefully stuffed the rope into the bag.

She drew the gloves off and handed them back to the girl, who took them and whirled away, sprinting into the darkness to disappear into one of the carts.

She came back just as quickly, though.

"What is that?" she asked, looking at the bag in disgusted fascination.

"An evil thing that sucks your energy." Ava's voice was still a whisper.

The noise coming from the campfire was loud enough to hide their conversation, but she was terrified Sirna or Evelyn would turn and see her.

"Please, don't go near it."

The little girl nodded solemnly. "What are you going to do now?"

"Destroy it." Only, she didn't know how.

"Would it burn?" the girl asked.

"Maybe." She really didn't know.

"Then throw it on the fire." The little girl waved toward it.

"I can't. Not while Sirna and Evelyn can see."

The little girl tilted her head. "Why not?"

"Who do you think put it on me?"

The child's mouth opened into a little round o.

Ava felt a spike of unease. Should she be telling a child these things? She didn't know.

She didn't feel like herself.

She was barely keeping herself conscious, but she felt she should be doing better than this.

"I'm sorry. I don't mean to frighten you. Why don't you go back to your parents?"

"It's just Da and me," the little girl whispered. "I didn't like the new people, but Da said I was to be polite. They said you were simple. You were tied to the seat on the cart when they joined us. They said you would wander off, otherwise."

Hah. So that was their story.

"What's your name?" Ava asked her.

"I'm Melodie. Who are you?"

"Avasu." Ava decided to use the name the Venyatux had given her. It felt safer. And it brought back memories of good times.

Ava tried to push herself up from her hands and knees, and collapsed, face first, in the hay.

"What are you doing now?" Melodie asked.

"I need to find something that looks like the rope to tie around myself, so that Sirna thinks it's still on me when he comes to check." She spoke into the hay, her voice muffled.

She thought she heard Melodie run off, but she drifted off and lost track.

It suddenly occurred to Ava that Melodie had known the rope was killing her. She wondered how, but then she blanked out again.

She woke to a gentle shake.

"Madam Croter uses this to hold open the curtains on her cart." The little voice whispering in her ear was sweet and low.

Ava bit back a groan as she turned, lifting her shoulder up, and saw Melodie was crouched back down in front of her, a thick velvet rope in her hand.

It was thicker than the magic rope, but it was black, and if she lay with the shawl on and hay covering her, she might get away with it.

"Thank you."

"You'll need to put it back before morning, or Madam Croter will notice. Her cart is the one with the red door." Melodie thrust the rope at her and then disappeared into the darkness, just as Ava heard a man with a deep voice call Melodie's name from the far side of the camp.

Everyone around the fire had been drinking some form of alcohol. Ava could hear it in their voices and in the rising volume of the conversation as she tied the velvet rope around her with shaking hands. But things seemed to be breaking up now, and fear had Ava turning to face the bag.

She was sure it had moved closer, but she managed to pluck handfuls of hay from the thick bed she was lying on and lay them between her and the bag. She also wound the shawl more tightly around herself, and covered her legs up to her waist in hay.

Her feet were freezing.

Sirna couldn't continue to let her go without clothes and shoes, but her more pressing problem was what to do with the magic rope.

She could wait until everyone was asleep and burn it, and she would do that.

No matter what she did next.

No matter the consequences.

Sirna would have to leave the caravan and go back to tying her up when he found the rope gone, or she could try to substitute the rope for something else. Try to fool him into thinking the rope was still on her.

As the people began calling their goodnights, a horse nickered close by, and Ava twisted slightly to see where it was.

Someone had tied all the horses near each other and she saw a tail swish to the side.

She had thought before that the rope looked as if it had been made from horse hair. If she could find a knife or scissors to cut horse hair with, and if she had the energy to do it, she could work through the night and make a rope of her own.

The energy part of it, in particular, worried her.

Just turning to look at the horses had tired her, and she closed her eyes and sank into a doze.

When she came awake again, it was to giggling.

"She's fine." Evelyn's voice was a little high-pitched.

"Course she's fine." Sirna gave a small burp. "She isn't fuzzy at the edges, is she?"

"The whole world is fuzzy at the edges," Evelyn said, and they found that very funny.

They laughed all the way back to the cart.

Something about that laughter got to her.

It ignited the first real feeling she'd had, other than gratitude toward Melodie, in days.

She waited for the camp to quieten. Then she waited a little longer, dipping in and out of a light doze.

A bird called suddenly from the bushes, its pure note repeated over and over, and it jerked her awake.

She sat up, hugging her knees, and then slowly, carefully, found her feet.

The bag definitely seemed to be closer than it had been.

Ava moved away from it, looking for its long strap in the hay, and then she walked toward the fire, using the strap to drag it behind her.

When she looked back, she could see the end of the rope had

come out of the bag, and she reluctantly lifted the strap up and held the bag out to her side.

She stepped between two logs that made up the seating around the fire, and then gave a start at the sight of an old man on the ground, leaning back against one of them.

She watched him for a long beat, heart hammering, but though his eyes weren't completely closed, his breathing was even and steady.

She moved to the fire.

It was low but still going.

Ava carefully pinched the cloth flap of the bag with her fingers and lifted it up. The end of the rope was still hanging out of the bag, and she thought it looked like more had come out since she'd first noticed it.

She gripped one bottom corner and tipped the bag over the fire.

The end of the rope swung up and brushed her wrist, but she jerked it away, avoiding the curling snare it threw out and then, as the first coil hit the flames, it contracted, as if in pain.

One end fell out of the fire pit, and Ava found a stick and flicked it back in.

The flames went green, and she thought she could hear a high-pitched hiss until the fire had consumed it all.

Her legs gave way, and she fell down.

She couldn't remember when last she'd drunk or eaten anything, and she wasn't sure if the sudden wave of dizziness was from the destruction of the rope, or her body's lack of sustenance.

She rolled away from the fire and forced herself onto her knees.

The relief at the rope's destruction welled up in her.

She would never have to face that again. She felt light as air.

When she got back to Fernwell, she would take the one General Ru had kept and she would burn it, too.

It should not exist.

Even if she couldn't fool Sirna with another rope, even if he realized she'd destroyed it, he could do nothing about it. The rope was gone.

And now she had a chance to rebuild her strength.

She thought for a moment of running right now. But she was breathing hard just from the short walk from her hay pile to the fire. She had no shoes to protect her from the rough road, no warm clothes, and no energy. There was also the Focus Sirna and *Himself* had spoken about. The magical lodestone that would find her no matter where she ran.

So, there would be no escaping for a few days at least. She was so far from normal, from the person she had been, she despaired.

In that moment, she wanted Luc so badly. The feel of his arms for comfort, the touch of his lips on her temple as he held her.

She blinked back tears.

Enough of this nonsense.

The rope had stolen more than her energy, it felt like.

It seemed as if it had stolen part of herself.

She hoped that was just her imagination, but the thought of it made her sick with fear.

Sap leaking from one of the logs in the fire exploded with a pop and the old man jerked, blinked at her, and then settled down again.

She stood stock-still, waiting for her heart to stop galloping, and brushed her tears away.

Time was moving on.

She turned slowly, looking for something sharp among the things left near the fire.

She found nothing.

She moved toward the carts, and then remembered she needed to return the rope around her waist, and unknotted it as she went.

The ground was cold and wet under her bare feet, and she wished for her boots. She drew the shawl more tightly around her and felt a surge of pure, hot hatred for Sirna.

The cart with the red door loomed out of the darkness and she wound the rope up and set it on the step.

There was a scrabble of sound which froze her in place, and then her eyes finally made out a black chicken in a wicker basket beside the steps. It fluffed out its feathers and gave a quiet cluck, then settled back to sleep.

Ava slowly let her limbs relax again, and began searching for something sharp.

Not a lot of things had been left out. These people didn't have much, and what they did have they kept safe inside their carts.

When she found a table where someone had set out a shallow basin, soap and a razor beside their door, she closed her eyes in relief and found herself clasping a fist to her chest in thanks to the Whispering Grasses, like the Venyatux she'd pretended to be for months.

With a silent apology to whoever owned it, she took the bone-handled razor and went toward the horses.

Five of the seven had black tails, or very dark tails. It was difficult to see the exact color when the only light came from the fire a little way off.

She lifted up a handful of tail hair from the top and cut a large piece from the middle of the tail, trying to hide what she'd done.

The horses didn't like it.

They stamped and a few nickered, but she was quick and she had a lot of horse tail hair by the time she was done.

She was sweating and shaking with effort, but she felt as if she were clutching her salvation.

She went back to the little table with the basin and soap, set her horse hair down carefully and ran the soap along the blade.

The river was close, so close she could hear the plop of frogs as they jumped in, and she made her way to the bank.

She knelt and carefully dipped the blade into the water, then rubbed the soap and bubbles off with the hem of her shift.

Then she set the razor down beside her and scooped up water with her hands to drink.

The touch of water to her throat hurt she was so thirsty.

She drank as much as she could and then staggered back to the table, hoping the shaver wouldn't notice a blunting of his blade.

He'd kept it very sharp.

When she finally sat down in front of the fire with her horse hair, she felt sick, as if the water in her stomach had swollen to twice the volume, but she didn't have a choice but to weave.

Not if she wanted to spend the next few days getting back to a semblance of herself and escaping.

She pinched a section of the big hank she had gathered off, used a single strand to secure the end, and began to plait the rope.

She worked for a few minutes, fingers a little clumsy, and then slowed as she realised something was wrong.

She wasn't working any magic into her braid.

She stared down at the braid in her hands in horror.

She couldn't remember a time when she hadn't woven magic into what she was doing. And when she didn't want to include magic, she had to actively stop herself, hold herself back with effort.

As the warm glow of the dying fire flickered, she felt the fear in her grow a little bigger.

Had the rope stolen her magic?

Had it eaten it up?

She choked back a strange sound that wanted to escape from her throat and rocked a little, comforting herself.

Although what comfort could she find in movement?

Even in her darkest days; hungry, thirsty, wishing for just a glimpse of blue sky, she had had her magic in Herron's dungeons.

It had been her only companion. Her only hope.

She was bereft without it.

Behind her, a horse stamped its hoof, and in front of her, the wood feeding the fire collapsed into coals.

Time was passing, and she had less than a hand's length of rope finished.

Sometimes, when she embroidered, she hummed. It helped the magic.

She couldn't risk humming aloud, but she forced herself to remember a song and sing it in her head as she worked.

And she thought of regaining her strength, of healing her spirit of the terrible damage she felt that the rope had inflicted on her.

But as the fire died, leaving her in deeper and deeper shadow, she lost the thread of the song more times than she cared to count, and her thoughts scattered, fear and loss and missing Luc and fear again spinning through her head instead of thoughts of strength and health.

Her eyes drooped and she jerked awake many times. The rope slid through her limp fingers to the ground often, and she had to unbraid it and redo it to keep it neat.

When the old man woke with a hacking cough just as dawn broke, she still had a short piece of unbraided hair left.

He looked at her, surprised, as he stood, scratching his stomach under his rough cotton shirt, and then he staggered off behind the horses to relieve himself.

While he was gone, terror at the lack of time left spurred her to finish the last bit. She wrapped one end around her waist, looping the bag across her chest and stuffing the rest into it.

It wasn't as long as the other rope, but as most of it would be in the bag, she wasn't worried about that. She was only concerned that it wouldn't look exactly like the one she'd burned.

The one way to keep Sirna's eyes from focusing too much on the rope was to make sure he found her where he expected to find her, so she staggered to her feet, almost crying out at the shooting pain of pins and needles in her legs from sitting for so long in one place.

She limped to the hay bed and found it was dew-covered and cold.

She forced herself to lie back down in it, and lay, shivering, waiting for the sun's rays to touch her and warm her a little.

When it finally did, she closed her eyes against their bright light and let herself fall into exhausted sleep.

CHAPTER 13

Luc saw the smoke first, rising above the trees, black against the pale blue of the autumn morning sky.

He rose up and twisted in his saddle, giving a short, sharp whistle to warn the rest of the unit.

As they'd moved closer and closer to the Jatan border, he'd taken front scout duty more and more.

Of everyone, he was the one with the most protections. Not that anyone knew that. They kept arguing he needed to be protected for the negotiations with the Jatan.

Massi suspected Ava was a spell caster, but Ava had never openly admitted it to her, and even so, Massi's suspicions hadn't stretched as far as thinking Luc was covered in her spells.

But he was.

From his cloak, to his tunic, to the crumpled kerchief tucked into his belt, to the skin on his forearm and his chest.

Ava kept telling him her workings may fade, that they wouldn't last forever, but they did not seem weaker to him, no matter how many weeks had gone by.

In the deep inside pocket of his cloak, each one held safe in its own little cloth pouch, were the workings Ava had given him before he'd left. She told him the one in the red pouch would foster cooperation, which he took to mean they would do whatever he suggested. The one in the white would make the recipient turn and leave, abandoning everything to go home, no matter what they were doing.

He would save the spells as much as possible, use them only when necessary, but with them in hand, along with the protections he had around him, he couldn't let anyone go into danger before he'd gone in himself.

It had been just over a week since they'd left Fernwell, and they'd made good time up through the plains and then into the northern forests, but if a Jatan attack was responsible for the fire up ahead, he was worried.

They'd come down much further than Kym had seen before she left to warn him of their movements. The mountains were visible in the distance, but they were a good week's ride away still.

This was bold.

Rev and Kikir thundered up to ride beside him, and he caught a glimpse of Massi through the trees, taking the higher ground with a few others who, like her, were experts with their bows.

They weren't following a path through the forest, but as they got closer to the column of smoke Luc saw one through the trees, a rough track that looked like it was maintained.

He urged his horse onto it and by the time he burst out of the woods into the fields that surrounded the small village, most of his soldiers were on the road behind him.

A woman was wailing.

That was the noise that stood out to Luc as he rode at a slower pace down the village's single street.

Her voice rose and fell with her breath, but she sounded as if she would go on until her throat closed up.

Luc kept on his mount, using the height it gave him to look into windows and check down the alleys between houses.

The fire was coming from a large building at the far end of the road. The flames had reached as high as the thatch roof, and the pall of smoke burned his nostrils as he breathed it in.

"Where is everyone?" Revek asked.

"There's one." Kikir pointed to the side, and Luc saw a man lying on his back near a door, a sword wound in his chest.

"Maybe most of them were able to hide before they were attacked?" Kym, the scout leading them to the border, had joined them as they'd entered the village.

Luc hoped she was right.

"Did you pass this way on your journey to Fernwell?" he asked her.

She shook her head. "I took the eastern edge of the forest."

The woman's wailing suddenly cut off, the silence so abrupt, it raised the hairs on the back of Luc's neck.

He'd drawn his sword as they'd ridden into the village, and now he gripped it carefully, looking for any sign of who had attacked this small community.

The attack looked like it had been carried out by someone who'd changed their minds halfway through.

Luc could see where doors had been smashed in, the blackened walls where fires had been lit but then quickly dowsed before the flames touched the thatch.

Aside from the one man lying dead behind them, there were no other bodies, although the way the woman had been crying, he could only assume she had done so over the body of a dead loved-one.

He moved in the direction the cries had come from, the flames still crackling overhead as they consumed the roof.

There was a sharp turn in the narrow lane, and suddenly he was back out among the fields.

A small group of people huddled on the far side of the open space against a fence, where the forest met the rich, ploughed soil.

Between where he stood and the villagers, a woman crouched beside a young man who lay on his side, eyes closed.

A man stood over her, and Luc guessed he was the one who made her stop crying earlier.

Every eye was turned toward him, and Luc glanced back to see where the rest of his people were.

Rev and Kikir were just behind him, some of the others were coming up from behind, but they knew not to trap themselves in the narrow lane, so Rafe would have the rest of them spread throughout the village.

Massi and the other four archers would be somewhere on high ground.

Luc shaded his eyes and looked for likely perches, and guessed some were to his right, on the low hill above the field, and others would be hidden high in the trees in front of him.

He moved forward, letting his horse pick its own way across the muddy ground.

An arrow shot at him, coming from the tight, huddled group in the corner.

It went wide, not even coming close, although someone behind him swore as it flew past them

He looked over his shoulder at his soldiers, to check if they were all right, and then turned back.

He could all but see the surprise, and then the fear, sweep over the group at his nonchalance.

A second arrow launched.

"Duck." He barked the order to those behind him, because while the arrow wouldn't hit him, it could hit one of them. He leaned to the side, aware that it was wise to at least look as if he were trying to avoid being hit, rather than explain the confidence he had that it simply wasn't a possibility.

The arrow flew past, lost momentum and dropped to the ground.

"Can you stop trying to kill me?" he called. "I have archers of my own, and the next time you shoot, they might decide to shoot back. Given how close you're all standing, it's not certain who they might hit."

Another ripple of shock went through the group.

But Luc had his eye on the man in the middle of the field, standing beside the woman who was now on her knees, resting her head on the chest of the young man she'd been crying over.

The man glanced briefly at the group in the corner. "Carvel, stop shooting." He widened his stance, putting himself between Luc and the Rising Wave and the rest of the village. "You've already taken everything, why did you come back?"

Luc studied him. The man was lying. Not everything had been taken.

There was a protectiveness about the man, and Luc guessed he'd be a lot more desperate if they were going into winter with nothing.

But it was a good lie.

If Luc and the Rising Wave *were* new marauders, coming in a second wave, it wasn't a stretch for the villagers to pretend they had been stripped of everything; that there was no more to take.

Luc respected that.

Massi stepped from the trees, just beyond the fence, and whistled to him.

He urged his horse forward, riding to the side, away from the huddled group, and met her at the wooden barrier.

"There's a stockpile of vegetables, probably harvested from these fields, hidden under a thick tarpaulin and covered with leaves, just through the trees." She paused as if to say more, then shook her head and disappeared back into the forest's gloom.

Luc turned his mount and rode back to the leader.

The man had been watching him talk to Massi, and his face looked worried as Luc approached.

Luc guessed he was wondering if she'd found their stash of food.

"My name is Luc Franck. I'm the commander of the Rising Wave. We have taken Fernwell, and we control Kassia."

There was a moment of silence as the man, and the people behind him, absorbed what he'd said. The woman crouched on the ground didn't seem to care.

"If you control Kassia, how come my village was attacked?" The man spoke bitterly.

"Because we can only be in one place at a time, and we were at Fernwell, securing our victory. But we heard the Jatan were coming down from the border, now that the Kassian army is gone, and we came to investigate. We saw the smoke."

The village leader considered his words. "It was the Jatan who attacked here," he admitted. "We thought you were another group of them. You look the same."

No uniforms, he meant. No insignia.

"Did your archer find our winter store?" He asked the question as if he wasn't able to hold it back.

"She did." Luc studied his face, then flicked his gaze to the group behind him. "We're not here to take your food. We saw the fire, as I said, and we came to help."

The man blinked up at him, as if unsure whether to believe him or not.

"Then that would be a change from the old guard, all right. The Queen's Herald came through here a few times on his way to the border and stripped us bare."

"The Queen's Herald is dead," Luc told him.

A sigh rose and fell at that.

"Now tell me, did you make a deal with the Jatan in return for them not burning the whole place down, or did you manage to move them on some other way."

The man looked down at the woman at his feet. She was brushing the hair from the boy's forehead, her fingers lingering on his cheek.

"I would have made a deal," he said at last. "I would have done anything to get them gone, and keep us safe, because I didn't think there was anyone coming to help us."

Luc waited and he eventually looked up.

"My name is Marcus. I'm the council leader here. We have someone watching from the hills most days, because the Queen's Herald comes through here sometimes, as I said. Just after dawn, the watcher gave the signal," he pointed to where Luc had guessed some of his archers were located. "They could hear a group coming, and we moved the winter store out to the forest. We didn't get everything, but we got most of it." He glanced beyond Luc, to the building which was still burning. Some of Luc's unit were attempting to douse the fire. "They swept in, looking thin and feral. Started bashing down doors and setting fires." He rubbed at the side of his head, and Luc noticed the bruise along his jaw.

"I tried to stop them. Told them we'd cooperate, that there was no need to destroy anything. But the leader hit me, put me on the ground, and they kept hunting for food."

"What stopped them?" Because either they were only playing at destruction, or someone had put an end to it.

"Another group came in." Marcus pointed across the field, to the road Luc and the others had taken. "An older commander. Also Jatan. He made them put out the fires, except for the hall, because the fire there was already too big. It would have taken them too much time and effort to put it out." His tone was bitter. "Then he let them take what food they could find and pulled them back. The young one, the one who hit me, didn't like it, but he listened." He hunched. "When you came, I thought it was him, coming back as soon as the older one's back was turned."

"They must have known you had food stored somewhere."

Marcus nodded. "We told them the Kassian soldiers had taken it on their way to Fernwell. I don't think they believed us, but they couldn't find it, and then they were ordered back."

"And you think the younger one will return?"

"I'm surprised he isn't back already. I can only think the older one is still keeping an eye on him."

Luc turned his mount and moved up next to Revek and Kikir.

"You think he's right? They might come back?" Revek's voice was low. He'd obviously been listening carefully to the exchange.

Luc lifted a shoulder. "If they're hungry and desperate, yes."

Rev turned and trotted back down the lane, to let the rest of the unit know to be wary.

Luc saw the word spread, but before he could make a decision on whether to move the unit on, to keep pressing north, or wait and protect the village, one of his archers on the hill gave a whistle.

They all went still.

Massi stepped out from between the trees again, and signalled to her archer on the hill, then disappeared.

Luc lifted his hand and twirled a finger.

His unit slipped out of sight.

"They're back." Marcus seemed to droop. "I knew it."

"How many of them were there?"

Marus lifted a hand, palm down, and waggled it side to side. "Fifty? Around that number."

That would mean the odds were in Luc's favor. Better if they held the advantage of surprise, as well.

"Stay here." Luc glanced over at the huddled crowd, then back at Marcus. "And keep quiet."

"Kill them." The woman spoke for the first time, looking up at him from her position crouched on the ground. Her eyes flashed pure hatred. "Kill them all."

Luc put a finger to his lips, then joined Kikir up against the building, out of sight of anyone taking the lane down to the back field.

Kill them all.

It might come to that, but he hoped not.

He didn't know yet what the Jatan had done in the north east. Whether his people were safe, or whether they were having to deal with the same type of raid that had just happened in this tiny Kassian village.

He needed to find out.

A bird's call came from down the street, near the burning hall.

Revek. He always had a way with bird calls.

It was a warning that the Jatan were in sight, coming from the woods behind the hall, from the back of the village.

They moved in silence, no talking or calling.

The sound of horses hooves and the clink of metal the only evidence of their approach.

Luc heard them come to a stop outside the hall, and waited for a reaction.

"Where are the villagers?" someone asked, his voice loud in the quiet.

He spoke Jatan, but it was close enough to Kassian as to simply be a different dialect.

"Getting the food they were hiding before, is my guess." The man who spoke sounded grim. "Seems we might catch them at it."

Luc felt his own anger begin to rise at that comment.

What right did this commander think he had to the winter store of an entire village?

He heard them come down the lane toward the back field, and then a group of ten horsemen trotted past his and Kikir's position.

Their gaze was fixed on Marcus and the woman, and the huddled villagers at the far end of the field. If they had looked to the left and back, they would have seen him, but they weren't expecting resistance or any trouble at all.

Two of the horses were each pulling a wooden cart.

They'd come back to steal the village's food supplies and cart it away.

That was their first mistake.

Their second was that they had only brought a small number of soldiers to do it.

Luc wondered if the rest had been left behind to fool the older commander, to pretend that his orders were being followed.

"Isn't this where we left you last time?" The Jatan soldier at the front of the group came to a stop close to the woman and the village leader.

Luc guessed he was the young captain.

"You haven't been gone that long." Marcus stepped back.

Just out of reach, Luc noted with approval.

"Spread out, the stores are either in the houses, or here on the field."

Some of the soldiers turned back toward the lane, and stopped dead at the sight of Luc.

He'd moved to the middle of the lane, Kikir by his side. The Skäddar was almost vibrating with eagerness for the confrontation. As soon as they had moved out from their position against the wall, Revek had emerged from a narrow lane and came down the lane to join them.

Luc caught a glimpse of a few of his unit further down toward the hall.

When Revek drew level and stopped, the three of them formed a solid barrier.

One of the soldiers finally found their voice and let out a yip of alarm. The captain turned.

He stared at Luc for a moment, eyes narrowed. "Who are you?"

"That's not how this works." Luc moved his horse toward them. "This is my country. These are my villagers. I ask the questions of interlopers, not the other way around."

There was a moment of shocked silence from the Jatan.

"Your country?" the captain tried to sneer, but Luc could see he was thinking hard behind the attitude.

"You still don't get the concept of who asks the questions. Who are you?" Over the officer's shoulder, Luc saw Massi swing up to a high branch in the tree closest to the field, and then dropped his gaze back to the threat in front of him.

"Lieutenant Hurst of the Fourth Jatan Regiment." Hurst spoke through gritted teeth, and Luc was surprised he'd answered at all.

He didn't like orders, this one.

He wondered how he'd progressed to lieutenant with that attitude, but Kym had said the Jatan had lost a lot of senior officers in their battles with the Kassian, so perhaps Hurst was the result of a shortage of good leaders.

"Lieutenant Hurst of the Jatan, what are you doing attacking a Kassian village so far from the Jatan border?"

"We are at war with Kassia, didn't you know?" Hurst was trying to be sarcastic.

"You look thin and desperate." Luc studied Hurst calmly. "You took advantage of my army's victory over the Kassian forces to move into territory I have taken. You will pay reparations to this village for the lives you took, the damage you have done, and the food you stole, and you will return to Jatan, or there will be consequences."

"They are Kassian, what do you care if you're Rising Wave?" The way Hurst flicked a quick look over Luc's shoulder told him he'd seen some of Luc's unit. Seen how outnumbered he was. "Aren't you all Cervantes?"

"I just told you. I've taken this territory and I take care of what is mine." Luc caught Marcus's eye and flicked a look behind him, to the rest of the villagers.

Marcus gave a nod, grabbed the woman's arm, and hauled her up before backing away, giving Luc room to fight if he needed to.

"We didn't realize you'd been successful in overcoming the Kassian army. Didn't know the war was won." Hurst lifted his shoulders and began to weave his horse through his soldiers and past the carts toward Luc. "And we needed supplies."

"Your fight with Kassia is over where the border lies and who controls which side of the mountains." Luc studied him, looking for the tell that said he was going to strike. No doubt about it, this one thought he was the best fighter in the room. "But here you are, far from the border and the mountains. Only a week's hard ride to Fernwell." He tilted his head. "Are the Jatan invading? Because that would be helpful to know."

"It's not my place to give an answer to that." Hurst's smile was insincere. "I am just a lieutenant."

"Then where is your superior officer?" Luc asked. "It seems I need a word."

Hurst moved.

Luc had noticed he'd released his reins while he'd been smiling, and his hand whipped back to grab his sword.

Luc moved faster.

The tip of his own sword rested under Hurst's chin before he'd managed to get a grip on his pommel.

"Tell your soldiers to dismount." Luc kept his tone even.

"You misunderstood me—"

One of Massi's arrows arced up and landed with a thud beside Hurst's horse's front hooves.

The horse blew out a breath and pawed the ground, and the edge of Luc's sword nicked the delicate skin beneath Hurst's chin.

A thin line of blood welled up.

The Jatan lieutenant's eyes wheeled a little in his head as he tried to see where the arrow had come from.

"We have archers, we have soldiers, we have you surrounded and we are unhappy at what we have found here. Tell your soldiers to dismount."

Hurst didn't have to tell them anything. All nine of them, five men and four women, slid off their horses, hands up, swords and bows still in their scabbards.

"Take their weapons and their horses," Luc called to Marcus.

The village councillor jogged over with a couple of villagers to obey.

"Kill them all," the woman screamed from the corner of the field. "I want them dead."

Everyone went still.

"Her son's body lies behind you," Luc said. "She has a right to want vengeance. These are not combatants. There was no honor or even logic in killing anyone here."

Hurst closed his eyes and grimaced. "He attacked us."

"What with, a stick?" Luc let the full contempt he felt for Hurst to come through in his tone. "So given your armor, your weapons, and the number of soldiers you had around you, is he dead because of your lack of control or your blood lust?"

One of Hurst's soldiers actually gasped and Hurst's eyes snapped open.

He looked at Luc as if he would like to kill him by any means possible.

Marcus and the handful of villagers had reached them, and two of them led the horses away, including the carts, while Marcus and the rest collected bows, arrows, swords and knives.

When they had everything except Hurst's gear, Luc flicked a sidelong look at Revek.

"With pleasure," Rev said. He didn't need Luc to spell it out. He dismounted, moved to Hurst and unstrapped his scabbard, tossing it, with the sword still inside, to Marcus. He patted Hurst down, collecting two knives, and then stepped back, his own sword out. "Off the horse."

Hurst glared at Luc, who withdrew his own sword so the lieutenant could slide off his saddle.

When he was on the ground, Marcus sent a young girl to collect the reins and lead the horse away.

"It doesn't make up for the two lives lost, but it's some compensation," Luc said.

Marcus nodded. "What'll you do with them?" He tilted his head toward the Jatan.

"As I said, I need to speak to their commanding officer. They can lead me to him."

Marcus hesitated. "Be careful. And thank you. I am happy that I never have to see the Queen's Herald again."

"Let's go." Revek gestured with an arm, and Hurst and his soldiers started walking through the mud of the field back to the lane. Revek swung back onto his horse and stopped close to Luc.

"That one wants you dead," he murmured, eyes on Hurst's stiff back.

"Oh, I know that."

Hurst could get in line behind everyone else who had tried and failed.

CHAPTER 14

Erdene Ru waited for the messenger Luc had sent back to leave the room before she turned to the small group around the table.

Since that first meeting where they'd decided to lie, she'd added two extra people to the group. Kurvin, her fourth lieutenant, and Talika, the Cervantes guard who'd been chosen to use the magic necklace and take on Ava's likeness.

"So the rumors in the city are being spread by some of the nobles."

"A bit more complicated than rumors, in that there *are* people going missing, but it's of their own free will." Dak pursed his lips.

"Should have known it was the nobles." Kurvin gave a snort. "When are they anything but trouble?"

He lifted his head and shared a quick look with Erdene. She suppressed a smile, but she recalled their roles in the not entirely peaceful transition from noble rule to common rule in Venyatu in their younger days.

"How do we combat it?" Fervanti was standing—always unable to sit unless it was on a horse, that one—and she leaned her hip against the table, eyes fierce.

"We counter it by talking about what happened at Lord Cynera's manor house. What Luc found, what Cynera had planned, the plot to sneak soldiers out to the countryside and even the plan to incite the Rising Wave to take revenge on country villages." Erdene leaned back in her chair.

All the chairs in this place were extremely uncomfortable.

Ava had mentioned the throne was no different.

Queen Freida of Kassia had most surely put pomp and grandeur ahead of usability.

Dak nodded. "Agreed. I'll call a meeting of my captains, have them spread the word, and let them know to discuss it freely within the city walls."

"If I may?" Talika was the least self-assured member of this little group, most likely because she had the lowest rank, but when she spoke, Erdene listened.

The Cervantes guard had suggested numerous ways to make her pretence as Ava less susceptible to discovery, and they were all good.

More importantly, so far, they had all worked.

Erdene wasn't the only one who was developing a respect for Talika, she noted, as every eye turned toward her.

Suddenly aware she was the center of attention, Talika seemed to draw in on herself, and then forced her shoulders down.

"I walk around the palace as myself for at least a couple of hours a day, to give the impression I'm still working as a guard outside the Queen's rooms, and I've been listening to the gossip in the kitchens. The nobles' servants say the nobles are suspicious they haven't had a meeting or function with Ava since Luc left five days ago. The Commander's message isn't just useful as a way to understand the rumors on the street, we can use it as a good explanation for why Ava hasn't mingled with the nobles, as well."

"That's true." Erdene gave a slow nod. "Dak, you and I need to order Cynera in to answer questions and explain the rumors and attacks."

Kurvin gave a chuckle. "I like that."

"I also suggest that you spend time together, walking around the upper apartments, and through the city to the tents outside." Dak tipped his head between Erdene and Talika. "That should put to rest the rumor that the general has locked her up, which is another one I've been hearing."

"Why have I locked her up, in this fantasy scenario?" Erdene shook her head.

"Why, because the Commander is gone," Dak said, a hint of humor in his voice. "So poor, weak Ava, all alone, has fallen prey to your machinations."

The thought of Ava as weak had Erdene shaking her head. "They don't know Ava very well, do they?"

The unfortunate thing was, they wouldn't be getting the chance to do so until they had Ava back. And she couldn't say when that would be.

So, they would do what they could to build this illusion.

"Let's start crushing all these different rumors." Erdene offered an arm to Talika. "Your majesty, would you care for a stroll?"

Talika touched the necklace at her throat and her face slowly changed to resemble Ava's. "There is nothing I would like more."

Something in her tone had Erdene sharpening her gaze on Talika's now altered features, and she thought she saw a glimmer of something warm and inviting in her eyes.

She cleared her throat, unaccountably at a loss, and with the light weight of Talika's hand on her forearm, stepped out into public view.

"LEAVE THE POOR SOUL ALONE."

The call was from a woman, the voice gravelly with age. Ava could hear her, but curled up as she was, she couldn't see her.

Sirna paused in shaking her and straightened up. "She needs to get up, otherwise she'll get left behind." There was a hard edge to his voice. A warning tone.

A touch of fear in there, too.

Ava guessed she looked bad. The way he'd stopped manhandling her at the woman's call told her he was nervous of attracting too much attention.

If what she'd seen last night was correct, at least a few of the carts in this caravan were owned by Grimwaldians. The brightly painted doors gave it away.

Grimwaldians took a dim view of anyone who mistreated those who were simple or had lost their wits.

It dated back to when some were born with magic they hadn't known how to direct or control. Or so she'd been told.

Nowadays it was rare to find young children unable to control their powers.

The accepted wisdom was that less and less spell casters were being born. Her father had thought more and more parents had decided to hide their children's gifts.

Whatever the truth of it, she found it curious that Sirna had weighed up the dangers and advantages of attaching himself to the caravan—and the watchful eyes of the men and women who were part of it—and decided it was worth his while to stay.

It meant he would have to treat her with at least a veneer of decency.

"There are other ways to wake someone who is unwell than rattling their teeth." The woman strode over, spry enough despite sounding old, and Ava sensed her crouching beside her.

She opened her eyes, fluttering them as if she had only just woken.

"There you go, my sweet." The woman's voice was soothing, and she stroked Ava's arm with a sun-browned, calloused hand, then drew back, outraged. "She's freezing!"

"We had a little too much to drink last night." Sirna shifted on the spot. "We forgot to get her a blanket."

"For shame." The woman bent over her again, and Sirna, as if suddenly realising she might accidentally touch the rope, brushed her aside.

"I'll sort her out." He lifted Ava to her feet, careful to stay on the opposite side to the bag of coiled rope, and holding her slightly away from his body.

"What's in that bag?" The old woman put out a hand, and Sirna yanked Ava away from her, so hard and fast, she stumbled.

"She doesn't like people touching it. She's a strange one, and once she starts screaming, it's hard to get her to stop." He pushed Ava in the direction of the cart.

"Well, she needs warmer clothes than what she's got. And some shoes. At a minimum." The woman's white hair hung over her shoulders, and her eyes were a light, almost silver blue. Ava wondered if she was Madame Croter, of the velvet curtains and braided rope that had saved her last night.

Sirna nodded but said nothing.

He was in a bind now. He had no clothes for her. She wondered what he was going to do about that.

He realized a response was required and cleared his throat. "She threw her clothes out yesterday. We didn't realize it until later." He spoke as if he was feeling his way into the lie, but warmed up as he got deeper into it. "I'll have to see if anyone here has clothes I could buy for her." He gave Ava another push toward the cart, and Evelyn appeared in the doorway.

Sirna's partner looked the worse for wear; her eyes were shadowed and her hair stuck up in disarray around her sulky face.

She'd heard the exchange, Ava guessed. And she was not happy about it. But even she must realize there was no way they could keep Ava in a thin shift with no shoes and not attract attention.

Her gaze landed on Ava, and she recoiled slightly, her eyes going wide.

She must look really bad, Ava guessed.

That was good.

The worse she looked, the less inclined Sirna was to suspect the rope was a fake.

And though she was exhausted after getting no sleep, she had the sense that she was more present in the world than she had been yesterday.

Not strong, but *here*.

It was something.

Better by far than the listless, uncaring state she'd been in before.

Her mind went back to her pitiful attempts at working magic into the braided rope around her waist by the fire, and she closed her eyes, shutting out the thought.

She had to believe she would recover in time.

She just needed to give herself some breathing room.

With people like Madame Croter, or whoever this woman was, keeping an eye on her, she might manage to do just that.

Her stomach growled, the sound clear as Sirna and Evelyn locked gazes with each other.

"I haven't eaten for a full day," Ava said, quietly. "And I don't think I can stand anymore." Her head had started spinning and her legs felt weak, and she let herself collapse.

Sirna caught her roughly at the shoulders, careful not to touch her waist. He gripped her too tight, his fingers digging into her upper arms in a way that would bruise.

He lowered her to the ground.

"Blanket," he snapped at Evelyn.

She glared at him and turned back into the cart.

They were both obviously feeling the effects of their drinking last night. It didn't help her for them to be snappy and bad-tempered; she would only get the brunt of it. She stayed where she was, compliant and unmoving, and Sirna settled the scratchy wool blanket over her shoulders.

"She needs food," he said.

"So make her some." Evelyn jumped down from the cart and stalked off, heading to the river.

Sirna took a deep breath in, and then hauled Ava up by one arm.

"You might want to be careful, there." A big, bearded man

stepped out from between the carts, with Melodie by his side. "We might think you're mistreating your companion."

Sirna tried to soften his grimace. "Tempers are a little short this morning, is all." He pushed Ava down onto the step at the back of the cart, and then moved past her carefully to go inside.

Ava lifted her feet and tucked the blanket under them, curling over her knees.

Melodie skipped up to her.

Ava gave the tiniest shake of her head and hoped the child understood she wanted to pretend they had never met.

"I'm Melodie, what's your name?" the little girl asked.

"Avasu," Ava said, voice hoarse. "Is that your father?"

"My da's name is Gregor. He's a blacksmith." Melodie skipped back. "Do you want to come and play?"

"Not now," her father said. "We'll have breakfast and then we are back on the road."

Melodie hesitated, on the verge of complaining, and then she darted forward, touched a hand to Ava's knee, and leaned in on a whisper. "It's good you aren't being eaten any more." She met Ava's gaze with solemn eyes and ran back to Gregor and took his hand.

Ava could hear her bright questions and tinkling laugh as they moved toward the fire pit.

"Don't let that child get close to you." Sirna appeared behind her at the top of the step.

Ava's heart leaped in her chest. Had he heard Melodie's soft comment?

She didn't think so. Hoped not.

She tried to turn to look up at him, gave up and bent her head. "I can't even stand on my own two feet. How am I supposed to do that?" Her voice was raw and faint.

Sirna didn't answer. Instead, he hooked his hands under her arms and hauled her up, dumping her on the floor just inside the cart's interior. It stank of sour beer and sweat.

He had the gloves waiting on the bed and he pulled them on.

"I'm taking the rope off you. I'll put it back on at night, maybe with a bit more fabric between it and your skin. But don't think that means you're free." He carefully unknotted the braid, his fingers clumsy with the gloves, and stuffed it into the bag. He lifted it up and carefully set it on the shelf and pushed it to the back. He stripped off the gloves and tossed them onto the crumpled bed, then crouched down in front of her.

"You're weak. I can almost see through you in some places, which is a problem more clothes will have to solve. That means you don't have a chance against me." He grabbed her chin with hard fingers and tilted her head up to look at him. "You keep quiet and keep your eyes on the ground while we're with these people. It suits me to use the caravan to hide in plain sight while there are people coming for you. I'm not quite as convinced as *Himself* that your people will follow the false trail he set. But they'll be looking for a lone traveller and a Grimwaldian." He put his hand into the inside of his coat and pulled out a knife, blade encased in a sheath. He slid the leather sheath off and the light coming in the doorway caught a curved, finely-honed blade.

"Luckily, I'm from Cattha. It's why *Himself* chose me. If I get caught, Grimwalt wouldn't get the blame. I also know one of the members of this caravan." His gaze lingered on his knife, and Ava remembered hearing something from her days with her parents about Catthans and their knives. The small principality lay to the east of Venyatu, along a section of the cliffs on Venyatu's coastline.

"You're weak enough, I don't think you can walk fast, let alone run." Sirna touched the knife to her cheek, skimming the cool edge down to her chin. "If you try, though, I'll catch you easily. I won't kill you. That would defeat the whole purpose of what I've done. But I'll cut you in a place the guards at the Grimwalt border won't see straight away. I'll cause you pain, I'll put you back in the rope all day, and I'll kill that old Croter woman and the child, at the very least."

She stared at him, her breathing harder and more labored.

He meant what he said.

She didn't have to worry about the rope either way, she

reminded herself as the fear blossomed and grew from her gut up through her throat, so she could barely swallow.

But Melodie and Madame Croter. He would kill them. And likely others, too.

It would inconvenience him, though.

It would lose him his hiding place and put him on the road alone with murder and death behind him.

And it would be risky.

He said someone in the caravan knew him—they would have told the others about him. That meant he could be identified as the killer by any of the survivors unless he truly meant to kill them all.

Also, Gregor, Melodie's father, didn't look like someone who would be easy to kill, and he didn't look like he'd take his daughter's death in stride. He'd hunt Sirna down, and she had to believe Sirna knew that.

It would help to stay his hand.

The thought calmed her and she felt a sudden flare of disgust at herself for the panic that had gripped her moments earlier.

The old her of just a week ago would have laughed in Sirna's face and turned his plots around on him.

But Sirna himself said he could almost see through her in parts.

She was not the woman of a week ago.

She was diminished.

The sound of a boot on the step stilled Sirna, and he turned his head.

Ava looked out from the corner of her eye, the knife still resting, sharp and dangerous, on the edge of her jaw.

"Having a little chat?" Evelyn smelled of river water and smoke.

"Just setting down the rules." Sirna slid the knife back into its sheath and rose to his feet. "I have a few for you, too, my dear." He kept his voice low, almost pleasant, but now that the blade was no longer against her skin and she could turn to watch, Ava saw Evelyn's nostrils flare.

She was afraid.

She tried to bluster through it. "Rules?"

"I'm trying to keep us safe. Drawing attention to us by treating her as a slave or a prisoner is working against that."

Evelyn's lips thinned. "I haven't done any more or less than you."

Sirna shifted, pushing right up against Evelyn, hand gripping her arm. "All I'm saying is we need to clothe her, feed her, and pretend she's your simple sister. Starting now."

"I don't see why she has to be my sister and not yours."

"Because," there was a level of icy anger to his tone, "Reckhart knows me. He knows I don't have a sister. Besides," he paused, tilting his head, "she looks like you. That's why *he* took you with him to Bartolo, remember?"

"All right." Evelyn shook herself loose. "But I'm not your servant."

Something moved in his eyes. Ava thought the headache from the drink the night before, and the sudden flare of temper between them, brought out the worst in him.

Evelyn went still, then she turned her head, looking behind her, and jumped to the ground. "I'll get breakfast going. We'll be leaving soon." She bent to pull a few wrapped food packs out of the leather sack either she or Sirna had set beside the steps, and walked away.

Ava braced herself. Sirna was angry. She could sense it. And she had no ability to fight back, or even to stand, right now.

"Keep the blanket on, I'll see what I can buy for you from the others." He yanked her to her feet. "And not a word from you. You stay silent, or I'll have to weigh up my options with the people here. This road is far enough out of the normal way of things, their bodies would not be found in a hurry."

As she stumbled down the stairs and let Sirna pull her along to the fire pit, she wondered if he had it in him to kill them all to keep himself safe from future retribution.

She didn't want to find out.

She now had the lives of everyone around her on her shoulders.

It was a pity those shoulders were so weak.

CHAPTER 15

A whistle from up ahead was the first sign they were coming close to the Jatan camp.

Luc could see their prisoners, walking in a group surrounded by the Rising Wave unit, try to hide their reactions, but it was clear.

Luc whistled as well, and everyone slowed to a stop.

"Who's your commander?" Luc asked.

Hurst's fists were clenched. He still couldn't believe he'd been taken prisoner and was now going to have to face his general on foot.

Revek was right.

This man would kill him if he could.

"General Tuart."

Luc moved his horse forward when he had the name, skirting the group of prisoners and making his way to the front.

"You'll need a few companions," Kikir said, coming up beside him.

Luc turned in his saddle. "Kym, you come with me, too, and Rafe. Revek, you're in charge here." He motioned with his hand,

and from the back, ten of his soldiers slipped away, on either side of the path, disappearing into the forest.

"You want me to listen to what the Jatan general has to say, and tell you later if it lines up with what I saw?" Kym asked, voice soft.

Luc nodded, waiting for Rafe to come abreast before moving slowly forward.

He called the general's name, and heard another whistle.

Eventually, a few riders appeared up ahead. As soon as he sighted them, Luc stopped, waiting for them to come to him.

He was aware of his hidden soldiers on either side of him, camouflaged by the gloom of the forest.

The Jatan moved slowly, nervous of an ambush, Luc guessed, and he sat patiently until they were close enough to speak without shouting.

"General Tuart?"

"That's me." Like the Rising Wave, the Jatan didn't wear uniforms. The Jatan nation was not so much a single country, but more a collection of fiercely independent regions with the same culture and dialect. When they needed to speak as one, they sent representatives from each region to what they called the Gathering.

The old Kassian queen had thought that lack of cohesion would mean less resistance as she tried to claim the mountains that formed the natural border between Kassia and Jatan, with their mines and their trade routes, for herself.

She had been wrong.

The Kassian offensive had poked the beast, and brought the regions together like nothing ever had.

But their individuality and their dislike of conformity meant uniforms were not favored.

The Rising Wave had never had the funds for a uniform, but Luc didn't think they would adopt one, even now they had access to Kassia's coffers.

The Jatan soldier who rode forward to speak was older, his clothing was well-made and of high quality. It made it likely he was a general. Or at least a senior officer.

"I would like to know what you're doing in my territory, General Tuart."

Luc could see his question had thrown Tuart. Whatever he was expecting, this was not it.

"Who are you? And how do you know my name?"

"I am the commander of the Rising Wave and now all of Kassia, Luc Franck."

There was a beat a silence.

"You won the war." The general's face flickered with surprise.

"We did."

"We were not sure who the victor would be, and given the Kassian army abandoned its position on our border, we decided to make a short incursion." The general sounded as if he had to think hard about each word he spoke.

"I have a letter here from the new queen of Kassia, Ava Valestri, for your own leaders." Luc tapped the side of his cloak.

"The new queen?" Tuart sounded incredulous. "Who is she?"

"She is the niece of the old queen, and my ally."

And so much more.

But that was none of the Jatan's business.

"Again, how did you know my name? How did you know where to find me to give this missive to me?" Tuart was finally over his initial shock.

Luc leaned forward. "We caught some of your soldiers raiding a small village to the south west of here. It was their second attack of the day, and my understanding is you were present for the first attack. Two civilians were murdered in that raid and their town hall was burned down. We imprisoned them and they led us to you. It was the price of their freedom."

General Tuart didn't just look surprised, now. He looked surprised and angry. "Where are these soldiers now?"

"Further back, being guarded."

"I would like to see them. Speak to them."

Luc nodded. "Come with us."

He narrowed his eyes when five other Jatan moved their mounts forward. Shook his head. "You can bring two with you. No more."

Rafe had put a hand to his sword when the soldiers had moved, but Kym was staring at the Jatan soldiers further back, her face pale with shock.

"What is it?" he asked her.

She stared blankly at him for a moment, then shook her head. "Nothing."

It didn't seem like nothing, but Tuart was watching them with interest, and Luc whistled, two sharp calls, and four of the Rising Wave soldiers hidden in the trees stepped out, two on each side.

Tuart flinched at the sight of them, turned and raised two fingers.

The Jatan looked unhappy about it, but only two of them nudged their mounts forward.

Rafe made room for them to pass and then blocked the way again, the four riders lining up with him to barricade the path.

Kym rode silently beside him, looking back at least twice.

Luc wondered who she'd seen that made her so twitchy.

She had been watching the Jatan border for months, it made sense she would recognize some of the soldiers. But why it would disturb her so much was something only she could answer.

When they reached the main unit, he saw Revek had allowed the prisoners to sit, surrounded by soldiers on horseback.

Hurst scrambled to his feet at the sight of Tuart, and his fellow soldiers followed his lead.

Tuart said nothing for a long moment as he stared down at them. Then he turned to Luc, without addressing his people at all. "Where are their mounts and weapons?"

"Given to the villagers for compensation for the harm done to them. Although, you and I both know that is not enough. We will send your Gathering a bill for the final compensation required when we return to Fernwell."

"It was my understanding that you are Cervantes. That Kassia annexed your region and enslaved your people, and that your fight was to free them, not to take control of Kassia."

In other words, Luc thought, he was asking why Luc gave a damn about harm done to a Kassian village.

"The way to keep Cervantes safe and let it heal is to control Kassia, and for Kassia to be as strong as possible. Strong societies treat everyone with the same respect. The rule of law cannot be for the protection of one group and not another. That leads to discontent. And look what my discontent has meant for Kassia." Luc leaned back on his horse, his gaze never leaving Tuart's face.

"All very well, but the Kassian people are the ones who pillaged your country in the first place."

Luc tilted his head. "Very few Kassians had anything to do with what happened to my people. The Queen and her Herald made the decisions. In fact, the village you just plundered was equally plundered by the Queen's Herald on his way to and from his border fortress. Many Kassians have no love for their former ruler."

"And you plan to unite them all, is that it?" Tuart seemed to sneer at the very idea, but Luc had the sense he was simply trying to provoke, to move the conversation on to another topic.

The general didn't want to address what Hurst and his soldiers had done. It could be seen as a declaration of war against the new rulers of Kassia. A war the Jatan were losing before, and would surely lose now.

"What I do or don't plan to do is none of your concern. The new queen and I will communicate with your Council." It was a slap-down on General Tuart's place in this game, and his eyes widened as he registered Luc's words as such. "You can be sure when we do, we will make it clear we consider what you and Captain Hurst did in that village as a provocation of war if an apology and adequate compensation are not forthcoming."

"My father will not—" Hurst's hands were fisted as his sides, his face red and his nostrils flared.

"Quiet." Tuart chopped a hand in the air, and for the first time, Luc sensed some nerves from the man.

So, Hurst was a senior officer's son. Someone at least the same rank as Tuart.

Hurst was chafing at facing some consequences.

The look he gave Tuart was as vicious and full of murderous intent as the one he'd given Luc.

Luc let the silence settle around them all for a moment. "I will let you take your people. Make your way back to Jatan, without molesting any other Kassian citizens along the way."

"We have no supplies." Hurst ground the words out.

"Funny that. When the Rising Wave was running low on supplies, we purchased what we needed from the towns and villages we passed. You might like to try that approach as you leave, as it is the only one acceptable to the new queen and I."

"You seem to speak very easily for the new queen." Tuart's attention had fastened on Luc again.

"That's right. The queen and I are very much aligned in our thinking. And you would do well to remember that." Luc pulled out the missive Ava had written just before he'd left and handed it over to Tuart.

He also had Ava's magic squares in the inside of his cloak pocket. His fingers had brushed over the little bags as he'd taken out the missive, and he'd considered using one of them, but Tuart seemed reasonable. No use wasting them when he didn't need to.

The general took the thin scroll, read it, and then carefully slid it into an inside pocket on his cloak.

Silence stretched again.

Luc gave a whistle, and waited for Rafe and the others to make their way back through the woods to join them.

Revek gave a signal, and the guards around Hurst and his soldiers moved out of the way so the small group could move forward.

"Where are you going?" Tuart watched them turn to face east.

"To Cervantes. I trust the Jatan haven't been foolish enough to try there what has been tried in north Kassia." He watched Tuart's face as he spoke and wondered if he was imagining the flicker of fear.

He had a sinking feeling he was not.

"In case there has been a misunderstanding of a similar nature, I think my unit should accompany you." Tuart watched Hurst and the others move past him and make their way toward the Jatan camp.

Now that he was free, Hurst moved slowly, clearly trying to overhear what was being said.

"I give you no leave to do so. Go home, General. And be glad I'm letting you go at all."

"The thing is . . ." Tuart looked off toward the horizon, avoiding Luc's eyes. "There may have been a few Jatan units who broke off and headed toward Cervantes. And it would be of use to you if I came along to command them back home."

Luc moved closer to him, and at last the general met his gaze. "What are you saying?"

"I'm saying that there have been a few promotions of junior officers who are not experienced enough to control their forces and if anything has gotten out of hand in Cervantes, then I have the authority over them to shut it down without bloodshed."

"Don't you mean, without more bloodshed?" Luc asked softly. "Because that's what you're afraid of, aren't you? That the Jatan have simply decided to follow in Kassia's footsteps when it comes to Cervantes."

"To be honest, I don't know, Commander. But I do know the Jatan cannot afford another war, certainly not with you. I also heard the Venyatux rode with you to Fernwell, and now I see Jatan's neighbour state, Skäddar, seems to have representatives embedded in your units, as well." His gaze flicked over Kikir, who tipped his head in acknowledgement.

"It would be very, very upsetting to me to find any harm has been done to my people." Luc let the spark of fury that had been growing in him since the general started speaking shine through his eyes.

"Then accept my company, Commander. And hopefully, we will be able to resolve this peacefully."

Tuart turned his horse and galloped away, his two guards following behind him.

"What do you think he's really up to?" Massi pulled up beside him.

"I think he knows full well his fellow generals are raiding Cervantes, and he's trying to work out what to do. He'll try to stall us. Try to cover up what he can."

"Then why let him come?" Rev asked.

Luc sighed. "Because I'm afraid he's also right. If there are Jatan forces attacking Cervantes, then he might be able to pull them back." He looked around at his unit. Everyone had pulled in as close as they could to hear him. "We are only eighty. We don't know how many we're going to face, and if Tuart is being honest, he'll be more of a help than a hindrance."

"*If* he's being honest," Massi said.

"If," Luc conceded. "We keep our eyes peeled. We trust no one except each other."

"Just like always," Revek said. There was a note of happiness in his voice.

"Just like always."

CHAPTER 16

A va tugged the too-long sleeves of her new shirt over her hands and folded the ends over her fingertips.

She tucked her hands under her armpits and let her cheek rest against her knees.

Since being abducted, she had either been curled up in pain, or to keep warm, or both.

It would be good to straighten up again and stand tall.

The caravan had stopped for a lunch break in a small open area to the side of the badly rutted road, and it was a relief to not be on the hard, rattling bench of the cart for a bit.

She had found a relatively sheltered spot where the sun filtered through the trees, slightly away from the others, the way Sirna liked her to. She closed her eyes to soak in the warmth.

"Here's some lunch." Melodie crouched beside her and Ava opened her eyes and turned to look at the little girl.

She was holding out a bowl of barley and lamb stew in one hand and a spoon in the other.

The whole caravan had bought the meat yesterday. Gregor had spotted the small farm just off their route and had ridden one of the horses to it, returning with a sack of neatly butchered lamb, several pats of butter and some fresh vegetables. Everyone had contributed to the purchases and the atmosphere had improved since then. Ava guessed they had been running low on fresh supplies.

She took the bowl and spoon with a nod of thanks, and began to eat slowly, savouring each bite.

Yesterday had been a blur. She had been given something at each meal, but she didn't think she'd eaten that much. She hadn't had the energy or the will.

Last night she'd slept outside again, although this time she'd been given a thick blanket.

She didn't complain, even though the air was cold enough to make each breath hurt.

They were having a cold snap.

"You're getting better." Melodie leaned in closer to whisper. "And the new rope you made, that you wear at night, is helping."

Ava paused with the spoon halfway to her mouth. "You can see that?"

Melodie squirmed a little and looked away. "My da says I mustn't say what I see. But it's hard sometimes. Because I do see it. And I need to tell. Like when that rope was eating you up."

Ava looked into her tiny, defiant face, and felt a chill sweep over her.

If this child could see magic, then Gregor was right. She needed to keep it a close-held secret.

But she was also only little. No more than four or five, Ava estimated. Trying to explain why she was in danger without making her constantly fearful was worth doing right.

"There are ways to help people without telling them how you know," Ava said, keeping her voice just as low. "Because your father is right. It's better to keep what you can see a secret, to protect yourself. You have to be resourceful."

Melodie looked up at her, interested. "Like how?"

"Well, like you were the other night. You helped me quietly, out of sight."

"I can't always do that." Melodie worried her lip.

"I would say until you're bigger, you should quietly tell your father what you see, and he can help you decide how to deal with it."

"I have, sometimes. Usually, he decides doing nothing is best." When she lifted her face to Ava's, Ava could see the glisten of tears.

She put out a hand, and Melodie set her own—small, a little sweaty, and smudged with dust—into it. Ava squeezed.

"Then you need to ask him why he decided to do that. You need to talk to him about how it makes you sad and why. Is it because you feel the person is in serious danger because of what you see? Is something evil being done to them? Or is it something they may not realize is harming them?"

"You speak to him." Melodie pulled her hand away and stood. "I don't know how to tell him right. It gets mixed up, and he just frowns and says no."

"I will try." Ava knew how it was to grow up with a gift that was suppressed. "But I need to grow a little stronger, first. So he'll listen to me."

Melodie watched her, and then gave a slow nod. "But you will?"

"I will."

She caught sight of movement between the carts, and scraped the last stew from her bowl.

"We need to move." Evelyn appeared, looking mean and unhappy.

Ava sighed inside. Sirna and his lover were growing less and less willing to tolerate each other.

They were supposed to be traveling across Venyatu, going home to Cattha. Not headed for Grimwalt with a prisoner.

It was grating on them both.

She gave a nod, uncurling slowly from her seat. She found her back was stiff, and she groaned as she tried to straighten up.

"Your father's looking for you, brat." Evelyn flicked her fingers at Melodie, and with a fulminating look, Melodie turned and skipped away.

"What were you talking about?" Evelyn lowered her voice to a hiss.

"She gave me lunch." Ava kept her words slow, her face confused. She held out the empty bowl. "Do you know where her mother is?"

Evelyn snatched the bowl from her fingers. "Dead. Died in childbirth, if that crone Croter is right." She started back. "Move it, or we'll leave without you."

Ava finally managed to stand completely straight, and bent back a little, easing her muscles. She smiled up at the sky as she did.

It was blue and clear.

Never make a threat you don't intend to carry out, her father had always said.

There was no way Sirna was leaving her behind.

She was the ticket to payment at the border.

She kept her pace slow and halting as she moved toward the carts. Evelyn had gone ahead, and she was leaning against Madame Croter's caravan, talking to the old woman, when Ava stepped out of the woods. She turned and sent Ava a smirk before she sauntered off.

The small fire that had been lit to warm their lunch had been extinguished, and final items were being packed away.

"Why don't you come sit with me, Blackie and Melodie, my dear?" Madame Croter patted the driver' bench of her cart. It was painted a bright red, like her door, and her massive black hen sat fluffed up next to her.

Ava nodded, letting her general vagueness work in her favor.

As she clambered up onto the seat beside the old Grimwaldian, Sirna noticed her.

"Hey!" His face darkened.

"Evelyn said she'd like to ride beside you and enjoy what little sun we have," Madame Croter said. "Plenty of room for Avasu here on the bench with me and Blackie. And Melodie is keeping us company, too."

Sirna couldn't hide his surprise. For the first time since Ava had met him, he seemed unsure. She could almost see the cogs in his head turning as he realized Evelyn had gone around him to arrange this. After being so insistent on riding in the back of the cart, now she wanted to sit in the sunshine up front, but didn't want Ava in the back, either.

Was it spite, Ava wondered, or just a marking of her territory? Except for yesterday, when Sirna had hauled her inside and taken off the rope she'd made, she hadn't set foot inside the cart.

Evelyn had made sure of it.

Madame Croter had turned away to give Melodie a hand up, accepting Sirna's silence as agreement, and Ava could see he realised objecting would seem strange.

He caught her eye and then lifted his knife in its sheath, pretending to adjust the belt it was tied to around his waist.

The message was clear.

She didn't nod in understanding, though. She just stared vacantly at him for a long beat, until in the end he was the one who looked away.

She faced the front, grabbing hold of the bench as the cart lurched forward at Madame Croter's snap of the reins, and then leaned to the side as the black hen fluttered its wings to keep its balance.

It amused her to give Sirna the blank looks and shuffling steps of someone who was no longer functioning normally.

There had been fear in his eyes just now, even though he was the one waving the knife.

He was worried she was so damaged, the Speaker would refuse to pay him.

He had waited late into the night, long after everyone else was asleep, to put the rope on her last night, and woke early to take it off. He'd wound a long scarf around her waist before he put it on, to dampen the effect he assumed it was having on her.

"Do you know how to braid hair, Avasu?" Madame Croter asked

her, and Ava suddenly realised she'd missed some of the conversation.

She gave a nod.

"Melodie needs her hair brushed and braided. Will you do it?"

Ava nodded again, and Melodie stepped over Madame Croter and wriggled in between her and Ava, holding out a hair brush.

Ava got to work, gently untangling the slightly curly golden brown of Melodie's hair until it fell in a shiny waves.

The cart rocked gently as they drove, and with the soft sunshine warming her head and shoulders, she felt better than she had in a while.

"Are you a prisoner?" Madame Croter asked softly as Ava smoothed a hand down Melodie's hair.

She jerked her gaze up, fear shattering her peace. She said nothing.

Madame Croter held her gaze, the reins loose in her hands as she let her horse lead the way. "Whatever they're doing to keep you so slow and tired, tell me. I'll help you."

Ava looked down, saw Melodie looking up at her.

The little girl looked ready to burst with the information she had on the subject.

She put a hand on Melodie's shoulder and Melodie shuddered with the effort of suppressing what she knew.

Ava looked back up at the old woman's kind, concerned eyes. "Patience," she whispered. "I will need to run soon, and I need my strength to do that. Letting me sit here with you is already helping."

"I knew it." Madame Croter sucked in a breath.

"I knew it first." Melodie couldn't contain herself. "I helped her!"

"You're a good-hearted child." Madame Croter stroked her hair.

"Be careful." Ava needed to impress this on her new friend. "Tell no one. He has made threats."

Madame Croter looked at her over the top of Melodie's head, and Ava ran a finger across her throat.

Madame Croter's eyes widened.

"Only if he thinks someone knows," Ava whispered, and with a grim nod, Madame Croter settled back in her seat.

Ava put the brush aside, now that Melodie's hair was glossy and tangle free.

She had become adept at braiding since the Rising Wave had taken Fernwell. She had sought out as many people in the camp as she could to learn their braiding techniques, and had created the rope of silence for her discussions with General Ru and Luc using what she'd learned. She had woven her horse hair rope the other night simply, but there were plenty of intricate patterns she'd learned which she was eager to try.

She hadn't thought to use them for braiding hair, though. Hers or someone else's.

She'd been focused on rope.

She ran a hand through her own tousled hair.

It was down to her shoulders now, no longer as short as her cousin had insisted it be kept, to stop her using her own hair as a substitute for thread.

She started to braid Melodie's hair, but her fingers were slow and clumsy and she had to adjust her idea of what she could do and choose something simple. As she plaited, she tried to think of protection for the child. Protection from knives. From cruel hands. From any form of damage.

She didn't feel the same spark she usually did when she worked her spell craft.

The fear of having lost her magic was a sick sensation in the pit of her stomach, but she took comfort in Melodie's proclamation that the rope she'd made from the horse hair was helping restore her energy.

She had clutched it as she slept, closing her hand over it in a fist, and hoped it gave her back something, even if just a little measure of what had been stripped from her.

If that poor piece of work had any spark, then hope was not lost.

Melodie's hair fell halfway down her back, and the simple braids Ava wove were long enough to fall below her shoulders.

Suddenly struck with an idea, Ava took a few of Blackie's feathers, which had stuck to her tunic when the hen had flapped her wings earlier, and wove them into the bottom of the braids.

Melodie touched them with delight. "Thank you. They look beautiful."

Ava knew the little girl was being generous with her praise. The braids were at least straight and even but nothing special. Still, she seemed to be pleased.

And if even a tiny spark of the protection she'd tried to work into the braids was there, it would be better than nothing.

She looked down at her hands. Her fingers didn't look right, but they were at least solid now. She could use them.

She wanted to ask for needle and thread from Madame Croter, but she had the feeling nothing she worked now would be of any use. It would be better to ask when she was a little stronger.

Again, the fear that even then, her workings would be barely useful darkened her thoughts, but she had to try.

Even if trying was all she could do.

Sirna had searched her last night before he'd carefully wound the rope around her.

She didn't know what he was looking for, what his mysterious master had told him, but neither of them seemed to know why the Speaker wanted her, so perhaps he was simply under orders that she should have nothing on her at all.

If she could work invisibility into her clothing just before she ran, that could mean the difference to her escape.

She reasoned travelers would all need to mend their clothes. Everyone should have a needle and thread available.

Any request she made for one before she needed it would expose her to discovery, though, so she would wait until the time was right.

And before then, she first had to find the mysterious Focus the man on the horse, *Himself*, had mentioned, and destroy it.

Because even if she could work invisibility into her too-big shirt and too-short trousers, Sirna would still be able to use it to find her, as he'd done before in Fernwell.

She needed to find a way to be inside the cart alone, with enough time to search it.

Evelyn represented a big roadblock to that.

She would have to think how she was going to shift it.

CHAPTER 17

Deni stared at the split in the road, and felt the same plunge of fear he'd felt a few days earlier in Bartolo when he'd split the team up for the first time.

"Which way do we go?" Carrie asked.

"Both ways." He knew he sounded grim. That's how he felt.

There was silence as everyone stared at the two roads.

One curved to the right. Toward Cervantes. No doubt it looped north, up through the foothills and into Grimwalt. The other went due north, up through northern Kassia and then most likely split again, right for Grimwalt, left for the mountains and Jatan.

Both looked well maintained and clear of debris. Well used.

Unlike the other kink in the road they'd passed yesterday afternoon.

Deni had dithered a little when they came across it, nothing more than a narrow track that left the main path, but he and Oscar had ridden down it a short way, and found it ill-maintained and rough.

They had both decided whoever had taken Ava would take the faster, clearer path to Grimwalt, would try and get within the safety of Grimwalt's borders as quickly as possible. They had rejoined the others ten minutes later, glad they'd eliminated the road and happy they wouldn't have to travel on it.

The choice that lay before Deni now was infinitely harder.

"Oscar will take one road, I'll take the other. Whoever gets the north road takes two along, whoever heads for Cervantes takes one."

"Because the north road heads toward Jatan?" Tras asked.

What was left unsaid was that was the more dangerous path.

Deni nodded. He swung out of his saddle, snapped off two piece of long grass and held them out to Oscar. "Let the Whispering Grasses decide. Long goes north, short goes east."

Oscar pulled one out and they measured the two against each other.

"Looks like I am headed north." Oscar stuck the grass into his mouth and chewed. "I'll take Tras and Carrie."

Deni nodded. "Let's stop here for a last meal together, and then we go our separate ways."

It wasn't ideal. But it was all he could do.

Whoever had Ava would be struggling with a captive Deni knew would fight every inch of the way. Avasu would never submit while she had breath in her body.

So the going would be slow.

They could catch up before her abductors reached Grimwalt, with its closed borders and corrupt Speaker.

They had to.

THEY WERE WALKING IN THE GARDENS WHEN ERDENE SPOTTED the group of nobles up ahead, coming toward herself and Talika.

They had a determined air about them.

"You need to have an argument with me." She slowed her steps as she spoke, putting a hand on Talika's forearm. She was surprisingly annoyed to have their walk interrupted, even though the point of these walks was to show the queen was present and accounted for.

Spending time with the Cervantes soldier had become something Erdene looked forward to more and more, and these walks, where they had privacy to speak without pretense, were her favorite.

Talika lifted her brows and glanced up ahead. Saw who was bearing down on them.

"They've met Ava?" she guessed.

Erdene nodded. "They've spent a few hours with her on a couple of occasions. They know her voice."

Talika nodded. She came to a stop and flicked Erdene's hold off her arm. With her other hand, she made a chopping motion, as if making an angry point.

"What are you going to say we were fighting about?" Talika stepped back and threw both hands up into the air.

Erdene turned toward her and gave a smile at her dramatics, lifting her own hands, palms out, in a placating gesture. "That Lord Cynera has yet to present himself for questioning, and you consider them all potential traitors."

"In other words, the truth." The corners of Talika's eyes crinkled in amusement.

With the necklace on, her eyes, her mouth, were Ava's, but she used them in her own way. Erdene thought she would know Talika now, no matter whose face she wore.

The thought startled her and she frowned at her fancy.

"Perhaps try to placate me a bit more?" Talika suggested.

With a snort at her own distraction, Erdene patted Talika's shoulder with a wink.

Talika winked back, a cheeky amusement in her eyes, and then she shrugged the hand off, turned on her heel, and stalked off, tossing her head as she went.

Erdene watched her go with regret. She didn't like to examine why, but she was in a suitably irritable mood when the nobles reached her.

Most of them ignored her, their eyes tracking Talika as she stalked out of the garden and through the doors to her private apartments.

"Lords. Ladies." Erdene eyed the group. They were dressed in silks and fine cottons, in line with their wealth, but these were not the frivolous young nobility, they were the harder-headed realists.

She had to deal with them sometime, she decided. Might as well be now.

"General Ru, we hoped to speak to the queen." Lord Haster's gaze was still over Erdene's shoulder, although Talika was long gone.

"Unfortunately, she didn't want to speak to you, Lord Haster." Erdene let her lips quirk into false regret. Haster glanced up in surprise that she knew his name, but Erdene had made it a point to learn the names and backgrounds of every one of the nobles since Luc had sent word of what was going on.

"And why is that?" Lady Elna's words were stiff. She saw Erdene as a foreign enemy, and she hated that she had to deal with her.

Most of them did.

Erdene smiled, because she enjoyed being a thorn in their side after what they and their queen had done to Venyatu.

"Because some of you are insurgents. You are bribing disaffected soldiers from the city, setting them up to attack Rising Wave units in the countryside, and trying to shift the blame to local villages. And then you have the gaul to spread rumours in Fernwell that the Rising Wave is behind the disappearances. That the soldiers who are missing have been killed, rather than living in your mansions, doing your bidding." Erdene drew herself up, not having to reach far for outrage. "Neither the queen nor I are very happy to have lies spread about us."

There was a beat of stunned silence.

"What are you talking about?" Lady Elna was the first to recover.

"I'm talking about Lord Cynera having arranged for some of the soldiers he's enticed from Fernwell into his service to lie in wait for the Commander and his unit to pass his estates on their way to Jatan, and then attack them."

"That fucking idiot." Lord Haster muttered the words softly, but Erdene heard them clear enough.

"Those soldiers could be anyone," Lord Frin said. "They could be locals retuned from the war. Who said Cynera had anything to do with it?"

Erdene looked at him pityingly. "The soldiers themselves said it. They took the Commander to Lord Cynera's mansion, where they were staying." She let the silence run for a long minute. "You seem well-versed in the story the soldiers told the Commander they were ordered to spread, Lord Frin."

He reared back. "Are you saying . . ." His bluster ran short.

"She's saying we are all suspects." Lady Elna drew herself up. "I had heard you wanted to speak to Cynera. I didn't know why."

"Cynera must have sent a rider out to his estates the moment he heard the Rising Wave was sending a group out to Jatan. They were ready and waiting for Luc's unit."

"Not ready enough, it seems." Haster was looking at her with a mix of frustration and respect.

"No." Erdene dipped her head to hide her smile of satisfaction. She lifted her chin and hardened her expression. "So have a little think about things, if you're part of this conspiracy to undermine your new queen. So far, it isn't going well, and we know about it now, so it'll be even harder to run. Until we know more, until we can be sure which of you is working with us in good faith, the queen will keep her distance. If you have a problem with that, take it up with Lord Cynera, who still hasn't come in to speak to us and explain, despite numerous requests."

Erdene gave a formal bow, turned on her heel, and walked away.

Up on the ramparts, she caught sight of Raun-Tu, keeping watch over her, his bow resting lightly on the wall.

She gave him a tiny nod, and he returned it.

She expected she would get homesick for Venyatu soon, and

they would eventually go home, when the deals with Ava, Luc, the Funabi and the Venyatu were finalized. But until then, she felt alive.

It was pleasant to be the victor, living in comfortable accommodation, no longer actively at war but still having to keep vigilant.

She was invigorated.

And if that thought brought Talika to mind, well, she was part of the game, wasn't she?

They had managed to keep the whole city from realising that the queen had been taken.

It couldn't last. But she could do nothing more than she already was doing to keep the secret.

She would have to trust Deni would find Ava. That she was unharmed.

And that she would be back in Fernwell soon.

CHAPTER 18

The Jatan had disappeared.

Luc dismounted and looked around at their empty campsite, evidence of a hasty departure everywhere, and wondered what Tuart was up to.

The Jatan general had forced himself and his small force on Luc. He'd insisted on riding in parallel to them, and then he'd disappeared in the night.

Vera, the scout who'd come to tell him their Jatan shadows had flitted away in the darkness, sat on her horse, her expression agitated.

"We should have noticed them leaving," she said when he finally looked up at her.

Luc inclined his head. "Maybe. But we weren't watching them in that way. They imposed themselves on us, so we had no suspicion they'd sneak off."

Her lips thinned. "I was on watch. I'm sorry I missed it."

He accepted her apology with a nod. "Anything stand out last night?"

She looked like she wanted to self-flagellate a little more, but stopped herself, looking toward the east, to Cervantes, as she thought about it.

Luc turned in the direction himself.

Along the edge of the clearing and up the side of the low foothills to their left, more than a few slender, white-trunked gimtali trees with their sage green leaves were studded amongst the pines and conifers.

The trees of Cervantes.

They were getting closer to home.

Luc knew he wasn't the only one feeling a lifting of his spirits at the sight of them.

He'd hoped to bring Ava home after they settled things in Fernwell, to show her the beauty of it.

He missed her so much it was an ache deep in his bones.

He knew she could manage whatever the city council and the nobles in Fernwell threw at her, and with Dak and General Ru as her allies she would be safe, but he would feel better with her by his side.

The only thing that helped distract him was physical exertion.

He'd pushed the unit hard the day before, and they'd made huge progress across the relatively open ground that skirted the heavily forested foothills.

He hadn't exactly been trying to shake the Jatan loose, but he had the feeling they'd kept up with a determined will, and it hadn't been easy for them.

The look in General Tuart's eyes when he'd insisted on accompanying them to Cervantes to see what the Jatan were up to there had set alarms tingling across Luc's skin and put a hard ball of worry in the pit of his stomach.

If he read Tuart correctly, the general was worried about what they would find, and if he was worried, Luc was terrified.

"Kym never signed off from guard duty," Vera said, breaking across his thoughts. "She told Hassini that she was going to wash by the river straight after her shift and asked him to sign her out when he got back to camp."

"That's not acceptable." Luc saw Rafe had arrived at the far side of the camp, moving his horse through the abandoned detritus with a considering look in his eye.

"That's what Hassini said. He refused to do it, but she never checked in anyway, so he told Revek what she'd asked him to do."

Luc remembered the look of Kym's face as she'd studied the Jatan soldiers yesterday. He had meant to ask her what she'd seen, but after Tuart gathered his troops and rode beside them, he realized she must have kept to the back of the unit. He hadn't seen her at all since yesterday afternoon.

"Fetch Kym for me now. And Hassini."

Vera nodded and galloped away.

Rafe reached him, but his gaze was on Vera as she left. "What are the Jatan playing at?"

"There is something going on here to do with our scouts at the border. I'll wait for confirmation from Vera, but my guess is Kym went with them last night, or they took her."

Rafe gaped at him. "Kym?"

"She saw something yesterday. Or rather, someone. I noticed it when she came with me to talk to Tuart. She said it was nothing, but it obviously was. Vera says last night she told a fellow guard to check in for her after her shift, that she was going to bathe in the river, and my guess is she slipped away to talk to someone in the Jatan unit."

He knew something was off with her reaction yesterday, but he had never followed up. He'd let her avoid him, and now she was either gone, or abducted.

He was angry with himself for the slip.

"You think whatever it was that was going on between her and the person she saw in Tuart's unit is why they left?"

Luc shrugged. "It seems extreme, but if not, then where is she?"

Maybe Vera would come back with Kym in tow, but he doubted it. An exclamation from across the clearing had him raising his head.

News of the Jatan's disappearance had obviously spread, because

Massi, Revek and Kikir had come to see for themselves, looking in surprise at the sight of the tents and other things the Jatan had left behind.

"Their need to slip away quietly was obviously greater than their need to pack all their equipment." Kikir stared narrow-eyed at the half-collapsed tents and bowls lying near the fire-pits.

"And they were ragtag enough as it was," Massi said. "They didn't look as if they could afford to leave much behind."

That was true. They had the hungry, desperate look of men and women who had been fighting without enough provisions for a long time.

So whatever they wished to hide from him, it had overridden every other consideration.

That worried Luc.

He worried about Kym, too, but the possibility remained she had gone with them willingly.

"What could she have seen on the border? Who could have been in Tuart's unit that caused the kind of distress I picked up from her?"

Rafe shook his head. "I have never had cause to doubt her. She is a loyal Cervantes."

"She said her fellow scouts had all disappeared. That was one of the reasons she felt she had to come find us and report in." Luc wondered if some of the scouts could have switched allegiances. It was possible she saw one of her friends amongst the Jatan soldiers yesterday.

"We need to press on as fast as we can." Cervantes was still in danger, and he was sure Tuart had not gone back to Jatan. He had wanted to get to Cervantes ahead of the Rising Wave.

What he intended to do when he got there was the mystery that was gnawing at Luc's gut.

As he took up his reins and swung back into the saddle, Vera appeared with Hassini in tow, and he waited for them.

"Kym is gone." Vera's lips were thin and tight. "Her tent is there, but she isn't in it."

He had thought as much. "What did she say to you, exactly?" He asked Hassini. "And how did she seem?"

"She wasn't herself." Hassini rubbed his breastbone in agitation. "She wasn't even supposed to be on guard duty, but she said she couldn't sleep, so she switched with Canril." He looked around the camp. "I told her it wasn't worth the trouble I'd get into to sign off for her after shift, that she was putting me in a bad position." He sighed. "She said, 'I'm in a bad position myself, Hass. So do this for me, please.' And then she just rode off."

"Luc." Kikir had been wandering around the camp on horseback, looking at the mess, but his voice sounded tight as he looked down at something.

Luc moved over, and the others followed.

The place where Kikir had stopped was red with blood. Luc could see the fine arterial spray of a cut throat, and the place where someone had scrabbled on the ground with their hands, desperate in their death throes.

"Look for a body," Luc said. "Whoever this was didn't survive." There was too much blood.

Without a word, all grim-faced, they began to search.

There was no sign of anyone, and no sign of disturbed earth where they might have buried someone, either.

"We have to move on. They may have taken the body with them." Luc felt the thump of every second, slipping through his hands.

"Why would they do that?" Kikir asked.

"Maybe we'd recognize the body," Massi said, voice low. "Maybe that's why they left. They'd killed one of our guards and they knew we'd retaliate."

"Killed Kym?" Revek looked like he wanted to deny it.

Massi shrugged.

The blood might be Kym's, Luc acknowledged, but it might be someone else's, someone Tuart suddenly realized might be familiar to them. Like another of the Cervantes scouts.

He shook the thoughts off. Speculating was no help. They had to go.

"I should have gone after her." Hassini looked miserable.

Luc remembered his fresh, open face. He'd been in his mid-teens when Luc had liberated him from one of the Chosen camps he'd been held in, and he was still painfully young.

"Kym was the one who should have come to me. Told me what she was doing." Or he should have found her. He was equally at fault there. "We don't know if this blood is hers, but if she'd asked for help, she wouldn't have come into this camp alone."

"What do you think happened?" Hassini's gaze went to the place where Kikir had found the blood.

Luc turned his mount in the direction of the Rising Wave camp. "There are too many possibilities to guess what's going on. So let's move and find out what it is they're up to."

The unit was on its way in less than ten minutes, and Luc thought if Kym had come off her shift after midnight, and only then gone to the Jatan camp, even if the Jatan had killed her immediately and then panicked and started packing their things, they could only be five hours ahead of them, at most.

They had been riding hard for an hour, Luc out front with Massi and Rev, when he saw a whirl of movement between the trees to his left.

"Did you—?" Massi kept her eyes ahead, but she had clearly seen it, too.

"I did."

"What?" Revek had missed it, but he was too experienced to look.

"A watcher. They've ridden away." Massi frowned.

"Tuart knows the direction we're going in. The only reason he'd have posted watchers is to find out how fast we're moving." Luc looked ahead, at the clear, open ground that hugged the foothills to the Jatan mountain range, and then to the right, to the area of rolling hills and valleys that the Kassian called the Thousand Hills. "So either the Jatan are doing something they need to finish before we arrive, or they're waiting for us to get somewhere and need to know the exact timing, maybe to ambush us."

Massi swore quietly. "I don't like this."

Neither did Luc. The sense of fear, of time running out, was a pounding beat in his head now. They needed to change their plans.

He rode into the middle of the open space and then pulled his horse to a stop. His gaze went up the hill in case the watcher had paused to study them a little longer, but there was no sign of them.

Still, when the whole unit slowed at the sight of him, and then stopped, gathering around him, he spoke quietly.

"The Jatan are watching us from the forest slopes." He was pleased to see no one looked in that direction. "They know where we're going, so it must be how fast we are going that is of interest to them."

More than one of the unit understood the implications of that immediately, whistling low under their breath.

"So what are we going to do?" Rafe asked.

"We're going to go via the Thousand Hills." Luc let that sink in. "It's a harder route, but there is less distance to go to reach Cervantes that way. If we push hard, but carefully, if we keep a steady pace, we can be home in less than two days, which is what we'd manage if we stuck to the foothills anyway."

"With the benefit of being out of the Jatan's sight," Massi said.

There was a murmur of agreement.

"Then let's go." Luc wheeled his mount around and raced to the right, toward the line of hills in the distance.

Whatever the Jatan were up to, he would thwart them at every turn.

THEY FLEW.

Luc was careful not to overextend, though.

They had to be ready for anything when they emerged from the wide flat valley with its undulating hills. They might have to engage in battle against the Jatan, or help their people in the aftermath of a possible attack.

On the second day, toward the late afternoon, a pillar of smoke in the distance gave him the sinking feeling it would be the latter.

The area up ahead would be on the very edge of Cervantes territory. The first place the Jatan would have reached if they'd come down into Kassia and swept to the east.

The smoke acted as a catalyst to the unit, and everyone went quiet, focused on riding hard, on reaching the first village while the sun was still in the sky.

The valley narrowed as they reached the end of it, so they emerged from between high cliffs and burst out onto an open plain dotted with gimtali trees.

"Who knows this village?" Luc called, and one of the soldiers lifted a hand.

"I'm from Bintinya, which isn't far from here."

"Come." Luc waited for him and they rode in front, while Rafe, Massi and Revek coordinated from behind, watching for lookouts or ambushes.

They reached the small settlement in the last gasp of the day.

A rough hut burned, the thatch smoking sullenly.

Luc had glimpsed movement as they approached, but when they drew to a halt and look around at the small village, there was no one in sight.

"My name is Frebo, from Bintinya." The soldier who'd ridden with Luc rose up in his stirrups, hands on either side of his mouth as he called out. "My aunt Greta trades here often."

"Ai, ai!" A man stepped out from behind a hut and walked slowly toward them. "The Rising Wave?"

"What happened?" Luc looked the length of the village, and saw to his relief people stepping out from behind the rough-built houses at the sound of the old man's greeting.

"The Jatan attacked. Took all our supplies." The man put both hands on his hips and looked up at them.

"Is anyone hurt?"

The man made a sound that Luc realised was a hacking laugh.

"The Kassian have been after us too long for us to be caught like that." He wiped away a tear as the smoke blew in their direction and irritated the eyes. "We have ways of disappearing that we've honed over many years of hiding our children from the Chosen camps." He looked at the soldier from Bintinya. "I think they were headed for Bintinya next."

Frebo looked at Luc, eyes wide.

"How long ago did they leave?"

"An hour." The man dropped his arms to his sides. "We suffered little but the loss of food and supplies. Go help Bintinya. And maybe get our things back, eh?"

"How many were there?"

The old man moved his head from side to side, considering. "Maybe twenty." His gaze flicked west, to where the rest of the unit was galloping toward them. "Not as many as you."

Luc nodded to Frebo. "Lead the way."

"Wait!" The man lifted a hand in supplication. "Who won? Who won the war?"

Luc tapped his chest. "We did. Kassia is ours."

With a whooping battle cry, Frebo turned his horse and raced away, with Luc following, and Luc could hear the man behind them whooping along.

As the rest of the unit thundered through, the soldiers took up the cry, and so did the other villagers, so there was a building victory call rising up behind him.

Joy to balance the hardship of the attack.

As he followed Frebo, he thought about timing.

They had just missed the raid.

That told Luc either this might have been done by a Jatan group who were already in the area, one of the break-away units Kym had worried about—the reason she'd come to Fernwell to warn him in the first place—or this was Tuart, under orders to attack, and just ahead of them because his unit had taken the easier route.

Either way, whichever Jatan force had done this, they had openly attacked Cervantes.

If it was Tuart, he would know what Luc's reaction to it would be.

And he'd done it anyway.

Now, there would be no quarter given.

CHAPTER 19

"W hat is that?"

Ava looked up from her place in front of the fire and found Gregor watching her.

She set down the thin piece of bark she had woven into a knot around one of Blackie's fluffy chest feathers and shrugged. "Nothing."

She was biding time until Evelyn left the cart.

She needed to find the Focus.

She kept her head down, careful to look absorbed in what she was doing, but Evelyn had said she was going to bathe in the river.

It was taking her a very long time to get her things together and leave.

Ava could feel the tension and frustration rise up in her, and she forced herself to look at the ground, to work on a blank expression.

"It draws the eye," Gregor said, and she lifted her gaze to meet his with a jerk.

That sounded like a warning.

She glanced down at what she had made, more or less without thinking, and studied it.

It was a thin, flexible piece of wood about the length of her hand from wrist to finger tip, and she had woven it into a complicated knot with the feather in the middle.

She had been thinking of rescue, however unlikely that possibility was, as she had bent and shaped the wood.

They were far from the main road, on back paths and barely-there tracks that she was slowly coming to realize were used regularly by traders to avoid the Kassian army.

That these hidden routes were so well known told her that traders had been avoiding the Kassian military for years. It made sense. Herron, her cousin and the Queen's Herald while he was alive, would have not stepped in to police his own soldiers if they took what they wanted from the trader caravans.

"It's just a piece of bark," she said, and flicked it off the tree stump she was using as a seat onto the ground behind her.

It never reached it, though.

Blackie's feather spiralled down, and then was lifted by the light breeze, and with a twirl, it lifted up and floated away.

She turned away from watching it.

General Ru would have sent people after her, but if they hadn't taken Evelyn and the Grimwaldian's bait at Bartolo and gone toward the coast, they would most likely be using the main roads.

Sirna had known what he was doing when he had taken the less-traveled route.

Her only hope might lie at the border.

If General Ru's rescue party was making better time than the caravan, they may be waiting for her there, watching the traffic going through the border post.

She already knew she needed to escape before they reached the border, but perhaps she should head there anyway, or make her escape just before they arrived. Whoever General Ru had sent, they would help her, protect her, and get her back to Fernwell.

It would be better than being on her own with no resources.

If she could find Luc . . .

She had had this thought more than once.

He had ridden north east a day before she'd been taken.

He would be close to Cervantes by now, if she had counted her days correctly.

He was much closer to her than Fernwell was.

She wondered if it really made sense to find him, given she had no real idea where he would be, or whether she just wanted to go to him, no matter the practicalities.

And then she wondered if she cared about the reason, one way or the other.

"If Melodie looked at it, I am sure she would say it wasn't just a piece of bark." Gregor's words were soft, breaking through her reverie.

Ava drew in a quick breath and turned her head to look at him, but he was staring into the fire.

"I don't think so," she whispered back. But there was a part of her that hoped she was wrong and he was right. It would mean her magic was coming back. "Even so, Melodie's . . . gift . . . is unusual."

And very, very useful. Just like her own.

"I know it." Gregor's eyes were dark and he seemed to search her face for something. "And what is your gift?" he asked.

She shook her head. That was a question she would not answer. Not to someone she didn't know. Not to someone she *did* know, come to that. "I have no gift." As she spoke, Evelyn stepped out of the cart.

At last.

Ava tore another strip of bark off the stump she was sitting on and began to weave it into a knot, keeping her head down as Evelyn gave her a long look as she skirted the fire pit.

"Your sister doesn't like you," Gregor said, consideringly.

Ava gave a tiny shake of her head, not to disagree but to end the conversation. Evelyn disappeared in-between the trees on the river bank.

It was time.

She rose to her feet, keeping her footsteps shuffling as she made her way to the cart.

Sirna had gone hunting with his friend, Reckhart, the one who'd let him join the caravan. They were armed with bow and arrow, looking for a deer for the fire tonight.

If she could shake Gregor loose, she could do a thorough search.

"Reckhart has let a viper into our midst, hasn't he?" Gregor was just behind her. "Sirna's done this to you. Made you ill."

Ava closed her eyes against his persistence. He needed to leave her alone.

And then she shrugged.

He seemed on her side. He probably wouldn't tell Sirna what she was up to.

She would look anyway.

This was the first chance she'd had to access the inside of the cart since the day before, and she was going to take it.

Gregor could watch her if he wanted to.

She pulled the door open and latched it in place to keep it from swinging shut.

She needed as much light as possible to do this fast.

"You're looking for something."

She turned to look at Gregor, lips in a sardonic twist, and he looked back at her, calm and patient.

"Why are you so interested?"

"Because I have a feeling that you are a good example of what might happen to Melodie in the future. So I'm trying to understand what brought you here, and why, so I can make sure she doesn't follow the same path."

Ava gave a low laugh as she pulled the bedding off the narrow bench and onto the floor. Then she lifted the wooden slats to look into the deep box below.

"You think this is a *path* I've taken?" She couldn't help the snort that escaped.

"Then what? Tell me." His voice was urgent.

She glanced at him over her shoulder as she sorted through the clothing, shoes, cloaks and other personal items in the box.

She tried to keep her features blank but something in her eyes must have given her away because he made a noise at the back of his throat, an angry, explosive sound.

"Is this what my girl has to look forward to?" He spoke through his teeth. "Being starved, left to sleep outside in the cold, stripped of her clothes, stripped of her wits, too?"

Ava sighed as she pulled the wooden slats back and smoothed the bedding out. It hadn't been neatly set to rights before, so she decided she could get away with leaving it messy.

"The answer is maybe." Both her and her mother were cautionary tales.

The pain in Gregor's eyes was evident. "I don't want her to live like that."

"There are ways to mitigate the risk." Ava knew she was not exactly a good example of how to do that. She stepped up onto the bed and began to take down the boxes on the shelf above one at a time, flipping the lids open, searching through, and then putting them back in place as she went.

One of them held tea, and she hesitated before closing the lid. Hadn't the Grimwaldian asked Sirna to give him the tea.

There was something about their exchange . . .

Another magical item, she would have to guess. Perhaps that's how Sirna had kept the diplomats under his thrall for weeks.

And Sirna had said he had handed over all of it.

Even the Grimwaldian hadn't known whether to trust him, but he'd been in too great a hurry to do anything else but take Sirna at his word.

Gregor was standing on the steps, leaning against the door as he watched her. His wide shoulders blocked the light, and she angled the box to get a better look inside.

"Is Melodie close by?" she asked.

Gregor narrowed his eyes. "Why?"

"I'd like her to look at this." She held out the box to him and he peered into it suspiciously and then shook his head.

"I don't want to expose her to more of this." Gregor's mouth was a hard line.

She set the box down, climbed back up onto the bed to take down the next one without putting the one with the tea back in its place.

She thought about his words. Thought about the lengths her mother had gone to to keep her safe by refusing to teach her about her gift. And what good that had done her.

She balanced on the edge of the bed as she pulled off the lid to the next box and jerked away, wrinkling her nose at the putrid smell that rose up out of it. She was again forced to hop down and angle the box into the light that managed to filter past Gregor through the doorway. As she peered inside, he bent his head to have a look as well. "What ever you think you know about me, I'll tell you this as one of the few things I know for sure." She kept her voice soft and low. "The more Melodie learns to control and use her gift, the safer she'll be. She can see the dangers in things that would trap other people. It will keep her safe, especially if she hones it."

Gregor stepped back, almost overbalancing on the narrow steps. He looked at her for a long beat, then he turned his head. "Melodie! Come here, sweetling."

Ava gave a nod of thanks. "What do you think this is?" She held out the box. She was afraid she knew, but hoped he had another explanation.

"A withered finger." Gregor narrowed his eyes. "Not preserved in any way. Just left in a box." He frowned. "Is this spell craft?"

"None that I've ever seen." Ava had never heard of using body parts in spells. But then, she barely understood her own magic. Who knew what other kinds there were in the world. She put the lid back on and placed the box back where she'd found it. Took down the next one.

"And what do I do about you?" Gregor gripped the doorway with his big hands. "I can't turn a blind eye to what Sirna and that sly piece of work Evelyn are doing to you. Not when what's happening to you could happen to my own daughter."

"Da?"

Gregor turned. "Sweetling. Come here." He lifted her up into his arms and turned back to face Ava.

She stepped off the bed and lifted the box with the tea up. "What do you see in here?" Ava asked her.

"Bad things." Melodie tucked her head under her father's neck. She reached out a hand toward the box, then her chubby fingers curled and she clamped her closed fist up against her chest. "It's like . . ." She tried to think of the words.

She was too little, Ava realized. She didn't have the vocabulary, or the world experience, to understand everything she saw.

"Like what, my sweet?" Gregor was staring at the tea.

Melodie shivered, and Ava saw Gregor's face harden. He didn't appreciate Reckhart bringing people into his daughter's orbit who were clearly dangerous.

"Like when you hurt yourself, like stubbing your toe, and then someone tells you it isn't so bad. But it is so bad. It hurts, and they tell you it doesn't, not really. They aren't you, it's not their toe, but they say you are the one who is wrong about how sore it is." She was obviously remembering an incident, and still hadn't let go of her resentment of whoever had dismissed her pain.

"Thank you, Melodie." Ava met Gregor's gaze. "Do you have a piece of cloth, or a handkerchief?"

He pulled one out and she tipped the tea into it, placed the lid back on and set the box back on the shelf.

"Burn it." She thought about it for a moment. "But try to do it when no one is looking. Magic things sometimes burn green."

He gave a nod, folded the tea into the kerchief and slid it into his pocket.

"What's going on here?"

Evelyn's voice was loud, but she wasn't at the cart yet. There was an edge of panic, and a strident, harsh blade to her tone.

Ava looked calmly around the interior, making a note of which boxes on the shelf she still had to examine.

She hadn't found what she was looking for, but everything was back in its place.

"I fainted," she whispered to Gregor, then let herself crumple to the ground, one arm grabbing at the bed linen, to make it look like any disturbance had been caused by her half-pulling it onto the ground with her.

"Your sister is ill." Gregor turned, Melodie still on his hip. "She collapsed and I carried her to your cart."

Evelyn shouldered past him, and Ava let her eyes flutter open a little to see Evelyn glaring down at her.

"She can't be in here." Evelyn turned to look at Gregor. "Carry her back to the fire."

"There's nothing for her to lie on there." Melodie piped up with her sweet little voice.

The thoughtfulness of it pricked tears into the back of Ava's eyes. She had managed to endure a great deal without ever shedding a tear, but the sweetness of a child seemed to cut her to the quick.

"That's life on the road." Evelyn only just kept her tone civil, and only because Gregor stood right in front of her. "And the fresh air will do her good."

"Go fetch a pallet from the back of our cart, sweetling," Gregor said.

"If you want me to carry her to the fire, you need to move."

Ava knew the moment he addressed Evelyn. His tone was cool and through her half-raised lashes, Ava saw Evelyn stiffen at the shift.

"I'm just thinking of what's best for her," she said defensively.

"Is that so?" Gregor leaned in when Evelyn had jumped down from the steps, out of the way, and scooped Ava up.

He carried her to the fire and stood waiting with her in his arms as Melodie tried to carry the pallet on her head, so it wouldn't touch the ground.

"I'll help you with that, sunshine." Vanin Gruger, the old man who had slept by the fire that first night while she braided the horse hair for her rope, hopped down from the back of his cart and lifted it out of her hands. "Now where do you need it?"

"At the fire, Mr. Gruger. Evelyn won't let Avasu lie down in the cart, even though she feels sick."

"How peculiar." He flicked Evelyn a look, and then set the pallet down at Gregor's feet.

Ava had noticed Vanin Gruger looking at her from under his bushy gray eyebrows a few times since that night, and she wondered how much of it he really had slept through.

He had never commented on his shaving blade being blunt, as she was sure it had been by the time she was finished with it. She wondered why not.

Although he didn't say much in general, so perhaps he simply preferred to keep his own council.

She thought there was tension in the camp. An uneasiness that she guessed had grown since Reckhart had invited Sirna to join them.

"There you go, Avasu." Melodie danced around her. "That will be more comfortable."

"I'm sure she's fine." Evelyn stared at the little girl, face hot, and then spun on her heel, her damp hair from her bath in the river flicking tiny drops of water as she turned and stomped to the cart.

Vanin Gruger wandered back to his cart and Melodie skipped after Blackie. For a moment, Ava was alone with Gregor again.

"Thank you."

He gave a stiff nod, and she knew it was because he thought she was refusing to be honest with him.

"Why do you think I'm like Melodie?" She first needed to know what he'd seen.

"The night Melodie was whispering with you, I was watching. I could see through part of your hand." His gaze settled on her hand for a moment, and his expression echoed the horror he must have felt at the sight. "And then you spoke to Melodie in such a matter-of-fact way. You knew she wasn't making it up." He hung his head, hands clasped between his knees. "She's stopped telling me things, because she thinks I don't listen. That I don't help people when I could."

Ava tucked her arm beneath her head and sighed. "I understand you're only protecting her with your choices."

"After I put Melodie to bed, I stood watching you."

Ava went still at his confession.

"I saw you throw that rope into the fire and watched it burn green. Then I saw you braiding a new rope, even though you could barely stand. Even though parts of you looked too translucent." He looked sideways at her. "Even if you aren't like Melodie, you understand her world better than I do."

Ava curled in on herself, closed her eyes against the sting of the smoke from the fire. "I don't understand it as well as I should, because my mother tried to shield me from it as much as possible, like you're doing to Melodie." She opened her eyes and held his gaze. "As you can see, that didn't work out very well."

He looked sick, as if he wanted to vomit. "What can I do?"

"Believe her. Let her know you believe her. And explain to her why you ignore some of the warnings she gives, but not all of them. She needs to understand and trust your decisions, or she'll end up giving herself away to the wrong person."

He nodded slowly. "And how can I help you? Because my conscience, and Melodie, won't let me do otherwise."

She thought about it. "I'm better than I was since I destroyed the rope, but I'm not as strong as I'll need to be to escape. You can help me by tucking a needle and plenty of thread somewhere on your cart that I can easily reach from the outside."

He frowned at that. "That's all?"

She nodded. "It is a lot. Why are you headed for Grimwalt? Is it to protect Melodie?"

"Yes." He clasped and unclasped his fingers. "She is going to expose herself sooner or later. I'd rather it be in a place like Grimwalt than anywhere else."

"I agree, but the border is supposed to be closed to everyone who isn't Grimwaldian. Do you have a place you are expected, a job you are going to?"

He shook his head. "Madame Croter is going to say she's invited me in to do some work for her in Taunen. She thinks they'll let us in because she knows the border guards well. Once we're through, I can work as a traveling blacksmith, but I have no fixed plans." He sounded grim and determined. "You're Grimwaldian, aren't you? I can hear it a little in your speech."

She nodded, thought through the offer that was dancing on the tip of her tongue. "I own a house in Grimwalt, in the Finster region. Ask for directions to the Yngstra estate. It will be empty. My grandmother's estate manager and her housekeeper should be there, but because the person who hired Sirna to capture me has a lot of power in Grimwalt, they have been arrested to keep them quiet. However, I don't think the house is being watched any more, and I would be pleased if someone could watch over it for me until I can find Tomas and Velda and bring them home."

She didn't know if her grandmother's estate could ever be home for her again. Wherever Luc was, she would be. And while the Speaker lived free, she would never be safe in Grimwalt.

She would not give it up, though. Not without a fight.

"So the danger for you has come from within Grimwalt?" He looked stricken. She saw the hope they would be safe there die in his eyes.

"The Speaker of the Grimwalt court wants me as his captive." She didn't say why, but she could see the understanding in Gregor's eyes. "He has hunted me for months. Spell casters should be safe in Grimwalt, and most of them are. But nowhere is truly safe."

Gregor studied her face. "This is information that is difficult to hear but important for me to know."

She was sorry to disillusion him, but he was right, he did need the unvarnished truth. "The offer is there for you to take when you get to Grimwalt, or not. As you think best."

He gave a curt nod and stood, took a few steps and crouched beside the fire. He looked over the camp site, a casual glance to check for watching eyes, and then pulled the handkerchief from his pocket. He flicked the tea in it onto the flames and some of them were caught by the swirl of hot air, and spiralled up in a glitter of green.

"What was it?" Gregor asked.

"I think it was a way to control minds."

He must have thought back to what Melodie had said in the cart. "She is special, isn't she?"

Ava nodded. "Make sure Sirna never knows."

Gregor met her gaze at that. "If I think he even suspects it, he won't live to see the end of this trip."

CHAPTER 20

They were too late.

Bintinya was burning, and from the hill above, Luc saw a group of soldiers riding away through the trees.

The village lay below, roofs smouldering. There was no sound other than the crackle of burning thatch.

"I don't see any Cervantes below. Where would your friends and family be hiding?" Luc asked Frebo, as much to steady him at the sight of the carnage as to get the information.

Frebo drew in a breath and pointed left and down. "There's a tunnel built into the hill on the far side. They'll be hiding in there."

"Then go find them, put out the fires, and tell Massi I've gone after the Jatan. I'll leave a trail for the unit to follow." Luc paused. "If you want to stay and help your village recover, I give you leave. You can join us later, or wait for us to fetch you on our way back."

Frebo opened his mouth, closed it, and then nodded. "Thank you."

Luc didn't waste any more time. He picked a path down to the village and easily picked up the Jatan's trail.

Their saddlebags must be overflowing, because they dropped a few things along the way.

If he were to guess, he was minutes behind them. Half an hour at the most.

Luc wondered if they were going to keep to the road, but within fifteen minutes of the village, they clearly turned north, through thick forests and rising hills.

They wouldn't be able to move quickly through this landscape, and they were weighed down with the things they had stolen from two villages.

There were enough of them choosing the same paths through the trees that staying on their trail was easy. In some places they had snapped off branches or cut them away to make passing through easier, and he had the benefit of their work.

It would slow them down, help him move faster.

He didn't know this part of Cervantes well. He had grown up on the central plains, deep inside the country's borders. But the trees were the same, and the birds he could hear calling were familiar.

And then they went silent.

He slowed his mount and moved more carefully through the trees, keeping to the shadows.

The way ahead became denser and denser, and eventually he had to slide off his horse and lead it behind a thick copse of bushes, and move forward on foot.

He could see boot prints in the damp soil, and followed them to a trail where the soldiers had had to dismount themselves and lead their horses in single-file beneath a tangled arch of branches.

He stepped off the narrow path, making his way through choked stands of trees to eventually find the Jatan camp.

It was an interesting choice for a mustering point.

There was nowhere to run here.

If they were attacked, they would be trapped.

But the Jatan's enemies would have to find them, first, and it would be difficult to mount a full assault. The camp was surrounded by thick forest and there was only one way in for horses. Any rider would have to be lying low in the saddle to avoid the overhead branches, making it difficult to attack.

Luc moved through the trees carefully, trying to judge how many Jatan were here.

Maybe a hundred, he guessed, when he'd made a full circle of it. At the very most.

That included Tuart's thirty soldiers. Luc had caught a glimpse of the general himself during his walk around the settlement, which meant Tuart had known about this place all along.

There was no way he could have come to this hidden place so unerringly in the time it had taken him to sneak off in the night and ride for Cervantes, unless he knew it was here.

Tuart could have been sent a guide, Luc acknowledged, but that would still mean he knew a camp had been established.

Which is what Luc had guessed anyway from his careful words.

However, Tuart had made out that any raids that might have been carried out would have been done by new officers, too undisciplined to know better.

This did not look like an undisciplined camp.

And the fact that Tuart was here belied his words, too.

Luc moved back through the trees to the place where he'd caught a glimpse of Tuart and hunkered down, leaning back against a trunk and pulling out a piece of bread and some cheese which he ate slowly as he settled in to watch.

It didn't take long for Tuart to appear again.

He thought the general looked harried. He looked behind him, waiting for someone, and then two of his soldiers appeared, holding on to Kym between them.

So she was alive.

And a prisoner, by the looks of things.

Luc could see a bruise high on her cheek and her lip was swollen, but she didn't appear to be badly hurt. She had been crying, though.

Her eyes were red, with dark rings around them.

She had gone willingly into Tuart's camp, so either she hadn't cared whether she would be caught or not, or she'd thought the Jatan wouldn't harm her.

Neither option made Luc think highly of her, but he didn't have all the facts.

He would try to rescue her unless he was sure she had betrayed the Rising Wave.

And seeing her, alive, if not exactly well, made him wonder whose blood they had found in the Jatan camp.

Clearly, it hadn't been hers.

Someone else had died, and they had taken the body with them.

It was likely they had discarded it along their way into Cervantes.

Luc had assumed they would, but the fact that they had not wanted the body found by him was suspicious.

Who had died, and by whose hand?

Tuart exchanged words with Kym, then ducked into a tent, and the soldiers pulled Kym in after him, then reappeared.

Luc decided he needed to hear what was going on in that tent.

He had hoped Massi and the rest of the unit would be here by now. He could only have been a half hour ahead of them when he'd left Bintinya, although he knew that they would have stopped at the village, and if they hadn't found Frebo straight away, there might have been some delay before they continued on after him.

It was close to an hour now since he found the camp, and he expected they would be here any moment.

Still, he needed to eavesdrop on Tuart and Kym's conversation and he couldn't wait.

He left his things tucked between the tree roots, pulling out the scarf Ava had worked for him weeks ago from his pack and wrapping it around his neck.

Even knowing it had the effect of making eyes pass over him without registering he was there, he was grateful that dusk was falling.

The shadows had lengthened, and he used them to make his way as close to the tent as he could through the trees, then he stepped out confidently into the camp.

There were soldiers walking around, talking softly as they prepared an evening meal, but none even looked his way.

Luc wondered if they would have sounded the alarm, even if they had seen him. There'd been no guards on duty. The Jatan must feel safe here, tucked away in the forest.

The tent Tuart and Kym had gone into was in the middle of the long, narrow clearing where the Jatan had settled, but it was still close enough to the tree line that he was standing at the back of it in moments.

He crouched down between it and the tent beside it, straining to hear what was said.

"Sit." The word was bitten out, curt and angry.

Luc didn't recognize the voice.

And then the screaming started.

The sound of the feminine cry of pain had him standing, every nerve, every sense, alert.

"Stop."

That was Tuart. Luc heard a scuffle as if there was some kind of fight.

Kym's cry cut off, and he could hear her ragged breathing.

"Tuart, get your hands off me." The unfamiliar voice came again.

"This is not the way, Carvill. She's part of the Rising Wave, and I've met her commander, Luc Franck. He is not someone we want to make an enemy of."

"From what you say, we've already made an enemy of him. What's one more crime?" Carvill's words were accompanied by the sound of someone pacing.

"I've already set up an explanation for the raids. I told him some of our younger officers have more ambition than brains, hinted they were off the leash. We can talk our way out of that, if we stop now and retreat. Harming one of his scouts on his own land? That is not going to be as easy to brush aside."

"We need to know about this new queen, though, and what her relationship with the Rising Wave is. And this soldier is going to tell us."

"I've already explained, I don't know." Kym spoke through her teeth, her voice shuddering. "I've been watching *you* for the last two months. I rode down to Fernwell not knowing if we'd won or lost, spent one night in a tent outside the city, and then saddle up to ride back out the next day."

Kym was being forthcoming, but Luc had to admit that nothing she said was a betrayal. Yet.

"You must have spoken to your fellow Cervantes soldiers, what do they say?" Carvill asked.

Luc was interested in hearing the answer to this, too.

Kym sucked in a breath, blew it out. "They say Ava is the queen's niece, and was imprisoned by the Queen's Herald with my Commander in a fortress on Kassia's border with Grimwalt. They escaped together and formed a deep friendship. That's all I know."

"See. No torture was necessary." Tuart's voice was tight. "And that explains a lot. I couldn't work out how Franck had managed to get close to the new queen, but the missteps of the Queen's Herald are legendary. That Herron would be foolish enough to put two of his enemies in a cell together to bond is perfectly within the bounds of what I've heard about him."

"Does she have the loyalty of the Kassians? This new queen?"

Kym was silent for a beat. "I don't know. I wasn't in Fernwell long enough. But one story I did hear is that she commanded the palace guards to open the gates to the Rising Wave, and they obeyed her. The Rising Wave didn't have to break down the city walls, they strolled in."

There was a sharp intake of breath at that.

"So for all intents and purposes, you're saying the Rising Wave has full control of Kassia now?" Carvill sounded nervous for the first time. "That this new queen used the Rising Wave to help her take the throne, and they are her source of strength?"

"That's what I have been telling you since I arrived." Tuart swore softly under his breath. "And Luc Franck and his soldiers are hot on my heels. They took a different path, I can only assume because they caught sight of one of my watchers, and I cannot say when they'll appear, but they *will* appear."

"He gave you a missive from the new queen for the Gathering?"

"Yes. We'll rest here tonight and then I'll take my unit back to Jatan to hand it over. And I strongly suggest you come with me. It's time to pack up here, Carvill, while you still can."

"I have to wait for Hurst."

Luc wondered why Carvill would have to wait for Hurst, a lieutenant in Tuart's own unit.

"His son wants to wait for him, too. And to be honest, I'm happy to be rid of the insolent little ratbag, if you're willing to let him stay, although I doubt he will if he knows we're going to the Gathering. He wouldn't pass up a chance to be in the heart of political power." Tuart lowered his voice, as if afraid of being overheard. "But even so, I urge you to come with me. General Hurst has gone off on his own, without Gathering consent or permission, and you have no obligation to wait for him. He certainly wouldn't do the same for you."

"Ah," Carvill's voice was just as soft, "but the Hursts are powerful and have a very long memory. If I don't wait for him, with supplies in hand, I will be lucky not to wake one night with a knife in my back."

Tuart sighed. "That's your decision to make, but don't discount Luc Franck's sword at your neck in your equation. Because that is a man I would not like to be near when he sees what Hurst has done to the Cervantes plains."

Luc almost missed the next words, his fury deafening him as it rose up from his chest.

"What do we do with the scout?" Carvill asked. "She's sat here quietly, listening to everything we just said, and now she knows about this camp."

"Nothing we've said is secret, and all of it will be more than obvious in a day or two. As for knowing about the camp, she came in blindfolded, so she can't lead anyone to it. When we're far enough away tomorrow on our way home, I'm letting her go."

Tuart's tone brooked no argument. "At least if I do encounter Franck, I can honestly say she's not a captive."

"If she's dead, you could say the same." Carvill must have lit a lantern as he spoke, because suddenly a light bloomed and the shadows of the two men were thrown across the tent wall.

"I don't kill for no good reason. I thought you didn't, either."

Carvill lifted his shoulders. "Fine. But make sure there's no way she can lead anyone back here."

Tuart didn't respond to that.

It was fully dark now, and Luc pulled the hood up on his cloak, tugged the scarf tighter around his neck.

Tuart was leaving the tent, a hand gripped around Kym's arm, as Luc rounded the side of it.

Kym had her other arm curled up tight against her chest, and Luc guessed that Carvill had hurt her hand.

He would remember that. Because that should not go unanswered.

Kym had answered truthfully, but nothing she had to say was to the Rising Wave's detriment. He would still need to find out why she'd walked into the Jatan camp on her own, but she had paid for it with the damage to her hand, and he could only think back to her face when she'd looked over at the Jatan soldiers back in northern Kassia—how shaken she was—to think she had been driven by some kind of strong emotion.

He followed behind Tuart as he hauled Kym to a tent which turned out to be the healer, thinking slightly better of the man that at least he was trying to get her help.

When the healer had done what she could to fix what turned out to be a mangled finger, Kym was pushed into a tent and a guard set to watch her.

Decisions, decisions, Luc thought as he moved back to the tree where he'd left his things.

He had just gathered them up when he heard the scuff of a boot nearby.

A bird began its evening call, a longing, melodic thrill, and Luc turned toward it with a grin.

He was already moving when he remembered the scarf around his neck.

He pulled it off and stuffed it into his pocket, before returning the bird call.

"Luc?" Massi's face appeared out of the the darkness. "We found your horse, so we knew you were somewhere here."

They embraced, a quick hug that had the tension in Massi's back ebbing away.

"Can you believe it?" she whispered, pointing at the camp.

He chuckled at the disbelief in her voice.

He followed her away from the tents, along a deer path that led down a slope to a small clearing.

About ten of his unit were packed into it. Rafe and Kikir were among them. He guessed Massi had left Revek with the others.

He gripped hands that stretched out to him in greeting, exchanged smiles.

"They have Kym, she's alive."

That grabbed their attention. He recounted what he'd heard.

"So do we rescue her, and tip our hand that we're here, or wait for them to release her tomorrow?" Massi mused.

"Rescue." Rafe had always had a soft spot for the scout.

"It's a difficult decision." Luc had been thinking about it since he'd seen Kym shoved into the tent and a guard set to watch her. He would prefer her safe, but the plan he had come up with did not make an early rescue possible. He looked over at Rafe. "She's in this situation because of her own choices. I'd prefer to rescue her, but there is no way we can do it without letting the Jatan know we're here."

"Tuart is leaving for Jatan tomorrow, you say?" Kikir asked.

Luc nodded.

"I need to leave for Skäddar. I should probably have left already. Following Tuart won't be far out of my way. I can shadow his unit until I'm sure Kym has been freed."

"You could send her to wait in Bintinya with Frebo," Rafe suggested. "We can collect her on our way back to Fernwell."

That made sense, but Luc wanted to know why she'd snuck into the Jatan camp sooner than that. He thought about it, decided it would be better for Kym to know Kikir would be watching for her. That she wasn't on her own.

He looked over at the Skäddar warrior. "I accept. Thank you. I need to get some information from her, though."

He turned to Massi. "Go back to the unit. I'll come join you as soon as I've spoken with Kym."

"You have a plan?" Massi's gaze flicked to the camp.

He nodded. "Where exactly is the rest of the unit?"

Massi shook her head. "Come back here and I'll lead you to them."

"I'll wait for you, too." Rafe's mouth was a hard line.

Kikir nodded in agreement.

He would have an entourage back to Revek.

Luc inclined his head, left his pack with Massi, and disappeared into the darkness.

As soon as he was out of sight, he looped his scarf back on and walked boldly into the camp by the most direct route. There was no time to sneak around.

He stepped around a few soldiers who were making their way to bed. No one even glanced at him.

The soldier guarding Kym's tent was yawning when he got there, but Luc didn't have time to wait for the woman to fall asleep.

If he understood Tuart and Carvill correctly, General Hurst was raiding villages in Cervantes. And he needed to be stopped.

He made his way behind the guard, looked around to make sure there was no one watching them, and pulled out the red pouch from his cloak. He pulled his sleeve over his fingers so he didn't touch it directly and worked the small fabric square out from inside it. Then he tugged his scarf off.

"Here." He moved beside the woman and held it out to her. He knew he could sound Jatan if he spoke as little as possible. It was similar to Kassian, if not exactly the same.

She froze in surprise, blinking at him as if trying to work out where he'd come from, but when he lifted the fabric up to her again, she took it.

"General Tuart has said I'm to relieve you. You can go sleep for four hours and then come back to keep watch."

The woman continued to stare. She hadn't spoken at all, and she frowned as if trying to work out what he'd just said.

"Sleep," he said. "Come back before dawn."

She nodded slowly and turned away from him, yawning again as she stumbled away.

It was a terrible power Ava had, Luc realised. Truly, it could do so much harm. And it was why Ava was continually looking over her shoulder, as those who wanted this power for themselves hounded her.

And yet, he felt no guilt whatsoever in using it now.

He moved to the back of the tent, looping his scarf back on.

"Kym."

"I thought that was your voice." Kym's whisper came from low down, as if she were lying on the ground. "How did you convince the guard to leave you with me?"

"She was falling asleep. I think she barely understood what I was saying." He hoped she believed him. He certainly wasn't going to tell her about Ava's magic fabric squares.

"She'll be in trouble when she's found sleeping and my tent in empty." Kym started to move, as if to lift the back of her tent up.

"Wait." Luc crouched lower. "Your tent isn't going to be empty. You're not coming with me."

She went still. "Because that would make them more wary."

Luc sighed. "Yes. I have a plan and I need them to think they're safe here for it to work. I heard Tuart say he'd release you tomorrow on his way to Jatan. Kikir will follow you to make sure he lets you go."

"And if he doesn't?"

"Kikir won't leave you. He'll get you out. You can go wait in Bintinya for us."

She was silent for a moment. "Thank you."

"Why did you go to the camp last night?" He didn't ask her if he could trust her. No matter whether he could or not, her answer would be the same.

"I saw . . ." She drew in a ragged breath. "I saw Joacim."

Luc had to think a moment who that was. "One of your fellow scouts? One of the ones who never met up with you at the appointed place?"

"Yes."

He could hear her voice was muffled, as if she was suppressing tears.

"He turned traitor?" Luc wondered why a Chosen camp survivor would do that.

"I wasn't sure." He could hear the intensity in her voice. "I didn't want to say anything until I could speak to him. It was possible he'd seen the Jatan moving into Kassia and toward Cervantes, and joined them to keep better watch, to find out what they were up to."

That was true, Luc decided. It would have been a daring move. A courageous one.

"And? Was that what he was doing?" Luc asked.

"He was captured, but he was able to persuade them that he was unhappy with the Rising Wave, at being left on the edges of the border. He told them he felt abandoned."

"So they just let him join them?" Luc didn't hide the skepticism in his voice.

"No." Her voice sounded small. "He had to give them information. About Kassia, about Cervantes, to keep himself alive."

Luc said nothing.

"He didn't know what to do. He'd compromised himself, and he was stuck. He didn't know if we'd won against the Kassians or whether we had been defeated. He was biding his time." She was crying, Luc realized.

"It was his blood we found?"

She drew in a shuddering breath. "They caught us together after I snuck into the camp, and he tried to protect me. Hurst, that officer we took prisoner in the village, he stabbed Joacim. He bled so much. He died holding my hand."

"What did he tell the Jatan? Do you know?"

She took a moment. "He told them Cervantes was vulnerable. That all the soldiers had joined the Rising Wave to march on Fernwell. That there would be no resistance."

"Why would he do something like that?" Luc couldn't understand it.

"I don't know. He was in a panic. He never thought they would venture this far from the Jatan border."

"But they did."

"He . . ." She spoke slowly, as if only now figuring it out herself. "He threw himself on Hurst's sword. Almost as if he were trying to die."

A heavy weight settled on Luc's chest. What a waste. What a terrible waste.

"Luc?"

"I'm here." He tapped the tent with his fingers. "Stay safe, Kym. Kikir will be shadowing you. He'll find you when Tuart lets you go."

"I'm sorry."

"Joacim was your heart's choice?" He couldn't think of any other reason she would have risked so much.

She didn't answer, but he could hear the quiet sound of her sobs.

"I'll see you in Bintinya." His words were not sufficient for the pain she was feeling, but no words would be.

Luc moved away from the tent and back through the trees to find Massi and the others waiting.

"What is it?" Massi was studying his face with concern.

"Nothing." Luc indicated to her to lead the way. War was war. And he was tired of it.

CHAPTER 21

Tuart left at dawn.

The Rising Wave had needed the night to rest and eat, and to wait for the reinforcements one of his soldiers had ridden back to Bintinya to collect, so even though Luc wanted to have left before Tuart emerged from the hidden camp, he accepted the necessity of waiting, pleased at least they were achieving several goals at once.

Kikir watched the small unit from atop his saddle, and as soon as they disappeared from sight, he turned, extending his hand.

Luc extended his own, clasping the Skäddar just below his elbow, and Kikir did the same. A warrior's farewell.

"I'll see you again." Kikir flicked his reins, and then galloped after Tuart, vanishing into the dawn shadows.

Kikir had been gone barely ten minutes when a low whistle from one of Luc's guards alerted him to the approach of horses from Bintinya.

As soon as he laid eyes on them, saw there were enough volunteers from the small village to make his plan workable, he rode off looking for Massi. He found her strapping the last of her things in her saddle bag.

"They're here?" she asked.

"Looks like twenty or maybe a bit more." He couldn't hide the satisfaction in his voice.

She nodded. "We'll chip away at their numbers, every time a raiding party leaves, we'll take them down."

He knew the easy way would be to kill them. But he was reluctant to take a step like that, and he could see Massi felt the same.

"Maybe the Bintinya volunteers will be able to suggest a good place to keep the Jatan prisoners. They'll know this area well."

She nodded and swung up into the saddle. "I'll go meet them. Lay out the plan."

He leaned over, pulled her to him in a one-armed hug. "Good luck."

"It'll be like spearing fish in a barrel, Luc. You're the one who needs luck."

He grinned. "I don't need luck." He had Ava's protections.

She grinned back, and then she was gone, calling in a low voice for the ten soldiers who were going to stay with her and the Bintinya villagers.

The plan was for them to ambush and capture the soldiers from the camp each time they ventured out. To whittle them down to nothing, and then surround them and keep them contained.

"Ready?" Rafe called to him in a low voice.

In answer, Luc gave a low whistle and started to ride.

The rest of the unit fell in around him, silent and serious as they headed deeper into Cervantes, to find General Hurst and put a halt to his raids.

It took them until midday before they saw the first evidence of violence.

There wasn't much between Bintinya and the Cervantes heartland, but the first village they came to, Druitte, a large sprawl of wooden houses on a slight rise, was silent and empty.

"They may be hiding. They might think we're Jatan," Revek murmured.

Eight of the soldiers in his group were from here.

But even when they called out, there was no answer, no movement or sign of life, and grim-faced, they rode on.

At least there were no bodies.

Luc wasn't the only one cataloguing the destruction, the burned-out homes and broken doors.

He could feel the rise in anger.

This village, and the two others they passed, equally abandoned, had been unable to defend themselves because most of the warriors from here had joined the Rising Wave and had fought their way to Fernwell with him.

Those that had come back with him now would be almost impossible to hold in check when they came face to face with the Jatan.

Luc didn't plan to, anyway.

"They've moved to safety somewhere else, because this is the Jatan's path to and from the camp," Revek said.

Luc nodded. He had guessed the same.

If the villagers had returned, they'd have been harassed over and over again, each time General Hurst returned to his safe haven.

"They might still be alive and well." Rev raised his voice so the other soldiers would hear him, but the dark swirl of violence-in-waiting did not lift.

They reached Versai in the late afternoon.

Luc had come through the small town many times.

When he was younger, he'd come with his mother, before he'd been taken to the Chosen camps, and then after he'd freed himself and the other Cervantes, he'd ridden through here every time he'd returned from building up support for the Rising Wave on his way home to Ta-lin, Cervantes' capital.

Versai was currently as silent as the other villages had been, but instead of calling out, as members of his unit who were locals had done each time they'd ridden through a village, one of the soldiers, a woman with long, braided hair and a stark look on her face, gave a whistle, as if calling a pet.

From further down the street, a dog began to bark, and then

raced out, and with a laugh of joy, the woman jumped down from her horse and crouched to greet her friend.

A cry of astonishment came from close by, and then people began appearing.

Luc watched them come forward, cataloguing the damage to the buildings around him.

Some Cervantes had left their villages completely during the years the Kassian army had spent abducting Cervantes children.

The Cervantes had fought against them, and fought hard—it was what they were good at, and partly why the Kassians were interested in their children in the first place. Though Luc had always suspected the capture and training of Cervantes children to fight for Kassia had been a side benefit.

What the Kassian had really been interested in was Cervantes' position along the border with Venyatu.

And the raids had managed to wear the Cervantes down. Kassia's numbers were greater, and they preferred to ambush and raid during the night. They avoided skirmishes and battles, and when they had enough children in the camps, they'd used the lives of those children as leverage against the warriors of the Cervantes, blackmailing them into laying down arms so the children weren't punished in retaliation.

Whole villages had chosen to disappear onto the plains and into the forests, becoming nomads and making it harder for the Kassian military to find the children that remained. But since Luc had freed every child and pushed the Kassians back from Cervantes, his people had begun to drift back to the homes they'd abandoned.

Versai had been one of the first to be repopulated, along with Ta-lin, being as they were in the heart of Cervantes.

A child began wailing, and Luc swung down and led his horse toward the sound.

This was the first sign of life they'd found since Bintinya, and he needed as much information as he could get.

The child's cry came from inside a small wooden house, and he knocked lightly and then peered inside.

"Luc?"

He went still at the sound of his name, peering into the gloom, and caught a glimpse of a woman leaning over. A lantern bloomed to life, illuminating the gloomy space.

"Sierra?"

She had fought with him in the camps. She was one of Massi's closest friends.

And she had left the Rising Wave when she fell pregnant, returning home.

Everyone had thought it was the safest thing for her.

Her heart's choice, Rory, had stayed to fight, and he was back in Fernwell.

Luc was grateful he wasn't here.

There would be no containing him.

"Your baby is hurt." That was an understatement. Luc could see blood seeping through a dressing on the child's shoulder.

"They came out of nowhere, in the early hours." Sierra spoke with a low voice. "I was up, because Roan was crying and I stepped outside with him, hoping the cool air would soothe him."

"They attacked a woman with a child?" Luc tried to keep his voice neutral.

"I think I surprised them. They were sneaking into the town, down side streets and along the sides of houses. I don't know who was more shocked when I came face-to-face with two Jatan soldiers, me or them. One held a sword to my neck to keep me quiet while I was holding Roan against my chest. I don't know if he wasn't paying attention or he was nervous, but it slipped. It cut Roan's shoulder and he started screaming. Then I started scream-ing." She smoothed her fingers over her son's feverish brow. "I fell backward, holding Roan, and they left us because people were coming out to help."

"Luc?" Rafe's call gave him an excuse to step away from Sierra for a moment, to try and contain his fury.

He waved to his captain, and then stepped back into Sierra's home to wait for him.

"They came through here early this morning. About fifty-strong," Rafe said as he stepped into the room. Luc didn't turn to look at him, but he felt his captain stiffen at the sight of Sierra and her baby.

"Sierra." Rafe's tone conveyed everything. Pain. Shock.

This is why they'd formed the Rising Wave and taken on the Kassians, even after they'd freed themselves from the camps and pushed the Kassian army out of Cervantes.

Because they had known they'd never be left alone while Kassia was still powerful.

And still, after everything; after taking Fernwell itself, their children were not safe.

"The cut is not that deep." Sierra watched them with eyes that glittered in the lantern light. She lifted the grizzling baby, holding him carefully against her chest. "An infection has set in, though. The blade was not clean, and he is so hot. I need to put him back in a cool bath."

The baby needed Ava, Luc thought.

She could fix this. She could heal this child.

And she was too far away.

"Where is your healer?" he asked. Cervantes' healers were good, using natural remedies to treat pain and fever, and most apprenticed for years to learn how to set bones and stitch cuts. Dorea, the Cervantes healer who'd traveled with the Rising Wave, had been invaluable in their march on Fernwell.

They hadn't brought her with them on this mission, though. He'd rightly expected the ride to be hard and fast, so Rafe had chosen some soldiers who'd spent some time learning field dressings and basic patch-ups from Dorea, rather than someone who might be useful after a fight but would slow them down.

"Our healers were taken." Sierra smoothed a hand down her baby's back. "Both of them. We were able to inflict a few injuries and it seems the Jatan didn't bring healers of their own."

"How did they know who your healers were?" Luc couldn't believe they would have had that level of information.

"They captured a few of the older people and threatened to kill them if our healers didn't step forward. Dagar and Calintha did so of their own accord."

"Where did they take them?" Revek had come in while Sierra had been talking, but Luc had seen him standing outside when Rafe had stepped in. He'd heard everything.

Luc could see his hands shook slightly.

Rev was almost as close to Sierra as Massi, and he kept his eyes averted from her, as if looking at her injured child would rip the last threads of his control away.

"Eduard followed them." Sierra dipped a cloth in cool water and brushed it over her baby's face and neck. "He returned less than an hour before you arrived. We thought you were the Jatan at first, that they'd seen him and followed him back. They've set up a camp under two hours away, just out of sight of Ta-lin. They seem to have lain low today and we're guessing they're planning to raid Ta-lin tonight."

"Bold," Rafe said.

"They've hardly encountered any resistance at all. They're confident." Luc shared a look with Rafe, as Revek was still concentrating on the floor.

That confidence was about to be crushed.

CHAPTER 22

"When do we kill them?" Revek hunkered down beside Luc, looking toward Hurst's camp, which was surprisingly quiet and dark.

Luc turned to look at him. "You can kill as many as you like, but only when it's time. If you're going to ignore the plan, I'd prefer you return to Versai and stand watch there."

Revek looked away.

Eventually he gave a nod, eyes still downcast.

They'd made good time from Versai, with Eduard leading the way directly to the shallow hollow where the Jatan had settled for the night. Luc thought the Jatan would be moving around by now, getting ready to raid Ta-lin, unless they'd already left, and he'd gotten here too late.

Revek's gaze kept going toward the camp and Luc suppressed a sigh. Revek would be difficult to control after seeing baby Roan's injuries.

He had to admit that he wasn't completely sure of his own control, either. But he had to be coolheaded if they were going to crush Hurst without any more deaths to his own people.

He didn't care how many Jatan died. All thoughts of long-term diplomacy were gone.

The Rising Wave would find it difficult to deal in good faith with the Jatan again.

"We'll need a distraction while we rescue the healers. I'm happy for you to be involved in that, but only if you think you're capable of pulling back when it's time." He intended to cripple Hurst's unit and take whoever was left alive as a prisoner.

The soldier who'd whistled for her dog, Tara, had ridden hard from Versai straight to Ta-lin, to warn them of what was coming.

Given how quiet things were here, Luc hoped they were just waiting until the early hours of the morning for their attack, and that Tara wasn't going to find the capital already under siege.

"Sierra needs the healers for her baby. We have to get them out before the fighting starts." Luc pressed the point home, and Revek gave a savage jerk of his head in acknowledgement.

Luc turned to Rafe, trusting his captain to have a cooler head, although he could tell the older soldier was deeply affected.

They all were.

"Hold things together here. We can't let them know we're here."

"What are you going to do?" Rafe lifted an eyebrow.

"I'm going into the camp to see where the healers are being held. If I can get them out while I'm down there, I will, otherwise I'll come back and let you know where we need the distraction in order to get them to safety."

"Why are you going, why not someone else?" Revek asked.

"Because I said that's how it's going to be." Luc turned his head and held Rev's gaze, and his friend gave a deep sigh and nodded his head.

"Don't take too long." Rafe's words were a warning that he wouldn't be able to hold back the rage and thirst for revenge that had been building in the unit throughout the day.

He acknowledged the comment with a nod, and disappeared into the darkness.

As soon as he was far enough away, he sent a thank you to Ava, hopefully sleeping peacefully in their rooms in Fernwell Palace, as he pulled out the scarf that let him go unseen and wound it around his neck.

Time was once again not on their side, so Luc did not bother to creep into the camp, he walked in boldly.

Soldiers lay asleep on the ground, curled up two to a pallet, and only three tents had been set up.

The horses had been corralled to one side, and there was a guard on duty watching them.

Luc moved toward them, getting close enough to see better. It would be useful to get the horses free and take them back to Versai, but first he needed to find the healers, Dagar and Calintha.

He heard the faint murmur of voices and headed in that direction.

The only light in the camp came from a fire at the far end, and he could see a few people sitting beside it.

"I need rilla powder," a woman said.

"You'll have to make do with what we have available." The answer was short.

"We could get some later in this big town of theirs," a man said.

"You think you can just ride into Ta-lin and take it?" A man Luc guessed was Dagar looked up from his place crouched beside an injured soldier.

The Jatan guard gave a derisive snort. "That's what we've done in every village we've come across."

"Ta-lin isn't a village," Dagar answered, but Luc could hear the fear and distress in his voice.

Calintha hunched her shoulders and then lifted a cloth to wipe away blood on a woman's stomach.

Two men watched over them from the fireside, their manner relaxed as they perched on rocks placed next to the fire pit, their swords lying on the ground beside them.

One of them stood, stretching and yawning. He turned and looked straight at Luc, moving his shoulders as if they were stiff.

"Can you fetch more water to boil?" Calintha asked. She wrung out the bloody cloth in her hand and then held out a small pot.

Grumbling, the guard took it and ambled off to the side, where Luc could hear the faint trickle of water.

Luc stared after him, then turned and looked back at the rest of the camp site.

It was still and quiet.

If these guards were eliminated, he could lead the healers straight out. It would be quick and quiet, and time was of the essence.

He considered killing the guard at the stream first, but both Calintha and Dagar had their backs to the second guard by the fire.

There wouldn't be a better time to strike while still using Ava's scarf.

The only alternative was to use one of Ava's worked squares, but he couldn't do that with the healers in earshot.

Anyway, his desire to avoid bloodshed had been eroded by the events of the last few days, and he couldn't muster any real regret that this was the least risky option.

Luc moved quietly behind the man, still sitting on his rock. He weighed the knife in his hand and then slit the guard's throat at the same time as clamping a hand over his mouth. It was a technique he'd been taught as a teenager in the Chosen camps, but never had any call to use before now.

The guard gave a grunt, and Luc lowered him backward from his perch, twisting him as he did to lie on his side.

Then he moved toward the stream.

He could hear the guard humming softly as he filled the pot.

Luc disposed of him in the same way.

He rinsed the small amount of blood he had on his hands in the cool water and then turned back to the camp.

Dagar had turned to look at the fire and Luc saw him go still at the sight of the guard sprawled out on the ground.

He hoped the healers wouldn't make any sound of surprise or

distress. He remembered to pull the scarf off and made his way back to them.

Dagar's head snapped toward him in fear as he noticed Luc in the flickering firelight. Luc put a finger to his lips and after a long moment, Dagar gave a nod and leaned across to grab Calintha's arm.

The other healer turned to him. "What is it?"

"Time to go." Luc spoke softly, and she gasped as she twisted to look at him over her shoulder. "Sierra's baby needs you."

Calintha let out a sigh of relief and stood. Her eyes went wide at the sight of the dead guard.

"Quickly now," Luc said. He started moving and the healers were silent as they fell in behind him.

He cut across the camp, reaching the edge of it as fast as possible. They were free of the sleeping soldiers and completely out of sight in less than a minute.

"You aren't from Versai." Calintha's voice was almost a whisper, even though they were far enough from the camp now that they wouldn't be heard.

"He's the Commander of the Rising Wave, Cally." Dagar's voice was just as soft. "I saw him eight months ago, coming through Versai on his way to Ta-lin. What are you doing here? Did we lose against the Kassians?"

"No, we won." Luc would never get tired of saying that. "I had scouts watching the Jatan border, and they were able to get the message to us that the Jatan had ventured into Kassia and Cervantes."

"You came to stop them?"

"Too late for Versai, but hopefully not for Ta-lin." Luc caught a movement up ahead, and gave a low call.

Rafe returned it. "You got them out?" He sounded surprised, but he allocated the two healers an escort and had them up in the saddle in moments.

They disappeared into the night, and the mood among the soldiers around Luc changed.

There was no reason to tread lightly anymore.

"Most of the Jatan are sleeping," he said, pitching his voice so everyone could hear him. "There are three tents; I'm assuming Hurst and his senior officers are using them."

Rafe tapped his forehead above his eye, and Luc reached up to his own forehead and rubbed there with his thumb. It came away bloody.

Every eye seemed to focus on it.

"Can we go now?" Revek asked, voice close to cracking.

"You can go now," Luc agreed.

And they went, silent with rage. Keeping their roar of fury trapped in their throats, to strengthen their arms and focus their aim.

CHAPTER 23

T hey were getting close to the Grimwalt border.

Ava could see it in the suppressed excitement that bubbled up as the caravan turned at a fork in the road, taking the better maintained track for once.

"We'll be there by tomorrow afternoon," Reckhart called to Sirna, and from her position next to him on the driver's bench, Ava noticed Sirna's mouth harden into a grim line.

He was worried.

She had let yesterday's pretence of a collapse continue, lying listlessly beside the fire through the evening, eating nothing. It was already mid afternoon and she had continued the charade, keeping her eyes unfocused and her movements jerky.

Last night, Sirna hadn't wound the rope around her, and she had seen panic in his eyes this morning when he'd had to wake her, give her a piece of bread to eat by the fire, and then lift her onto to the cart.

Evelyn had circled around them, not engaging but not ignoring what was happening, either.

She seemed both resentful of Ava's state, and angry with Sirna, and Ava hadn't heard a civil word between the two since she woke.

Her sharp decline had spurred the rest of the caravan into some sort of action.

Madame Croter kept offering Sirna advice, Gregor was openly rude to both Sirna and Evelyn, and although Vanin Gruger was his usual, silent self, he shared some of his food with Ava at lunch, reaching across Sirna to hand the fruit and nuts to her in a deliberate snub.

The only person who seemed determined to ignore the problem in front of them was Reckhart. And even he kept shooting nervous glances at his friend.

Ava let her head loll forward as she sat on the driver's bench. The afternoon sun warmed her, countering the chill breeze, but the long run of clear skies seemed about to end.

So were the choices available to her.

She had balanced regaining her strength against proximity to the border.

Now the gap had almost closed.

The closer she was to Grimwalt, the more people would be available to hunt for her when she ran.

But she might find help there, too.

And every hour that passed where she didn't have to run, to survive on her own, was another hour to build her strength.

She began to braid her hair. It was clean enough, she'd managed to wash in a stream yesterday, and she'd been thinking since she'd braided Melodie's hair that weaving workings into her hair was a good idea.

It couldn't be stripped from her. It was not an obvious place for a working to be. No need for thread of any kind.

She focused on strength and health for the right side, pausing often as her fingers ached after a while. Once the right side was done, she rested a little, then lifted arms that felt leaden to the left side, and worked in protection. From knives, especially, but also fists, and arrows. Reckhart was good with his bow and arrow, and she didn't know which side he would land on if a confrontation erupted.

She would have to make her first move tonight.

Find the Focus, or come up with another plan.

Dark clouds rose up ahead, purple and gray in the distance, and Ava wondered what Evelyn would do with her when it began to rain.

She still clung to her deep-seated objection to Ava being in the cart.

That suited Ava. She couldn't escape if she was inside the cart with Sirna and Evelyn.

It would be hard to sneak out under Sirna's nose. He watched her carefully, even though she slept in a nest of hay and blankets near the fire each night and he was in the cart with Evelyn.

She had woken a number of times with him looming over her, staring down at her with the same mix of accusation, fear and rage on his face, as if her weakness, even her existence, was a deliberate act of defiance.

It worried her each time she caught him that she hadn't sensed him. That she was still so weak and tired that he could be right beside her without her knowing.

She was improving, though. When she'd woken this morning, stiff with cold and feeling every muscle, she'd missed working with her needle and thread for the first time since the rope had been tightened around her waist.

It gave her a sweet, painful stab of hope.

But she faced the hard truth. Even with the improvements she'd made, she couldn't run fast enough. If she couldn't get rid of the Focus, it would lead Sirna to her and she would be dragged back.

Unfortunately, the chances of getting another look inside the cart were slim.

Evelyn had been even more protective of her territory since Ava had been in there yesterday.

Far in the distance, lightning flashed and then she heard the low rumble of thunder.

The air felt charged, and the dark purple of the clouds began to take on a greenish tinge. The scent of rain filled the air, and Ava filled her lungs.

A few drops of rain hit her cheeks, then stopped, and Ava looked up between half-closed eyes.

The clouds were not directly overhead yet, but she could see the rain falling in sheets in the distance.

The carts kept moving, directly into the storm, but before they reached it, Reckhart gave a piercing whistle and led them off the track, into a clearing that was surrounded and sheltered by big, established trees, their branches arching over the elongated space to form a natural shelter.

"And if the branches snap off in the wind?" Evelyn asked, sourly. She had come out of the cart when it had stopped and walked up to Sirna's spot on the driver's bench.

"You'd prefer we kept riding?" Sirna asked, and they stared each other down.

"What are we going to do with her when it rains?" Evelyn asked, voice low. "She's not coming into the cart."

Sirna gritted his teeth. Ava could see his jaw clench under his stubble.

"Where will we put her then?" he hissed. He looked over at the other travellers, talking to each other in laughing voices as they set up for bad weather.

"That's what I asked you!" Evelyn leaned closer to him. "Under the cart, maybe?"

"Not without a pallet. We've drawn enough attention to ourselves where she's concerned as it is." As he spoke, the rain hit, thundering into the leaves overhead, hitting the roof of the cart in a sudden cacophony.

Ava hunched over, curling over her thighs. The branches overhead protected them from the worst of it, but rain was still getting through.

With a curse, Sirna jumped down from the bench and disappeared, and after a moment, Ava could hear him in the cart behind her.

"You ruin everything." The words were said with a venomous hiss. Ava looked up and saw Evelyn hadn't moved, she was staring at Ava from beside the cart.

"Let me go, then," Ava mumbled.

A sudden bright flicker of lightning and the almost immediate sound of thunder on its heels jerked Evelyn's attention upward.

"Get her down," Sirna shouted and she reached up, grabbed Ava's arm, and yanked her down.

Ava let herself fall to her knees, head bowed.

"Are you sure she's your sister?" Gregor loomed out of the rain. "You treat her like a prisoner."

"Tempers are just a little raw," Sirna's excuse for every interaction was starting to wear a little thin. Even he seemed to offer it with less conviction as he stepped up behind Evelyn.

"I can lend you a tent for Avasu. Melodie and I use it when we have to leave the cart somewhere for repairs."

"Thank you." Sirna's relief and gratitude were genuine. "I didn't know how the pallet would hold up on the wet ground."

"You can put it in the tent and it'll stay dry," Gregor told him, and then nodded to Sirna and held one end of the tent out to him.

It took Sirna a moment to realize he wanted help putting it up, but the narrow-eyed stare Gregor gave him galvanised him into action.

When she was finally installed inside it, lying on Sirna and Evelyn's comfortable pallet, dry and warm with a blanket from Madame Croter tucked around her, Ava finally let herself grin.

The burst of amusement left her feeling light and energised.

A shadow darkened the tent's entrance, and she forced the smile off her face and turned.

Gregor poked his head inside.

"It's not leaking?" he asked.

She shook her head.

"I can't keep watching the abuse, Avasu. I need to get you free of them." His voice was low.

She held the blanket tight around herself and rose to her knees to face him. "If you hide me in your cart, or try to separate me from Sirna, he *will* retaliate. Maybe you'll beat him, but maybe he'll hurt a few people before that happens." She lifted her shoulders. "If Reckhart stands with him, it'll be you against the two of them. Madame Croter and Vanin Gruger won't be much help against them. They're just liable to be hurt. And Sirna will keep following me. There's too much on the line for him not to. I can't risk going across into Grimwalt, not with the people waiting for me there, so you'll have to leave me in Kassia at some point, and as soon as you do, he'll grab me again. I don't currently have the strength to outrun him."

"There are plenty of places to hide in the forest. You wouldn't have to outrun him." Gregor's face showed that her words of caution about a direct confrontation with Sirna were something he'd already considered.

She hesitated. "I will either have to outrun him, or find the item he used to capture me in the first place. The Grimwaldian who hired him to grab me called it a Focus. It can track me somehow. It's in the cart."

"That's what you were looking for yesterday?"

She nodded. "If you want to help me, wait until dinner, send Melodie to find me, and have her proclaim me missing. Help search the camp for me, and watch closely to see if Sirna takes anything out of the cart to come looking for me in the forest."

"Will you be missing?" he asked.

She shook her head. "I'll have 'collapsed' by the stream. I don't have the stamina yet to outpace him. I need to get rid of the Focus, then I can disappear." If her magic was up to it. If it wasn't, she was in serious trouble.

Rain was running in rivulets down Gregor's face, plastering his thick dark hair to his head and dripping off his beard. He nodded, eyes sparking at the notion of finally doing something.

He withdrew, but Ava had barely settled back onto the pallet when Melodie crouched in front of the tent. "Can I come in?"

Ava nodded, sitting up and scooting over to give her space to sit next to her. She turned, so the little girl sat close, with her back to Ava. She tucked the blanket around them both and began to comb her hair with her fingers.

Since she had braided her own hair, she felt an urgent need to do the same for Melodie.

"Are you going to put magic in my hair again, like you've put into your?"

Ava paused. "I'm glad you see the magic in my hair. The rope took a lot of my magic from me, so it's good to hear it's coming back."

"It looks strong," Melodie told her, voice serious. "And pretty."

"I hope what I put in your hair will be just as strong and pretty." She focused on protection in both braids, though, trying to think of everything Sirna, Evelyn and Reckhart could do to her and protecting against it.

When she was done, they sat quietly for a while, listening to the rain on the canvas and the rumble of thunder.

"Da says he's going to send me to get you from the tent at dinner and you won't be here, and I'm to make a big fuss." Melodie sounded excited, and Ava felt a lurch of fear.

"Yes," she whispered back.

"Why?"

She thought about her answer. Decided to be truthful. It's what she'd recommended to Gregor in his handling of his daughter. She would be a hypocrite not to do the same.

"I'm still not strong enough to run away, so I'll have to escape Sirna by hiding in the forest. But I can't do that until I get rid of or damage something he has that can find me no matter where I am."

"Something magic?" she asked.

Ava nodded. "I heard the man who gave it to him talking about it. It's something they took from my home in Grimwalt and then spelled to find me."

"So you want him to be forced to use it to find you tonight so you know what it is?" Melodie was quick.

"I've asked your father to watch him closely and see what he takes out of the cart when he comes to find me."

"What if it's small, like something that fits in his pocket?"

Ava grimaced. "That would be extremely unfortunate." Because if they were going to reach the border by tomorrow, she didn't have time to get stronger. She'd have to run, no matter how weak she felt.

"I'll watch, too. My da can't see what things have magic on them, but I can."

Ava slowly leaned over and lay on her side, propping herself up on an elbow so she could look at Melodie's face. "I am like you. And I know it's hard to believe looking at me now, but I was very strong, in my magic and in my body." She held Melodie's fascinated gaze for a long beat. "Sirna got me anyway. Yes, he used tricks, and things stolen from my home, but he got me. If he wants to get you, even with your father standing in his way, he might just succeed. I don't say this to frighten you, but to warn you to be very, very careful. Because if anything happened to you while you were helping me, it will be a burden I'll bear for the rest of my life."

Melodie returned the stare. "You spoke to my da, didn't you? About me? About how we can keep me safe and still help people?"

Ava gave a nod.

"That was good. I won't put myself in danger. Sirna doesn't notice me, anyway. He thinks I'm nothing more than an ann . . . annoyance." She stumbled over the big word, then smiled when she got it right. Then she cocked her head. "Da's calling me." She scrambled for the entrance, then paused and gave Ava's foot a comforting pat. "Don't worry about not being strong anymore. You sparkle brighter every day. It's beautiful."

With a wiggle, she was out.

Ava stared after her, hoping beyond anything that what she saw was true.

AVA GRIMACED AS MUDDY WATER RAN OVER HER LEGS.

She hoped Sirna found her soon.

She had lain down beside the narrow stream, in a pretence of collapse, but the heavy rains had swollen its banks in the twenty minutes since she'd been there, and the water pushed at her, dirty and cold.

She heard a faint shout coming from the trees, and closed her eyes, hoping the bank would hold long enough for them to arrive, or she was going in the water.

The rain was still relentless, although at least the wind had died down.

"Avasu!" The shout came from Gregor, and Ava made sure she was completely limp as the search group reached her.

"Let's get her up." Gregor bent over her, and with the addition of his and Sirna's weight, the bank finally gave way.

Ava landed in the swirling, freezing water, and opened her eyes.

Sirna had gone into the water with her and Gregor, and he went under, then came up spluttering.

Gregor planted his feet, still hanging onto her, then he lifted her up like a child in his arms and stood firm as debris flowed all around him.

Sirna was flaying his arms, trying to get purchase with his feet.

He was holding a baby's dress in his hand—her baby dress, she realized—and he let it go to push away a branch with sharp points that came at him. The movement toppled him over and he went under again.

Ava leaned over in Gregor's arms and snatched the tiny dress up as it floated on the surface, curling into Gregor's chest with it balled in her hands.

Sirna came up with a shout.

"Did he see me—?" She kept herself turned away from Sirna, her body shielding the Focus.

"No." Gregor waited a moment, then took it from her and palmed it into the pocket of his big coat. "You all right, Sirna?"

Sirna swore, and with a grunt, Gregor waded downstream a little way and then climbed back up onto dry land, holding her as if she weighed no more than Melodie.

Reckhart appeared out of the rain and darkness and pushed past them to put a hand out to Sirna, who must have been following behind.

He struggled up on hands and knees, head bowed.

Gregor turned to look at him, and Ava felt a moment of satisfaction at seeing Sirna coughing up dirty river water.

Then Gregor headed back to the camp.

Ava hadn't gone far and they reached it in less than five minutes.

Vanin Gruger and Madame Croter were standing beside a fire they'd lit beneath an open-sided canvas shelter.

It was a clever idea.

Ava was almost tearful with gratitude as Gregor set her down beside it and Madame Croter began to pour hot water from a pot beside the fire into a bowl.

She had brought being cold and wet on herself, and she was sorry Gregor was in a similar condition, shivering and bedraggled. But with the Focus safely out of Sirna's hands, she couldn't regret it.

"Come now, let's get you to my cart. I'll clean you up and get you warm." Madame Croter jerked her head at Gregor and he obligingly lifted Ava again, bending over her to shield her from the rain once they were out from under the canvas covering until he had her inside Madame Croter's cart.

"Thank you." She whispered it into his ear as he set her down. "If you have a chance to burn that dress when no one can see you, please do it."

He nodded. "Melodie told me it was what you were looking for."

Then he backed out, and Madame Croter came in. She sponged Ava down with hot, clean water and soap, and then rubbed her dry with a rough towel.

It was the first hot water she'd had to wash in since she'd been taken, and the feeling of being clean *and* warm was indescribable.

Madame Croter took the dirty water and stepped out of the cart.

Ava was naked, and she burrowed deeper in the blanket she'd been given and took the opportunity to have a good look around the interior.

She hadn't asked what Madame Croter did for her living, but now she could see she was a merchant.

There were boxes set into carefully designed shelves along both walls of the cart, containing hats.

Or Ava thought the closed boxes contained hats. There were plenty of hats of all kinds not in boxes, sitting on racks. Two carved wooden heads, the necks set on sturdy wooden bases, each sported a jaunty wide-brimmed hat.

Gregor poked his head back in. "You look better."

He stepped inside.

"You, too."

He was in dry clothes, and no longer looked bedraggled.

"Thank you."

He nodded. Patted his pocket. "I can't burn it now, but when they go to bed . . ."

She closed her eyes in relief. Gave a nod. "Tell Melodie goodbye from me. And that offer is still open. Go stay at my grandmother's house for as long as you wish, if it suits you."

He hesitated, then gave a nod. "You're going tonight?"

"Yes. That needle and thread that I asked you about . . . "

"Tucked behind the back wheel. There's a little box set under the cart where I keep tools in case something gets caught in the spokes. It's in there."

She reached out and took his hands, squeezed them. "If you ever need help, or Melodie does, you can go to the Rising Wave, ask for whoever is in charge, and say Ava sent you."

He stared at her in surprise, then gave a slow nod. "I feel like there is something else I could do."

She thought about it for a moment. "Try to get Sirna and Evelyn drunk tonight. That would help."

His lips quirked up but he didn't answer, turning his head a little as if he could hear someone coming. Then he hopped down and stepped aside to let Madame Croter back in.

"I'll dress you, and then Sirna wants you back in your tent." She spoke loudly, as if for other ears, then closed the door.

As soon as it clicked shut, she sent Ava a big smile and began hauling out boxes from under her bed.

She handed Ava wide-legged pants that seemed to have been made in another era, a big shirt that she told Ava she had once found in a camp site, had washed and kept aside, just in case, and a heavy wool jacket.

Of everything, Ava was most reluctant to accept the jacket. It was well made, if old, and would be warm and valuable.

"My guess is, you're hesitating over that jacket because you're worried I need it, and you're planning to run tonight." Madame Croter's voice was whisper quiet.

Ava hesitated before she nodded.

"That's why I've saved it until now, girl," the old woman gave a low chuckle. "Found it in an inn in northern Kassia years ago. Kept it, like the shirt, just in case. I wanted to give it to you so many times before today, but I was afraid that evil man and his harpy of a partner would take it from you. You take it with my blessing."

She gave Ava warm socks and tucked another pair into the pocket of the jacket.

There was nothing Ava could do about her boots. They were wet from her plunge into the stream, but she had no other pair and was lucky Sirna had forced Evelyn to give her these as it was. She would have to pretend to sleep in the tent for a little while, so she would set the boots by the fire to dry a little in the meanwhile.

"One last thing." Madame Croter opened a drawer, and pulled out some simple knitted caps. She had seen the Skäddar warrior, Kikir, wearing one, and had wanted to try to knit one herself, but had never had the time.

Too busy bringing Kassia to its knees.

She smiled as she rubbed the soft wool between her fingers.

This is what she could use to sew her invisibility into. Something easy to take on and off.

"If you are ever in Fernwell," she said, and slid the cap into her pocket, "please come to the palace, give your name, and say Avasu sent you."

Madame Croter studied her. "I don't think I'll get back to Fernwell. This trip has taught me that it's time to settle down. I'll find a place to set up shop in Taunen and rest my weary bones. Reckhart promised we'd be safer together in company on this old track, away from armies and unrest, when we left Bartolo, and then he let that evil in. I'll not expose myself to this again."

"Then may you find rest and comfort in Taunen." Ava leaned forward and kissed her cheek.

"Is she ready?" Sirna banged on the door and then opened it.

Madame Croter stood. "Careful with my door." She gave a sniff and then turned back to look at Ava. "You ready?"

Ava had made herself limp, and looked over at Sirna with an unfocused gaze and said nothing.

With a grunt of disgust, he reached in and pulled her out, supporting her weight as he dragged her to the tent.

"Wander off again and I'll hunt you down and make you wish you were dead." He hissed the words in her ear as he shoved her inside.

The pallet was gone, and he frowned. "Where did you put it?"

She shook her head and then collapsed onto the hard ground and he paused, obviously working out Evelyn must have taken it back while he'd been out searching.

He shook his head, she wasn't sure if it was in disgust or in admiration for Evelyn's single-minded focus on her own comfort.

The blanket, which had been loaned by Madame Croter, was still inside.

"You'll be dry and warm enough." Sirna tossed the blanket over her and went quiet.

Ava could feel his eyes on her and simply closed hers, shutting him out.

"I mean it," he said in a low voice, obviously unwilling to leave without emphasizing his point. "Make it difficult for me to get my money, and you'll be sorry you were born."

CHAPTER 24

Ava hovered behind one of the trees on the roadside where the caravan had pulled over and watched Sirna lose his temper.

The sky was clear again, the storm had blown over, but the air was even crisper than it had been the day before. She was glad of the thick coat and the knitted cap that covered her ears, and she huddled into them as the drama unfolded.

It had taken Sirna until now, at the midday stop, to realize she was gone.

Even if she had run, with him still in possession of the Focus, she might actually have had a chance, she realized.

Gregor had done an excellent job the night before, breaking out a bottle of spirits that had kept the laughter and shouting going late into the night.

Vanin Gruger and Gregor had been up first, and they had packed up everything, including her tent, and urged the others to get moving, so that Sirna had merely stumbled from the back of the cart onto the driver's seat, and had sat, sipping the hot brew Vanin Gruger had passed around to everyone before he doused the fire, as the horse pulled them ever closer to Grimwalt's border.

Ava had weighed her escape options all night as she sewed invisibility into the knitted cap, and protection and healing into the shirt, pants and coat. She had rebraided her hair, loose from being washed by Madame Croter, and she didn't need Melodie to tell her the spark was back this time. She could feel it for herself.

The braiding actually felt a little stronger than the embroidery.

She would need more time to build up the kind of protections she'd had before, the layer upon layer that she had perfected with her cloaks, but she knew what to focus on, what was most important.

She'd also realized, as she'd bound off the last stitch and crept out of the tent, that she couldn't simply walk away without making sure Sirna didn't hurt her friends.

She would have to follow and keep watch.

Shadowing the caravan was a good idea on two fronts.

She could make sure those who'd helped her were safe, and she could see who might be waiting for her at the border.

General Ru *would* have sent someone. The question was whether they had managed to get ahead of the caravan in time.

She hoped so. She desperately needed allies.

There was risk, though.

Her magic was not as strong as it had been. She could feel the difference in her workings. It was not something she would have noticed before she had been sucked dry, but she was well aware of it now.

She would need to keep renewing her work, bolstering it. And hope it didn't fail at the wrong moment.

She also didn't know who might be waiting at the border for Sirna in anticipation of him handing her over.

If it was the spell caster who'd created the rope and the Focus, she had a problem, because he or she was strong.

Most likely, given her current weakness, stronger than her.

And possibly capable of seeing through any working she might have created.

She would have to walk a fine line between keeping her distance from those who meant her harm and getting close enough to see who might be her friend. With the Grimwalt border closed to everyone who wasn't Grimwaldian, the Rising Wave soldiers would not be allowed entrance. If they had decided to wait and see who came through, she might get lucky.

Gregor hopped down from his cart and looked back down the road, almost as if searching for a sign of her, ignoring the growing argument behind him.

She hoped he had managed to burn the tiny dress she guessed the Speaker had had someone take from her grandmother's house. Something about it, though, about the feel of it in her hands, nagged at a memory in the back of her mind.

Something important.

Whatever it was, was just out of reach.

She did wonder, though, that if the Speaker had access to a spell caster with enough magic to create the rope, the net that had caught her, the Focus, and the necklace that changed someone's very appearance, why he needed her at all.

She was no more talented than whoever was helping to find her and bring her in as a prisoner.

"I thought Avasu was sitting with you." Sirna was not taking the discovery that no one had seen Ava all morning well, and he was pointing an accusing finger at Madame Croter, who's cart had been two ahead of his own all morning. "I heard you call out that you had her."

"I can't help what you thought, Sirna. I was calling to Gregor, and I said that I had Melodie riding with me. I found the blanket I'd lent Avasu on my step this morning, and saw the tent had been packed up. If that wasn't you, who was it?"

Vanin Gruger coughed. "Gregor and I took the tent down. Avasu wasn't inside, and neither was the pallet, so we assumed you were up already and had packed it back in your cart." He looked blandly at Sirna, his face holding the same calm expression he always seemed to have.

There was a moment of silence and Evelyn and Sirna exchanged a glance.

Evelyn's lips thinned in anger. She wasn't going to admit to having taken the pallet back the evening before, leaving Ava to spend the night on the ground.

Ava leaned against the tree, amused at her misdirection.

She had, in fact, traveled with them by sitting on the back step of Madame Croter's cart. Vanin Gruger had been the next cart along in the caravan, and she had watched him carefully as he'd sat on the driver's bench, but the only time she'd worried he'd seen her was when the cart's rough passage over poorly-maintained roads had forced Ava to stand and give her backside a break. He seemed to start as she stood and held onto the side of the cart for balance.

She'd frozen in place, and after a moment he'd relaxed again.

Maybe he had caught sight of something, some shadow as she stood, maybe it was coincidence.

With Vanin Gruger, she never really knew.

"The girl probably wandered off again, and you left her behind." Madame Croter's voice took on an accusatory edge. "Didn't you think to check on her this morning? You knew she was cold and disorientated from last night."

Sirna stood, the movement aggressive, and Gregor got to his feet slowly as well.

Melodie had been sitting with Blackie on Madame Croter's step, and she looked straight at Ava, her eyes going suddenly wide.

Ava stared back, putting a finger to her lips and then beckoned her over.

Melodie hopped down and skipped into the trees closest to Madame Crater's cart. Ava moved behind the tree to wait for her to make her way through the wood, shielded from view.

"I thought you were running away." The little girl whispered the words as she darted forward.

"I decided to follow you to make sure Sirna doesn't hurt anyone, and to see if some of my friends are waiting to help me at the border."

Melodie blinked at her. "Is that why you've made your cap like that?"

"Like what?" She was interested to know how Melodie saw her workings.

"Telling eyes not to see you."

"Yes."

Melodie gave a slow nod. "I'll pretend not to see you, too, then." She glanced over her shoulder uneasily as the tone of the conversation ratcheted up.

"Tell your father I'm here, if you can do it quietly."

She looked up at Ava, frowning. "So he knows he has help if Sirna does something bad?"

The little girl was sharp, Ava acknowledged. "That's right."

"Okay." She barrelled forward, gave Ava a clumsy hug and then began working her way back through the trees to Madame Croter's cart.

"We'll have to go back and look for her." Sirna's fists were clenched at his side.

"I thought you said you lost—" Evelyn cut off what she was going to say as Sirna sent her a vicious look.

"She's probably wandering along the track, looking for us, poor thing." Madame Croter stood and brushed crumbs from her dress. "I hope you can find her."

"You're not going to help us look?" Sirna asked.

"Not if we want to make the border before sun down." Vanin Gruger shrugged. "They close it from dusk. If you don't get there in time, you have to wait until morning to get through."

"In fact, we should be getting on, if we're going to make it," Gregor said.

"Fair enough." Sirna spoke congenially. Too congenially.

Ava tensed, waiting to see what he would do.

"It sounds as if this is goodbye, if we don't find Avasu in time to catch up with you. So if you have time for one last cup of tea together, I'd like to treat you to a special blend from my home country, Cattha." Sirna walked to the cart and emerged in a moment with a box in his hands.

The others looked like they'd prefer to leave, but good manners meant they were stuck with accepting Sirna's hospitality.

Ava caught sight of Gregor's face at the mention of tea, and when he saw the box, his eyes narrowed.

Melodie reached out a hand and patted his arm, and he glanced at her.

She smiled at him, her eyes dancing, and he slowly smiled back, then lifted her onto his lap. She whispered in his ear, and Ava saw him go still.

Message received. He knew she was watching.

He lifted his head and did a slow sweep of the clearing, his eyes passing over her.

He wasn't able to see where she was, she thought with relief. Her working was still holding. For now.

"This must be the wrong box." Sirna tried to smile as he looked down into what was now an empty container. "Or did you use it?" He looked at Evelyn, his jaw tight.

"No. Maybe that's the wrong box." She spoke brightly, but she was frowning, and when her gaze met Sirna's she gave a tiny shake of her head. She got up and disappeared into the cart, taking so long that Vanin Gruger stood and began packing up.

"We'll have to use our normal stash," Sirna said, giving a nervous laugh.

"If it's all the same to you, we need to move," Reckhart said, clapping him on the back in an overly-hearty way. "And you'll be worried about Avasu and want to find her as soon as possible."

"True." Sirna nodded, but he looked angry. "Thank you for your company this last week."

Gregor grunted in response to that, and Vanin Gruger and Madame Croter said nothing.

While the others doused the fire and packed away their lunch, Sirna grabbed Evelyn's arm and dragged her amongst the trees.

They ended up standing close to the tree where Ava had

stationed herself. She crouched down, keeping to the shadows even with her invisibility working, and waited.

"Where is it?" Sirna gave Evelyn a shake.

She ripped her arm out of his hold. "I. Don't. Know. I haven't touched it. You're the one who's so keen on using it, not me."

"It was in that box."

"*Himself*." Evelyn hunched over, arms crossed over her chest. "It was probably him."

"Did he go into the cart?" Sirna looked up, his face slack as he tried to remember.

"He demanded the tea back, and you got it for him. But he was in the cart dealing with *her*. So he was in there alone." Evelyn rubbed her upper arms.

"He told me that I would regret it if I hadn't given it all back." Sirna tapped his chin. "If he knew I hadn't, why didn't he just say?"

"Because he wanted you to bring her to the border for him. If you knew he would be waiting to accuse you of stealing from him when you got there, you wouldn't have done it, would you?" Evelyn sniffed and turned away.

"I'm still not sure it was him. Maybe it was Ava."

Evelyn gave a laugh. "What about her makes you think she can even walk in a straight line, let alone reach the box and empty it without us seeing. I haven't let her in there alone, ever."

"It's the rope. We used it too much. And even if she isn't translucent, like she was in the beginning, she isn't right. The way she stares at me, absolutely blank and empty." He shivered. "That old hag is right, she's probably wandering around among the trees, trying to find the road or something."

"Pity you lost the Focus." Evelyn's voice took on a sharp edge.

"I fell into the fucking river." Sirna's nostrils flared as he snarled the words. "It was in my hand one moment, gone the next."

"Another reason not to bother to show up at the border." Evelyn watched him with cynical eyes. "*Himself* told me in Bartolo he had to pay a former bodyguard of the Queen's Herald a lot of money to break into the palace and steal that Focus from Herron's old rooms. And you've gone and lost it."

That was interesting.

Ava felt a buzz along her arms at the information.

She had sensed something when she'd held the dress . . .

How had Herron got it? He had never been to Grimwalt, let alone to her parents or her grandparents' house, that she knew of.

She had wondered many, many times how her parents had known where she was being held. They had been ambushed on their way to rescue her. Her father had been killed, her mother captured and used by Herron in the same way he had wanted to use her.

Her parents had seemed to know where she was being kept.

Either her mother or her grandmother must have created the Focus to find her. And when Herron had captured her mother, he had taken it, and not left it in the fortress where she was being held.

For some reason, he had taken it back to Fernwell with him, and kept it in his rooms. Most likely because he didn't trust anyone else with it.

He didn't want anyone else to be able to find her except him.

There was no spell caster who had invaded her grandmother's estate, as she'd feared, no one had been through her things and stolen something to find her.

The rope, the necklace, the net. They could all be old pieces, loaned to Sirna for this abduction.

The spell caster she feared might not exist.

It lifted a huge weight off her shoulders.

"They owe me."

She realized while she had been processing what Eveyln had said, Sirna had started to pace.

Evelyn was right, Ava thought. There would be nothing good waiting for Sirna at the border, even if he had her in hand.

His dream of full payment was just that. A dream.

"I'm not walking away from what I'm owed." Sirna's lips thinned and took on a stubborn line.

"Then we better go get her." Evelyn sighed, but she was shaking her head. "Although, given the way the rest of them cluck and fuss around her, I'm surprised they didn't notice she was gone, either."

Sirna went still, slowly turning his head to look at her. "You're right." A look passed over his face, and it was not a nice one.

Ava went cold. This was what she had worried about. This was the danger she had anticipated.

"Sirna. We're leaving, but you'll need to move your cart." Reckhart's shout turned them both toward the camp.

"What are you going to do?" Eveyln had noticed the change in him, too, and she licked her lips nervously.

"Where do you think they've put her?" Sirna asked as he walked back toward the makeshift camp.

"That old bitch's cart, maybe. Or the surly blacksmith with the brat." Evelyn spoke with her usual venom, but she was frightened, Ava thought. Wary. "Do you think Reckhart is in on it? *If* they have her, that is?"

"I don't know." Sirna sounded bemused. "And they definitely have her. I can't believe I fell for that little act for even a moment."

Ava followed behind them, moving out from the protection of the trees as they strode toward the small group waiting for them.

She was pleased to see that Melodie still had her braids from the day before in place. That was good.

Because there was about to be trouble.

But Sirna exchanged goodbyes with Reckhart, and he and Evelyn manoeuvred the cart out of the way and rode off with a wave.

There was a beat of silence after they turned the corner and disappeared.

"You let someone very bad into our group, Reckhart." Madame Croter spoke first. "I won't travel with you again."

"Agreed." Vanin Gruger slapped the side of his cart. "Watching the way those two treated Avasu will weigh on me for a long time. It's not acceptable."

"I didn't know—"

"My daughter should not have had to see that." Gregor cut Reckhart off. "Don't pretend you didn't notice."

Ava listened to them with half an ear, her focus on the road Sirna had taken.

There was a sharp bend in the tree-lined road, and they could have stopped just around the corner.

They had not just driven off, she knew that.

Maybe the others should know that, too.

She made her way over to Gregor, and thought how to tell him. Melodie had passed on the message that she was there and watching, but he didn't necessarily know she was invisible. And he was a strong man with good reflexes. She would not like for him to react badly and hurt her, for both their sakes.

Melodie wasn't standing in the group, and Ava guessed Gregor had sent her to the cart already, as far from Sirna as she could get.

She would be the best way to get the message across.

Ava moved around the small group, headed for Gregor's cart, when the sound of Melodie's scream cut the air.

Everybody spun toward the sound. Before Ava could sprint toward it, Sirna came around the back, arm around Melodie, holding her up against his chest, her feet dangling in the air.

She had hoped the braids would protect the little girl from being grabbed. That they hadn't sent her heart plummeting.

"He said he'd kill Blackie if I didn't come to him." The little girl reached a hand out to her father in explanation. "I'm sorry, Da."

Gregor swore, and something in Ava became a little lighter. Her braids had worked. He had had to persuade Melodie to give herself up, he hadn't been able to catch her.

Which meant he couldn't stab her, and couldn't strangle her. She tried to remember everything else she had woven into Melodie's hair.

"Where's Evelyn?" Madame Croter asked him.

Sirna ignored her, and Ava wondered if Evelyn had refused to be part of this. She might actually be holding the cart around the corner, pretending what she couldn't see, hadn't happened.

"Where is Avasu?" Sirna hefted Melodie a little higher and lifted a knife to her throat. "She isn't in your cart, blacksmith, so where are you hiding her?"

Reckhart stepped forward, face flushed with anger. "Sirna, what are you doing? No one has Avasu. Put Melodie down."

"Someone has her. Do you think I'm stupid?" His spittle sprayed out. "The way you watch me with her. The way you pander to her. One of you has her, and I want her back."

"Go ahead and search, then," Madame Croter said, with an imperious wave of her hand. "Go ahead and look."

Except, it would be difficult to look while he held Melodie, and it would mean trapping himself in a small space. And holding Melodie hostage meant there was no one here who was not against him.

Still, he didn't look too concerned.

"Evelyn." He gave a shout and she stomped through the trees to him.

So she had been persuaded to participate.

Ava had thought she was too uneasy with what Sirna planned, but obviously she was able to overcome her finer feelings.

"Look in the carts. Every one."

Evelyn looked at everyone with a cold stare and then began searching, taking her time while Sirna stood with Melodie, knife almost touching her throat.

Did he mean it to rest on her skin? If so, he hadn't noticed it wasn't.

Hopefully because it could not.

She had focused on knives while she had woven the braid. She knew they were Sirna's preferred weapon.

And it was time she found a weapon of her own.

Sirna held everyone still with the threat to Melodie, especially her father, so she was on her own.

She moved to Gregor's cart and slipped inside, hunting for his tool box.

She found a long knife on a high shelf, the blade almost as long as her forearm, and a long-handled hammer.

She held both close to her body, and moved back out to join the others.

"She's not here." Evelyn emerged from Reckhart's cart, the last one she'd searched, and put her hands on her hips.

"She has to be." Sirna tightened his hold on Melodie. "There is no way you don't know where she is."

Ava reached Gregor. She tapped the back of his hand with the handle of the knife, deciding it would be easier for him to hide it against his leg than the hammer.

He glanced sharply at her, and when he saw nothing, his eyes widened. Not sure what else to do, Ava crouched down and slid the knife into the top of his boot.

He went still, then flexed his hand, his attention going back to Sirna.

Ava leaned right up against him, and though he flinched, he held still.

"I spelled a protection against knives into her braid," she whispered into his ear. "If you look closely, the blade isn't touching her, and I think he means it to."

She would let Gregor take his own risk assessment on whether to trust her working with his daughter's life or not.

She wasn't completely certain of it herself.

But Sirna would hurt her—or try to—very soon.

He was losing his calm.

It was an ugly thing to watch.

"Tell me where she is." He screamed so loudly, Melodie hunched away from him as best she could, the shout in her ear obviously painful.

"Put my daughter down." Gregor had his attention, and Ava decided there wouldn't be a better time.

She had been moving around the back of Sirna since she'd given Gregor the message about Melodie's protections.

The little girl was following her movement. She could tell by the quick little glances she threw her way.

She caught her gaze deliberately as soon as she was behind him.

"Get ready," she mouthed. Then she lifted the long hammer and slammed it into the back of Sirna's knee.

He went down with a shout, slashing his knife across Melodie's throat as he fell.

Ava saw him do it, and it was quite deliberate.

Rage flared up in her, even as she registered Melodie had thrown herself out of his arms and was rolling away from him. She scrambled to her feet, completely unharmed.

Ava lifted the hammer again, so angry she found it hard to concentrate on the shouts and exclamations of the others. She was quite prepared to slam it into Sirna's head, but Gregor beat her to it.

The knife was in his hand as he leaped forward. He jerked Sirna up from where he knelt on the ground by the throat.

"You tried to kill my daughter." He said the words quite calmly, and then he plunged the blade into Sirna's gut. He held him there, with the same ease Sirna had held Melodie, and then he threw him down on the ground.

Evelyn started to scream, and Madame Croter turned on her.

"Shut up. Or do you want to be next?"

The threat did the job. Evelyn backed away, her gaze fastened on Sirna, on the pool of blood widening around him, as she edged away. As soon as she was clear, she started running down the road to where they must have left the cart.

"You want me to fetch her back?" Vanin Gruger asked.

Gregor shook his head. "Let her go. She's no threat anymore."

They all turned back to Sirna, whose hands were trying to stem the bleeding.

"Are you going to help me?" His words were garbled, and there was blood on his lips. His eyes were fixed on Reckhart.

"You tried to kill a little girl," Reckhart said, voice strained. "No. I'm not going to help you."

No one moved, no one said anything, they just watched until Sirna's eyes closed.

Then Gregor grabbed his shirt again, and dragged him amongst the trees.

When he came back out, Vanin Gruger uncapped a water skin, and Gregor held out his bloody hands and rubbed them together as water was poured over them.

He shook the droplets off as if the matter was now done.

"If we don't leave for the border right away, we won't get through," Madame Croter said, the practicality of it jarring after what had just happened.

They all began to move, quiet now. Subdued.

Melodie had stood beside Madame Croter, watching her father drag Sirna into the forest. When he emerged, she stood still and submitted to a thorough examination, her father's now clean hands smoothing over her, making sure she was completely unharmed.

Ava left them to it, heading for their cart. She clambered onto the driver's seat and realised she still held the hammer in her hand.

She set it down beside her and leaned back, closing her eyes against the warm sun.

She had finally escaped her captors. And they were gone for good.

She heard a noise and turned, opening her eyes. Melodie stared up at her from the ground. She reached down a hand, and pulled the little girl up beside her.

"How strong is the hat's message?" she whispered.

"It's still saying not to look at you, but more in a normal voice now, not a shout."

Ava nodded. She'd have to sneak off at the next stop and work some new embroidery into it, to bolster it for the border station.

But the hard part was done.

She was free.

CHAPTER 25

I t was a power move, but Luc knew from experience a show of strength was sometimes what was needed.

The bedraggled survivors of their raid on General Hurst's regiment, as well as what was left of the hidden camp that Massi had whittled down and then rooted out, marched before him, hemmed in on both sides by the Rising Wave.

The Jatan forces waiting on the Jatan side of the border to meet them were forced to watch their soldiers brought very low; horse-less, weapon-less. Unkempt.

"They won't be happy with this sight," Massi said from beside him. She didn't sound overly concerned about it, though.

"No, they won't. I'm surprised there are so many of them, to be honest." The sight of at least double the number of his own soldiers gave him pause, but it wasn't completely unexpected. They'd had time to assemble, and they would want to make a show of strength themselves.

He'd let one soldier go after they had rounded up their captives, giving her a missive for the Jatan Gathering that stated his displea-sure in no uncertain terms. In it, he'd insisted he be met by someone of authority at the Roali Gap, one of the most open sections of the Jatan / Kassia border. He made it clear the Jatan Gathering needed to arrive with a plan for restitution and a commitment to stay on their side of the border, or they would not be getting their people back.

The Jatan would feel the sting of that.

He knew they would want to push back, which is why he didn't just have the unit he'd set out with from Fernwell, now.

He'd acquired many older warriors, from Ta-lin, Versai, and even Bintinya—those who had left the Rising Wave's march on Fernwell because of family responsibilities.

The ire of the Cervantes had been roused, and many wanted blood.

Some of them had gotten it, and still, they wanted to see the Jatan sent back home with their tails between their legs.

His eighty-strong unit had swelled to nearly a hundred and fifty.

He kept his eye on General Carvill and General Hurst, who were walking at the front of the prisoners, gauging their reactions as they approached the Jatan troops.

Both had survived the decimation of their units.

Luc didn't know if it was by luck, or lack of valor.

Carvill had earned a little of his respect over the last day since they'd joined up with Massi and then headed straight for the Jatan border.

The Jatan general had accepted his defeat with dignity, and had instructed his soldiers to cooperate in order to keep them safe.

Hurst, on the other hand, had raged, incensed that he'd been bested, and had blustered about consequences and how sorry Luc would be for his treatment. He'd done nothing for his soldiers, leaving them to their own devices, but most had followed General Carvill's lead, and had not made any trouble.

They were frightened, Luc knew, and that soothed something inside him.

They should be frightened.

It would make them think long and hard before they attacked his people again.

In the center of the long line of mounted soldiers that waited up ahead was a small group in robes, rather than the soldier's standard of pants, shirt and heavy jacket. They had all dismounted from their horses, and stood watching the Rising Wave approach.

Three women and three men.

Behind them were three officers who held themselves a little apart, and Luc's good eyesight recognized one as General Tuart.

So he had made it home and must have delivered Luc's missive.

When he saw Luc, he raised a hand and moved his mount around the robed figures to approach, but he was called back.

Luc could not hear the conversation, but it seemed heated, and he wondered if Tuart had wanted to have a quick talk with him in private before he met with what was surely the Jatan Gathering's representatives.

To try and smooth over his own mistakes, Luc wondered? Or Hurst's?

It was time to slow down the forward momentum and make sure there was enough open ground between the two sides.

He put his fingers to his lips and gave a piercing whistle.

Up ahead, at the tip of the right flank, Rafe acknowledged the signal and began to move across, cutting the prisoners off and leading enough soldiers to form a barrier, so their Jatan captives were completely surrounded.

"What now?" Revek asked as he came up beside Luc and Massi.

"I think it's best Massi and I go forward and talk. You and Rafe will have to keep watch for anyone who might decide it would be a good idea to try to make a break for the border and their friends on the other side."

Revek smiled, and it wasn't friendly.

"Don't kill unnecessarily," Luc warned, and Rev gave a grunt in response.

It would have to do.

Luc moved his mount to the side and Massi joined him, skirting the Rising Wave left flank and coming round the front of the square they'd created with the prisoners inside.

Luc glanced at Rafe and he gave a nod of understanding.

There were enough seasoned warriors making up the front line that Luc felt confident his people had control.

He and Massi approached the Gathering representatives, ignoring Tuart, even though the general tried to signal him.

If Tuart wanted him alone, then he wanted the opposite.

"The Turncoat King?" One of the old men in front of him, in a gray robe, asked.

"Commander of the Rising Wave, Luc Franck," Luc responded. He no longer had time for the title the Kassians had given him. They were defeated and their moniker could be buried with them. "And you are?"

The man acknowledged the edge to Luc's question with a nod. "Didier, of the Restina."

The other five introduced themselves, each giving a personal name and a Jatan tribe name.

"This is Massi, one of my lieutenants."

They greeted her respectfully.

"Will you not dismount, so we can talk more easily?" One of the councillors, a woman who'd introduced herself as Fallicia of the Ectare, asked.

"My experience so far with the Jatan is that you cannot be trusted at your word, so no." Luc tipped his head toward Tuart, who had edged forward as close as he could on his horse. "I don't think a single word General Tuart spoke to me turned out to be true."

The six councillors turned to looked at Tuart, and the general became stoney-faced.

"That is a grave insult."

"No, it is simply the truth," Massi said, keeping her voice even. "You said if there were Jatan soldiers raiding Cervantes, it was out-of-control officers, too young to know better. And what did we find? Two senior generals, hiding in secret camps and running raids so deep into Cervantes territory as to get within a two hour ride of our capital."

Tuart blinked. "I may have been misinformed. I didn't know that information was wrong when I gave it."

Luc studied him, letting the silence drag on until Tuart found it difficult to keep still.

"I was eavesdropping on your conversation with General Carvill in the secret camp. That time that Carvill was trying to torture information out of one of my scouts." Luc twisted his lips in a wry smile. "Would you like to amend your assertion that you thought you were telling the truth when you said the raids were unsanctioned. Because that's not what you said that night."

Tuart's eyes widened. "You were there? How?"

"There was a reason the Kassians wanted us as their soldiers," Luc said. "You might consider that, and how it ended for them, next time you think to attack us." He looked back at the Rising Wave behind him. "And how it ended for Hurst and Carvill."

"Will you let our people go?" The man who spoke had been hovering just behind Tuart. Luc had noticed him from the start, flanked by a man with similar bearing to Tuart. He wore a heavy ring on his finger and a thick chain around his neck.

If Luc were to guess, this was the commander of the Jatan forces, the general who oversaw the troops sent in by all the tribes.

He stared at the man without answering, and Didier stepped forward, his expression thoughtful. "This is High-general Baclar." He shot Baclar a look, as if to admonish him for not introducing himself.

"I will let your people go when I've seen some restitution for the damage, theft and harm that has been done to the villages of northern Kassia and Cervantes by you, as well a signed treaty that you will cease your aggression against us and return to your side of the border."

"Or else?" Baclar asked, voice soft.

"Or else the Rising Wave, Kassia, Venyatu, Funabi and Skäddar will be at war with the Jatan."

There was an audible gasp from the councillors.

Baclar blinked in response. "Do you have the right to make that threat?"

"I do." Luc gave him a slow smile. He turned to the councillors. "Have you not read the missive from the queen of Kassia?"

"We have." Fallicia bowed her head, refusing to meet his gaze. "We had not heard that Kassia had crowned a new queen."

So that was the excuse they were going to use. That they hadn't heard of Ava. That they would not take her demands seriously.

But Kym had told Tuart about her. He knew full well there was a new queen.

He wasn't going to stand around and deal with liars. Those days were gone.

"Well, then your information is sadly lacking. When you are ready to do what is right, and offer compensation for your crimes, when you're willing to live beside us peacefully, you can send a missive to Fernwell, and we will consider your deal." He turned, and Massi turned with him, her face serene at his decision.

She approved.

The Rising Wave soldiers on the front line who could hear him approved, too. He could see it in their expressions.

"Wait." Tuart's call stopped him, and he turned to look back over his shoulder.

"We have your scout, Kym, or had you forgotten?"

It was a last, desperate effort for some non-existent leverage.

Luc laughed. "Do you ever speak a single word of truth? I know you let her go. We had someone shadowing you until you did. You seem to have already forgotten that I was listening in on your conversation with General Carvill in the camp."

Tuart had forgotten. Luc saw it in his flinch.

"You will have to bring the money you plan to offer as compensation with you when you finally come to the table, not just promises of it," Luc said to the councillors. "Because I do not take your word as good."

"What will you do now?" Didier was glaring at Tuart.

"We will take our prisoners away and secure them. And then we will plan for war."

He began to move again.

"We didn't know the Rising Wave had taken Fernwell when we crossed the border." Fallicia's voice rose to be heard.

Luc stopped again. "That doesn't excuse your attack on small villages, on non-combatants, and the theft of their supplies."

He clicked his tongue and began riding again, with Massi already slightly ahead of him.

A cry went up from the Jatan prisoners, as they realized there would be no freedom for them today.

"I could shoot you in the back." Baclar's voice was clear enough over the noise.

Luc didn't stop, but he did turn to look over his shoulder. "And then we wouldn't just be planning for war, we would be *at* war. And you would stand alone against all your neighbours. Can Jatan afford that, after fighting Kassia for so long?"

If Kym was right about their numbers and their reserves, the force ranged against him now was their last gasp.

They had no more depth than this.

A sudden scream forced his attention back toward the Rising Wave and their prisoners.

One of the Cervantes soldiers on the right flank was being yanked from his horse by General Hurst, who slashed at him with a knife.

He must have hidden it and bided his time for a moment like this.

The Cervantes soldier fell, blood pouring from his arm, but he still tried to grab Hurst, to hold on to him as he tried to heave himself into the saddle.

And then Revek was on him, sword swinging as he separated Hurst's head from his shoulders.

There was a moment of absolute silence, and then a roar from the Jatan side, and the responding roar from the Rising Wave.

Luc had a sudden, inexplicable urge to lean forward over his

239

horse's neck, and he went with it, recognising the feel of Ava's magic tingling against his skin.

An arrow passed over his shoulder as he bent.

He glanced at Massi as he straightened, to find her lifting her hand back from her bow, return shot already taken.

A mounted archer near Tuart and Baclar gave a hoarse shout as he fell with an arrow in his eye.

"Stop!"

Didier, the councillor, shouted the word as he walked forward with his five fellow elders, hands waving.

The elder turned to Baclar, staring him down, and with a tight nod, the high-general waved at a soldier to his left and she raised a horn to her lips and blew.

As the last note sounded, the Jatan officers had control of their soldiers again.

Luc had simply put out his hand and made the gesture for hold, and the Rising Wave had obeyed.

When the noise was just a background hum, Didier walked toward him, Fallicia beside him.

"That was . . . unfortunate."

"Your high-general said he would shoot me in the back, and then someone right beside him tried to do just that. I would say that was more than just unfortunate." Luc glanced down at him, then up at Baclar, who was moving toward them, as well, Tuart at his side.

"I know I threatened to do it, but I swear that I did not order the archer to shoot. I don't know why he did." Baclar actually looked like he was telling the truth, and the invisible lines on his skin, the magic Ava had sewn into him, agreed.

But still . . .

"I can't believe you. Your people have done nothing but lie since I encountered them."

Tuart heaved a sigh. "I was trying to shield my fellow officers from their poor decisions, and I would do so again, but there is no excuse for shooting you in the back. We are not stupid enough to court a war with not only the Rising Wave but all your allies."

"And we can't ask the archer why he acted as he did, because your lieutenant is obviously a much better shot than he was." Baclar looked over at Massi with interest.

"Perhaps he thought you would be pleased with his actions, after what you said." Massi bared her teeth at him.

"Perhaps," Baclar acknowledged. "It was a foolish thing to say." He shook his head. "Your last comment before Hurst turned this into a near bloodbath makes me think you already know how close we are living to the edge of disaster. The Kassians have bled us almost dry, and we cannot fight a war with you, let alone Venyatu and Skäddar."

"We will need time to gather funds as recompense," Didier said, voice soft. "We are not saying your demands are not valid, but the thought of it worried us, and made us stupid, because we have very little left. We have obviously heard of the new Kassian queen, and we know you are in accord with each other." He looked over at where the Rising Wave soldiers were dragging Hurst's body toward them, with Revek holding the general's head by its hair. "Hurst should not have been in Cervantes, and he most definitely should not have been attacking civilians. But he is one of our generals, and we have to take responsibility for him."

Fallacia stepped up beside her fellow councillor and put her hands together, cupped palms facing upward in the universal gesture for peace. "Let us each go settle our people, and the generals and councillors will discuss a way forward. Will you join us for dinner tonight?" Fallicia moved her arm behind her to the open field that straddled the border. "We can make a fire in the open and resolve our issues without bloodshed. And negotiate for our people's return."

She winced as Hurst's body was dropped beside her. Baclar took Hurst's head from Revek with a look on his face that said he'd rather be doing anything else.

"Luc." Massi looked worried.

But Luc knew there were times you had to put your rage aside, just as sometimes blood was the only answer.

"I'll join you for a meal and a negotiation. But I'll have my people watching my back. If you don't know why one of your people shot at me, you may have more in your ranks with similar ideas."

"I'll speak to them," Baclar said. "But I agree. Have as many people as you like."

Luc gave a nod, twirled a finger in the air, and the Rising Wave began to move.

"That was nearly a full battle," Revek said when they were out of earshot.

Luc grunted in acknowledgement.

"We still won, though." Massi patted Rev's arm. She had always been more attuned to his feelings, and Luc guessed he had not come away from decapitating Hurst unscathed.

"We won that round," he agreed. "Now let's see if we can win the next."

CHAPTER 26

I lloa, the small village that straddled the Kassian-Grimwalt border, offering accommodation for people on both sides who missed the evening cut-off, was bathed in late afternoon light as the caravan came over the hill.

Ava had given Melodie and Gregor a farewell hug and dropped down from Gregor's cart just before the caravan crested the hill. She hung back to work a little more invisibility into her cap and then followed behind on foot as the four carts took the winding road down into the valley.

She would rather have a little distance in case there were people waiting for her in Illoa who were looking out for a caravan.

A massive rock stood in the river that separated Kassia from Grimwalt, its smooth, pale surface alight with the dancing reflections of the sun off the clear water.

She had been through here before with her parents, many years ago, and she was suddenly overwhelmed with nostalgia and a deep sense of loss. Herron had taken her parents at the prime of their lives, and she brushed away a tear as she thought of what could have been.

The carts rumbled through the town, slowing when they

reached the busy streets and making it easy for Ava to catch up enough to walk a cart's length behind. Gregor led the way, taking the direct route to the border post, and they all came to a stop at the bridge that separated Kassia from Grimwalt.

Two buildings stood, one on each side of the bridge, with a metal portcullis set between them. It was raised, as there were still a few hours before it needed to be lowered for the day.

There were guards milling around, but if one of them was paying close attention to the travelers, they were careful not to stand out.

Ava edged closer as her friends spoke with the border guards, and then moved to one side, watching, to be sure they were able to get over safely.

Reckhart was allowed through first and then Vanin Gruger, although both stopped just over the line, on the bridge itself, waiting for Madame Croter and Gregor to get approval.

Whatever Madame Croter said about her need for Gregor's help in Taunen must have been convincing enough, because eventually they let her and Gregor through.

As soon as they started moving across the bridge, Ava lifted a hand to wave goodbye and then lowered it abruptly.

They couldn't see her, and only Melodie and Gregor had known she was still with them, anyway.

She wondered if she would see Evelyn on the Kassian side of Illoa after the sun set. After all, where else could she go? The alternative was back the way they'd come, but Ava doubted she would want to get off the smoother, main road they had turned onto, and navigate the rough track on her own to find another way to Cattha.

Gregor's cart finally reached the far side, and then all four carts disappeared from sight. Ava turned away and pulled her coat closer around her, shivering as an icy breeze blew through the streets, off the high snow-capped mountains on the Grimwalt side.

The bustle of stalls providing food and clothing drew her deeper into the village, and as she neared them, she realized she had no money. She wished she'd been able to take some from Sirna before she'd escaped, but that would have made him aware that she wasn't as addled or confused as she'd seemed.

She would have to steal to survive, but she would try to find a way to compensate the merchants she took from when she was safely back in Fernwell.

She slipped some fruit and a pie from stalls that were packing up for the day, hoping that what she took would have been difficult to sell the next day, anyway.

Then she headed for the stables beside the tavern.

It was quiet. Long past the midday meal, but not day's end quite yet.

If she was going to hear any news, it would be at the stables, or, failing that, in the tavern itself. But she might have to wait for the evening crowd for that to happen.

If some of her friends from Fernwell were here, looking for her, she might recognize their livery on the saddles stored in the stable's tack room.

She ate as she walked, slipping around pedestrians, listening out for any talk that might help her.

There were a few conversations about the Rising Wave's victory at Fernwell, some speculation about whether the Kassian defeat would mean the Grimwaldian border would open to foreigners again, but nothing that told her who might be waiting for her in town; friend or foe.

As she got closer, she caught sight of someone walking from the tavern toward the big, open double doors of the stable entrance, and stumbled to a stop, heart hammering in her chest.

Deni?

Could it be?

She heaved in a quick breath so sharp her heart hurt and stumbled the first few steps as she followed him.

The inside of the stable was well-lit, the open doors making the entrance light and big windows along the outside wall letting in the afternoon sun.

They illuminated the long line of stalls, the clean floor, and the neat rows of equipment hanging from hooks.

Deni had walked to the fourth stall down and was leaning in, a carrot on his outstretched palm.

Ava stopped for a moment and felt some of the weight on her shoulders lift a little.

General Ru had not just sent anyone, she had sent Deni.

One of the few people who knew her secrets.

She wondered if Oscar were here, too, and felt her throat close as emotion swamped her.

For the second time tonight she brushed away a tear, but this time it was from happiness.

A low murmur of voices came from the tack room to her left—the stable workers, no doubt, relaxing in their office.

There was no one else near the horses other than Deni, and Ava made her way over to him.

Something about the way he leaned on the stall door, and the weariness on his face, made her think he was carrying a heavy weight.

"Deni." She used a whisper, standing far enough away from him that he wouldn't get a fright at a disembodied voice in his ear. "It's Ava."

He got a fright, anyway, dropping the carrot before his horse could take it, and spinning around to face her, eyes darting everywhere.

"I'm invisible. And think I should stay that way in public." She still could hardly believe how good it was to see him.

"Avasu?" He spoke on a sigh, as if in relief.

"It's me." She stepped closer, and he held out his arms. As soon as she was close enough to touch, he hauled her in, squeezing her hard.

She squeezed back. "I cannot tell you how happy I am to see you, my friend."

"When did you—?" He stopped short, stepping back and looking around. "Follow me to my room. We can talk there."

He led the way back across the open courtyard, through a side door to the tavern that bypassed the main tap room, taking them up a narrow staircase to the upper floor, to a long passage with doors on either side.

Deni stopped outside one of them, hand raised, and then lowered it and turned in her direction. "Taira is with me. You'll have to take off whatever is making you invisible before I call her." He kept his voice soft, and moved on to the next door along and opened it.

Ava slipped passed him, and once she was inside, pulled her cap off.

Deni made a sound in the back of his throat at the sight of her and hugged her close again, then turned back toward his door to fetch Taira.

"Wait." Ava reached out and put a hand on his arm. "It would be better if I travel with you wearing this." She held up the hat. "That would mean explaining to Taira—"

"Deni, did I hear you outside my—?" Taira was suddenly in the doorway, and she gave a gasp as the sight of Ava.

Before she could say anything, Deni yanked her into the room and slammed the door shut, putting a finger to his lips.

"Avasu." Taira's whisper wobbled with emotion.

Ava hugged her, and felt her eyes sting again.

This was clearly a day for tears.

"How long have you been in Illoa?" Deni asked when they finally pulled back a little.

"About an hour?" Ava lifted her shoulders. "We got here just before dusk."

"We?" Taira was still holding her arms, and her grip tightened.

"It's a long story."

Deni pulled a chair out for her to sit on, and she lowered herself down.

"Let's hear it. And we have news, ourselves."

She could see from the way Deni said it, the news wasn't good, but right now, in the company of friends, she felt they could over-come anything.

"THOSE BASTARDS." DENI STARED AT HER, THEN CROUCHED down, lifting a hand to her cheek. "I thought you looked gaunt. You're saying that magical rope sucked your life force? That they could literally see through you?"

She nodded. She had considered downplaying her weakness, but that wasn't fair to either of them. They needed to know she was not as capable as she was before. That she was still a long way from full strength.

"Avasu, I'm so sorry we didn't find you sooner." Taira crouched on her other side. "You definitely destroyed the rope?" She looked stricken that such a thing could exist, and even when Ava nodded, she still looked frightened at the thought.

"It was my decision not to take the back trail, and my mistake." Deni shook his head in dismay. "We would have found you sooner if I had."

"No." Ava put her hands on each of their shoulders. "You made the best choices you could, and here we are, together. How long have you been waiting in Illoa?"

"Only a day and a half," Deni admitted. "We got here early morning yesterday. I've been watching the bridge to see who was coming and going, and Taira spent her time talking to the locals, trying to get news or find out if you'd come through earlier."

"That's how we found out that the Jatan have been attacking villages in Cervantes. Someone who'd just been in Ta-lin was in the tavern last night. They were passing through Cervantes for Illoa, and that's all anyone in Ta-lin is talking about. Luc, Massi and Revek fought a battle a little to the south of the capital and captured a Jatan force. Word is they're marching them to the Jatan border for an exchange. Compensation for the attacks in return for the prisoners."

"How far are we from where they're having this exchange?" Ava's heart lifted. To be able to meet up with Luc . . .

She felt a prick of conscience at the thought that Tomas and Velda were still in a prison somewhere in Grimwalt. That she had yet to do a thing about rescuing them.

Still, crossing into Grimwalt now, by herself, with no official power behind her . . . that was a good way to get caught by the Speaker, rather than rescue her friends.

"It's about half a day's ride. And if we go that way, we will probably meet up with Oscar, Tras and Carrie. They took the northern route when the road split." Deni looked down at the ground, then back up at her. "But if I were being logical, I'd say we need to head for Fernwell now. General Ru has had nearly two weeks of trying to hide the fact that the queen of Kassia is gone. She'll be under huge strain keeping up the facade."

She had been so tired, so worn down, she'd barely given a thought to what consequences her disappearance would have caused for the general and the council of Kassia. They had been in the middle of delicate negotiations. That would have stopped, and General Ru would have had to come up with a believable lie as to why Ava was no longer able to attend to her duties.

"You're right." But she didn't want him to be. This was when duty and honor had to come before personal wishes. It was hard, though.

Very hard.

And even so, she wanted to find a way to go to Luc.

"You say you expect the Grimwaldians are waiting for the man who took you in Fernwell to come through here, though? That they're watching for you?" Taira looked up at her.

Ava nodded.

"Then traveling back to Fernwell with Luc and the soldiers of Rising Wave would be safer." Taira touched her knee and then rose from her crouch. "We know these people are desperate to get you. If Luc is only a half day's ride away, even if his business with the Jatan isn't finished by the time we get there, he'll be able to send some guards back with us. It will take us on a different route out of Illoa, as well. One they won't expect Ava to be on." She turned to Deni. "I'd prefer to have more protection for Ava than just you and me. She's still not fully recovered from what they did to her."

"That is very true." Deni gave a slow nod. "And traveling with a Rising Wave contingent will mean we can take a main route, not hide on backroads to avoid being seen." Deni glanced at her as if looking for approval. "That alone would save us much more than half a day."

She could have it all, after all.

Ava gave them both a bright smile. "Let's go."

CHAPTER 27

"You can't all come." Luc looked over the more than twenty soldiers who'd volunteered to protect him while he ate dinner and negotiated with the Jatan.

"Yes, they can." Massi was strapping on her quiver of arrows. "Either Baclar is lying about ordering that shot, or they have some internal conflict. Someone there wants you dead. And I won't let them try."

"The more eyes the better." Hallis, the man who spoke, was an old friend of Luc's mother. Younger than her by a few years but of her generation. Deep wrinkles radiated from his dark eyes, but he was still fit, and Luc knew those eyes missed very little.

The group who'd presented themselves for duty were a mix of young and old, some were experienced by their time in the Chosen camps, others by the long battle to keep the children who were left from the Kassians clutches.

Everyone had too much battle experience, Luc realized. The Cervantes had been plunged into twelve years of continuous fighting, and he wanted it to end.

Which only strengthened his resolve to make this negotiation work.

"Don't let the thought of more war make you consider a bad deal." Rafe spoke up, and Luc wondered what the captain had seen on his face to make such an astute comment. "We are tired, it's true, but we know our worth. What's another few weeks of fighting, compared to getting what we are owed? Because that's all the fight this lot has in them. If that."

There was a murmur of agreement.

Luc sighed. "All right. But some of you try to keep watch out of sight. It'll be better if they think there's only half of you there."

"I'll sort it out," Massi said.

Luc nodded. "Rafe, you stay here and manage the prisoners with Revek. After this afternoon's escape attempt, we can't have them trying again. It'll just ramp up the tension."

"I think they'll think long and hard before trying something like that again, after Rev's response." Rafe closed his hand over the hilt of his sword.

"How is Terrick?" The soldier who'd been attacked by Hurst was seriously injured, but last Luc heard, he was holding on.

"It's a deep wound." Rafe shrugged. They all knew it could go either way.

If Ava were here . . . Luc tried to push the wellspring of longing that rose up in him at the thought back down.

Wishing was not reality.

She was over a week's ride away, and there was no way he would want her in this volatile, dangerous situation, anyway.

He moved through the trees they had put between themselves and the Jatan, and saw a massive fire had been lit in the middle of the open field.

He left the situation of the guards to Massi, as she'd asked, trusting her to have his back covered. Two guards followed him, a pace or two behind, and when he swung down from his horse, he handed the reins to one of them.

All six councillors sat on low tree stumps that had been placed to the side of the fire. There were four other seats, and he saw Tuart and Baclar standing, waiting for him.

"We thought you might bring your lieutenant with you," Baclar said, indicating the fourth seat.

"She's close if I need her," Luc said in response, and Baclar looked out into the darkness.

Luc assumed he wouldn't catch sight of her, but he focused over Luc's shoulder and Luc saw his face change slightly.

He turned.

Massi sat easily in the saddle, her bow in her hand, arrow notched.

The soldiers who'd come with her were arranged in a semi-circle on either side of her, covering the whole Kassian side of the field.

The raw lust in Baclar's gaze as he studied Massi pricked Luc's anger. He knew his friend was beautiful. Her dark hair was pulled back in one of the complicated braids the Venyatux had taught her, and she sat straight and lethal on her mount, the firelight dancing over her face.

"Pity for you, you lead the army that harmed the newborn baby of one of her best friends," Luc murmured, and Baclar's gaze snapped to his, his face going blank as if he had not wanted to reveal quite so much.

"A baby?" Tuart repeated softly. "Surely not."

Luc swept his hand out toward the soldiers holding the line behind him. "I started this journey with eighty warriors. I now have many more. The injury to that baby has meant I've had to turn warriors away who wanted to join me."

Baclar swore. "Hurst always was a little shit. He didn't die a moment too soon."

Luc had a feeling if Hurst's head had lain at his feet at that moment, Baclar would have kicked it.

"Shall we get down to business?" Didier rose from where he and the other councillors had been sitting, watching and listening to the exchange.

Luc inclined his head and took a seat across from them, making sure his back was facing his own people. The two generals settled beside him to his left.

They talked about reparations, about border rights, and about what the old Kassian queen, Freida, had done to the Jatan in her effort to annex their mines.

"What is the situation at the mines?" Luc asked. "Are they being run by Kassian miners?"

There was a moment of hesitation.

Luc raised his brows. "You killed them?"

"Not all of them," Baclar was quick to state. "But some, yes."

"And the rest? Where are they?"

"Prisoners." Falacia glanced at the other councillors. "Some were very cruel to our miners, who'd been conscripted to keep working the shafts for the Kassians."

"If they are put on trial, and the trial is fair in accordance with your laws, I have no issue with them being punished for their crimes." Luc would not interfere in Jatan justice. "But some of them would surely have been simply under orders of the queen, and there through no fault of their own?"

"We undertake to sort the innocent from the guilty. And yes, it would be good to have trials. It would soothe the anger, I think." Didier noted the point down, as he had done since they started negotiating.

"We did not know the new queen would be so unlike her aunt," Tuart said.

"You didn't ask," Luc answered, and after a moment, he acknowledged the point with a nod.

They had been served a vegetable soup, and then roasted chicken flavoured with a tangy spice rub, and finally presented with coal bread, the bread cooked in cast iron camp ovens common through the whole continent. It took the place of dessert, served as it was with butter and jam.

Nothing lavish, but then Luc's unit wouldn't have been able to provide anything better than this, and Luc guessed even this meal was stretching the Jatan's provisions.

Finally, a young soldier moved about, offering mugs of ale.

The invisible line on Luc's forearm fizzled, igniting his skin, and he realized with a start he was rubbing his chest where the arrow had once pierced him.

He watched the soldier closely, looking for where his weapon might be hidden.

The soldier was closer to a boy than a man, seventeen, perhaps, and he was clearly nervous, but then, that would be normal, given the circumstances.

Luc lifted the mug of ale to his lips and took a shallow sip, keeping track as the boy moved to hand a mug to Fallacia.

As the ale hit the back of his throat, it began to burn.

He felt immobilized, stuck for a long moment in a strange confusion.

Then he managed to choke out the word that had leaped onto his tongue. "Poison."

As he said it, Baclar pitched forward, and he heard screams. He was surprised to find himself lying on the ground, and when he managed to glance up, it was to see Massi standing over him, bow held high. Some of her dark hair had escaped its braid and was blowing back in the wind. She looked like an avenging goddess, face cold and fierce.

And then he knew nothing more.

CHAPTER 28

After traveling north west for hours, they had slept for only two before they moved on.

Ava would have chosen not to sleep at all, but she felt better when they mounted their horses again, and she conceded Deni had been right to insist.

She had sewn energy and strength into her shirt before she'd settled onto the thin pallet by the fire Deni had built, and she hoped some of her increased vigour was as a result of her workings.

That would please her more than anything, other than reaching Luc as soon as they could.

She had also pulled out her braid, which had come loose, and redone it, refreshing the working in that, as well.

She wondered what it would look like to Melodie.

Some of the urgency was simply her need to get to Luc as quickly as she could, but both Deni and Taira were sure there had been someone suspicious nosing around the yard when they'd gone down to negotiate for another horse from the stable master.

Deni had ended up spinning a story of needing to meet a friend who's own horse had gone lame further up the road to explain why he needed to buy another mount.

From the way he and Taira spoke, the stranger had unsettled them, and she wondered if it was *Himself*. The mysterious man from Grimwalt.

Maybe he was getting impatient for Sirna to arrive and had crossed the bridge to the Kassian side for a look around.

Deni and Taira had ridden out of Illoa with the extra horse and met her in the forest to the north of the village, looking over their shoulders the whole way. There had been no argument from them when she'd set a punishing pace.

Now dawn had broken, making the ride even easier, although the road was in good condition and clear of traffic. They had passed no one so far.

"Look." Taira pointed up at the sky. "Smoke."

It wasn't the black of a burning roof or building. Ava sniffed the air and thought she caught the scent of pine. But it was a big fire, bigger than one would expect for a small camp.

"Keep back, Ava. Stay in the trees." Deni touched his head when Taira wasn't looking, to remind Ava to wear her knitted cap when she was out of sight, and she nodded.

She carried on with them for a little way longer, but when the sound of shouting, of fighting, filtered to them on the breeze, she lifted a hand to forestall Deni's admonishment, and pointed her horse into the thick forest that ran on either side of the road.

The forest wasn't deep.

Once she was amongst the trees she could see where the tree line ended. The disturbance was coming from that direction.

Luc was meeting the Jatan, Deni had said. That had the possibility of going badly, and whatever was happening up ahead definitely wasn't going well. But she thought they were still hours away from reaching the Rising Wave.

Perhaps they had made better time than she realized.

As soon as she was a few trees away from what seemed to be an open field, she slid off her horse and left it to pull on the long grass while she moved ahead on foot.

She had her cap pulled down on her head before she stepped

out into the open, and she stood for a moment in the sunlight, trying to work out what she was looking at.

A disaster was the first description to come to mind.

Two armies faced off against each other, both focused on something just out of her view in the space that lay between the two opposing sides.

That was where the smoke was coming from.

Ava began to walk around the Rising Wave soldiers, recognising some of the faces. It lifted her spirits just to see them again, despite the situation.

She checked to her right, to where the road emerged from between the trees, but either Deni and Taira were hanging back to assess the situation first, or the loop the road took was longer than she'd thought. Perhaps she had taken a shortcut by moving through the forest.

There seemed to be a lot more soldiers in the Rising Wave than had left with Luc from Fernwell, but some were wearing more homespun clothing and she guessed Luc had picked up extra fighters in Cervantes, keen to protect their country from the Jatan.

Even though the Rising Wave numbers had swelled significantly, they were still outnumbered two to one by the army on the other side of the field.

The Jatan were thinner, though, more ragged.

That might make them more dangerous, though, not less.

They looked desperate.

At last she rounded the front of the line, hunting for any sign of Luc. She saw Revek and Rafe, their horses a few paces in front of everyone else's, both watchful and tense.

Luc was nowhere in sight. Which, knowing him and his lead-from-the-front attitude, seemed impossible.

That is when she finally caught sight of what held the attention of both sides.

A small group of people were huddled together around a fire in the middle of the field. The fire was going strong, and only when she got closer did she see the reason.

Two round wooden stumps, the kind often used as seats around a fire pit, had rolled or been kicked into the fire and had caught alight.

They were burning in the sullen, smoky way of over-large pieces of dry wood.

People lay on the ground, some curled over, others spread-eagled.

One of the people curled over in a foetal position was Luc.

She was running before she even registered the fact.

Massi was there, she noticed peripherally, standing close to Luc, arrow pointing down, but everything about the way she stood projected a readiness to fire at a moment's notice.

Four other warriors that she guessed were Rising Wave stood with her, and one held a long knife to the throat of a young soldier kneeling in front of him.

Some of the people in the small group were wearing robes, and a few looked like senior officers. She guessed from the situation they were Jatan, but she didn't try to make sense of it, yet.

Everyone looked tired, and she sensed this had not just happened.

It was a stand-off that had dragged on for hours, and the breaking point was fast approaching.

She slowed her pace as she reached the small group, catching her breath so no one would hear her, and then slid silently through the bodies and the guards to kneel behind Luc, crouching at his back. Massi might step back and stand on her if she went to his front.

He was breathing, but his breath was labored.

She reached a hand around to place it against his chest, and she could feel the raspy rattle in his lungs.

She gave herself a moment to feel the hot, fiery rush of rage against Sirna and his rope.

She was much better, stronger, but she was still not what she was.

And she wanted all the power she could have to help her heart's choice.

If Sirna hadn't been dead already, she would have found a way to kill him again, and it would not have bothered her conscience at all.

But that type of thinking would not help Luc, so she drew in a quiet, deep breath and took out her needle and thread. As she did, she looked around at the other victims and saw a few were just hanging on to life, others were dead.

From the mugs of ale lying beside them, she guessed poison, and she wondered who wanted to poison both the Jatan and the Rising Wave.

Unless this was some kind of internal Jatan conflict.

She knew the Jatan had only come together to fight the Kassians. Perhaps one of the groups had decided that now was a good time to stage a takeover.

"Let our medics come over," someone shouted from the Jatan side.

"So they can finish our Commander off? I think not." Massi's derisive words were clear in the early morning air.

"Whoever has done this has done this to both of us." The officer shouting across sounded weary, as if this was not the first time he had said this.

"Obviously. But it was done by one of your people. So it could be the person you send over. How am I to know?" Massi called back.

There was silence.

Ava embroidered a garland of visilli flowers down the inside length of Luc's shirt hem, hoping no one in the Rising Wave front line would notice that his shirt was lifting up at the back.

Dried visilli flowers were one of the ingredients Dorea, the Rising Wave healer, had lost in a fire set by Kassian spies while the Rising Wave made its way to Fernwell, and one of the cures she had been most upset about losing.

She had told Ava that they were good at drawing poisons out of the body, and one of the first things Ava had done when they had taken Fernwell was give Dorea access to the palace apothecary, where she could restock what she had lost.

It took time to make the flowers realistic, although she worked faster and faster as her fingers learned the shape of the petals.

She wondered for the hundredth time, as she tied off her thread and pressed the embroidery against Luc's back, if it truly mattered what she chose to embroider. Whether it was her intention alone, or a combination of intention and the image she created, that made the magic work.

She had not been able to test it properly, but when she and Luc returned home, she would get serious about working it out.

If it meant she could work quicker, do less complicated embroidery to accomplish the same task, it could save lives.

But now was not the time to try. Not when lives hung in the balance. Especially the most precious life to her of all.

She had been aware of Massi and the Jatan officer exchanging more words with each other as she worked, the temper in both their voices and the huskiness in Massi's told her that they had been dancing with each other for a while. Their argument created a perception of progress, when really they were stalling for time, both playing the same game, waiting for something to tip the balance.

No one wanted to make the first move.

Massi was in a position to harm their leaders, those who were still alive, the Jatan were in a position to engage in serious battle, where the odds were in their favor.

Ava tuned out the discussion as she put her hand on Luc's back.

Was his breath a little easier?

She didn't know if she wanted it to be so much, she was imagining the progress.

But since she'd started to recover from the rope, her workings were becoming more effective.

No one had noticed her yet. There were no gasps of surprise at her having made it to the fire pit, which meant her invisibility held.

She smoothed her hand over the hem of Luc's shirt again, pressing it onto his skin. Maybe he needed more.

She moved on her knees to his head and twisted the fabric on the back of his shirt, along the neckline, to start working there. From the corner of her eye, she caught sight of Massi lifting her bow, and then turned her head to look as Massi shot off an arrow.

The Jatan officer stopped a few paces from the Jatan front line, the arrow quivering in the ground at his feet.

He lifted both hands and stepped back.

Luc sudddenly sucked in a deeper breath, and Massi went still, slowly turning her head to look down at him. "Luc?"

He was still fighting the poison, still unconscious, and Massi turned back, but Ava thought she was a little less stiff at this indication that Luc was doing better.

The success of her visilli flowers spurred her on to work faster on the second embroidery at the back of his neck. Relief made her fingers tremble a little at the evidence she was making a difference.

She tied off a garland of three flowers, pressed the shirt down against his skin, and then leaned over him, awkwardly lifting the cuff of his sleeve. She was forced to lean against his back and use his side to support her body so she could use both hands.

The sound coming from both armies had risen since the Jatan officer had tried to breach the distance and Massi had shot her arrow.

It swelled, and she had a horrible feeling that it was rising to a crescendo that would break in ways that no one would like.

She just embroidered one flower under his cuff. She could feel Luc's rib cage move up and down where she leaned against him, and she was afraid she was hurting him.

When she finished, she bent to bite off the thread with her teeth and a small movement made her turn her head. Her face was close to his and she looked directly into his eyes, which were open in narrow slits.

Heart racing, she pressed his cuff down deliberately onto the skin of his inner wrist, holding it there, and then reached out with her other hand and put a finger lightly against his lips.

He had told her before he could see her when she was wearing her invisibility workings, not clearly, but as a shadowy shape.

He would know it was her.

He parted cracked lips and gently bit the top of her finger.

She drew in a quick breath, fighting a sob, and Massi turned back again, worry on her face.

Luc coughed to cover for her, and then struggled to sit up.

Ava moved back to give him space, looping an arm around his shoulder and squeezing tight for a moment, her heart so full of relief, she struggled not to tremble.

"I'll go and see if I can help those who are still alive," she whispered in his ear, and he gave a tiny nod.

She scooted back, shaking out the tension that had gripped her until now, and then rose to her feet and walked to the next person, a soldier of some seniority, she guessed, by the style and formality of his clothing.

He was breathing, but only just, and seemed in worse condition than Luc had been.

She knelt beside him and got to work.

CHAPTER 29

A va had felt . . . frail.

Luc could only see her as a faint shadow, but he was sure he felt her ribs as she leaned against him to sew healing into his sleeve. Her weight had hardly registered.

He didn't understand how she was here. Had she come with another unit from Fernwell?

Massi put a hand down to help him up, and he could see the stark relief on her face as he pushed up to sitting.

Standing might be a stretch for now, but at least he was conscious and able to participate in what looked to have been a night-long stand-off.

He could see the exhaustion in Massi's eyes.

He opened his mouth to speak and started coughing again. It hurt, and tears leaked out of the corners of his eyes as he bent over, trying to suck in air.

Whatever the poison had been, it had affected his lungs, freezing them.

He had come slowly back to consciousness, felt the tight iron band around his chest begin to loosen, while Ava had been sewing a working into his collar.

Now, while the tightness was still there, it was lifting with every breath, and he spent a moment just relishing being able to drag air into his lungs.

He studied the Jatan when he was finally able to lift his head again, looking for who among the senior officers in the front line might not be so happy at his recovery.

He glanced at the other victims lying around him, all the councillors, as well as Baclar and Tuart, and saw that he was in the best shape.

Didier was clearly dead, his eyes open and staring up at the sky.

A shadow hovered over Fallacia, which meant Ava was sewing something into her clothing. The councillor must be hanging on.

General Tuart shifted position and started to cough. He guessed Ava had already seen to him, although the Jatan's eyes were still closed.

"The poison is wearing off." Massi's legs were quivering, and Luc wondered if she had been standing over him like that all night.

He had a feeling she had.

He circled his wrist with his thumb and fingers, pressing the embroidery Ava had stitched under his cuff hard against his skin, and took another deep breath.

He got onto his knees and slowly pushed himself up, looking back to the Rising Wave. He couldn't see any new troops there, so the question rose up again. Where had Ava come from?

Someone made a strange sound, like a trapped animal, and he turned in that direction.

Eduard, one of the veteran Cervantes warriors who'd come with them from Versai, was standing with a knife to a young soldier's throat.

Luc stared at him, and then realization hit.

This was the boy who'd served them the ale.

"Who poisoned the ale?" he asked.

Eduard's gaze snapped across to him briefly, and he saw the flare of relief in the old warrior's eyes.

The boy hunched his shoulders and said nothing.

"He hasn't spoken a word," Eduard said.

"Luc!"

Luc turned and saw Revek had dismounted and was walking toward him across the field.

A flurry of movement exploded on the Jatan side, with bows drawn and swords pulled from scabbards.

"No further!"

Luc recognized the voice of the Jatan officer who shouted to Revek. He had heard it while Ava crouched over him, working her magic, in a back and forth with Massi.

Revek stopped and slowly backed away, into the front line.

"Who is that one?" he asked Massi, nodding to the Jatan.

She lifted a shoulder. "Says he's Baclar's aide. Captain Bartholomew."

Luc studied the man. He was agitated, and his gaze kept going to Baclar.

Ava was bent over the high-general now, he saw by the shadow that blurred the high-general's right side.

If he were to take a guess as to who was responsible for this mess from the Jatan camp, he'd choose Lieutenant Hurst. His father had been killed yesterday, and Luc had a feeling the lieutenant would have been thirsty for revenge.

Interesting that he had gone after not only Luc, but his own leaders, as well.

He moved even closer to Massi, and breathed into her ear. "Where is the unit that Ava came with? Is it enough to tip the balance of numbers in our favor?"

She turned her head, looking him straight in the eye. "What are you talking about?"

"Ava." He was on dangerous ground here, but Massi had indicated in the past she suspected Ava was a spell caster, although Ava had never taken her into her confidence.

Massi had been in the grip of a spell when she had first met Ava, and she had not been her normal, welcoming self to his heart's choice.

It had caused a distance between the two women he was closest to, and it would take more time than they had had so far since they took Fernwell to bridge it.

"Ava is here." He had to tell her this. If Ava had not come with a unit, he didn't understand what was going on, and Massi had at least been awake and aware since last night, unlike himself. "How else do you think I'm standing right now?"

Massi narrowed her eyes. "You think Ava's here and she healed you?"

"I know Ava's here, I spoke to her, she healed me, and she's healing Baclar right now."

Massi looked over at Baclar.

The shadow that was Ava was still bent over the high-general.

Massi looked back at him, worry in her gaze.

She thought he was hallucinating.

"Let's say I'm right, how would Ava have gotten here? Has a new unit arrived?"

"No." Massi shook her head, glanced at the slowly recovering Jatan, looked back at him again. "She's here?"

He nodded.

"How do I not see her?"

He wiggled his fingers, and she snorted out a laugh.

"Is that your way of saying spell craft?"

They had kept their voices pitched to the low, almost inaudible level they had used when they were in the Chosen camps together, where talking to each other could get them punished.

"What's going on?" The shout came from Bartholomew.

Luc stepped in front of Massi and gestured to the Jatan officer to approach.

"I won't get an arrow in my foot?" Bartholomew asked, gaze flicking over Luc's shoulder.

Massi smiled, cold and sharp. "If you were going to have an arrow in your foot, it would already be there."

Bartholomew walked forward and Luc met him halfway, barring

the captain's access to his boss, but letting him get a closer look at him.

"I have to say, this has all the markings of jura poisoning but I've never known anyone to recover from it." Bartholomew studied his face, as if looking for some reason for his recovery.

"I saw the boy's nerves, the one serving the ale, and I barely took a sip of my drink, watching to see if he went for a weapon." Luc lifted a shoulder. "I didn't realize the weapon was already deployed."

"Still," Bartholomew shook his head. "Even the smallest amount is deadly, it just takes the recipient longer to die."

Luc didn't respond, refusing to offer any explanation as to his survival. "We all seem to be recovering. Those of us who aren't already dead." He paused, decided to distract the captain. "Do you Jatan carry around poison as a matter of course?"

Bartholomew glowered. "It's a common root found in the mountains. Anyone could have picked some, if they were intent on mischief."

Intent on murder, more like, but Luc didn't correct him.

Tuart began coughing again, and curled in on himself a little tighter.

Fallacia's eyes were open now, and she had rolled herself over onto her side, panting.

Baclar's breathing was audible, a deep sawing in and out of air, but he was still unconscious.

Two other councillors were starting to recover, another was dead, like Didier. Ava hadn't reached the final one, yet, although he still seemed to be breathing.

"You question the boy," Luc invited. "He won't speak to us." He turned and motioned to Eduard, who dragged the boy forward.

"What's your name?" Bartholomew asked.

The boy looked wildly at the captain, then flicked his gaze into the crowd of Jatan a little way back. "Simon."

"This was a peaceful meeting, Simon, meant to secure the future of Jatan. Why would you jeopardise that?"

"I thought it was just him." Simon jerked his head toward Luc. "They said the poison was at the bottom of his cup, that only he would fall."

"Who's they?"

Again, his gaze flicked to the line of Jatan soldiers. "I don't know."

The lie was so obvious, Bartholomew lost his friendliness. "I won't ask you again. Who's they?"

An arrow smacked into Simon's chest, and the young soldier staggered back into Eduard's arms.

"Was it Hurst?" Luc asked Simon as Eduard lowered him down.

Bartholomew looked at him sharply, but Luc's attention was on the boy. Blood bubbled on his lips and he turned and coughed some up.

"Was it Hurst?" Luc bent down on one knee, but Simon gave a sigh and went limp.

"He's gone," Eduard said.

Bartholomew rose up, and Luc saw absolute fury in his eyes as he turned to his own army. "Who shot that arrow?" His voice quivered with outrage.

There was silence in response, except for a shuffling nervousness from the soldiers in the line.

"Someone here tried to kill all our councillors, the high-general and General Tuart." Bartholomew sounded incredulous. "Why would you protect someone like that? Someone who doesn't even have the courage of their convictions to admit they're responsible, who kills a boy rather than have their name known."

"It was Lieutenant Hurst!" The shout came from a few rows back from the front line.

A moment passed and then Hurst pushed his way out from the line. "I have the courage of my convictions."

"Of course." Luc swept his arm at the victims behind him, and at the dead boy at his feet. "Only after you're outed, you come forward. You poison and you ambush. You're a real prince."

"I'm a strategist." Hurst's tone was defensive. He obviously thought he held a certain amount of sway among the troops, and he risked losing them if they saw him as a coward.

"No, you're a traitor." Bartholomew glanced back at Baclar, but the captain's boss was still lying on the ground. "What were you hoping to achieve?"

"They were going to sell us out." Hurst flicked his hand at the councillors. "We can't afford reparations. We were at war, and we needed supplies. There was no shame in what we did, raiding villages for food."

"And your father's death, caused by his own arrogance and stupidity, didn't figure in to your decision?" Massi had stepped closer, as well, and she scoffed at Hurst. "Why don't you admit this is a personal vendetta? You thought the councillors would all die, your soldiers would kill the rest of us, and somehow you would walk out of this with your father's place in the army, and power in the running of Jatan."

Bartholomew looked at her with interest. "That's a neat summary." He looked at Hurst. "Your mistake was using poison that didn't kill them all straight away. Then, I admit, it would have been a bloodbath."

"Jura makes everything taste too bitter. It had to be diluted. But they should all be dying, if not dead." Hurst seemed at a loss. "I've never heard of anyone surviving jura poisoning before."

As he said the words, Baclar pushed himself to his hands and knees.

Bartholomew looked at Luc and he gave a nod. The captain ran over to his general and knelt beside him.

A prickle of warning ran over Luc, a tingling of his skin, and he swung to face the Jatan, moving in front of Baclar as another arrow flew from between the Jatan rows toward the high-general and his aide.

He was slow, not his usual self, but he was fast enough to put himself in the way.

The arrow lodged in his chest and he pulled it out from where it had caught in his cloak, snapped it in two with both hands, and threw it on the ground.

Massi had raised her bow as soon as the shot was fired, but there was no clear target. The Jatan had closed ranks.

"As I said," Luc sneered at Hurst. "A coward."

The soldiers in the front line stared at him, wide-eyed.

They would think he was wearing protective armor beneath his cloak, and in a way, they were right. His woolen tunic, thanks to Ava, *was* the protective armor.

"I didn't order that shot." Hurst lifted both hands. "I was standing here the whole time."

"Hear that?" Massi called out to the soldiers in front of them. "He'll let you dangle for that, pretend he didn't tell you to take a shot if Baclar looked like he was actually going to live."

"Enough. We need to attack them now." Hurst stepped back behind the line, away from the aim of Massi's bow, although his voice was still clear. "We need to secure Jatan's future, and we can't do that if we're in debt to Kassia." He raised his voice. "They were the ones who attacked us first, remember?"

"That regime has passed," Luc said. "We're the reason the Kassians withdrew from your border to begin with. Do you really want to go to war with us and the rest of the region over Hurst's revenge for his father's death and his personal pursuit of power?"

"Don't listen to him." Hurst's voice rose even higher. "This is our enemy, and we outnumber his army two to one. If we fight now, we won't have to fight again later."

Luc looked over at Baclar, waiting for him to say something, but the high-general was still coughing, hanging his head as he tried to draw in breath.

He felt the touch of a hand on his own, and angled himself toward the shadow beside him.

Ava leaned up against him, going up on tiptoe to reach his ear. "I've done what I can, but I'm not at full strength."

Again, he sensed she was thinner, less substantial than she'd been before. He turned to face the Rising Wave, so the Jatan wouldn't see his lips move. "How did you get here? Is there another unit in the area?"

"No." She turned with him. "I came with Taira and Deni, but that's all. It's a long story."

They were going to have to fight. He sensed it in the tension behind him.

The Jatan knew they had caught themselves in a trap.

It would be easier for them to simply throw themselves into a battle they thought they had a good chance of winning, and pretend it was inevitable if they ever had to justify it to their leaders back in Jatan.

Except Luc thought the Rising Wave would win.

They were Cervantes, after all, and they were rested, fed and angry.

They had the advantage, although the Jatan didn't realize it.

But there would be losses and Luc was tired of losses. He was reluctant to engage when there was a peaceful way out.

"Ava, go hide in the woods." She was a superb fighter, but he had the feeling she wasn't as capable as she had been when she'd been beating her Venyatux friends in ring fights every night for sport. Not with the delicate feel of her body against his right now. Bird-like and fragile.

"I won't leave you." She murmured the words as she stood beside him, turning to face the Jatan again.

"If you stay safe in the woods, you can help with the healing when it's over. And there will be plenty of healing to do." He heard the grimness in his own tone.

She held still, then sighed. "I am invisible. I'm not up to my usual strength, but I'll stab the Jatan in the back, or even in the front, if I get the chance."

"Ava."

"I'll make myself small and no one will know I'm here. I won't hide while everyone else fights." She brushed her lips against his neck—all she could reach without him bending down—and that would just look strange to those watching him. "If it makes you feel better, I'll go stand near the Jatan councillors, keep an eye on them."

He acknowledged the wisdom in that. "Their survival would help us," he admitted. "But be careful."

"Always." Her fingers squeezed his hand and then he felt her leave. He ached where her body had pressed, warm, against his. He wanted to call her back, to tell her not to take any chances, but there was no way to do that.

"Luc." Massi was watching him. "All right?"

He moved toward her. "Ava has done what she can to purge the poison," he murmured to her. "She's going to stay hidden and watch over the Jatan councillors, Baclar and Tuart. We can't move them without Hurst using it as an excuse to attack. But you and your team should go to the back of the line. You haven't slept in a day's cycle. If you have to do something, organize the archers. Delegate."

Her eyes had dark bruises under them. "I'll get my team to the back, but I'm not going to sit and bark orders, Luc." She rubbed her eyes. "I am tired, but there will be no rest for me while we're under attack."

The inevitability of what was about to happen settled on his shoulders, heavy as a robe of chain mail, as Massi ordered Eduard and the other three to the back.

When they saw she wasn't going, they were unhappy about it, but they went.

Tuart and Baclar were trying to sit up, Bartholomew helping them. Both of them were so much better than they had been, but Luc wondered how long they would last with Hurst's assassins in the Jatan line. The moment they engaged, the two generals would be completely vulnerable—Bartholomew couldn't protect them both against so many.

Luc could sense the moment of battle was almost upon them.

The Jatan's second row was already fitting arrows to bows all down the line, and Massi lifted her arm and gave a signal.

Luc didn't look back, but he knew his own archers would have just responded in kind.

"Stand behind me," he said to her. "You can shoot over my shoulder."

She moved slowly to do just that, as if every step weighed on her. "What is it that you're wearing under there?" she asked, touching his back. "And where did you get it?"

Massi hadn't been in Fernwell when he'd survived at least ten arrows shot at him in the street, she'd been securing their victory in Bartolo with Raun-Tu, and until now, he'd been able to give a convincing performance of ducking or bending at just the right moment, the arrow never actually touching him.

The arrow directly to his chest had eliminated that option.

"Special armor." That wasn't a lie.

"Ava?" she asked after a long pause.

He sighed. "Yes."

"Maybe she and I will be friends one day and she'll make some for me."

"Maybe." He hoped that would definitely happen, but now was not the time to discuss it.

The Jatan side looked like they were waiting for an order to attack, but Luc wondered if Hurst would commit that far. He would not want any of the blood that would soon be spilled to be linked back to him. Especially not the councillors and Baclar's blood.

Luc glanced over at the high-general.

Bartholomew had been helping him, but when the archers had begun to pull their bows, he stumbled to his feet.

"Traitors," he screamed at them, and Luc saw a number of them flinch. "When the armies of the Rising Wave come crashing down on your villages, will you be able to look your children in the eye and admit that the reason they are there is because of what you did today?"

Some of the soldiers lowered their weapons, and Luc sensed a deep unease move through the ranks.

This was not a united force, clear in their purpose.

Hurst may have whipped up some resentment for the councillors, and even Baclar, but he wasn't leading anymore. Not when it came down to hard action.

Some of them might just be wondering why.

Others, though, were feeling enough nerves to do something stupid.

Luc's soldiers behind him were quiet, they would have spread out on silent feet.

The tinder was dry, and the smallest of sparks would set it off.

He was aware of the stakes, but he was the commander of the enemy force. There was no way anything he said would sway the Jatan.

"Get ready," he murmured to Massi, and then turned his head to where the councillors lay, where Ava was crouched, a wispy shadow amongst the sick and dead.

"Lower your weapons," Bartholomew ordered, but he had already reached everyone he was going to reach. The rest were not going to listen to him.

One of the soldiers in the front line lifted their sword up and back, ready to run forward, and behind him, Luc heard the rattle of Massi's quiver.

A sound wafted toward them on the light breeze, a deep, mournful cry that Luc at first thought had been made by some strange animal.

Then it came again, and he recognized it as a horn.

It meant nothing to him, but the Jatan recognized it.

They faltered in their focus, turning left toward the call, which came a third time from the road through the forest.

An army appeared.

Or, not an army, but at least twenty soldiers, maybe a little more, with blue and green patterns on their faces, riding the small, hardy ponies from the Skäddar mountains.

Kikir rode at the front with a man and a woman on either side of him, and he caught Luc's gaze and rode straight toward him, using a signal to order the rest of his unit to join the Rising Wave.

The Skäddar's arrival, their immediate support for the Rising Wave, had a devastating effect on the Jatan.

They lowered their weapons.

Some placed their swords on the ground in a more obvious surrender.

"We still outnumber them." Hurst's words were furious.

"Is that you, Hurst? All the way at the back of the line?" Bartholomew called.

His jeer was met with silence, as many of the Jatan turned to look for Hurst's place among them.

"My friend, it seems we are just in time." Kikir extended his hand down from his seat in the saddle, and Luc grinned up at him, clasping it in his own.

"Your timing is impeccable."

Kikir looked across at the Jatan forces, then at the bodies and the recovering victims close to Luc. "I cannot wait to hear this story," he said.

"I will be happy to tell it," Luc said. "But how did you come to be here?" The last he had heard, Kikir was headed home to Skäddar to press the case for an alliance with the Rising Wave. That had been less than a week ago. It seemed impossible he would have managed to win over the Skäddar Collective so quickly.

Kikir lifted his shoulder. "Some of my people became worried about me, about my long absence, and they began to hear rumors of our victory over the Kassians. They sent a small party to investigate, and we met where the Kassian border touches both Jatan and Grimwalt."

Luc could see from Kikir's expression that had been a very good reunion.

"You didn't keep on going, back to Skäddar?"

"No." Kikir seemed uncomfortable all of a sudden. As if unsure of himself. "We planned to, but while we were camped for the night, just inside Kassia's northern-most edge, I found something." He shrugged, looking away. "I had the feeling Ava needed help."

"Ava?" Luc's gaze flicked to the Jatan councillors again, but the thin shadow was gone.

Kikir put a hand in his pocket and held something out. Luc took it, frowning. A twist of thin bark around a black feather.

The moment he touched it, he felt a sudden, tight grip of pressure. Of a need to make sure Ava was safe.

He looked up at the Skäddar warrior. "She is here. And she is safe." His voice was strained, as if something was constricting his throat.

Kikir blew out a breath and lifted his shoulders, as if he had been relieved of a burden. "I would like to hear that story, too. I fought my better judgment all the way through the forests. I don't know why I had such a strong feeling that Ava had made that, and that she needed help. It floated to us on the wind, and it was just out of curiosity that I caught it as it floated by. It could have come from anywhere." He looked back at his own unit, who were silent as they spread along the Rising Wave line. "We decided to head for Illoa, where there's a bridge from Kassia into Grimwalt, to see what news we could find there, but sometime yesterday I had the sense we should go west, and then we heard from a traveller about your meeting with the Jatan, so we headed here as fast as we could."

Luc nodded, without giving anything away.

"Who's that with General Tuart?" Kikir asked, his gaze moving to Baclar and Tuart, who were now sitting up, with Bartholomew hovering over them.

"The Jatan high-general, Baclar, and his aide."

"The story gets more interesting by the minute," Kikir said, and slid from his horse.

Luc looked down at the twist of bark on his palm. "Yes, it does."

CHAPTER 30

Ava watched from the trees as Luc and Kikir walked over to Baclar, crouching in front of him.

The conversation was short. Bartholomew helped his boss up, calling to soldiers in the Jatan front line for help.

Three of them ran forward, one to take Baclar's other side, the others to assist Tuart, and after a short while, a man and a woman strode through the Jatan army from the back, both wearing robes rather than the trousers and jackets of the soldiers, to bend over the four surviving councillors.

Ava had done all she could for them. Three would definitely make it, but the oldest survivor, a grizzled man with white hair and dark eyes, might not.

She tried to make peace with the fact.

He would find the strength to fight, or he would decide his time had come.

She turned away, picking through the forest to where she'd left her horse.

She moved silently, and was glad she had when she found Deni and Taira waiting beside her horse.

She pulled off her cap and stuffed it into the inner pocket of her coat before she strode toward them, making more noise.

"Thank goodness." Taira leaned back against a tree, obviously relieved to see her. "We hid in the forest when we heard horses, but Deni went to look and says it's the Skäddar?"

Ava nodded. "I was watching the situation with the Jatan, hoping to help, but then Kikir and his friends arrived and tipped the balance in our favor."

Deni nodded. "The Jatan saw the wisdom in stepping back from hostilities, before they would be forced to surrender."

"True." Ava gave it some thought. "They're in a better position now than if they'd attacked. But it was close."

"Very close." Deni sounded a little shaky.

"Well, let's go see our old friends." Ava let herself smile. "It's been hard to watch instead of standing with them."

They led their horses out into the open, and Ava smiled at the guards who turned their arrows on them, faces set.

"They remind me of you, Deni. The first time we met." She lifted a hand and waved.

Rafe walked toward them, face stern, and she laughed as he nearly stumbled when he realized who it was.

"What are you—?" He stopped, mouth open, and signaled to the guards to lower their bows.

Her gaze skipped over him, though, because Luc was walking toward her, face unreadable, although she sensed a tension in him.

She didn't understand it, but it didn't matter, he was here, he was unharmed, and they were together again.

Nothing else mattered.

She dropped her reins, knowing Deni would take them, and moved toward him.

Crouching over the poison victims, and the energy it had taken to embroider the flowers, had made her stiff. Not to mention the hard ride they had made to get here. She was dismayed to find that she wasn't able to move as fast as she wanted to.

She almost fell into his arms, despite the fact that they had spoken, touched, just half an hour before.

She thought she was done with tears, but she found that wasn't true.

It was so unlike her, she kept her face pressed against his shirt, and if he felt the damp evidence against his skin, he said nothing, content to brush one hand down her back and hold her close with the other.

They were left alone.

Except . . . She forced herself to look up at Luc. "Don't let Deni and Taira say anything about how I got here." She thought of General Ru, of everything she would have done to keep Ava' disappearance quiet, and knew they had to protect the lie.

"Deni." Luc's voice rose above the exclamations of shock and surprise coming from the Rising Wave unit.

"Commander." Deni stepped close, and Ava turned to him.

If he was surprised to see the tears on her cheeks, he didn't show it.

"We need a story to explain my presence," she told him softly.

"I have one. Raun-Tu and I worked it out together before I left, in case you were seen after we found you. You were needed up on the border to negotiate a deal with the Jatan. And here you are." He studied her face, and then gave a nod when she inclined her head in agreement.

"And here I am." She knew it would take a bit of work to be believable, but it was good enough.

Deni walked off, calling out a teasing insult to one of the Cervantes soldiers, and again, Ava and Luc were alone.

"What is the truth?" Luc studied her, and she could see he was trying not to let his true emotions show.

"I was taken from Fernwell by people working for Grimwalt's Speaker." She said nothing more, but his nostrils flared.

"Did Deni and Taira rescue you?"

She shook her head. "I rescued myself, but I knew General Ru would have sent someone to find me, and so I looked for them in

Illoa. We heard there that you were meeting with the Jatan on the border here, and we rode through the night to get here."

"Ava." He seemed unable to say anything more, but there was death in his eyes. Cold, black death.

"You will have to wait in line," she told him, lifting a hand to cup the back of his neck. "Harm was done to me, and I do not intend to forget."

She slid her thumb under his collar, found her visilli flower embroidery and pressed it into his nape. "How do you feel?"

"Better." He glanced over at the Jatan councillors, who were now lying on comfortable pallets, watched over by healers. "I was the least affected, and I know your magic is the reason." He stepped back, hands still on her, as if he were afraid to let her go. "We cannot let this stand, Ava. Grimwalt has all but declared war on us by kidnapping you."

She inclined her head. "Except, I don't think many in Grimwalt know. This was a private mission by the Speaker. He wants to use me to keep control of the Grimwalt court. If we confront them, I think we'll find that most of the court's representatives will be horrified."

His mouth formed a stubborn line. "I'd rather not be at war with Grimwalt, especially as our relationship with Jatan is precarious, but the Speaker cannot be allowed to walk away from this. If I have to go into Grimwalt and kill him myself, he will not escape justice."

"Agreed. This has to end." And she would like to do that ending herself. Especially as Velda and Tomas might be in danger because of the Speaker, as well. She needed to make sure her friends were safe.

She caught sight of Kikir, who had just finished speaking to Revek and Rafe, and she waved to him.

"Having the Skäddar come to support you as allies really took the Jatan's legs out from under them," she said to Luc. "That was a masterstroke."

Luc gave a low chuckle at that, but before she could ask him what was so funny, Kikir strode over, enveloping her in a hug.

"You are safe," he said it so fervently, she wondered if he knew something about her abduction. He stepped back, eyes narrowing. "Although you are not well, Avasu. What has happened?"

"It's a long story, but all is well now."

"Good." He turned to Luc and seemed about to ask something, when one of his fellow warriors called to him, and he reluctantly strode off.

Luc put a hand in his pocket and brought something out.

"Do you recognize this?"

She stared at it in amazement. "Where did you get it?"

"Kikir found it floating through his camp just before he and his Skäddar friends were set to return home. It compelled him back into Kassia, all the way here."

Ava lifted her eyes to his, shocked and speechless.

"I thought I had almost no power when I made that," she whispered. "I felt so weak."

"What did they do to you?" Luc sounded cold, but she could see from the expression on his face he was anything but.

"They used a rope, like the one they used in the camp when they tried to take me before. Something that sucks the energy out of you, makes you too weak to fight. It sucked everything out of me. My magic, my energy, my will to keep going. I managed to destroy it, to substitute it with a fake, but it still took me a long time to regain enough strength to escape, and at times, I thought I'd never be the same."

"Ava." He pulled her back into his arms and she realized she was shivering. "It's all right," he crooned. "I will kill them all."

CHAPTER 31

There was nothing to do but wait for Baclar and at least some of the councillors to recover.

Hurst had disappeared, according to Bartholomew, and Luc believed him. Unless the captain had murdered Hurst and pretended he couldn't find him.

Either way, the lieutenant was gone, and he was Baclar's problem now.

Luc wanted to be done with the Jatan. He was sick of them and their pathetic excuses, but the time to strike a deal with them was now, while they were weak, on the defensive, and very much aware of the rapport between the Skäddar and the Rising Wave.

It would be foolish to leave without a treaty, and he was no fool, even though General Ru was holding the fort in Fernwell, no doubt on the razor's edge between truce and war, and Grimwalt sat, a day's ride away, deserving of all his wrath.

Still, it wouldn't hurt Ava to have a good night's rest. She said very little about her time in her captor's care, but he could see from the gaunt hollows in her cheeks that she had not been well-treated.

He had to push the thought from his mind, because it nearly

overwhelmed him with rage each time he glimpsed the painful thinness of her wrists, or the dark smudges beneath her eyes.

She sat by the fire beside him now, finishing the last of her evening meal, chatting happily with old friends and drawing the warriors from Cervantes who she didn't know, and some of Kikir's Skäddar unit, into the conversation as well. She seemed not to notice the worry in the eyes of everyone around her, but he saw it.

More than one person flicked a look at him, searching for an answer as to her condition, and he had given a tiny shake of his head in response.

Massi emerged near the end of the meal, having been persuaded earlier to sleep for a few hours, and she took a bowl of stew and sat on his other side, yawning, content to eat and listen to the conversation swirling around her.

She hadn't said anything more to him about Ava since this morning, but he sensed her focus sharpening when she'd scraped her bowl clean and slid off the log they were sitting on to lean back against it, listening to the chatter.

The conversation turned to Fernwell, to what was going on there, and Ava kept her answers vague, getting quieter and quieter, until Luc stood and she lifted a hand for him to pull her up without saying anything.

"Time to rest."

"I'll come with you," Massi said, pushing herself to her feet. "There're a few things I need to discuss."

They walked to where the tents were set up, and Luc led the way to his one, which was indistinguishable from the others.

"What do I need to know?" Massi asked when they got there, keeping her voice low.

Luc thought about it. It was better if someone other than just Deni, Taira and him knew the situation. "The Speaker of Grimwalt finally succeeded in abducting Ava."

Massi's sharp inhalation was audible.

"Ava managed to get away. General Ru sent Deni after her." Luc thought about it, and turned to Ava. "She didn't just send Deni and Taira, did she?"

Ava shook her head. "There was a whole team. But the abductors left a false trail in Bartolo, and Deni split the team up there. Then they reached a fork in the road, and split again. By the time I found them in Illoa, it was just him and Taira. Oscar and two others shouldn't be far from us, actually, if they stayed on the route Deni thinks they did."

"General Ru didn't think to send a message to us?" Massi asked.

Luc had wondered about that, but on reflection, he didn't think anyone could have caught them, the speed they had been going since meeting up with the Jatan force.

Massi must have come to that conclusion herself, because she let it go with a lifted shoulder.

"So will they come looking for you?" Massi asked.

Ava was silent for a long beat. "Hard to say. Of the two transporting me from Fernwell, one is dead, the other on the run home to Cattha."

"Why are Catthans involved in this?" Luc wondered how many countries they'd have to add to their enemies list.

"I think to give the Speaker the ability to deny Grimwalt's involvement. There is a contingent waiting for me on the Grimwalt side of the Illoan bridge. They have the coin Sirna was promised for kidnapping me there, and they may decide to come looking when Sirna doesn't arrive with me."

"How many?"

She shook her head. "I don't know. There's a man, I didn't get much of a sense of him, I was very weak when he joined us after laying the false trail in Bartolo, but he was obviously in charge, and taking his orders directly from the Speaker."

Luc could see the strain on her face. He wondered what the man had done to her.

His rage wanted to rise up out of him on fiery wings and lift him into the sky, so he could rain down his fury from above.

"So he might come looking for you when you fail to arrive?" Massi was looking at Ava with concern.

"From what I gathered about him," Ava said, "he will be beyond angry when I'm not delivered at the border."

"How did they even get you in Fernwell?" Massi asked.

Luc wondered the same. And they would need to know, to stop it happening again.

"The Queen's Herald, my cousin Herron, had something in his apartments in the palace. A spelled item of my clothing from when I was a baby that my mother used to find me when Herron abducted me years ago. It's called a Focus. Sirna was the cart driver for the Grimwaldian delegation that came to Fernwell just before you left to deal with the Jatan. He was given the Focus by the man from Grimwalt, who paid one of Herron's old guards to break in and steal it. They used it to track me and take me when I stepped out of the palace gates."

Luc and Massi shared a look. Rafe had told him of the break-in the day Kym had arrived with her news about the Jatan coming over the border.

He hadn't thought about it since.

"Where is it now?" he asked. It needed to be destroyed.

"Gone. I couldn't risk escaping while Sirna still had it."

Luc felt himself relax a little.

"So what's the plan?" Massi asked. "Once we've finished up here?"

"We go to Illoa." Luc looked at Ava, to see if she would object, but she simply nodded.

"And do what?" Massi wanted to know.

"And tell them they've started a war."

CHAPTER 32

"We can't actually tell some random border guards on the bridge in Illoa that Grimwalt has started a war with Kassia," Ava said as she watched Luc pull his shirt over his head. "Not without first knowing what General Ru's been saying about where I've been all this time."

Luc looked like he didn't care too much about that, but he crawled into bed and gathered her close. "What do you suggest?"

"I think I need to send a number of missives to Taunen, to people I think can be trusted, and to some of the old established families in the provinces who knew my grandparents and my parents." She yawned, her jaw cracking, and snuggled against him, closing her eyes at the feel of his skin against her cheek. "It needs to be done quietly and quickly, before the Speaker has the chance to slip away or somehow twist what he's done."

He didn't disagree, but she could feel the tightness in his muscles. He didn't want to send missives, he wanted to draw blood.

"I didn't even suspect you were in trouble." The words were stark. "I had no idea."

She lifted her head to look at him, surprised. "How could you have?"

MICHELLE DIENER

He touched his forearm.

She didn't understand for a moment, and then enlightenment struck. "You think my magic should have told you?"

He shook his head, then shrugged. "Maybe? I thought it did, once before."

She traced where she had sewn his wound together. "When was this?"

"In Fernwell the day we took the city. It was as if the protections you had made for me understood part of my wellbeing was tied to your wellbeing. I knew you were in trouble, and where you were."

She frowned. "You never told me."

"Too much happened that day. I didn't think of it again." He moved, leaning over her, one hand anchoring in her hair beneath her braid.

"It could have faded. Magic doesn't last forever." She quirked her lips. "Thank goodness."

"Can you make me something like that, though? Something that will tell me when you're in trouble?"

She pondered it. "I can try. Why not?"

He gave a nod. "Good." Then he bent down and brushed his lips against hers.

The low smolder of desire she'd felt since he'd pulled his shirt over his head ignited into something hot and needy, and she deepened the kiss, holding his head between her hands.

He undressed her as they kissed, his hands sliding and stroking as he did so, pausing here and there.

She tugged on his trousers and he helped her remove them. When they were skin on skin together, she reveled in every caress, every sound he made as she touched him, every gasp she could not contain when he touched her.

When they lay at last beside each other, panting for breath, he rose up over her again, and tugged at her braid.

"They starved you."

"In the beginning, I wasn't able to lift my head, let alone eat, but yes," she looked down at herself, at the sharp angle of her bones through her skin, "they were not careful with me."

"I want to kill them." He pulled her hair tie off and started loosening her hair, sliding it through his fingers.

"Sirna is already dead, and Evelyn . . ." She thought about what she would do. "I think she's headed for Cattha as fast as she can go.

"They are just the little people." Luc twirled a strand of her hair around his finger. "I'm talking about this man from Grimwalt who was in charge, and the Speaker, the person who set this in motion."

She closed her eyes and relaxed into the pallet. "They will need to be dealt with." She couldn't go through life looking over her shoulder for them.

"Agreed." He flopped back down beside her and drew her close, so her head rested on his chest.

She must have fallen asleep, although she didn't remember doing so, because she was awoken as Luc extracted himself from the circle of her arms, with someone speaking to him in a low voice just outside the tent.

"What is it?" she fought her fatigue, lifting her head as he crouched at her feet, pulling his shirt on.

"One of the Jatan prisoners wants to speak to me. General Carvill." He leaned over her, and brushed a kiss to her temple. "Try to get back to sleep."

He left with his boots in his hands, and it was only after he'd gone that she saw his tunic was still in the tent.

He must not have thought it was a serious problem if he hadn't put it on, but it worried her.

These people had tried to kill him today.

She lay back down, and slowly drew on her own clothes, feeling too vulnerable and cold to lie naked without Luc beside her.

Eventually, aware she wasn't going to get back to sleep unless she took him the tunic, she sat up, redoing the braid Luc had undone, giving herself protection and stealth.

Like Luc, she carried her boots out of the tent, stepping into them once she was outside.

The night was quiet, almost too quiet if there was a problem with the prisoners.

She knew where they were being kept. The soldiers had spoken about it over dinner this evening, talking about how glad they would be to hand them back to the Jatan tomorrow, after the deal had been signed.

She headed toward it, moving between the tents.

She looked around for guards, but she couldn't see any, and she supposed that wasn't unusual. They would be patrolling the perimeter, not the camp itself.

She tried to shake the feeling that there was something wrong.

A shout of laughter came from the fire to her right, and she relaxed a little at the sound. At least in some parts of the camp there was noise and people.

She moved to the prisoners' enclosure with more confident steps after that, leaving the tents behind her. Ahead, she heard the low murmur of voices, and saw a line of lanterns that must define the area where the prisoners were being kept.

She slowed a little, looking down at the tunic in her hand and wondering if Luc would be teased for having his lover come running after him with a warm garment while he dealt with his duties.

She shrugged. So be it.

She had come this far.

He had broad enough shoulders to take some ribbing.

She nearly tripped over the guard who lay in her path, stumbling and righting herself just in time.

She crouched beside the woman, putting a hand to her throat to check for a pulse, but she was dead, an arrow embedded in her heart.

She should have brought her invisibility cap, or found someone and asked if they knew why Luc had been called away, but she hadn't done either of those things, and now she could just make out, in the weak lantern light, Luc standing with his back to her, facing a man with a sword, flanked by two archers.

There was another body lying off to the left, and she guessed there were more she couldn't see, otherwise someone would have called the alarm.

The prisoners seemed to be gone.

Escaped.

The general they were holding, Ava couldn't remember his name, must have had outside help. He'd asked to speak to Luc, so a guard came to fetch him.

They must have quietly shot the other guards, released the prisoners, and waited for Luc to come to them.

They wouldn't have found his tent amongst the many in camp, so they had to lure him out.

It meant there was more going on here, and they wanted Luc specifically.

They would not have him.

She thought through her options, but she didn't have many, and she needed to get Luc into the tunic.

At the very least.

One of the archers lifted their bow and aimed at him.

She had run out of time.

She strode forward, eyes on Luc. "You were gone so long, sweetheart, I was worried you'd be cold."

She threw the tunic at him, saw the surprise and fear for her that flitted across his face as he caught the woollen garment one handed.

"It's chilly at night this time of year," she admonished him. "Especially this far north."

"Who are you?"

The man with the sword stared at her, perplexed.

"What do you mean, who am I?" She frowned at him and put a hand on her hip. "What's going on here?" She pretended she'd only just noticed the archers.

"I thought you were sharing pillows with the Queen of Kassia," the man with the sword said, looking over at Luc. "At least, that's the impression you gave when we first met. But instead you seem to be doing so with . . ." He trailed off and tilted his head toward Ava, a smirk on his face. "Are *you* the queen of Kassia?"

Ava laughed and flipped her short braid. "I'm a Venyatux soldier."

Out of the corner of her eye, she saw Luc had pulled the tunic over his head.

"You want to be warm before you die, Commander?" The man watched him put it on with the same smirk.

Ava smiled brightly at him, some of her fear evaporating as Luc became impervious to both arrow and sword. "Wearing the right clothing is important. Especially on campaign. Comfort is just as important as function, don't you think?" She lifted her hands and brushed them down the front of her shirt. "I personally won't wear anything that feels scratchy. Life's too short for that, you know?"

"Are you stupid, girl?" The man with the sword took a step forward. "You and your commander are about to die, and you're babbling on about clothes?"

Ava gave a half-turn as Luc passed her in a blur, and just for form's sake, in case someone was watching, she bent to the side as the archer closest to her shot at her, his action more out of panic at Luc's sudden explosive launch at them than out of fear for her, she guessed.

The arrow missed her by an arm's length.

She wasn't up to her old level of fitness—she had made peace with that. She knew she would be more in the way than useful if she tried to jump in and help, so she simply stood back and watched as Luc reached the sword man and slammed a palm into his face as he tried to chop at Luc's chest. The blade glanced off him, and he ripped the sword from the Jatan's grasp and swung it at his neck.

At least it was sharp, Ava thought with a wince. It was a clean job.

Luc spun, lifting the sword to block as an arrow came straight for him at close range. It struck the blade and ricocheted off, and the archer threw his bow down and knelt, arms wide, in a gesture of surrender.

Luc left him, spinning the other way and impaling the second archer, who was desperately trying to notch another arrow.

He turned again, facing the camp, and let out a piercing whistle.

While he waited for help to come, he searched the surviving archer, and when he had the man lying face down, arms extended, he finally looked up at her, blue eyes blazing.

"Ava."

She shrugged. "You really shouldn't go out in the cold without a warm tunic."

He threw back his head and laughed.

CHAPTER 33

He had been foolish to think Hurst was no longer a problem.

He'd killed guards, broken free the prisoners, and tried to kill Luc and Ava.

Luc was coldly angry, as much with himself as with Hurst.

Not that Hurst would be a problem ever again.

After he killed him and his pet archer, his whistle brought Rafe and Rev and Massi and everyone who heard it, and they went hunting.

They rounded up most of the escapees in less than half an hour.

The Jatan prisoners had moved into the forest after Hurst had set them free, intent on working their way around the Rising Wave camp to find the Jatan army, and in the dark, most hadn't got very far.

The anger amongst the Cervantes was palpable.

Of the guards, four were dead, and two were just hanging on to life.

Luc looked over everyone who'd been recaptured, and was sorry to see General Carvill was not among them.

Then Rafe had whistled for attention, and they found the

general dead, a knife buried in his throat, almost right next to the place where the prisoners had been held.

Hurst again, Luc guessed.

Maybe Hurst hadn't thought Carvill had helped his father enough while they were prisoners.

He would have been tempted to kill Carvill himself given the loss of the guards, so he found it difficult to care, either way.

When the prisoners were back in place, and the number of guards were triple what they'd been, he walked over to where Ava waited for the field medics, really just soldiers Dorea had spent a little time instructing, to clean the wounds.

When they were done, she bent over them with her needle and thread.

"What's she murmuring over and over?" Massi asked Luc, coming to stand beside him.

"'Healthy, and a beautiful straight scar.'"

Massi looked at him, eyebrows raised. "Why?"

Then she looked down at his arm, the one she'd seen open to the bone, which was now smooth and scar free.

He watched her face change, as she slowly worked out Ava was protecting herself by making sure there was a scar at all.

"Will you take her to Roan?"

He knew he shouldn't. They had rescued the two Versai healers, and they had surely managed to help the little boy, but he didn't want to take the chance. "Yes."

General Ru would have to wait a day longer for them to arrive.

Massi relaxed, as if she was afraid he might have chosen to go straight to Fernwell.

"We need to send someone into Grimwalt with some warning missives." He'd been thinking about it while he hunted Jatan prisoners in the woods. "Ava has friends and old allies of her family who need to know what's happening with the Speaker. We can't keep defending against him. We need to start pushing back."

"I'm surprised you're not going in there yourself." She looked at him sidelong.

"I want to." He couldn't hide the fierce longing for blood in his voice. "But General Ru has had to hold things in Fernwell on her own for weeks, and the longer we leave her exposed, the closer we come to undoing everything we fought for the last two years."

Massi's gaze drifted back to Ava, who had finished stitching the first guard, and was moving on to the second. "If she's not exposed already."

"Yes. Which means I am taking a huge chance by swinging past Versai on my way back, but none of the fighting and loss would be worth it if Roan doesn't live. That was the whole point of the Rising Wave to begin with."

"Yes." Massi sighed. She rubbed the back of her neck. "I'll go to Grimwalt. The sooner we move, the better."

That was true, but he didn't want her to.

It would be dangerous. Very dangerous.

And she was precious to him.

"It can't be Rafe or Revek. They don't know . . ." Massi waved in Ava's direction. "Don't know exactly what the Speaker's obsession with her is all about."

That she was right didn't make it any easier. Luc turned to her, but before he could speak, he was hailed by Rafe.

"Bartholomew wants to speak to you. My guess is a few of the prisoners we didn't catch have made it to the Jatan camp."

Luc hesitated. He didn't want to let Ava out of his sight.

Rafe gripped his shoulder. "I'll watch her. No harm will come to her, I promise."

Luc nodded and without needing an invitation, Massi fell into step with him.

He glanced across at her. "Bartholomew is interested in you."

She gave a quick, throaty laugh. "So is his boss. Not sure what that's about."

Luc grinned at her. "They obviously like dangerous women."

When they reached the line where Bartholomew was waiting, though, flirting with Massi seemed to be the last thing on his mind.

"What just happened?" The high-general's aide got straight to the point.

"I'm not sure of all the details, but Lieutenant Hurst and two of your archers crept up on our Jatan prisoners tonight and quietly killed a few of our guards. With the guards on one side out of the way, he managed to speak to General Carvill and persuade him to ask one of the guards on the other side of the area they were being held in to call me, then they killed or tried to kill all the other guards and set the prisoners free.

"When I arrived, they shot the guard who'd gone to fetch me in the heart, and tried to kill me. I killed Hurst and one of the archers. The other is now a prisoner with the rest. We found Carvill's body among the trees, and he wasn't killed by us, so I'm guessing that was Hurst, too. Oh, and we rounded up most of the escapees, but I'm guessing a few made it to your camp, which is why you're here?"

"Shit." Bartholomew spun around, facing his camp, and then turned back. "This wasn't any plan of ours."

Luc studied him for a long moment. "I'm prepared to believe that. Hurst has looked after his own interests since I first met him. The meeting is still on for this morning. Let's get it done early, so we can all go home."

Bartholomew stared at him. "You're being serious?"

"What part of me looks like I want to stay here another second?"

Bartholomew blew out a breath that was half laughter, half relief. "Fair enough. I'll see you at our little fire pit for breakfast. Everyone brings their own food and drink."

"I think that will be best." Luc started to turn, and then stopped. "Oh, the queen arrived earlier this evening. So she will be present and able to sign the treaty herself, rather than use me as proxy."

"The queen?" Bartholomew frowned. "The queen of Kassia?"

"The queen of Kassia," Luc agreed. "See you in a few hours."

"I STILL CAN'T DECIDE HOW THAT WENT." AVA LOOKED DOWN AT her hands and noticed for the first time how thin her wrists were. "I felt like a child playing dress-up."

"You behaved and looked like a warrior queen," Luc said.

The tone of his voice told Ava that he was slightly wary of her mood, and she guessed her nerves at the first treaty she'd signed as queen of Kassia had made her edgy.

The document was sealed, both parties had a copy, but even hours later she still felt a little sick.

After the Rising Wave had taken Fernwell, and by extension, the whole of Kassia, both she and Luc had slowly worked out a peaceful transfer of power from her to a council was not going to happen in a hurry. Not when doing so risked undoing all the gains they had fought so hard to attain.

So she had committed Kassia to a truce with Jatan, agreeing to Kassia's withdrawal of their claim to the Jatan's mines. In exchange, Jatan committed to paying reparations for their raids and staying on their side of the border, unless they asked and were granted permission.

"The look on Baclar's face." Massi was on her other side, and she chuckled softly. "He acted as though we'd just dressed up a foot soldier and said she was queen, and then you gave him that haughty look and he changed his tune almost straight away."

That had been a touch and go moment, Ava conceded. "Some of it might have been Kikir's indignation. He was very convincing when he swore I was the queen."

"The job would certainly have been harder if you had arrived to the meeting in those ancient pants and old wool jacket of yours," Massi said. "Good thing we had enough clothes among the women to dress you up to at least look like a fighter."

"What did Baclar pull you aside to ask you afterward?" Ava looked over at Luc.

"He wanted to ask about some embroidery he found on the

underside of his shirt," Luc said. "I told him I didn't know what he was talking about."

Ava's shoulders tensed, but then she remembered she had been invisible when she'd done the sewing. No one could point the finger at her.

"Did he accept that?" Massi asked.

"He didn't press the subject, if that's what you mean. He simply said it was exquisite work, and he was surprised he hadn't noticed it before."

"Well, they aren't our problem any more." Massi sounded relieved.

"Grimwalt still is." Luc had told Ava that Massi had volunteered to go to Grimwalt and deliver messages of warning from her to the representatives she knew had been at court a few years ago, before she'd been captured by Herron and locked away.

She needed to get the word out to as many people as she could.

The Speaker could not have control over everyone—if he did, he wouldn't need her.

"We'll overcome Grimwalt, just like we've overcome Kassia and Jatan." Luc sounded completely sure of himself.

She hoped that was true.

She turned to Massi. "Luc says you'll ride with us until we reach Versai, and then double back to Grimwalt from there, so I have time to write the letters you're going to deliver."

Massi's mission would be dangerous. Ava would have to work some protection into her cloak.

"And if you find out anything about my friends, Tomas and Velda, please see what you can do to rescue them." She paused, because that might put Massi in more danger than was fair. She drew in a breath. "Or rather, send a message or make a note of where they may be, so when you get back, I can see what I can do about getting them home."

"They're important to you?" Massi asked.

She nodded.

"Then I will do what I can."

CHAPTER 34

The second time they approached Fernwell, it was as troops coming home, rather than besiegers.

Some of the Rising Wave, including some riding with them now, Ava knew, would be heading back to Cervantes as soon as they could, but for now the mood was light and eager, and their welcome was assumed.

She hoped that was true, that General Ru had managed to keep her grip on the slippery hammer handle of power while she and Luc had both been absent.

Their numbers had swelled—more were coming back than had left, but that was because some of the old warriors had wanted to see Fernwell and the Rising Wave's victory with their own eyes, after years of guerrilla warfare with the Kassians.

Some of Kikir's fellow Skäddar had asked for permission to accompany them, too, to see Fernwell and to integrate with the Rising Wave, and although Kikir had not come with them, needing to finally get home and speak to the Skäddar Collective, she and Luc had happily agreed to their request.

Two of their new members rode beside her and Luc—Sierra and her baby, Roan. They had decided to come with the Rising Wave to

Fernwell because Sierra's heart's choice, Roan's father, Rory, was here. And everyone knew he would leave immediately to go home when he heard the news of Roan's injury.

"Why not go to him, so he can see all is well straight away, instead?" Sierra had asked, and Luc had conceded the point.

They had reached Versai the same day Ava had signed the treaty with the Jatan, arriving late in the night.

The healers Luc had rescued had been treating the cut with moss and pastes, and the baby was much better, so she had waited until the next morning to stitch the wound.

She had sewn in healing and strength, but she hadn't thought of the scar, she realized afterward. She had been so intent on working quickly to minimise his discomfort that he may not have one.

Hopefully it would be put down to his being young.

They had parted ways with Massi and left for Fernwell straight after, and had ridden hard.

Happily, because Deni and Taira were considering going to look for them, they had met up with Oscar, Carrie and Tras on the second day. Their relief at finding her safe was palpable, and she had ridden with them for hours, exchanging stories with them in low voices, because they were still trying to pretend to everyone else that Deni had brought her up to the border to sign the treaty with the Jatan.

Six days after they'd left Versai, in the late afternoon, the walls of Fernwell loomed before them.

Clustered near the gate was the tent city that housed the Rising Wave troops, and with a whoop of happiness, some of the unit raced ahead, ululating as they approached.

A cry went up, and from the walls, Ava heard a horn blowing.

"Since when do we use a horn?" She couldn't help the sudden acceleration of nerves.

"The soldiers in the camp wouldn't be acting like they are if there was a change in who was in charge," Luc said, but his eyes were narrowed and he was taking in everything.

"Let us go ahead," Ava told Sierra. "Get someone to show you where Rory's tent is in the camp, and wait to hear it's safe before you go into the city."

Sierra nodded, calling to a friend in the unit, and peeled off, so it was Revek, Rafe, Ava and Luc who rode through the gates first.

The people they passed reacted, but as far as Ava could see, it wasn't in a hostile way. Their gaze was focused on Luc, not her, and she wasn't surprised. She had not had a lot of time before she was taken to move about the city as the queen.

Likely no one realized who she was.

They reached the palace, rode into the courtyard in front of the massive entrance, and slid off their mounts.

The guards at the door gave a whoop at the sight of them, and one called out questions about what had happened, whether there had been trouble with the Jatan.

One raced off inside the palace, and Dak appeared in the doorway, smiling broadly at the sight of Luc.

When he noticed Ava he stumbled, eyes wide. He obviously wanted to say something, but didn't want to speak in front of an audience.

He seemed to take stock of the situation, and then bounded down the stairs, ordering a guard to go to the stables and let them know to collect the horses, ordering another to fetch Raun-Tu.

He stood with his back to Ava while he issued his orders, blocking her in a way that made Ava think it was deliberate.

The moment they were alone, he spun to face her.

"General Ru and you are in the throne room right now, facing off against a delegation of angry nobles and councillors."

"General Ru and . . . me?" She frowned.

"Someone pretending to be you, wearing the necklace that Grimwaldian used to break in and abduct you last time." He grabbed her arm and hustled her up the steps, and Luc was suddenly on her other side.

Dak looked down at where his hand grasped her and dropped it. "They starved you?" His voice was shocked.

"Later," she said, dismissing the question. "What do you mean, facing off?"

Raun-Tu appeared at the end of the long, wide corridor, and he sprinted to meet them.

He and Dak exchanged looks.

"The nobles and councillors are insisting you speak for yourself, which hasn't been possible since you were taken. General Ru has been speaking for you, and they are now suspicious you're nothing but her puppet. I don't think the excuses we've been making over the last few weeks are going to hold much longer. And the woman playing you just doesn't sound anything like you. They're going to know something is very wrong, very soon."

Ava increased her pace, heading for the throne room.

"Ava, you can't walk in there. They'll see two of you!" Raun-Tu blocked her way. "Including the guards at the door."

She stopped short. "We need to get whoever is pretending to be me out of there, so we can switch."

"How are we going to do that?" Dak hissed.

Ava looked over at Luc. "I know if I had been here this whole time, and Luc had just come home, I would take a few minutes, at least, to welcome him back."

"That . . . could work." Dak blew out a breath.

"Take me to that room off to the side of the throne room and bring the happily reunited couple in there," Ava said. "Raun-Tu, you walk in and whisper in my double's ear about what's happening, then Luc can make a big entrance." She eyed her heart's choice. "You'll have to make it convincing."

"I can do that." Luc's lips quirked up. He looked over at Rafe and Revek. "You can flank me, make sure no one tries to stop the reunion."

"Shield you from those nobles?" Revek asked. He cracked his knuckles. "That sounds like fun."

Rafe snorted a laugh, but gave a nod of agreement.

"We have to do this right now." Raun-Tu's sense of urgency was catching, and Ava guessed General Ru was in serious trouble.

She let Dak lead the way down a few twisting corridors and sneak them through a side door to the throne room's antechamber.

They both moved to the door to the throne room and Ava noticed for the first time there was a place to watch what was going on set into the door itself, a thick mesh that allowed just enough visibility to make out the throne and those nearest it, as well as made it easy to hear what was going on.

"Must have been so the servants knew when things were about to wrap up," she said to Dak, but he simply grunted in response, eyes riveted to the scene in front of them.

Raun-Tu had entered at a fast clip, walking up the middle of the throne room, ignoring a noblewoman who was speaking, and bending to whisper in the ear of the woman on the throne.

Her.

Ava was astonished at how like her the woman looked, but then, she'd know the necklace had that ability. It was amazing seeing her own face on someone else, though.

The woman gasped, rising to her feet.

At that moment, the door to the throne room open and Luc stepped through, Rev and Rafe one step behind on either side of him.

With a cry of joy—or was it heartfelt relief?—the fake Ava ran down the few steps on the dais and hurled herself into Luc's arms.

Luc swept her up, holding her close to his chest, and Dak shooed Ava back, behind the door, and opened it, sweeping his arm to invite them inside.

A cry of protest rose up from the audience.

As soon as the door closed, with Rafe and Revek standing guard in front of it, blocking her view of what was happening in the room, Ava spun around and started pulling her shirt over her head.

"Quickly," she said to her double, and with a chuckle, the woman unclipped the necklace at her throat and Talika appeared.

"Talika." Luc's surprise was palpable. "Well done."

Ava was already out of her clothes, and Talika turned so Ava could help her unbutton the back of her dress.

"They're about to revolt," her former guard said. "It's been touch and go for days, but they have reached the end of their patience now."

"Were you in public view for the last five days or so?" Luc asked her.

Talika shook her head. "We said I was indisposed, because just the sight of me made them angry that I wouldn't meet and talk about the way forward for Kassia."

"That's good." Ava picked up the dress the moment it landed on the floor, and stepped into it, her gaze going to Luc. "If no one saw me at the palace for a while, we can definitely say I was at the border signing the treaty." Then she thought about Luc's dramatic entrance. "Then again, if I was with you dealing with the Jatan, how do we explain the touching reunion they just saw?"

"We don't explain it. Let them think what they like." Luc looked like he would relish being asked about it.

Talika buttoned the dress for her quickly, but Ava could feel her fingers trembling as the shouting on the other side of the door got louder.

"It's going to turn violent." Dak stood, eyes on the throne room beyond. "You look visibly thinner than Talika, but you need to go now."

There was a lot going on here, Ava realized. The strain on everyone's faces told a story of a group holding the line beyond all hope.

"Done." Talika gave her a little push, and Ava strode to the door.

Dak opened it, and Luc was suddenly behind her, a hand on her lower back.

She stopped and looked back over her shoulder. "When did you step into the throne room today? How long ago?"

"About half an hour ago." Talika frowned. "Why?"

Ava looked up at Luc and he nodded. "Who will check when exactly we rode through the gates?"

Also, if the agitated audience had only just arrived themselves, maybe they wouldn't notice how much thinner she was now than five minutes ago.

They walked into the throne room, and the noise rose.

Ava ignored it, walking to the throne and sitting.

Luc took up his usual position on her right.

She said nothing, waiting, until eventually the noise died out.

"I have just come from the Jatan border," she said, keeping her voice to a normal level, forcing everyone to stay quiet. But her words were too much for some of those present, and the chatter rose, then fell again when she said nothing more.

"Why weren't we told?" Ava recognized Lady Elna, the noble who'd been speaking when Raun-Tu had first entered the room.

That was a good question. Or it would be, if she really had left a few days ago for the Jatan border.

Ava had a feeling she didn't have enough information to answer correctly.

General Ru bent over as she hesitated, and Ava saw her hands were shaking, just a little. "Because some of the nobles have been conspiring against the Rising Wave, and they might have tried to make trouble with you gone," she whispered.

Ava nodded.

"What's that fork-tongued Venyatux whispering in your ear, your majesty?" Lord Haster was someone Ava remembered well. He seemed relatively forthright, but he was also power hungry and bitter that his power was about to be diluted.

"General Ru, who saved my life many times on my journey to Fernwell, and is an honorable and trustworthy ally, was updating me on what her intelligence agents have uncovered in my short absence." Ava finally rose. "What do you think the nobles who do not want change to come to Kassia would have done if they had known I was traveling to deal with the Jatan?"

The councillors, made up of the normal citizens of the city and its surroundings, were on the right side of the room, the nobles on the left. Ava noticed the commoners looking across the aisle with speculation.

"General Ru has not produced an ounce of proof of any insurgency—"

"That is because I was the one who uncovered it." Luc spoke for the first time.

A lot of the nobles jerked their gaze to look at him, then looked down. Ava wondered why they kept forgetting who and what he was.

The most dangerous and powerful man in the room.

It was as if they didn't want to acknowledge that he had bested them.

"On my way to deal with the Jatan, I personally came across the troops who were lured off the streets of Fernwell to cause trouble in the countryside. They were instructed to shoot me on sight." He turned to General Ru. "What has Lord Cynera had to say for himself about that?"

"He has gone on the run, rather than answer the questions we had for him." General Ru rocked back on her heels.

"Have the soldiers we found come back to Fernwell, and given themselves in?" Luc asked Dak, who was still standing by the door to the antechamber.

"Some." He nodded, and Ava thought she saw amusement in his gaze. "As well as some soldiers who fought us on the plains. They said you'd told them it was safe."

"That's good." He let the silence stretch out.

"Why did you need to make a deal with the Jatan?" Lady Elna obviously saw the trap of pursuing questions about the nobles' loyalty, and decided to move on.

"They had breached the border, and were raiding Kassian villages in the north, going down as far as Cervantes." Ava clasped her hands together. "The Commander rode out to assess the situation, as you would be aware, and he sent back a messenger to say they were willing to deal."

"You had no right to deal on our behalf," one of the councillors, Jitco May, said, his voice cutting through the murmurs.

"I had every right." Ava drew herself up, and turned to him.

"The Jatan needed to be certain they were dealing with someone in a position to deliver what was agreed. They were killing Kassian civilians. We here in Fernwell were not at the point in our negotiations where a new governing body could ratify an agreement, and let me remind you, these talks are at my instigation. I am the duly crowned queen, and if I choose, I could remain so. This was not a normal succession. It was hard fought, and the people who led the fighting are standing on either side of me. I have offered Kassia a more collaborative system, in the interests of the whole region, but until that system is strong and fair, the hard decisions devolve to me. Or do you say otherwise?"

Jitco May watched her for a beat, then lowered his gaze. "No."

"Good. Then I can tell you that the Jatan are returning to their side of the border with no more fighting, and they will pay reparations. We, in turn, will withdraw our claim to their mines, and return to our side."

"Those mines are worth a lot," Lord Haster muttered.

"Those mines are not ours," Ava replied. "Now, I have been riding for days. Our supplies were washed away when we crossed a river in full flood, and for three of those days, there was no food." She looked down at herself ruefully, lifting the loose fabric of her dress away from her body as if in illustration. "I will ask your leave for a day to recover, and then we can meet again to start our talks in earnest."

There was a general murmur of agreement.

"Wait." Luc's strong voice cut through the noise. "First, before the queen talks to the nobles, Lord Cynera must appear to answer publicly for what he's been up to. Otherwise, I don't see why they should be included."

"You mean, you will still speak with us?" Jitco May asked, gesturing to the councillors. "And exclude the nobles?"

"I will." Ava looked over at the shocked faces of the nobles to her left, saw the satisfied smiles of the councillors.

"That's unfair, I haven't seen Cynera in weeks," Lady Elna said.

"You haven't *seen* him," General Ru said. "That's doublespeak.

You must know where he is. And if you don't, you know where to find him. Start pulling your weight."

She held out her arm to Ava, and Ava curled her fingers around her elbow and let the general lead her back into the antechamber.

As soon as they were through, the general dropped her arm and ran a hand down her face.

She was suddenly enveloped in a hug from Talika.

"That was close."

General Ru lifted her head and smiled, brighter than Ava had ever seen her smile before. She pulled Talika closer, curling an arm around her shoulder, and kissed her brow. Then she turned to look over at Ava and Luc.

"I don't know how your timing was so good, or how you arrived together, but I am very, very grateful."

CHAPTER 35

Dinner was a small affair.

Just General Ru, Talika, Raun-Tu, Dak and Revek joined Ava and Luc in the living space in their palace apartment.

Luc sprawled back in his chair, his fingers touching Ava's hand where it rested next to her empty plate.

"So Massi is in Grimwalt." General Ru sounded pleased. "What's the plan?"

"Massi will send a message as soon as she has a sense of what's going on behind the Grimwalt border."

"What of the Grimwaldian diplomats?" Ava asked General Ru. "Are they still here?"

The general nodded. "They're still recovering. It took them a while before they could remember why they were even here most days. It was as if their minds had been muddled."

"They were given a special tea every day by Sirna. There was some kind of mind control magic infused in the leaves." Ava turned her hand palm up, and Luc covered it with his own.

"He tried it on you?" Raun-Tu asked, leaning forward.

She shook her head. "He didn't need to confuse me, only make me too weak to run. He did try to use it on the other travellers who we were with, when he wanted them to help search for me the day I escaped."

"How did it work?" General Ru asked.

Ava tightened her grip on his hand. "It didn't. One of my fellow travellers had helped me destroy the tea a few days before."

"You could only know he tried to use it on them if you didn't actually run." Luc tried to keep his voice even. She should have gotten away as fast as she could.

She shot him a quick look. "I needed a lift to Illoa, and the group was headed there. I wasn't strong enough to walk the whole way. I was waiting for Sirna to go chasing after me, and then planned to hop in a cart and let the others take me where I needed to go."

Dak gave a chuckle. "And it worked?"

Luc felt her still beneath his hand. She sucked in a quick breath.

"He decided they were hiding me." She lifted a shoulder. "Some of them did know I planned to run, but not where I was. He held a knife to a five-year-old's throat to get them to give me up."

"Which they couldn't do, because they didn't know where you were." Talika's eyes were wide with distress.

She nodded her head in a sharp jerk. "But the little girl's father was not someone Sirna should have been antagonizing." She tightened her grip on his hand. "The little girl is fine, Sirna is now lying dead in the forest, and his partner, Evelyn, is no doubt riding as fast as she can back to Cattha."

"What did they use to keep you weak?" General Ru asked. She was sitting on Ava's other side, and she touched Ava's painfully thin wrist lightly with her fingertips.

"A rope like the one you have in the drawer of the queen's office downstairs," Ava said. "I'm sorry, I know you think it could be useful, but it must be destroyed."

The general looked like she wanted to object, but when she lifted her gaze from Ava's thin arms to her face, she went still and then gave a slow nod. "All right."

"It doesn't just suck the energy out of you, it sucks your life force." Ava's voice was low. Quiet. "I thought I would never be the same, even after I rid myself of it. I'm still not what I was."

They were all quiet after that, and Luc moved his chair closer to Ava's, lifted their combined hands and kissed the back of hers.

"You need to walk around the city more," Dak said, out of the blue in the silence. "You need to be seen. They are hungry for stories of you. Hungry for a relationship with their new queen."

She nodded, although Luc wanted to argue against it.

"I know."

"We also need some good news." Raun-Tu bit into a slice of apple he'd taken off the cheese board, and looked around the table. "Something everyone can get behind."

"How about a formal heart's choice ceremony?" Luc suggested, and Ava turned her head, gaze fixed on his.

"You and me?" she asked.

"You and me. If you will have me."

Their joined hands were still raised, and she moved them to her mouth so that she could kiss the back of his hand. "I will."

"Sorry to break the moment, but I don't think that's a good idea." General Ru's sigh was heartfelt. "The nobles and the councillors are already too nervous about the Rising Wave's influence on their queen. It's better to wait until the negotiations are finished before you make your partnership official."

Ava hadn't looked away from him. "I'll do it, anyway, if that's what you want."

He felt the warmth of her words spread through him, and he dipped his chin. "Good. But I already know my heart. If it's better to wait, then we can wait."

She nodded, and he saw General Ru relax a little.

"There still can be a heart's choice ceremony." Talika spoke up, and Luc turned to her in surprise.

He caught the sudden stiffening of General Ru's spine at her words, and wondered what was troubling her.

Talika stood, and in the Cervantes way, clasped her hands

together between her breasts and just under her chin. "I claim you for my heart's choice, Erdene Ru. And I ask you for your agreement in front of witnesses on a day of your choosing."

General Ru seemed speechless, and then she stood in a rush, hands out, cupped together. "I will give my agreement."

After a moment of shocked silence, there was much joking about the circumstances of the courtship of a Cervantes guard and the general of the Venyatux army, and much arguing about the date of the ceremony, but after the toasts were over, Ava leaned against him as they waved to their departing guests from the balcony.

"Do you mind that we have to wait?"

"No. I'm patient."

She turned to him and grinned. "No, you're not."

"Well, no, I'm not." He lifted her up, his heart catching a little at how much lighter she was now. "But I am disciplined."

"How disciplined?" she murmured as he lay her gently down on their bed.

"Well, now. How about we find out?"

ACKNOWLEDGMENTS

A huge thank you to Claire and Jo, who help me make my stories the best they can be, as well as the eagle eyes of Diane and Jess from my readers' group. Thank you also to Book Coverology for the amazing cover.

ABOUT THE AUTHOR

Michelle Diener is an award winning author of historical fiction, science fiction and fantasy.

Michelle was born in London and currently lives in Australia with her husband and children.

You can contact Michelle through her website or sign up to receive notification when she has a new book out on her New Release Notification page.

Connect with Michelle
www.michellediener.com